Change The Game Publications

Presents

Dutchess

A Novel By Dutchess

Change The Game
Flint, MI 48505
810-210-7957

The characters in this novel are made up individuals. Some of the scenes in this story might seem like real life events, but again this is a book of fiction.

Change The Game Publications
Published by Change The Game Publications
For more information please feel free to contact Jeremy Drummond at 810-210-7957 or visit our web-site www.dutchessbook.com or e-mail Dutchessbook@gmail.com
Cover design by Marion Designs.
Manuscript edited by Dutchess

ISBN 1451529902
EAN-13 9781451529906

From Milan to Smilin'
"Anything is Possible"

Dutchess

Dutchess

Crack invades, causing despair
Pungent aroma
Fills the air
Broken Promises
Lost Dreams
And Goals.
Broken Skin
Punctured with needles
Leaving holes.
Cocaine Base, whipped to perfection
Shared tools
Passing Infection.
Pregant women, searching high
Child in womb
Will surely die.
Poison Manufactured, distrubuted
To Blacks
Mothers sellin' daughters
All for that pack.
Freakish sex, perverted and foul
Power to control another
In a tiny vial.
A dope fiends abuse
Sickness From Seperation
Promotes prolonged use.
No matter where you from
Look around
There is always
A Devil's Playground.

@Jeremy Drummond@ 2008

CHAPTER ONE

HIGHLAND PARK ILLINOIS

"So how is the Baptiste case coming along?" Lawrence Blackwell questioned his wife, while holding a copy of the Chicago Tribune with his eyes glued to the front page. His cup of hot white caramel mocha coffee from Star Bucks sits on the nearby table. He has been subtly trying to get her to drop the case.

"It's coming along. So far, so good we have two star witnesses who are willing to cooperate and testify against Kennytha Baptiste." Cheryl Blackwell replied as she places a large stack of court documents into her black leather Gucci briefcase.

Cheryl Blackwell is a federal prosecutor, who has spent most of her adult life prosecuting high profile drug cases. She is in her mid-forties, an attractive African-American woman, with strong Indian features. She usually keeps her long, black hair pinned in a bun, as the strange color of her eyes hides behind a dull pair of black, horn-rimmed prescription reading glasses.

Lawrence Blackwell is in his late forties, dark complexioned and has a solid build. He has a touch of gray hair around his temples while the rest is dark and curly.

He claims that his hair is naturally curly without the use of an S-Curl kit.

He is a DEA agent, with a severe gambling addiction. While on the Vice Unit, he began accepting money from local street dealers to support his habit. After ten years on the Vice Squad he was recruited and given a promotion by the Drug Enforcement Administration. At this point, he began working with an organized, sophisticated drug operation, which earned him a few hundred thousand in tax free dollars. Lawrence is on Baptiste's payroll and he isn't trying to lose out on the money.

"Why don't you let Al handle the case, Baptiste is dangerous?" He is referring to her boss Al Sorensten.

"He's no more dangerous than Melvin." Melvin was the leader of the Black Disciples, who she convicted last year.

"But he has a lot of workers, I just don't want anything to happen-."

"So what, Melvin had a whole army," She blurted, cutting him off in mid-sentence. "You know once I start a case I finish it to the end, no matter what." He knew very well, she is stubborn like that. It is one of the qualities that attract her to him. Still he has to try again.

"But-"

"Don't worry," She said, "Nothing is going to happen, I'm prepared for the consequences." Lawrence falls into heavy silence. He knows that there is nothing that he can do to manipulate her decision. Even when the threats over the phone had begun a month ago, she stuck to her guns. She didn't tell him about them either. "As long as the witnesses stick to their stories on the stand, we got him", she said with a smile.

"Hopefully, they don't end up dead like the witnesses on his last trial." Lawrence said, rising from the glass kitchen table with his nine millimeter resting under his armpit.

He removes his grey Brooks Brothers blazer from the

back of his chair and puts it on. The phone rings, seizing her attention. Cheryl struts away to answer the phone.

"Hello", she answered. A sinister voice responds.

"Bitch, this is your last warning, drop the case or lose-." She hangs up on the caller. Lawrence watches as her face crinkles.

"Who was that?"

"Wrong number," she lied. ***No sense in making him worry, if he knew that I've been receiving threats, there's no way he would let me finish this case, I have to think about my career.*** She thought.

"Well I guess it's time for me to prepare for a long day of work, and get these criminals off the streets." Lawrence stated, walking over to Cheryl.

"That makes two of us," she added, rising from her seat with briefcase in hand. Immaculately dressed in a beige, two piece Armani skirt suit that exposes her long, muscular legs. She has the style and sophistication of a fortune five hundred business mogul.

Lawrence's six foot frame, towers over Cheryl as they stand face to face. He leans forward and plants a soft, warm, tantalizing kiss on her full lips while his hand brushes her silky hair behind one ear. "Mmmm," Cheryl purrs, with her eyes partially closed. With his other hand, he cups her round, firm backside. "Baby you're going to start something we can't-."

"Now ya'll know ya'll too old for all that." Sade Lynell Blackwell interrupts her parents in the middle of their passionate moment. Startled, they both show embarrassing expressions.

Sade is the younger version of her mother, only thicker. She has just turned eighteen three days ago on August 2nd. She has a butter-scotch complexioned, with long shoulder length black hair. She has funny light brown, almost greenish eyes, like her mother. She stands five feet seven inches tall, one hundred and forty pounds, with a small waistline.

Sade stands in the doorway of their massive sized kitchen with her hands on her wide hips of her Apple Bottom jeans. "Uh, Uh, Uh. Shame on ya'll," Sade added, rocking her head from side to side with a smile on her face.

"How do you think we made you?" Lawrence jokingly asked. Cheryl hit him on the shoulder, further embarrassed.

"I think we better get going before we are late". Cheryl stated, ignoring both of their remarks.

"I think we better get going before we be late." Lawrence stated, staring at his beautiful creation.

"Naw daddy, I'm off on Mondays."

"Oh yeah, I forgot."

"Well, I'll see you two later." Cheryl said.

"Bye ma."

Cheryl heads for the door, exiting their million dollar four bedroom home in Hawthorn Meadows. The distant sound of her black Vintage, high heel pumps, clicks against the concrete driveway.

"Let me get going too. I got a long day ahead of me. I don't want my boss yelling at me for being too late. I have a big meeting to attend to this morning." Lawrence kisses Sade on the forehead. "I'll see you later Poohbear."

"A'ight dad, don't forget my graduation is later on tonight."

"Forget, I wouldn't miss it for the world."

"You promise?"

"Yea, I promise."

Sade stands in the doorway watching the only man she has ever loved. The man who raised her, taught her how to ride a bike and drive a car. Despite being a crooked agent, he is a good father. He has always given Sade unconditional love and made many sacrifices for her and her mother. She knows that there is nothing in the world that her father wouldn't do for her.

Sade peers through the screened front door watching her mother pullout of the driveway, while waving bye to her father. An older white woman jogs pass their residence with her puppy running along the side of her. The rearend of her mother's pearl white Lexus GS430 is no longer in view.

The tranquil neighborhood only allows you to hear the rustling sound of trees being slapped by the warm spring breeze. Lawrence climbs into his navy blue Range Rover and places the key into the ignition. He blows a kiss to his pride and joy. As he turns the key slowly, ***Kaboooom!!!*** The truck explodes shaking the earth with a loud, thunderous rumble. Blazing fragments of Lawrence's shredded truck showers the well manicured lawn and driveway. It appears as if it is the last days, raining fire. The impact of the explosion knocks Sade back. Her hands are in front of her face as she cringes on the cold floor. She gets up and rushes outside. The ablazed truck with its top blown open becomes a silhouette, dancing in her eyes.

The curious neighbors step outside, staring at the burning truck in disbelief. All that can be heard is the faraway sound of sirens. Sade falls to the ground, unable to stand. "Noooo! Daddy! Noooo!" Sade cries uncontrollably, feeling dizzy and sick to her stomach. "Noooo!" She continues to cry, swaying her head as if she has just been defeated. The smell of burnt metal lingers in the air, as thick, black smoke billows from the remnants of the truck. Sade hits the ground with her fist. "You promised me!" She cried.

A black Mercedes Benz with limo tint is parked a half a block away from the Blackwell's residence. The back door is ajar for the dog. The man takes off the white wig once he climbs into the car. He puts on his communication head set, while making observations through a pair of binoculars. "1-8-7." He speaks into the headset tossing the binoculars in the back seat, startling the poodle. He pulls off in a casual manner as a fire truck races by him.

Detective Carlos Herra was the first to arrive at the scene. A veteran to the homicide department and a personal friend of Lawrence. He is short and stocky, with bushy eyebrows. He signaled to the paramedics to assist Sade off the ground. "Get this place cleaned up," he yelled to the other uniformed officers that were just arriving. "Rope the area off, talk with the neighbors; find out if anyone has seen anything suspicious." Herra walks to his cruiser, and shakes his head. "Damn it Lawrence, what have you gotten yourself into now," he mumbles to himself. Herra puts out a call to Lawrence's partner. The phone rings repeatedly and goes to the voicemail. Someone has to break the news to his wife and he doesn't want to be the one, but it has to be done. He speeds off, headed for the Federal Building.

MCC CHICAGO

A MCC correctional officer struts to Kennytha Baptiste's cell block carrying multiple lunch bags on a metal cart. "Lunch time inmate Baptiste." The burly, freckled faced, white correctional officer announced, stationed in front of the cell block in his uniform. Baptiste rises from his bed, approaching the secured door.

Kennytha Baptiste is a well known Haitian drug lord from the West Indies. He has short dreads, charcoal color skin and even darker eyes. He is tall, with a muscular frame. He is dressed in his orange, jail issued jumpsuit with MCC stamped across the back of it.

He came to the United States of America at the age of ten and was introduced to the drug trade at the age of sixteen. He began his criminal career as a mule, transporting small amounts of heroin into the country for his uncle.

The C.O. hands Baptiste the lunch bag through the open slot on the steel door. The officer closes the slot and stares through the window, locking eyes with Kennytha. They nod their heads at each other and the C.O. struts away, passing out the remainder of the lunch bags to the other inmates housed in the segregated unit.

Baptiste is perched on the edge of his bed, fishing through his lunch bag. He removes two dry baloney sandwiches, throwing them to the dirty concrete floor. He cracks a wicked smile as he pulls out the prepaid Sch-i830 Samsung cellular phone. He presses the power button, bringing the phone to life. He dials a number and places the phone to his ear.

DEA agent Timothy Cohart opens his eyes in complete darkness. He is lying on his back, unaware of his placement. The sedation of the chloroform that was injected into his system, no longer has an effect on him. Timothy Cohart, is Lawrence Blackwell's partner.

Timothy feels around the tight spaceless casket, trying to feel out his environment. As his hand traces the interior of the closed casket, he feels a furry rabbit sized creature. He becomes frightened as he feels many more furry rabbit sized creatures that seem to be lifeless.

A cellular phone illuminates the casket with a green glow, chiming a customized ringtone. Scarface's "You gotta minute to pray and a second to die", plays, gaining Timothy's attention. As the cellular phone shines, he can see the outline of the numerous rats scattered all over. He answers the phone. "Good Afternoon. Me know you probably surprised to hear from me," Kennytha said in his thick Haitian accent.

"Come on Kennytha, please let me live. I'm telling you, it wasn't my fault. I told Lawrence to make his bitch drop the case. Please man, let's work this out." Timothy begged.

"Me sorry Mr. Cohart, dis is a non-negotiable situation. Me told you from day one, if you crossed me, me will kill you muthafucka. God say, thou shall not kill, but me write me own fuckin' commandments." He was screaming now. "This is my muthafuckin' world and me want everything in it!" Timothy can feel the movement of the rodents coming to life, as the chloroform they were injected with wears off.

"Please Kennytha. Please spare my life. I got two precious daughters to go home to and a wife. Please, I'll do anything".

"Me knew betta to mess with a blue eyed devil. The rats inside the casket 'bout to wake. Them not eat in several days."

The hungry rodents begin to move rapidly, eating into Timothy's flesh. "Aaarrgghh! Please. Noooo! Somebody help me." Timothy grimaces in pain as the rats enjoy their feast. He can see the many red eyes of the rodents glowing in the darkness. An inhuman scream escapes from his lungs as he attempts to shake the filthy creatures from his frame. He is nearing hysteria.

"Me told you me reach is long. Me hands reach all around the world." Timothy does not hear him, he has dropped the phone long ago. Being unable to endure the pain, he passes out and begins to dream.

He can see the casket being opened up. It's Lawrence. "I knew you would come for me." Then Lawrence did a strange thing, he threw a gun into the casket and closed it back. Timothy picked it up and placed it to his head, pulling the trigger. He didn't wake up from his dream.

Kennytha can only hear the squeaking of the rats feasting on flesh. He presses end on his phone with a wicked laugh dispersing from his vocal cords as he begins to sing his version of, "He Got The Whole World in His Hands." "Me got the whole world, in me hands. Me got the whole world in me hands. Me got judges and witnesses in me hands. Me got the whole world in me handddds."

Members of Kennytha's organization are burying DEA agent Timothy Cohart's body, six feet deep, never to be found.

Cheryl Blackwell enters into the Federal building. She passes through the security gate and the guard hands her back her purse. "Excuse me Mrs. Blackwell, Mr. Sorensten wants to see you in his office." A young blonde intern informs her."

"Thank you." Cheryl heads for his office. She knocks on the door before entering.

"Come in." The voice is crisp and authorative. Mr. Sorensten sits behind his desk. He is a gaunt man, in his late fifties, with balding, silver hair that he keeps slicked to the sides. He waves her to have a seat in the mahogany chair. "Listen, the bigwigs are breathing down my back. They want you to go into some sort of protection program." Cheryl crinkles her face, an old habit when she's upset about something. "Cheryl, I see that look, it'll be just be until the case is over."

"No, I'm not doing it. I'm not going to let some two-bit, criminal run me into hiding."

"I figured you would say as much. Well it's your decision and your safety on the line. I wish you would give it more thought, but I know your mind is made up and we all know once that happens." Sorensten threw his hands in the air shaking his head.

"Are we finished here?" Cheryl asked.

"That's all I had to say and oh, someone from the security detail is suppose to be stopping by to visit you. Inform them of your decision."

With that being said, Cheryl walked to her office. She had a trial to prepare for.

Detective Herra ran the different scenarios through his head as he turned down Dearborn Street. "***Hi, you don't know me, but I was a friend of your husbands. By the way, he's dead.***" No, that wouldn't work, he thought out loud. Neither would, "***What day will you have Lawrence's funeral, he would want me to be there.***" Herra ran his hands down his face, as he parked the cruiser. It was no use trying to think of the right words to say in such a situation. "There are none," he said to himself as he walks into the building.

The elderly black guard greeted him as he approached the security gate. "Sir, you're going to have to check your gun in until you come out."

"What? Oh, no problem." Herra passes him his revolver.

"You here for probation?"

"No, actually, I'm here to see Mrs. Blackwell."

"Just keep going straight, it's the second door on your left."

"Thanks."

Herra found the door, it was slightly cracked. He knocked anyways. "Just a minute. Ok, come in." She greeted him at the door. "Hi, I was expecting you Mr. Uh-."

"Herra," he shook her outstretched hand in confusion. "You were?"

"Yeah, I know why you are here. I just want to let you know I'm fine."

"You are?" He said, perplexed by her response. Herra stared at her in disbelief. He had heard of people coping with losses quickly, but this was insane.

"Yep, so you can save the speech. I'm a tough girl." Herra was scratching his head.

"And I'm going to assume you know your daughter was taken to the Highland Park hospital." Cheryl's face goes blank. "She wasn't harmed in the explosion," he added.

"Explosion? What? You're not here from the security detail are you?"

"No ma'am, I'm with the Chicago Homicide department. Your husband was killed today in a truck bomb explosion." Her face crinkles.

"What? Get out of here!" She shouts, pushing him in the chest. "Get out of my office. Lawrence isn't dead, I just left him. Shame on you!" Herra tries to fend off the vicious blows that she's throwing. He reaches in his pocket and takes out his card. He tries handing it to her and she knocks it out of his hand. The paper card falls silently to the carpet. "Get out of here you monster!" Herra turns around and exits the office. He grabs his revolver from the guard and goes to sit in his car.

"Well, that went well," he said to himself. "So much for the preparation." There is nothing he can do now. "She has my card, she'll call if she needs me," he said.

Cheryl slams her door as Detective Herra makes his exit. "***What a day. First, they tried to put me in a protection program, then some clown comes in with some sick joke about Lawrence being dead.***" She didn't give it a second thought. She had too much work to do for the upcoming case. She had to have everything finished by four o'clock. That's the time Lawrence always calls and tells her he loves her. ***"I will finish my work, no breaks for me, unless I take a break to go and tell Mr. Sorensten we need to hire a different guard. Old man Arnold is getting to old,"*** *she reasoned.* ***"He's letting any quack that comes through in. He probably wasn't even with the police."***

She sits down in front of her computer and begins to prepare the files for the Baptiste case. At 3:59 sharp, she shuts down her computer and waits for Lawrence's call. At 4:23, she decides, ***"He must be in a meeting. Sometimes they run long,"*** she told herself. At 7:10 p.m. she turns off the lights in her office and heads home. Lawrence still hadn't called. ***"He's probably at home by now."***

It didn't dawn on her until she saw the yellow tape surrounding her lawn. The charred, black concrete where the truck had been, and burnt blue fragments of the truck stuck in the grass. She screams as the reality of the tragic event invades her. ***"Lawrence is dead"***, she thought. One minute later she stopped. Then she thought about the man who told her that Sade was in the hospital. The screaming continues.

Cheryl's teared, stained face, looks like a scene from a scary movie not yet invented. Her mascara is smeared carelessly on her face like it is Halloween. She approaches the reception desk and startles the nurse stationed behind the counter.

"Oh my, can I help you?"

"This frog looking bitch got a lot of nerves. Even on my worst day I look better than her." Thought Cheryl, taking offense from the woman's reaction. "I'm looking for my daughter."

"Name please?"

"Sade Blackwell." The woman types the information from the woman's reaction into computer.

"Hmm."

"What is it?" Cheryl asked, with fear written all over her face.

"Well, it says here that, she was transferred from the trauma unit, but it doesn't say where. Gimme a sec, let me call." The woman picks up the phone and scribbles a note on a little piece of paper. It reads, Psychiatric ward, room 203a. "Just take the elevator behind you to the seventh floor." She hands Cheryl the paper. When Cheryl left the woman thought to herself, ***"It must run in the family."***

Cheryl rushes to the elevator as it is just about to close. She reaches her hand out to stop it. She steps inside and a man is coughing profusely. The black nurse with him tells him to quit and he stops instantly. A woman in a wheelchair says to Cheryl, "These aren't my legs. I have another pair." Cheryl contemplates on telling the nurse to press seven then changes her mind.

"They got to be going to my floor," she said to herself.

The psychiatric ward is bright. Everything is white, from the nurses and doctors uniforms, down to the computer equipment. Cheryl walks pass a nurse reprimanding a sixty year old man. "How many times do I have to tell you, you are not Spiderman." A clean cut Jewish doctor approaches the nurse.

"What he do this time?"

"I found him in his room hanging upside down from the shower again." The doctor gives the man a disapproving look.

"Excuse me doc." Cheryl interrupted, gaining his attention.

"Yes ma'am, what can I do for you?" Cheryl glances at the piece of paper.

"I'm looking for room 203a, my daughter was brought here. Is she okay?" He looks at the ceiling trying to recall which patient is in that room.

"Let me see," He glances at the clipboard. "Ah, the new arrival. Well, if you mean, okay, as if she's sane, than yes. She was sent to this floor because the hospital was running short on rooms. Just follow the hall we're in now and you'll run right into it. Is that all ma'am?"

"Yes, thank you doctor."

"No problem, glad I could help."

Cheryl follows the hall around the curve. She hears multiple animal sounds coming from the open rooms.

Every zoo species is equally represented. She enters into the room and finds Sade lying in the bed in a fetal position crying. "Sade." Sade turns over, her puffy, red eyes stare back at her mother. Cheryl rushes to her side and embraces her in a hug. They share a tearful and emotional moment.

"Why mama, why?"

"I don't know baby," she answered rocking Sade in her arms."I just don't know." Then the conversation with Lawrence pops into her head.

"Why don't you let Al handle the case? Baptiste is dangerous."

"He's no more dangerous than Melvin."

"But... I just don't want anything to happen-"

"Don't worry, nothing is going to happen, I'm prepared for the consequences."

The guilt that she is feeling made her cry even harder. Her mind is clouded with a million, 'ifs'. "If only I would have told him about the threats. If only I would have dropped the case like he asked me to." She knew very well who had been making the threats and why Lawrence had been killed. Rather or not, she is going to admit it is another question.

"Come on Sade baby, let's go home." As they walk out the door, Cheryl makes a vow to herself. ***"I'm going to make sure that bastard spends the rest of his life behind bars."***

Chapter Two

ONE MONTH LATER

Sade moves rapidly along with her co-worker Olivia, counting their drawers, ending a hard day of work at the currency exchange in Englewood, on 63rd and Racine. The security guard awaits them as they place the money into the safe.

Loud thunderous bass causes the windows of the check cashing place to vibrate attracting their attention. Olivia's boyfriend Ice pulls up in the front in a Sunkist orange Hummer H2 on 30 inch chrome LX116 rims. The multiple television screens inside the truck illuminates the peanut butter interior, outlining his facial features as he converses on his cell phone. The diamond bezel on his Amaswiss watch and his iced out platinum teeth twinkles.

"I can't believe this nigga finally made it on time for a change." Olivia stated, grabbing her Dooney and Bourkes purse.

Sade peers through the bulletproof glass admiring Ice's truck. Ice buys Olivia anything she wants. He even told Olivia that she doesn't have to work if she does not want to, but she chooses to work because she knows that the game Ice is playing is a temporary game and it all comes to an end. Olivia has dated several drug dealers in the past. She always tries to convince Ice to change his game and do something different with his money, but his infatuation with money, sex, power, and fame will not allow him to diversify.

Sade always notices the lustful stares that he flashes every time they cross each other's path. The armed security guard escorts them outside as he secures the establishment. "I'll see you later girl. You take it easy and keep your head up. I know it has been hard on you lately. You know if you need me you can always call me." Olivia stated.

"I appreciate that Olivia, but I'll be alright." Sade replied, unlocking the door of her Mazda 626.

"Okay, you be safe."

"You too."

Olivia Climbs into Ice's truck waving bye to Sade.

Sade puts her Keisha Cole CD into the disc player. Sade has always had a lust for the street life after watching her cousin Pirelli obtain the finer things in life. Pirelli is on his way back home after serving a short period of confinement. Due to Sade research, in her mother's personal law library, she managed to assist him at getting a lighter sentence.

Her high school sweetheart Deangelo, always laughs at her when she talks about her fantasy and tells her that the game is not for a woman. He encourages her to pursue going to college to study law, along with her parents, but Sade just is not ready for anymore schooling at this time.

Sade stares at Ice's truck as it turns out of the parking lot. It's chunky, chrome rims glisten and chop, reflecting on the smooth pavement. ***"I know if that nigga can get major bread, than a bitch like me can get paid."*** Sade thought, making her way through traffic.

Many spectators mingle together, cramming the Dirksen Federal courthouse, in branch 32, room 207, awaiting the results of Kennytha Baptiste's trial. The courtroom is in complete silence as Kennytha's multi-million dollar defense team, takes the stage. The young, beak-faced, beady-eyed Jewish lawyer from Steingold & Steingold, rises from the defense table.

"Your Honor, I would like to move for a dismissal, due to a lack of evidence, and the witnesses' failure of appearance. The government has been given, in my opinion, substantial amount of time to bring forth their witnesses' and other substantial evidence." He adjusts his tie and prances around the courtroom like he owns it. "Furthermore, without these ghost appearances, the government is unable to prove their case, beyond a reasonable doubt. According to my files, a Mr. Timothy Cohart, was scheduled to testify and he's nowhere in sight." The lawyer looks around the room, then towards the door as if he expects Timothy to walk in. "I submit, that my client, is nothing more than a tax paying citizen." Attorney Markkus Steingold advocated. Mrs. Blackwell scowls at the points during attorney Steingold's presentation. Attorney Steingold, stands tall, in his tailor made Zanetti suit, with strong confidence. "With all due respect your Honor, for the foregoing reasons, I ask that all charges against my client be dismissed." Attorney Steingold finished. Kennytha smiles slightly as he plasters his eyes on Mrs. Blackwell.

"Who does this drug dealing, murdering bastard think he is? He will not get away with this." Mrs. Blackwell thought.

"Prosecution, do you have anything you would like to add, before I make my decision?" Judge Milton inquired, sitting behind the desk, in his black robe, with his receding hair line.

"Yes your Honor. The government would like to request more time to locate the witnesses." Mrs. Blackwell stated, hoping that the judge would grant her request. She continued. "As in his last case, we're sure he is responsible for the missing-."

"Objection your Honor," Steingold was up in a flash. "My client was never found guilty of any of those charges and what she's saying is pure speculation. It has no use in the courtroom."

"Sustained," said Judge Milton. "I'm going to agree with the defense here. Your walking on a very tight rope here Mrs. Blackwell, so be careful. Do you have anything you wish to say?"

"Sorry your honor, just for more time."

"I see. I have to come to a decision people of the courts. Mr. Steingold, I have to grant your motion for dismissal."

The courtroom erupts into an uproar before Judge Milton could finish delivering his decision. Cheryl listens in disbelief, with her face crinkled. A clatter of contending conversations dominates the courtroom. Judge Milton bangs his gavel. "Order in the court! Order in the court!" Judge Milton amplifies his voice, regulating the disorderly courtroom. Kennytha leans back in his chair smiling. He winks his eye at Mrs. Blackwell, taunting her.

"Me coming for you next," he silently mouths. Attorney Steingold places his hands on Kennytha1s shoulder, proud of himself for a job well done. "Get me out of here. Orange is not me color."

Two hours later, Kennytha exits the front entrance of MCC Chicago. He inhales the fresh breeze. He's dressed in a wrinkled Polo khaki suit, with no laces in his Havanna Joes.

News reporters and cameramen from channel 9 and 7 news rush in the direction of the reputed kingpin as he makes his way to the silver Porsche. A channel 7 reporter questions Kennytha. "Mr. Baptiste, is it true that your organization paid off federal witnesses?"

Another news reporter from channel 9 asked, "Isn't it true that your organization is responsible for the assassination of at least one DEA agent? And the possible disappearance of another?"

Kennytha pushes all of the cameras and microphones away from him, disregarding their questions. "Get them fuckin' cameras out of me face!" he bellowed, breaking through the large disorderly crowd. He opens the door of the sports car, climbing into the passenger seat. He presses the power button on the door panel and the tinted window descends. "This is how me feel about the federal government!" he shouted out the window to the news reporters, elevating his middle finger. Kennytha activates the sound system. The sweet melody of his favorite reggae artist, legendary Bob Marley blares from the speakers.

Kennytha knows that the dismissal of his case has caused a lot of controversy. He knows that the federal government will not rest until he is either dead or behind bars. "Did you bring me personal?" Kennytha asked the driver.

"It's in the glove compartment boss." Reno informed. Kennytha opens the glove compartment and pulls out a quarter ounce of uncut cocaine, which looks like crushed glass. He unties the plastic bag eagerly, ready to feed his nose. He sticks his pinky finger into the bag, scooping out a small portion of its fine flakes. He places his pinky finger close to his nose, snorting the cocaine. He feeds each nostril and lie back in the leather seats, with his eyes closed. His face becomes numb within seconds, as he embraces the instant gratification. Hearing the sound of the reggae, he feels like he is in another world.

"Step on it. Me know them cockroaches followin' us." Kennytha blurts, feeling invincible from his victory against the federal government. Reno follows his order and smashes down on the gas causing their bodies to jerk back. The car reaches top speed, plastering their backs to the seats. They detour through traffic, vanishing out of sight.

The sound effects of the movie 'State Property' escapes from the surround sound speakers in Bianca's Englewood apartment. Bianca is accompanied by Sade and Carmen. The trio has been friends since middle school. Bianca and Carmen always considered Sade lucky, being that they both came from single parent homes. Now, for the first time in life Sade can really relate with the two on how it feels to be fatherless. After hearing how Bianca and Carmen fathers had cut out on their mothers and left them to struggle on their own, Sade is grateful for the time she did get to spend with her father.

Lawrence always blessed her with the latest fashions, and she looked out for her girls. There were times he had helped out both of their parents financially and for that they were forever grateful. To them, he was the perfect father figure they wish they had.

Carmen Young had one child, a two year old daughter named Renee. She conceived her at the young age of sixteen, which is her reason for dropping out of school. She found employment at a local hair salon. She has a pretty face, but is a little on the chubby side, which she blames on her pregnancy. She has dark, milk chocolate skin, brown eyes, and shoulder length microbraids.

Bianca Nunez graduated from high school, but never was able to attend college. Her mother couldn't afford to send her to college. Blanca promised herself that she will go to college one day. She is short and fine. She has brown eyes that are pecan shaped, high cheek bones, with thick full lips like Angelina Jolie. Her sandy brown hair is cut short and is blended with red highlights.

Sade sits on the carpeted living room floor Indian style with her back against the tattered leather sofa. "Y'all know what? I've been thinkin' about making me some fast money," Sade claimed, seizing the attention of her friends.

"Girl you trippin', I don't know what's gotten into you

lately," Carmen stated. "I know this movie ain't having an influence on you."

"Yeah mami, you trippin' fo' real," Bianca added.

The television illuminates the living room, causing shadows to cast on the ceiling. "Naw, I'm not trippin'. I'm serious. It's time for a bitch to get paid. If them niggas out here getting money, why can't I. If they can do it I can do it even better." Sade sincerely stressed, with a solemn expression, gazing at the two bewildered women.

"Those streets are not made for a woman," Carmen stated. "Why you just want go to college and study law like your mother wanted you to do? Just like you helped your cousin Pirelli, you can help somebody else. You know your moms will pay for your tuition."

"Ha! Ha! College, yeah right Carmen. What is college going to do for me, except get me a nine to five bustin' my ass everyday for peanuts."

"Still Sade, you shouldn't pass on an opportunity to go to college mami," chimes in Bianca "Do you know how many people wish they could go and don't get the chance?" Bianca being one of those people could relate, and her grades weren't high enough to get a scholarship.

"Well, I'm going to fall back so those people ya'll talkin' about can get their chance. I'd just be takin' up space."

Bianca rolls her eyes at Sade, but she does not notice. ***"Forever the spoiled brat,"*** she thought to herself.

"I'm show these niggas how a true bitch get down. All I got to do is find me good connect. I got somebody in mind I'mma holla at. The nigga mad paid too girl. So y'all either gon' get down or lay down?" Sade mocked the movie, smiling at her girls.

"You see Bianca, I told you we should have rented 'Maid In Manhattan'," Carmen said. They all roll on the floor in laughter.

"Naw, but fo' real mami, I hope you know what you're

about to get into," Bianca stated. "They giving out a lot of time for that shit."

"Yeah, I know the consequences. But most people that go down do so because of greed. For me, it's about more than just money."

"Oh yeah, than what else is it about?" asked Bianca.

"It's about-, it's about-" Sade could not find the words.

"My point exactly, it's always money," Bianca proclaimed.

Sade stands up yawning, extending her hands towards the ceiling "Let me head out, it's getting late." the distant sound of Carmen's daughter crying in the back room. "I'll call y'all and let y'all know I made it home safe."

"A'ight girl, you be careful," Carmen advised.

"Alright mami," Bianca said.

Sade climbs inside her car. She looks into the rearview mirror and questions herself. ***"If it ain't only about the money, than what else is it about?"*** a inner voice answered the question she had trouble with answering. ***"It's about this being my only chance to get close to the man who killed daddy."*** As she drives home, she figured out the other reason why she wants to be in the game. The question is what is she going to do when she find him.

Sade peels her clothes off preparing herself for a hot bubble bath. Her black satin Arak's dress tumbles to the ivory tiled floor with a soft clump. She dips her foot into the tub and the water makes her cringe slightly. She removes her foot quickly as steam vapors rises from the tub. Slowly she eases her way into the tub and her body adapts to the water temperature. She relaxes with her eyes closed, mulling things over in her mind with the bubbles covering half her chest.

"What type of gun is this Sade?" Lawrence Blackwell asked, holding the black and chrome revolver out to his ten year old daughter. The blindfold covers her cinnamon brown eyes as she handles the weapon in the privacy of their spacious backyard.

Sade has been handling weapons since the age of six, and often practices at the built in fire range inside the shed located on their property. Mrs. Blackwell does not know that Lawrence has allowed Sade to fire weapons in his presence. The secret staying safe between father and daughter.

Sade spins the weapon in her tiny hands, feeling the grooves as the sun beams down, giving an added glow to her yellow sundress.

"Umm, a Beretta Cougar .32 automatic." She replies with a smile plastered on her face.

"Good, and what about this one?" Lawrence takes the gun and replaces it with one of the similar weight. Sade studies the weapon carefully. Her eyebrows furry upward, right above the red covering of her face. "Give up?" Lawrence asked.

"No daddy," She giggled, "I know the answer, I just sometimes get confused."

"So you saying that you don't know?" Lawrence questioned.

"I didn't say that. I know it's between the Colt and the Sauer." She stammered.

"Which one is it quick?"

"Uhh, the Colt."

"Wrong."

"You didn't let me finish. I was about to say the Colt is not the one." She replied giggling. They are interrupted in their training session by Sade's mother.

"Lawrence, don't be out there letting my baby hold no guns. She needs to be playing with the Barbie dolls

I bought her." Cheryl Blackwell screamed through the patio screen.

"She don't want to play with no Barbie dolls Cheryl. I got to show her how to protect herself from all the little boys that's going to be after her cause she's so pretty." Lawrence ruffles her long jet black hair.

"Stop it daddy, yuck boys, I can't stand them."

Her cellular phone chimes, snapping her out of her trance. "Who's callin' me this late at night? It's probably either Bianca or Carmen calling to lecture a bitch," Sade theorized. "Hello."

"That's all I get is a hello," Deangelo said. Sade shifts her body in the tub. Her left hand disappeared somewhere beneath the water.

"Hey baby, I was just thinking about you," she lied.

"Oh, you was? What was you thinking about?" Small ripples form in the water.

"Just how neglected my body has been since you went away to college."

Deangelo is Sade's high school sweet heart. He is one year older than she is. "I'mma have to make that up to you."

"You better."

"Anyways, speaking of college, have you decided where you're going? I was hoping you come to USC with me. You can get a degree in law here. That way we can spend more time together."

"***Damn, here he go lecturing a bitch, fuckin' up my flow. I wonder did Bianca put him up to this***." Her hand shot out of the water. "You know I would like to baby, but my mom would never let me come out to California. I'm all she got left." ***"It was partly true"***, she thought.

"I know, I know," he agreed, saddened by the news, but understanding. "So, how you doing?"

"I'm doing okay. You know me baby. I miss you Deangelo."

"I miss you, too sweetheart. That's why I was callin' you to tell you I got a surprise for you."

"And what's that?"

"If I tell you it won't be a surprise."

"Alright. So when will I see you again?"

"Real soon baby. College life ain't easy. My professor keeps me busy. All of this shit is almost over with."

"Besides college, how is life in Cali."

"It's a'ight. It can be better with you by my side."

"I hear that baby."

"Well, let me go baby. I got work tomorrow. With that new promotion I got, it means more money, but the hours is longer. I'mma need my rest. Love you Sade."

"I love you too Dee." Sade hangs up the phone and lies back, wishing Deangelo was right beside her, to satisfy her with his warm touch. "Oh well," Sade said aloud, frustrated. She has work tomorrow as well. Her hand disappears under the water again and she closes her eyes.

Sade and Olivia are stationed behind the bulletproof glass of the semi-crowed currency exchange. The two young women satisfy the request of the awaiting customers. The line slowly disperses one by one, leaving the establishment empty.

Sade grabs her bag having free time. She removes a new urban novel she purchased from Barnes & Noble entitled 'Change The Game'. "Gurl, what you know about that book you reading?" Olivia inquired. Olivia is a devoted urban novel fan. She has the same book at home in her collection.

"I know Niko be doin' it big. So far this book is off the chain."

"Just wait until you get to the end. It's gon' fuck you

up gurl." Olivia said enthusiastically. "Ole boy Niko is ..." Olivia continued, being cut short in mid-sentence before she can say anymore.

"Don't tell me. Let me finish reading it," Sade suggested.

"My bad gurl. I just got a little carried away," Olivia apologized.

Olivia peers through the window noticing a man approaching with two dozen pink roses in his hand and a small green suede box. "It looks like somebody got a surprise," Olivia proclaimed, smiling on the inside.

The man steps to Olivia's booth. Olivia smiles at the man. "I have a special delivery for a Ms. Sade Blackwell. Would that be you young lady?" Olivia's smile fades away.

"That's probably what Deangelo was talking about." Sade thought, unable to hear what the man is saying to Olivia. She points to Sade booth. Sade flashes a delightful smile, as the man makes his approach.

"Would you please sign this receipt to show that you recieved the package." He places the receipt into the slot. After Sade signs the receipt, she had to unlock the side door and walk around to get the package. The delivery man hands her the gifts and watches as she walks back into the work station.

"My, my, my, I don't know what they puttin' in the water these days, but I sho' wish they would have did it in my generation," He thinks to himself as he exits the building.

Sade returns to her seat and inhales the sweet fragrance of the pink roses. Olivia stares at the small box with curiosity.

"Hurry up gurl, open the box."

"Damn Olivia, you sure this ain't for you?" Sade opens the box being blinded by the pink diamond bracelet. Olivia gasps, staring at the extravagant piece of jewelry.

"Gurl you must be puttin' that pussy on some nigga for him to buy you a bracelet like that. It almost looks like the bracelet Ice bought me for Valentine's Day, except mines have white diamonds."

Sade doesn't even hear a word she is saying. She is deep in her own thoughts. ***"Damn, how Deangelo afford something like this,"*** she thought. Than she remembered him telling her about his promotion. Sade finds a folded piece of paper inside the box that reads: ***Surprise! Call me at 9:00 p.m., 454-5111***. A small crowd of customers pour into the check cashing place and Sade stashes her gifts.

Sade hangs up her cell phone after calling the number in the jewelry box. She analyzes the pink diamond bracelet as she waits patiently in the parking lot of Harold's Chicken, on 73rd and Stoney. She turns up the sounds listening to Beyonce's 'Upgrade'. As she bobs her head, a brown Chrysler Imperial pulls beside her with tinted windows, attracting her attention. The chrome 24 inch Giovanna blades shimmer along with the low profile Toyo tires, glazed with BlackMagic.

Sade's cell phone vibrates in her lap. The screen on the face of her phone glows, displaying private caller. "Yeah, who this?" Sade answered.

"Damn, is that how you always answer yo' phone baby," the caller asked in his deep voice.

"I don't like to answer private calls."

"My bad sweetheart. I apologize. Get out and holla at me. This me right on the side of you."

Sade climbs out of the car, wearing a pair of tight fitting Ecko Red jeans and a matching Ecko Red halter top, stealing the man's attention. Sade opens the door and the interior lights shine, revealing the two-tone brown and crème leather interior. She closes the door and the lights dim slowly. "You never expected it to be me that sent you those roses and the bracelet huh?" Ice inquired with his fifty thousand dollar smile.

"Naw, I didn't expect it to be you," Sade replied. She stares at him like he is crazy. ***Niggas know they ain't no good. He must think I'm like the rest of these hoes. Like I seriously didn't know who it was, when he sent the same bracelet***, Sade thought to herself.

"I didn't think you would want to go on a date so quick." Ice stated, staring at her with lust burning in the depths of his eyes. Sade had to admit he is cute with his long braids, freshly corn rowed, but she isn't here for all that.

"Look, let me get straight down to business and keep it real with you. The only reason why I agreed to meet with you is because I'm ready to get paid. I was gon' have Olivia holla at you, but you made it easier." Sade stressed. Ice looks at her with his face contorted.

"I know you ain't talkin' about hustlin'?"

"What, you don't think a woman can get down out here?"

Ice chuckles, taking Sade for a joke. "If you would be my woman, you wouldn't have to worry about selling drugs."

"And what exactly would you have me do? Barely make ends meet like Olivia and wait on yo' gifts. Thanks, but no thanks. I was taught to be independent and pay my own way." Sade informed, placing the bracelet in his palm.

"What you know about the streets baby? You heard what James Brown said. This is a man's world," Ice snaps, as she crushes his pride. "From what I heard, you was born with a silv-, make that a platinum spoon in yo' mouth. You don't know nothin' about this game. You wouldn't last six months. Seriously, what nigga gon' respect you. Let me know so I can rob his bitch ass."

Ice grew up in the Ida B. Wells Projects. He's known throughout the projects as a certified baller. "I see you take me for a joke. I'm not like the rest of these bitches you deal with. I don't need no man to take care of me. Sorry for wasting yo' precious time. I know you got a lot of business to attend too." Sade stated, opening the door to his car. She jumps into her car and pulls off. ***"I still got my cousin, he'll be home in a couple of days."*** She thought to herself. Her cousin Pirelli wasn't getting it like that, but he would be a start. "I'mma be the baddest bitch that ever touched the streets of Chicago," she said aloud with strong confidence. Ice's rejection only did one thing for her, it caused her drive to increase. Sade knows with her intellect, beauty, and skills, she can dominate the game.

TWO WEEKS LATER

Sade and her cousin Pirelli navigates through the energetic city in Pirelli's red bubble Riviera he purchased his first week home, after serving two and a half years in Joliet State Penitentiary for possession of illegal narcotics. Pirelli was facing 15 years, but with Sade's ability to interpret the law, Pirelli walked away with 5 years, only having to serve half of it with his good time.

Sade can't believe how much he resembles his father, only without the curly hair. They pull into the parking lot of Victory Faith Baptist Church. "What we doing here? Don't tell me you let prison turn you into a church boy." Sade stated, lounging in the passenger seat. Pirelli lets out a short chuckle.

"Church boy. Naw'll, you know cuzzo ain't changed.

Just sit back and relax. I got this fam," Pirelli proclaimed, climbing out of the car. "Just sit tight, I'll be right back".

Pirelli enters the empty church from the rear entrance scanning the scenery. He hears a combination of musical notes producing a smooth melody. He spots Pastor Moore seated beneath a large bronze crucifix, playing the organ and humming praise his name. Pirelli struts down the burgundy carpeted aisle in Pastor Mario's direction. The smooth melody and harmonized humming ceases as Pastor Moore turns around, aware of Pirelli's presence.

"I'm glad you finally made it son," Pastor Moore admitted, removing his silk handkerchief from the pocket of his suit jacket. He uses it to wipe the perspiration from his forehead. "What you got for me?" Pastor Moore asked, glad to see Pirelli.

"You said you wanted an eightball didn't you?"

"That's right. Let's hurry up, I have another speech to deliver shortly." Pastor Moore grabs a hundred dollars in various denominations from the silver collection plate. He drops the money into Pirelli's hand. Pirelli retrieves a sack of different sized rocks from his crotch area, handing the Pastor an eightball. Pastor Mario's eyes glow with anticipation. "God bless you son." Pirelli stares at the Pastor in disgust.

"***Fuckin' hypocrite***," he thought, as he places the sack back into his crotch area. "Just hit me and I'll be at yo' service to answer yo' prayers faster than Jesus," Pirelli retorted as he heads for the exit.

Pastor Moore grabs his glass pipe from underneath the organ hurriedly. He seats himself in the front row of the sanctuary and places a yellow chunk into his pipe. It has been a few days since he were able to get high. The services of the church has kept him busy. "My God, my God, why have you forsaken me," he quotes Jesus, holding his blazing lighter in front of his glass pipe, taking a hit. The burning crack crackles and pops, like a bowl of Rice Crispy cereal. The instant gratification from the crack rejuvenates his soul. With his eyes closed, he blows out a cloud of smoke feeling as if he was just filled with the Holy Spirit. He opens his eyes and stares at the large crucifix hanging above him. "Thank you Jesus. Hallelujah."

Pirelli reclines in the driver's seat chatting with Sade. "Boy you goin' to hell for selling dope in a church," tears escape from her eyes as she laughs uncontrollably.

"Hell. I don't believe in that shit. The only thing I believe in is these Benjamin's."

A white Pontiac Grand Prix GT catches their attention. "Where the bread at? That's my man right there." Sade reaches inside her Coach purse pulling out a wad of unorganized bills. "Shit Sade, you suppose to have all the faces facing the same way." Pirelli informed, grabbing the money.

"My fault. Next time I'll have it in order," Sade apologized. Pirelli shakes his head.

"Rookie."

"I got yo' rookie," Sade replied. He jumps into the car with his connect, conversing briefly. "***All I got to do now is talk my uncle into letting me use his apartment. As long as I break him off, he shouldn't have no problem with it***," Sade mused.

Pirelli gets back into the car and hands Sade two ounces of pure white crystal flakes individually wrapped. She wanted to ask him is that all, but didn't want to sound like a rookie. "***I'll just ask my uncle Amos***," she thought to herself.

"That's that good white right there cuz," Pirelli bragged, "When you fry those you should get a little extras." Pirelli stated, enthusiastically. "If you keep shopping wit' him, he'll give it to you for the low, low."

"I'mma be right back at him," she responded, not having a clue on who she is going to sell it to, or for how much.

Carmen steps inside of her small two bedroom apartment exhausted from a long day of work at the hair salon. Her nostrils are immediately slapped with the strong odor of marijuana. The father of her daughter lounges on the sofa playing NBA Live 2010' on Playstation 3 game system. Aware of her presence, he glimpses at her.

"Tyrone, I thought I told you not to smoke that shit in my house with my daughter here. That's all you do is smoke weed and play that damn game all day, while I bust my ass every day. I'm sick of this." Carmen emphasized.

"Stop all that muthafuckin' bitchin'! I don't wanna hear that shit!" Tyrone roared. "I told you I didn't want my daughter around that Puerto-black hoe, but she stopped by today to get Renee."

"Hold up, who you think you talking to like that? This is my fuckin' house. I pay the damn bills around here. The reason I need Bianca to watch Renee is because yo' sorry ass won't watch her or do nothin' fo' her." Carmen snapped.

Tyrone rises from the sofa snarling and charging towards Carmen. He snatches her by the shirt collar aggressively. "Bitch, didn't I tell you, I don't wanna hear that shit?" Tyrone barked, striking her with a powerful back hand. She staggers backwards, crashing against the wall landing on her butt, shielding her face with her hands. Tears stream down her face.

For the past two years of their relationship, Tyrone has been very abusive to Carmen.

"Fuck you and this raggedy ass apartment." Tyrone snatches his Pelle Pelle jacket off the sofa and storms out of the apartment, slamming the door. The pictures on the wall rattle as Carmen remains on the floor, crying and sniffling.

Across town several high ranking political figures congregate at the Pure Heaven Social Club. The aroma of freshly brewed coffee lingers in the atmosphere, commingling with that of cigars and cigarettes.

"It's amazing that the world believes that an organization as superior as ours is extinct," states Judge Milton, "the ignorance of society as a whole. We took off them white robes and put on black ones. We stopped setting wood on fire and sat on benches." He smiled. "And people are none the wiser. You see, when people think of the Klan, they think of red neck southern hillbillies, not sophisticated gentlemen, such as ourselves." Judge Milton expressed to his comrades. He crushes the remainder of his Marlboro cigarette in the ashtray.

"Can you believe," began C.I.A agent Nathan Regan, "that they once viewed us as a terrorist organization? The brotherhood has always attempted to do what was right to keep America safe. Where our ancestors went wrong was in giving them niggers a false sense of citizenship. But one good thing we did was invented the 100 and 1 crack law, which has the prisons full of minorities."

Senator Donald Hennings shakes his head in agreement as Regan continues.

"Now, I'll admit, it has had its advantages, but they don't outweigh the negatives. They just don't know their place anymore. There was a time they wouldn't dare look a white man in the eyes. Now days, that fear has been replaced with open hostility." Agent Regan ranted.

"I agree," said the Senator scanning the sea of pink faces before him. "It's believed that we fell as an organized body, but our agenda moves forward. Our presence is strong throughout the country. We have infiltrated the highest levels of government. We are winning this covert war." The Senator concluded.

"It's amazing; some darkie hasn't tried to join the organization citing affirmative action and other anti-discrimination laws." Sheriff Adams joked, causing the members to chuckle.

"On a more serious note," Judge Milton spoke, "as you all know I just finished up the Baptiste case. I, for one, never want to see that murdering, dope peddling, son of a bitch, off the streets. He gives the little ones in the ghetto something to aspire to. He represents success. He's a hero to his kind. The problem is the prosecutor in his case. She's filing all types of appeals to the seventh circuit, about my ruling. I can't afford to have one of those black judges reviewing the case, 'cause I didn't exactly follow the rules. This is where I was hoping your people can lend me some help Nathan."

"Why don't you just make a call to Sorensten?" Agent Regan asked.

"Who AI, the modern day nigger lover, sometimes Klansman. No sir, you never know what type of sheet he's wearing and this is too important."

"I see, I'll check into it and see if my people can find her alternate employment." He said with a devious smile.

The congregation rises from their seats, pouring out of the room, preparing for their work at hand.

The Foyer Square housing project is located a few blocks south of Wicker Park, on Divsion Street. Outside of the graffiti scarred building with various gang emblems and pitch forks. Junkies roam the trash riddled streets, looking for lost change and bottles.

Sade parks her car next to a gutted out green Ford Tempo. She gets out walking pass a man stretched out in the back seat resting. She looks up at the, dingy red bricks of the high rise building, before going in. She immediately covers her nose with the sleeve of her Prada jacket, after inhaling the dank malodorous scent of the building. She walks quickly to the elevator and presses the button.

"It don't work," said a dark skinned woman with wild hair. A little girl, not more than three years old, wearing a diaper, a dirty pink shirt, and no shoes and socks, tags onto her leg. Sade stares at the girl with dried snot under her nose in discomfort, before returning her attention back to the woman talking. "You gotta take the stairs." She said pointing. "Bring yo' ass on Kisha," the woman yelled to her daughter, whose baby brown eyes are begging Sade to save her. She scurries off in the direction of her mother, looking back at as she enters the stairwell.

A drunk bum is lying in the middle of the stairway, which reminds Sade of a movie she had seen a long time ago called, 'Coming To America'.

After going up the five flights of stairs, she exits into the hallway. The carpet which was once crème in color is now a new shade of brown.

Sade knocks on the door of apartment 5B, waiting patiently for someone to answer. It has been two years since Sade stepped foot in her uncle Amos' apartment. When Pirelli was incarcerated she never had a reason to go to visit Amos. Pirelli had warned Sade about his father's disloyalty. Amos stole Pirelli's stash when he was arrested, leaving him for dead, with a public defender, who tried to sell him out and convince him into taking a bogus plea bargain. After calling Sade to do some research for him, he fired his attorney and was appointed to a new one.

Sade can hear someone fumbling behind the door with the chain. Amos opens the door, greeting Sade with a crater face and an off white smile.

"I can't believe it, my favorite niece. What blows you this way?"

"I need to talk to you about somethin'." Sade replied, scrutinizing her uncle, seeing signs of advancing age.

"Come in, and talk to me." He ushers her into his rundown one bedroom apartment. Amos has always been labeled the black sheep of his family. He clears some off the dirty clothes off of an old tattered chair, giving her a place to sit. He takes a deep breath. "So, I assume this must be about yo' father," Amos assumed, taking a seat in the chair across from her. "I wanted to go to the funeral and see my baby brother for the last time, but we both know he wouldn't have wanted me there."

"I understand, but naw unc, this ain't about my father. This is about me gettin' paid. I need you to let me rent out yo' apartment and help me get this off," Sade explained, placing the two ounces of cocaine on the cocktail table. Amos' eyes enlarged in surprise, as he craves for his next hit.

"I know this rich white boy from up north in yo' area. He's a plastic surgeon and I'm tellin' you, the boy is paiddd.

He comes down here every weekend coping at least an ounce of powder. I usually get it from a guy that lives in this building and take a little out for myself before I give it to him. On top of that, I charge him a couple hundred more for my pocket." Amos picks up one of the ounces, examining it. "This stuff you got here, we can easily sow up this building. But we have one problem though."

"What's that?" Sade asked in confusion.

"This ain't enough, the white boy will cop an ounce himself alone," Amos informed.

"That's cool unc, I'll just call my connect again and get some more."

"Most people around here like it hard. I got some other white friends with money who comes here and stay over all weekend. They be running to the ATM machine all night long. They be doin' they thang." Amos said walking into the kitchen, with the two packages. He removes a calculator sized digital scale from his cabinet and a box of Arm & Hammer baking soda. Sade makes a steady observation. She use to watch Pirelli the same way when she would go by his spot.

"What you doin' unc?"

"I'mma 'bout to cook one of these up for my people and have me a wake up. You know unc gotta test the product. My man normally keep some good shit. Know what I mean?" Sade didn't have a clue, it sounds like to her, he is just trying to get another free hit. He already told her the product she got is capable of sowing up the building.

"***Fuck it, let him do what he do. I'll make it back up in the long run***." Sade said to herself. "Yeah unc, I know what you mean." Sade responded recognizing game.

Amos resembles Sammuel L. Jackson. He removes all the utensils he needs to cook the cocaine. He empties one of the packages and pours out the crystal powder, into a glass Pyrex tube. He sprinkles a small amount of baking soda into the tube, mixing it with the soft white flakes. He adds a little water and stations himself in front of the stove.

"***I have to keep my eyes on unc. Family don't mean shit when it comes to that white dust***," Sade thinks as she continues to watch him closely. Amos holds the Pyrex tube over the fire. The cocaine bubbles, becoming foamy, breaking down slowly transforming into oil base. Now that the dope is in its liquid form, he walks over to the sink and turn on the cold water. He drops a small amount of water into the Pyrex tube; He twirls the tube in a circular motion. The oil base solidifies, turning into a golf ball sized boulder. He holds the rim of it with his thumb and index finger. The white rock makes a clacking sound, bumping against the inside of the tube.

"There you go baby, let daddy rock you," Amos blurted, proud of his work. Amos drops the boulder on the scale and it reads, 29.5 grams. "When this dries up, it looks like you might end up with an extra gram," Amos admitted, hoping that Sade will give him the extras.

"How much the white boy paying unc?"

Amos thinks to himself before replying. "***Should I keep it real or lie? Fuck it, I'mma keep it real wit' my niece and short the white boy.***" "You can tax him eleven hundred an ounce," He answered. Sade becomes excited knowing that fifteen hundred is what she paid for the two ounces.

"***That mean the other ounce I only paid four hundred dollars for. That mean I'mma 'bout to make a nice profit. I'mma take the first fifteen hundred I make and hit Pirelli back, so he can call his man for me,***" She mused. "Look unc, gon' and take the extras and leave me with 28 grams. Once I turn this over a couple times I'mma hit yo' hand real good." Amos smiles from ear to ear.

"I knew it was a reason why I chose you as my favorite niece."

Sade sits in the kitchen at the table as Amos takes a hit. He splashes rubbing alcohol on the glass table top and drops a match. The fire blazes dancing on the table, as he leans forward with his pipe taking a hit. He becomes silent and calmly leans back in the chair. His lips begin to twitch, which is an indication of a good product. Enjoying the cocaine a loud powerful knock at the door startles him and Sade, bringing him back to reality.

Black Jesus navigates his black, big body Mercedes Benz S600 through traffic, heading for a suburban area North of Chicago called Libertyville, Illinois. He is a well groomed Jamaican, with a dark complexion and long tamed dreads. He was educated in the United States. He majored in business and philosophy. Many people say that he's the brains behind Baptiste's organization. Being that he is Kennytha's right hand man provided him with lots of luxuries. However, those gifts didn't come without their share of problems.

He assumes that the federal government will follow him, now that Kennytha has won his trial. In addition to law enforcement, a person of Black Jesus' caliber has to watch out for the wolves, as well as the thirsty thugs on the street corners that are not eating. He had come to respect their hustle, considering the fact that he was once on them same street corners struggling.

Occassionally, he glimpses in the rearview mirrors paranoid, as the rain drums on the windsheild. He knows that if he slips one time it can cost him his freedom or his life. He feels a sense of relief as he enters the subdivison. He passes by the many elegant mansions. It's a couple of kids playing outside in the rain. A man up ahead walks in the rain with no umbrella, then more kids.

"***Wait a minute***," his mind alerts him as the man reaches into his pocket, Boom! A loud thump bangs against the passenger door. With quick reflexes, he ducks down in his seat. The Benz swerves, trampling over a well manicured lawn, leaving tire tracks in the grass. The tires let out a short screech, as he smashes on the gas. He gazes into the rearview mirror and sees a basketball bouncing in the middle of the street. The young kid glances over his shoulders, noticing that the car is far away. He runs into the street chasing the ball. He scoops the ball up and runs back to accompany his friends.

"***Bad ass kids. I should turn around and whip they little ass fo' hittin' my car***," Black Jesus contemplated, he chuckles at his thought. He is happy it was only a basketball and not a bullet.

He pulls up to Kennytha's estate facing the gated entry and presses a button that is positioned in front of a security camera. Kennytha's estate is equipped with a sophisticated security system. If a squirrel comes on his property he knows about it.

The security gates open slowly allowing him to enter. He drives down the winding driveway that leads to Kennytha's French colonial style home. He climbs out of his car making his way to the columned front entrance. He glances at the stone lined pond. He marvels at the 8 foot mahogany door, with its antique solid brass knocker. He signs heavily, "One day," he tells himself.

Before he is able to knock on the door, one of Kennytha's body guards, with a burly build and clean shaven baldhead opens the door, flexing his jaw muscles, gripping an AR-15 assualt rifle, with a strap attached to it. He's already familiar with Black Jesus. He sweeps the air with his hand ushering him inside. He escorts Black Jesus through the extravagant foyer, with its dramatic skylight. They strut across the Brazilian walnut floors. Black Jesus scans the luxurious interior of the mansion. He admires the stone water fountain in the livingroom area, and the catheral ceilings. A large chandelier reflects off a glossy top cherry oakwood 20 seat dining room table.

"Hold up a second," the tamed gorilla instructed, breaking the silence. He opens a cabinet and tosses him a pair of swimming trunks, with the price tag hanging from them, along with a drying cloth. "I think you gon' be needin' those. You can change in there." He points to a dressingroom adjacent to the hallway that leads to a set of glass doors.

He changes over and trails behind the man, stepping on the cold Saturina marble floor in his barefeet. He hears the soft roar of water cascading from a distance. He steps through the glass doors with his muscular structure exposed. Kennytha stands in the 78 foot by 40 foot marbled bottom indoor heated pool. The water sparkles, being illuminated by the dim sunlight that penetrates the glass walls, that sheilds the indoor pool. Three stoned waterfalls cascades.

A beautiful topless Asian chick massages Kennytha's shoulders. An 80 inch projection screen overlooks the stainless steel wetbar; playing 'Shottas' Kennytha takes a toke of his blunt and gazes at Black Jesus through the haze of his ascending smoke, with bloodshot red eyes.

"Come, join me rude boy," Kennytha instructed in his heavy accent, his voice echoing. He eases his way into the pool adjusting to the cool tempature of the water. The Asian woman appraises Black Jesus' solid frame and stares at it in mesmeration.

Kennytha and Black Jesus never discuss business over any electronic devices. Having Black Jesus climb into the pool with him is his way of reassuring himself that it's safe to talk. Although Black Jesus is Kennytha's right hand man, he trusts no one.

"So, did ya have them get rid of the body?"

"Yeah, I handled that right away. He'll never be found," he answered. Kennytha cracks an evil smile.

"That's what me talk about. I think it's time we celebrate me victory." Kennytha snaps his fingers and a beautiful spanish fly prances along the deck in a zebra striped bathing suit, looking like the coming of dawn. She walks behind the wetbar and grabs a bottle of Louis 13 Black Pearl and cracks it open.

"***Now that's what you call eye candy***," Black Jesus thinks to himself, as he traces her viciously curved body. Black Jesus leans against the edge of the deck watching her, as she steps into the pool. She places the bottle to his lips and he clutches it, taking a swig. A smile decorates her honey toned unblemished face as they lock eyes on each other. Black Jesus places the bottle on the deck, with her steadying hands upon his chest. She licks her lips in a circular motion, stroking his love muscle into a throbbing erection. He pulls her close, cupping the bottom of her bubble shaped ass. Her soft firm titties flattens against his chest.

"You want me papi?"

"Do I want you? Baby you damn right I want you." he retorted. She plant's soft genlte kisses on his neck and traces down his chest with her tongue, working her way down. She disappears underneath the water and deep throats him. A warm sensation flows through his bloodstream. He closes his eyes and tilts his head back faintly groaning. Black Jesus' knees become weak as he enjoys her hellified head game. It was as if she got a degree at Brain University, in brainology. Kennytha watches the couple and blurts out.

"Now that's what me call celebrating."

Chief Lawson of the Drug Enforcement Agency fields chants on the phone with one of his superiors, as he's grilled about the disappearance of Timothy Cohart.

"I know sir, he's not on vacation...Yes, we're doing everything in our power to find him." While he's on the phone, a young DEA agent enters into his office. He signals for him to sit down, while he finishes his call. Lawson knows that whatever the agent has to say, has to be significant, because nobody comes into his office unannounced like the agent did, without knocking. Lawson's coal black eyes stare at the agent as he hangs up the phone.

"Now, what's up?"

"Just recieved a tip sir." The agent fills him in with the details.

"Very well, get a team together, and go check it out."

"Okay boss." Lawson smiles to himself as the agent leaves. The news has filled him with hope.

Who is it?" Amos shouted, hoping that it's not law enforcement. Sade gathers up the dope and rushes to the bathroom. She inserts the packaged drugs into her vagina. It causes her to feel uncomfortable. She hears the distant sound of her uncle in a dispute with an unfamiliar voice. She feels relieved, knowing that it's not the police. She steps out of the bathroom, hearing all of the commotion.

"Muthafucka gimme my money, for I fuck you up!" The man yelled, aiming his gun handgun at Amos' chest.

"Unc, what's going on here?" Sade inquired.

"He owe me five hundred, that's what the fuck is going on!" The man shouted, waving the gun frantically.

"I told you, I'mma pay you Donnavan." Amos said, trying to pacify the man.

"You ain't gon' keep tellin' me the same shit! Sade reaches into her purse to take control of the situation, as Donnavan focuses on Amos.

"Put the gun down!" Sade shouted, with her hand extended in front of her. Donnavan calms down seeing the wad of money in Sade's hand. He tucks his gun back into his waistline. He is dark skinned, with a clean shaven head, and resembles DMX.

“Here go yo’ five hundred. I’m paying his debt, but from today on, he no longer needs yo’ services. He owe me now.”

“One thing I’ve always learned is to respect the game.” Donnavan replied.

“Good, now I’m asking you to respect my game, like I respected yo’ game.” He looks at the beautiful goddess, surprisingly shock to see a woman with so much game about herself.

“I guess I don’t have a choice baby. Seeing that you about yo’ money, maybe we can hook up one day.”

“I’ll think about it.”

“So, what’s yo’ name sweetheart?”

“Dutchess.”

“Dutchess uh, I like that.”

“Well Donnavan, my unc got a lot of work to put in.”

“I feel you. I know you tryna break bread. I can’t knock yo’ hustle sweetheart, but you be careful out here. You know the haters always on their job. And you being a woman, niggas will try and take advantage of… “

Cock! Cock! Dutchess produces a chrome .45 automatic. “A bitch lookin’ fo’ seventeen reasons,” Dutchess proclaimed. Donnavan blows out a short whistle.

“That’s a pretty mutha fucka right there Joe.” Donnavan examines the burner in admiration. Dutchess cocks the gun again and a bullet flies out the chamber landing on the carpet next to Donnavan’s feet.

“No disrespect baby, that one right there could’ve been you, so you make sure you be careful. Don’t ever let a pretty face fool you.”

“Damn, sweetheart, who taught you how to handle that heater like that?”

“It’s a long story, and right now I got business to attend to.”

“Well, maybe we’ll bump into each other again in the long run.”

"Maybe." Dutchess replied cordially.

"A'ight, you be easy out here." Donnavan said, as he exits the door.

"Handle that unc. Get that white boy down here and do what you gotta do. Just get mine."

"Okay niece. I appreciate what you just did for me." Dutchess doesn't respond. Her mind is many miles away. She suppose to go out to dinner with her mother.

"***Why my mom ain't called me yet***." She wondered.

"Sade, why did you tell Donnavan your name is Dutchess when it's Sade?"

"Well unc, you know everybody in the streets have a street name and that was the first name that came to mind," Dutchess said, still thinking about her mother. "So fo' now own, my name is Dutchess."

"That's fine with me, Dutchess."

The sun shines brightly, with its orange glow producing a brilliant contrast against the cloudless baby blue sky. A jamacian man is seated in the driver's seat of a BMW 760 with a Rasta Safari hat sheilding his dread-locks. He rants on his cell phone in his heavy accent, as the veins in his neck bulges. His face crinkles as he scolds the person on the other end.

A Chrysler with tinted windows pulls into the parking lot of Oak Street Beach. The occupant of the Chrysler touches his waistline to reassure himself that he is on point. He knows that if a man plays his cards wrong one time, he may never get to reshuffle the deck. In the game he plays, he never leaves home without his artillery.

He trudges over to the BMW, dressed in a grey Sean John hoodie velour sweat suit, with his wheat colored Timberlands crunching the gravel on the pavement. His shadowed beard accentuates his dark complexion. The gold necklace around his neck dangles in the the rythmn of his stride. He examines the scenery meticulously calculating his every move. The six years he served in the federal penitentiary allowed him to polish his street game. He made a promise to himself that he will never get caught slipping again.

He drums on the paassenger window of the BMW with his fingertips, captivating the driver's attention. He makes a gesture with his hand, summoning for him to get out. The man flips his phone closed and steps out of the car to accompany Black Jesus.

"Sup Rasta?" Black Jesus greeted. The two embraces each other with a manly hug, with one elbow between them keeping their distance.

"Ain't nuttin' mon, jes tired of dese silly bomba klaats. Anyway mon, watcha wanna see me about mon?" Ganja questioned, as they saunter side by side, with the cool breeze fluttering their attire.

"I'm tryna put a heavy move down," Black Jesus answered, glimpsing around with his hands in the pockets of his hoodie.

"What dat move be like?"

"I need ten tons of that good green."

"That's e large order rude boy. You know me gonna need half up front and de other half on delivery."

"Ain't no problem, I know how it go. My man already handled that. Seven hundred and fifty thous in the trunk of yo' car." Ganja's face creases in shock, wondering how did Black Jesus managed to get into his trunk without his knowledge.

"Me not gonna ask. That's why I like you mon. Ya always on point. I like a mon who can drop one point five like it's nuttin'."

"So, when you gon' drop that load off on me?"

"Give me few days. I call you wit' de pick up spot."

"Fo' sho' Rasta."

Dutchess arrives back home only to find her mother sleeping, with her cell phone turned off. Ever since Lawrence died, she's been sleeping a lot lately. It has been two weeks since she took abscence from work.

Dutchess wakes her up. Cheryl stirs in the covers, agitated by the disturbance. "What time is it?"

"Twenty minutes after six," Dutchess responded.

"I'm late, how come you didn't call me to wake me?"

"I tried." Cheryl picks up her Nextel and looks at the screen.

"My battery must of died out," She says, pressing the power button to no avail. Dutchess' phone ring and Cheryl still half sleep, thinks it's hers. "Hello ... ello," the words echoed as they answered simultaneously. Dutchess laughs at her mother.

"What up Bianca? .. Naw, I can't, me and my mom suppose to be going out to eat ... Bianca said hello ma."

"Tell her I said hi," replied Cheryl

"She said what up?...I don't know, hold on let me see." Dutchess turns to her mother. "Ma, is we still going out?"

"Yeah, why? You trying to dump me for one of your friends?"

"Naw, Bianca wanna go get something to eat too."

"Tell her she can go with us. By time she gets here, I'll be dressed." Dutchess relays the massage to Bianca, as she leaves her mother to get ready. Dutchess stashes the money she made underneath her mattress.

Cheryl takes a quick shower and changes into one of her simple blue business suits. She takes a look at herself in the mirror, and decides to change. She has let her appearance go down slightly, since the death of her husband, opting for jogging pants and keeping her hair pinned up. Even still, she is very attractive.

She digs into her shared closet. The scent of Lawrence's body lingers in the air. She smells one of his suits hugging the material, as the fragrance of Cool Water cologne stirs her nostrils. Running the suit across her face, she feels the hard object in the blazer. The black box is from Geneva Seal. Inside the box is a pink diamond tennis bracelet. Engraved on the clasp is 10-23-84, the date of their first anniversary. Her eyes become misty as she finishes reading the creme card, with gold letters that came with the jewelry.

To my wife, my lover, and best friend
Life is a journey, best shared between two people. I'm thankful to be spending it with you,
You are my sun, when there is no light,
the pulse to my beating heart, and the quench to my thirst.

Happy Anniversary,
Your hubby

A large tear drop falls to the card, leaving a moist circle "I love you Lawrence," the muscles in her face trembles, as she cries, being choked with her own tears. "Lawrence would want me to live," She said to herself. She takes out a gold sequence dress and puts it on. She fixes her make up and takes another look in the mirror. She removes her glasses, revealing her pretty eyes. She could do without them, but they keep her with the ability to see things at a distance. Finally, she unpins her sleek hair, letting it fall to her shoulders. The last thing she does before she leaves the room, is put on the bracelet.

Dutchess studies her mother as she prances in her direction. Dutchess stares at her speechless, before finding her voice.

"Dang mama, you look nice. Let me go change up out of these jeans real quick," She said getting up heading for her room.

"You don't have time, Bianca will be here in a minute. Besides, we didn't tell her to dress up."

"Think about who we talkin' about, when have you ever known Bianca not to be dressed to impress? I'll only take a second." Cheryl thinks about it, then says, "Hurry up, I'm starving."

As Cheryl waits for Dutchess to come back down, the doorbell rings. Bianca is wearing a red lace, strapless minidress, with floral print. Cheryl greets her at the door and ushers her in.

"You look nice Mrs. Blackwell." Bianca complemented.

"Thank you, and so do you." The vainess in Bianca's voice wants to respond, "I know," instead she politely smiles. "Come on Sade, Bianca is here," Cheryl yelled. Dutchess comes down wearing a black satin dress with spaghetti straps.

Upon seeing Bianca, Dutchess says, "I forgot something."

"No, let's go," said Cheryl.

"Yeah mami, you look fine," Bianca proclaimed, inspecting Dutchess up and down.

Dutchess concedes and the trio exits the house, getting into Cheryl's Lexus. Cheryl takes them to Chicago 312, off Rush Street. Her status within the city allows them to bypass the long line. The hostess takes them to an open booth by the window. The restaurant is frequented by every top broker and politican in the city.

"Can I offer you ladies any beverages?" The dark haired Italian waiter asked.

"Water for now, please sir, and we'll take three menus," said Cheryl.

The waiter returned promptly. "I'll be right over there

when you're ready, just signal me." He politely stated with a friendly smile pulling at the corners of his mouth.

"Actually, we're ready now," Cheryl informed.

"Oh, well in that case," he pauses, "Starting with you." He stations himself beside Bianca. "What would you like?" She browses through the menu once more, before deciding to go with the buttered salmon, over rice pilaf, with fresh steamed vegatables.

"You not gonna write that down?" She asked.

He smiles, "I have a very good memory, and for you ma'am." He points to Dutchess. Cheryl speaks up for her.

"We'll both have the goat cheese ravioli, with mushroom sauce."

"Yeah, whatever she said." Dutchess told him a little angry that her mother still dictates what she eats, like she's still a little girl. Dutchess had her mind set on the parmasean chicken dish.

The waiter returns with their food and Dutchess ends up liking the ravioli. They talk girl talk over the meals and make jokes about the people coming in and out of the restaurant.

"Can I offer you ladies dessert?"

"Thanks, but no thanks," they answer in unison as Cheryl picks up the check. As they walk to the car Cheryl says, "Well that was fun. We got to do that more often." Dutchess and Bianca agreed. Bianca is always down for a free meal.

They turn out the parking lot going west on Rush Street. A few turns and lights later, they enter onto the expressway. Dutchess is busy scanning through the radio stations and Bianca is in the back seat, adding more make up to her face, with aide of a compact mirror. Suddenly a dark sedan cuts in front of Cheryl sharply causing her to slam on the breaks to aviod a collision. The motion causes Bianca to smear a black line down her cheek, with her eyeliner, as she hurls forward into Dutchess seat.

"Stupid bastard," Cheryl shouted, as she watches the car swing in front of two other drivers to merge to the exit. "Are you two okay?" Cheryl asked the girls as she gets the car moving again.

"Yeah we alright," Said Dutchess, 1ooking into the back seat at Bianca, who is wiping her face off and talking aloud at the same time.

"Marticon, pinchy cabron," she cursed. Three exits down, the sedan reappears, merging fast off the ramp and slams into the passenger side knocking them hard into the concrete divider.

Cheryl regains control of the wheel and steps down on the accelerator. Bianca looks out the back window as the sedan gains speed coming closer. "Can't this thing go any faster!" Cheryl yelled in fear.

"Ahhh," They scream as the back window shatters.

"Get down," Cheryl commands Bianca and Dutchess, who is already one step ahead. Flashes of fire erupts from the sedan again, this time logding in the trunk. Cheryl with her head halfway down, keeps the pressure on the gas pedal. They zoom pass a state trooper, who flicks on his lights. The driver of the sedan spots the state trooper and slows its pace. The crusier is now behind Cheryl, beckoning her to pullover. As Cheryl slows down, Bianca lifts her head, as the sedan rolls by. "Get the plate number," she screamed. Cheryl tries her best to read the liscense number. She can't see from the faraway distance. She cursed herself for not wearing her glasses. The state trooper approaches the car and taps on the window looking at a startled Cheryl. He studies the disheveled women.

"Ma'am, you were going one forty in a sixty five per hour zone," the blonde haired crew cut officer stated.

"Officer, we were being chased by a black Volvo," Cheryl explains inbetween breaths, "Look at my window, whoever it was shot at us." Cheryl is out of breath and glad that the experience is over. The state trooper inspects the window, and sends an all points bulletin out through his walkie talkie that's attached to the shoulder area of his uniform.

The dispatcher alerts all avaialable patrol, to be on a look out for the Volvo. The state trooper writes down the statements from the women and escorts them back to the Blackwell's residence.

Cheryl is thinking that Kennytha Baptiste had to be behind it, because of the threat he made to her in court. Dutchess thinks about what Donnavan had warned her about. "You being a woman, niggas will try you." Bianca is thinking, "I have to get as far away from them as I can, before I get killed."

A discovery has been made. A group of men are huddled up in the darkness, dressed in all black, wearing steel-toed boots. They are busy at the GraceWorld private cemetery, digging up a gravesite.

CHAPTER THREE

TWO HOURS LATER

Pirelli thinks about the conversation he had with Dutchess earlier in the day when he dropped her off at his father's apartment, as he rides down the dark road. Dutchess had tried getting him to go in at least to talk with Amos, but he wasn't buying it. "***Fuck that nigga. Any man can become a daddy, but it takes a real man to be a father***." Pirelli thought to himself. As far as he was concerned, Amos was dead like Lawrence, dead.

Pirelli merges onto 1-94 and heads to his dope spot in Hyde Park. He is carrying two ounces he cooked up earlier from the four in a half ounces he copped. He sold a half ounce in grams. The other two went to Dutchess. He blends in with traffic, keeping his speed limit two miles per hour below the posted limited of sixty five. A yellow Camaro speeds by him, doing well over eighty with a young female in the driver's seat, not caring about the law.

Pirelli is passing quite a few cars himself, but he pays no attention as he nods his head to "Make Me Better",

Fabulous and Ne-yo's cut. Despite the speedometer reading sixty five, he is gaining on the yellow Camaro.

Seconds later, he is passing the car with the fine red

bone behind the wheel. As he passes her, he looks back to get another look. “Damn,” Pirelli whispers to himself noticing a car parked in the emergency lane. The car is on the side of the road with its door ajar. A uniformed officer leans across the hood of a patrol car slightly visible, behind tall grass, holding a radar gun. He shoots out the x band signal, tracking the Riveria’s speed. The signal returns, reading eighty-three miles per hour, he jumps into pursuit.

Pirelli checks his speedometer once more, he remains at sixty three. “Oh, I’m straight, but I gotta be careful,” He tells himself. His confidence drops down, as he watches the cruiser out of his rearview mirror, quickly gaining speed.

The chirping sound of crickets, commingle with the crunching sound of shovels digging into the earth’s surface. The leader of the crew stands next to a mountain of dirt.

He expels a loud breath and wipes the perspiration from his forehead, with the back of his hand. His comrades move simultaneously in their dirt stained attire. The man aims his flashlight directly into the hole, now able to see the top of a pearl green coffin. He signals to one of the men.

“Call the boss, we found it.”

The man seats himself on the tombstone, situated in front of the hole. One of the other men retrieves a fresh pack of Newports from his shirt pocket and taps the pack against his palm, removing a cigarette.

The lights from a truck blares as it pulls into the cemetery moving slowly around a snaky driveway, with precise timing. The man smoking flicks his burning cigarette to the ground, and assists his comrades, at removing the casket from the ground.

They elevate the casket bringing it to the surface. The men gather around the coffin as the man opens it up, exposing fifty individually wrapped bricks of cocaine, sealed with beige wrapping and duct tape.

Mr.Taylor, the crooked funeral director that let them on the premises walks up to the group of men.

"Which one of you is Black Jesus?" The man who opened the casket went off to talk to him. Black Jesus pays him for his services. Hauling dead bodies from city to city didn't pay a fraction of what he recieved from drugs.

The men carry the kilos to the truck. GraceWorld cemetery stays under surveillence 24 hours a day. Mr. Taylor kept the tapes running that night for insurance. In his opinion, drug dealers were like dead bodies, cold.

"Fuckin' raggedy muthafucka!" Pirelli snapped at his car, as he realizes the speedometer is broken. He closes his eyes for a second and opens them. The officer is still on his tail, approaching at a fast pace. "A'ight think about it baby." He talks to himself, as he deliberates. There was really nothing to think about. It is either pullover and die in prison, or hit the accelerator and risk dying in the streets. The voices of good and evil begins talking to him at once.

"Pullover P, all you have to do is explain to the officer, you speedometer is broken, he'll understand," said the good voice.

"Don't listen to that good samaritan shit, you on paper. With two ounces of hard in the car," said the evil voice.

"But, if you play it cool, what's the odds of him asking to search the vehicle? Your license and tags are fine," reasoned the good voice.

"Fuck all that, you betta be worrying about what's the

odds of Judge Milton giving you the high end of the federal guideline range when this cop find them drugs, cause he gon' search," stated evil.

"Trust me, worst case scenario you're lookin' at a couple of years, if you plead guilty and accept responsibility, you might get probation," said the good voice.

"P, this nigga lost like most of the niggas out here peddling this shit, and he's trying to sell you a dream like the lawyers that represent them. You're riding around with 56 grams of cocaine base. I know it don't sound like much, but even a first time offender is looking at no less than ten years. With you being a second time offender and your prior history, you'll be at a level 32, category six, which carries 210-262 months, all thanks to the cracklaw. If you take it to trial and lose you face a mandatory life sentence." said evil.

"But you can cooperate," said the good voice, "Recieve less time."

"Don't tell me you're thinkin' about snitchin; you know what you got to do," said evil.

Through the whipping of the wind, from his partially cracked window, he hears the sound of the siren. It snaps him back to the reality of things. The red and blue lights swirl frantically in repetitious movements. Without further thought, he pulls to the side of the road. Many vehicles fly by him, but the one that catches his eye is the Camaro. The officer pulls up behind him. He calls the plates in and steps out of the patrol car. Pirelli leans his head back on the headrest, as the officer makes his approach. His peaceful thoughts are interrupted by the knock on his window. He hears the annoying voice of the overweight officer.

"Driver's license and registra-" Errrk! "Heyy, come back here." The officer shouted, reaching for his walkie talkie. Pirelli's engine roars to life. The Riveria jerks, burning rubber as the tires screech, leaving the officer running to his patrol car, far behind. He is now doing a hundred miles per hour, maybe even one twenty. He does not know the speedometer is stuck on sixty-three. His only indicator of how fast he is really going comes, as he catches up to the camaro, passing by it. He looks back, and sees the Crown Victoria, catching up to him.

"***Damn, I gotta get off at the next exit.***"

He merges recklessly across two lanes, just barely missing an Astro van. The cruiser duplicates his movements, from only two car lengths back. Pirelli reaches under his seat, grabbing an ounce. He rolls his window down, and tosses it out the window. The car behind him, rolls over the package, crushing it. He tries to get his hand on the other package, but it slides out of reach. He grabs the steering wheel with both hands, gripping it like a Nascar driver. The cruiser is now directly behind him. He exits the freeway quickly, with the officer right on his rear-end. One sharp turn, takes him down a one-way street. The blaring sounds of horns, and frightened expressions on the other driver's faces, does not scare him. He yanks back the steering column, with precision, avoiding a near fatal collision with a rig, carrying gas.

The officer navigates the cruiser effectively, bumping his fender against Pirelli's bumper. The car careens out of control.

Pirelli regains control, exiting the one-way. A couple sharp right turns, puts him on Oakwood Blvd. He is very familiar with the area. Swiftly bending the corner on Oakwood, he ends up on Drexel. He takes it around as Washington Park comes into view.

The officer with one last desperate attempt, smashes into the side of Pirelli's car, causing him to lose control. The car does a 360 degree spin, smacking into a telephone pole, totaling it.

With the speed of a jack rabbit, Pirelli jumps from the damaged car, staggering and takes off sprinting. The officer knows he has no chance of catching him on foot. Luckily for him, the backup he has called is quickly filling the area.

Pirelli jumps a fence, ripping a hole in his pants. His eyes search frantically around, looking for a place to hide. His forehead is drenched with perspiration. A trickle of blood rolls from a small gash on his forehead from the accident. His lungs burn, as he dashes underneath a parked Toyota Camry, on 55th street. As he catches his breath, blood leaks from his leg as well, from where the fence had cut him. He nervously looks on trembling, as two cruisers circle the block.

He can barely hear a voice talking to someone. “Is Vollmer far from here?” Pirelli hears, as the scooby-doo voice muffles. Pirelli knows that Vollmer road is close to Chicago Heights. It is a strange question, considering where he is now. Then he hears the voice again. This time, loud and clear. “He’s under the car”. Panic swells inside of him.

Pirelli reacts quick springing from underneath the car. Before the officer has time to react, he is on his feet again. An old lady points in his direction from her porch. “Stop, or I’ll shoot,” the officer bellows.

Pirelli keeps running, as the police issued 9 millimeter barks. A bullet spirals in his general direction, making contact with...

“Baptiste, I give you my personal promise that I won’t miss again. I had her until the unfortunate occurrence of the state trooper saved her. To express my apologies about the blotched job, I’m going to throw somebody else in, for no extra charge”. The assassin hangs up the phone. He throws a knife at a wall with Cheryl’s picture. The knife strikes, sticking right between her eyes. A wicked smile, creases his lips.

Despite the odds, Pirelli dives, missing the bullet as it makes contact with an Expedition truck parked on the side of the road. Pirelli's heart beat races as the near miss excels his level of adrenalin. A little further and he'll be safe.

Pirelli increases his speed as the entrance to the campus of the University of Chicago comes into view. He runs into a building, and exits out the back door, blending in with the mixed throng of students taking night classes.

FOUR HOURS LATER, (3:27 A.M.)

Several white rig trucks pull into a warehouse off Royce road, in Naperville, Illinois. A handful of Mexican immigrant workers wearing masks help unload the noisy pigs that are running around in a customized bed. The acrid smell of pig shit goes unnoticed to them as they work meticulously to complete the task. After removing the pigs, a lever at the bottom of each truck is pulled, allowing the beds to be removed. The secret compartment underneath holds many bricks of individually wrapped cocaine packages.

As the workers remove the dope, a loud ear piercing scream is heard as a vehicle makes its way down the winding dirt road.

The alert comes from a ten year old boy, startling everyone. He is shirtless, with tight jeans, exposing his frail chest. His unruly, dark hair sways in the wind.

Panic and then fear goes into their eyes as the vehicle nears. A few workers pour out the warehouse as the boy continues to yell in his native tongue.

"El jefe es aqui," he reants, repeating the words, "The boss is here."

The workers that ran out the warehouse wait patiently to greet Black Jesus. He steps out of the rented Astro van with his light green Stacy Adams, which kicks up dust as his feet drums against the ground. He places his matching suit coat back into the vehicle, sporting only the tailored made pants, shirt, and vest.

The workers are all nervous, because this is the first time the, 'proclaimed boss', has decided to pay a visit. They instantly think that something is wrong. Very few of them speak any English at all, and the ones that do, don't very well.

Black Jesus' driver waits for him in the van while he directs the Mexicans inside the warehouse on where to send each shipment. Sheilding his nose from the smell of the warehouse, he steps back outside. He takes a deep breath, happy to be out of the warehouse. The country air offers little help as it smells of manure, with the faint scent of something burning in the distance. The wind softly blows, causing the smell of smoke to grow stronger as he walks toward the van. Moments later the van slides onto the highway traffic, heading north. The roads are relatively dead, except for a few vehicles heading in the opposite direction.

Black Jesus enjoys the power he yields as an acting boss. So much so, that he craves the real thing. "***If only Baptiste was out of the way***," he thinks to himself, as he reclines in the passenger seat. He dozes off and makes up his mind that he will do whatever it takes to get Baptiste out of the way.

While Black Jesus is sound asleep, twenty undercover agents get ready to rush the building he has left, acting on a tip.

"Squadron one, move on my command." DEA agent

Thomas Rains whispers into his wireless headset. Searchlights wash the warehouse, dispersing globes of bright light.

"La policia, La policia," the young Mexican boy cries out, giving the others a warning.

"Get down, get down on the ground, get the fuck down!" yelled a combination of voices, drowning out the boys high-pitched baritone.

Tiny red laser beams chop through the darkness, finding their intended targets. A helicopter roars, hovering over the premise, kicking up dust and blocking the sounds of clicking guns, as agents swarm from every angle. Women, men, and children alike, are being escorted from the warehouse.

Agents comb through the warehouse removing bundles of kilos. A young field agent approaches Rains. "We've secured the premise, and searched every room, there's no sign of him." Agent Rains let out a deep sign.

"Damn, we must've just missed him." Placing his hands over his eyes, he shakes his head. "Chief Lawson isn't going to be happy about this."

A Mexican worker wearing handcuffs behind his back passes by, with an agent following him. The deep cut above his eye leaks blood.

"Hey, what happened to him?" Rains inquired.

"He resisted," the agent replied smiling.

Frustrated, Rains stop the next Mexican going by, grabbing his arm. "Hey you, where's your boss?" The man shrugs his shoulders.

"No hablo ingles." Rain grits his teeth.

"I just fuckin' bet you don't speak no english."

An agent enters the warehouse breathing heavily. "He got away."

"No shit."

"No, not Black Jesus, I menat the boy."

"Don't worry about it, he can't out run a car. We'll get him, we'll get them all." He proclaimed with a promising look on his face.

The sound of "Rick Ross' "Everyday I'm Hustlin" plays, as Bricks sits at the red light in his Denali XL. He considers the truck to be his trapper. The light turns green, he glimpses in the rearview mirror. A grey Buick, that seems to be trailing him from a distance, catches his eyes. He removes the triangle barrel Glock .40, out of the console, while staring at the suspicious automobile. He makes a right turn, attempting to lose the car. The car follows his course, making its mission evident.

Bricks smashes down on the gas pedal and a short ear-piercing screech escapes the tires. He maneuvers the S.U.V through an alley and exits onto a side street losing the car.

"There's only one rule, don't get caught," Young Jeezy proclaims from Bricks' burnt mix CD.

"***I hope that wasn't those people. It's time for me to lay low.***" Bricks mulled, pulling into his Hyde Park neighborhood. He circulates throughout the neighborhood, scrutinizing the scenery. He pulls up to his stash house, attentively, calculating his every move. He trudges to the front entrance, dressed in a grey and baby blue Phatfarm velour jogging suit, suede baby blue Havanna Joes, with grey bottoms. The platinum necklace swings on his neck, as the two three carat rocks in his earlobe twinkle, accentuating his dark complexion.

He struts into the house securing the door. The distance sound of his two tamed beast barking, reverberates from behind the bedroom door. He can hear the scratching of their paws against the wooden floor as he nears. He opens the bedroom door and the two Muscular

King Corsos rushes him. They look as if they are on steriods. Bricks' face crinkles at the sight of the disorderly room, cluttered with torn boxes, plastic, and money scattered all over. He notices one of the dogs chewing on a bundle of money.

"Get out of here! Shit!.. Damn dogs chewin' up my fuckin' money!" Bricks rebuked. The two tan beast scurry out of the room, sensing the anger in their master's voice. Bricks' cell phone rings, stealing his focus. He looks at the screen of his caller's ID, and sees an unknown caller. "Yeah...what up?" A feminie, automated voice appears on the line.

"This is a pre-paid call. You will not be charged for this call. This call is from, "Moe." An inmate at a federal Correctional Facility. To accept this call press five." Click! Click!

"Yo' what up my nigga?"

"Nothin' much. What about yo' self?"

"Rollin' wit' the punches, trapped in the belly of the beast, about to touch down in the next thirty days." Moe replied.

"Come on home baby, we waitin' on ya." Bricks said, sinking into the butter soft leather sofa, in front of the 42 inch plasma screen.

"Good lookin' out on those flicks you sent me. You always kept it real wit' a nigga from day one."

"Like you always said, real niggas do real thangs." Bricks added.

"You know you like the brother I never had. I got mad love for you. I don't know how I could ever repay you fo' lookin' out for my shorties over the years," Moe sincerely expressed, with heartfelt words.

"Don't trip. I know you'd do the same for me if it came down to it. If it whatn't for you, I wouldn't have a lot of shit I got. Beside half of this shit is yours too."

The feminie voice interrupts their conversation. "This call is from a federal correctional institution."

"Check this out Bricks. A lot of people look at situations like these as setbacks, but in reality this is all a come back. This was just a time for me to do some meditation and evaluations. These circumstances only awakened the beast in me. You continue to watch yo' back and yo' front 'cause them dirty, no money gettin' niggas waitin' for you to slip."

"I feel you, believe that," Bricks agreed, knowing that Moe is telling the truth, and that the street game is filled with many different obstacles.

"Hold it down out there. I'mma 'bout to touch down on them haters and artificial individuals who turned their backs on a real trooper when he was standin' on his tippy toes. But you know how that goes."

In unison, they finish the sentence. "If they knew betta, they'd do betta." They burst out in laughter.

"Yo' you know they only give us three hundred minutes a month, so I'mma holla at you in a few."

"A'ight. No doubt. Keep yo' head up and if you need me to do somethin' for you before you touch just hit me, I gotcha."

"Good lookin' out beloved. I might need you to pick me up at the bus station wit' two of the baddest freaks in the city."

"Ha! Ha! A'ight fam, you got that."

"One."

Many customers traverse the sidewalk in front of the check cashing place. Dutchess exits the building checking out from work. A man stares at her from a distance, in an outdated sedan. He discretely climbs out of the car, approaching her from the rear, with one hand behind his back.

Dutchess opens her car door, unaware of the intruder. He cups his hand over her eyes startling her. She recedes and a short scream escapes her vocal cords, piercing the air.

The harmony escaping Ganja's cell phone garners his attention as he navigates the powder blue BMW 760 into the gas station on 75th and Stoney. Reggae music croons from the factory car system.

"Yo' what up mon? ..A'ight, hurry mon." He slides the phone closed and removes a half of blunt out of the ashtray, blazing it up. Marijuana smoke floats in the air as he watches the pedestrains traverse the lot, briskly sheilding themselves from the light rain.

Usually Ganja doesn't transact any business after eight o'clock pm. But today he made an exception, due to the sixty five thousand dollar debt that has been well over due.

"***What's takin' this bomba klaat so long***," He thinks to himself, frustrated glancing at his diamond bezeled Cartier watch. "***Maybe I should catch Chaos at anotha time***," he mulled, running out of patience.

Prepared to pull off, Ganja notices Chaos trudging to his car. "***Why didn't he pull up in his car? Normally him don't do dis. Me havin' a bad feelin' 'bout dis***." He eases his hand under the seat grabbing his blue stainless steel 9 millimeter. He places it in close reach.

Chaos approaches the passenger side of the car with a bookbag in his hand. Chaos has been conducting business with Ganja for 9 months. Ganja presses the power button on the door panel allowing him inside.

"What up Rasta? Sorry 'bout the delay," Chaos apologized.

Chaos is brown skinned with a medium build and short

braids that don't hang much below his shoulders.

"No problem. What ya got for me mon?" Ganja inquired, with his gaze locked on the bookbag in Chaos' lap. Chaos tosses the bulgy bag in Ganja's lap. "How much is dis mon?" Ganja questioned, unzipping the bag.

"Forty five."

"Forty five." Ganja's face crinkles in disappointment as he stares inside the bookbag containing shredded newspapers.

"That's what I said." Ganja turns his head, staring into the barrel of a nickel plated .44 magnum. A red dot shines on his forehead, as rain taps on the windsheild, like soft music. They glare at each other.

"What dat fuck ya doin' mon?"

"You know what the fuck this is! Break yo' mutha fuckin' self!" Chaos barked, in his raspy voice.

"Me die fo' me shit ya bomba klaat!" Ganja rebelliously snapped, as he reaches for his artillery. Chaos squeezes the trigger. Blocka! The .44 mag throws up, silencing him, with a bullet to the head. Ganja's body folds up, he crashes against the steering wheel face first. The horn blares, seizing the attention of the bystanders. Chaos adjusts Ganja's body, laying him back in the driver's seat. A custom platinum iced out necklace twinkles on Ganja's neck.

"You wont be needin' this no mo'." Chaos yanks the neclace off his neck. "You won't be needin' this either." He removes Ganja's diamond bezeled watch from around his wrist. He wipes the door handle with the sleeve of his shirt, and exits the car, vanishing into the darkness.

Dutchess piercing scream comes to an halt as Deangelo reveals the dozen red roses. He turns Dutchess face to face with him, gazing into her almond shaped eyes. With a smile stretched across his face, he says, "Surprise baby."

"Boy you almost got hurt walkin' up on me like that." Her fear turns into happiness, seeing that it's Deangelo. She feels that she has been slipping lately. She promises herself that she will be on point next time. Considering the situation that occurred the other day when leaving the restaurant, with her mother and Bianca.

"Oh yeah. And what was you gon' do to me?" Deangelo inquired, smiling at a beautiful Dutchess who he has been dating for many of years. Dutchess is the only woman to ever have his heart.

"You don't waana know that," Ducthess answered, locking eyes with him. She gives him a passionate kiss on the lips, her hands loops around his neck. They saunter away holding hands conversing.

"I'm only gon' be here for two weeks, so we got a lot of catching up to do, if you know what I mean."

"Believe me, I know," Dutchess admitted, followed by a flirtatious smile.

"Let's go get somethin' to eat baby girl, and do some catching up. What do you say?"

"That sounds good to me."

"Just leave yo' car parked and we'll take mine. We'll come back and get yo' car later." Deangelo suggested.

"That's cool with me." Dutchess agreed.

Deangelo walks to the passenger side of his outdated BMW and opens the door for Dutchess.

"Awww, your such a gentlemen," Dutchess stated, smiling at him. Deangelo always treats her with respect.

They ease through the heavy traffic, engaging in a profound conversation. A thunderous noise attracts their attention. They examine the scenery in curiousity, trying to identify the rumbling volcanic sound that's shaking the earth.

A black Cadillac ESV sitting on 26 inch flat face rims,

pulls up close to the rear of them, playing Rick Ross "Push It to The Limit."

Dutchess gazes into the rearview mirror, scrutinizing the personalized plate that reads "Govenor." Dutchess examines a beautiful pecan complexiond woman with long, black silky hair. She is wearing a familiar looking bracelet around her wrist. She maneuvers the truck parallel to the passenger's side of Deangelo's car. A trailor is attached to the trucks rearend. Dutchess notices a matching black Cadillac XLR, with the top dropped, resting on 20 inch

Lexani's with the rims spinning. The truck slowly moves forward and Dutchess recognizes a familiar man sitting in the driver's seat of the convertible Cadillac talking on his cell phone.

Ice makes eye contact with Dutchess and lifts his Prada sunglasses, revealing his light brown eyes. He winks his eye at her and drops his sunglasses down, sheilding his eyes. He cracks a smile at her, the fading sun rays strikes his diamond mouth piece, obscuring her vision. The light turns green, and the truck pulls off. A black Impala with limo tinted windows trails behind Ice, on security.

"Damn, what was that all about? You must know that nigga?" Deangelo blurted, with jealousy written all across his face.

"Yeah, I know him, but believe me, it ain't what you think." Dutchess defensively proclaimed.

"What you mean by that?"

"That's Ice, my friend Olivia's no good ass boyfriend.

He tried to talk to me behind Olivia's back. I told him I don't get down like that. He tried to buy me like I'm some type of hoodrat or one of those bitches he be dealin' with. I refused his gift and let it be known, I got a man." Dutchess stretches the truth and leans over and kisses Deangelo on the cheek.

"Yeah, you know better. You don't want no drama up in here."

"My man knows who boss."

"He do, huh. We gon' find out later on," he flirted.

Later that day (10 P.M.)

"I think ol' boy Bricks, caught on to us. Everytime we get close to em' he always slips through our fingers".

"Don't worry about it. We'll catch him on the rebound." The two unknown men sit in an apartment plotting their next move. Bringing the twenty minute conversation to an end, they exchange a handshake, with a strong manly hug.

"Aight Joe I'mma holla at you later."

"What you about to do?"

"Go and fuck wit' this bitch Mimi, I just met."

"I feel that, aight, One."

"One".

Dutchess and Deangelo exit the Loews Theater located on 8th and South Walbash, carrying a gust of fresh butter popcorn from the inside, into the cool night's air.

Dutchess takes a sip from the extra large cherry coke, which they shared during the movie, and then passes it to Deangelo.

On their way out the door, Dutchess spots her girl Olivia, and Ice coming in. Ice is dressed to impress

in an all-black Armani suit, with matching big block Mauri gators, while Olivia sports a shimmering black dress by Roberto Cavalli.

Ice hits the alarm on his shiny Hummer H2, sealing the deal.

"Heyyy Girl!" Olivia and Dutchess hug each other.

"Olivia, this is Deangelo, Deangelo, this is Olivia and Ice."

Ice shakes Deangelo's hand. "What up my man?"

The diamonds from Ice's platinum Rolex watch blinds him in the process, making him uncomfortably aware of his own fake platinum watch. He rolls his sleeve down, on his Roca Wear jean jacket, covering the piece.

"***That's a damn shame, just earlier, he was with anotha' chick***," thought Dutchess. She wants to ask him, who the other girl he was with, and bust him out, but instead, she says, "Ya'll lookin' good, dressed like ya'll ready for a ball or somethin'." There is a slight tinge of jealousy in her voice. Olivia doesn't notice it. Olivia's dress alone made Dutchess' Gucci jeans, and pink V-neck tee shirt look like it was donated by the Salvation Army. The large one carat vvsl clarity diamond earrings she wore, added insult to injury.

"Oh, this, girl this ain't nothing", she boasted.

Couples traverse the parking lot holding hands, walking over candy wrappers, and little white ticket stubs.

"You shoulda' told Olivia you were going to the movies, it could have been a double date," Ice said, staring a

little too long for Deangelo's liking. Deangelo waits to mention it. Dutchess can feel Ice staring at her through his Cartier frames, piercing a hole through her body.

"Yea Girl," chimed in Olivia with a pout, mad because her girl didn't let her know she was going out. She is oblivious to her man's ulterior motives. "What ya'll go see anyways?"

"We went to see Dream Girls, didn't know Beyonce could act like that."

"Is it good," asked Ice. The way he said it, made Dutchess unsure if he was talking about the movie, or her goodies. If he was flirting, she was getting ready to shut him down.

"Deangelo said he like it."

"Oh yea, in that case I need to hurry up and buy me a

ticket. How much does it cost?"

"***Oh no this nigga didn't***," Dutchess thought, as Deangelo, answers for her.

"$8 a ticket, but if ya'll tryna' see it," he glances back into the theater, at the clock, avoiding his watch. "It started already, so you betta go now."

"I'll talk to you later girl," said Olivia, pulling Ice by the arm. Her high heels clicks against the pavement as they make their way inside.

Dutchess and Deangelo enter his 1992 blue 5 series beamer.

"What was that about?" he immediately asked.

"What was what?" Dutchess inquired.

"I seen the way that nigga was lookin' at you," Deangelo snarls.

"Baby, I can't stop people from lookin' at me, but all you need to be concerned with is I'm yours and I ain't going no where," Dutchess replies, kissing him passionately.

Deangelo puts Ice out of his mind as he drives to the hotel.

Pulling into the parking lot, they opt not to pay for valet service, and park a couple of rows back from the entrance. The bellhops are busy carrying in suitcases, for the other customers. They approach the clerk behind the desk and Deangelo slips her a fifty dollar bill. They take the elevator to the third floor then get off, turning left, finding their room.

The room is narrow and long. A mirror set above the dresser and a television was attached to a small wood table. The bed sits in the center of the room and this is what Dutchess sees first. Her eyes enlarge as she sees the numerous stuffed animals that are lying on the bed. The organic smell of vanilla scented candles aromatize the room as they burn from little glass holders. Sharing the bed with the teddy bears, are tiny crushed rose petals that are neatly spaced out, forming the shape of a heart. Dutchess heart melts, as she turns to face Deangelo.

"Awww you did all this for me?"

"I keep tellin' you I love you Sade."

They embrace in a passionate kiss, as Maxwell's "A woman's worth" spews from the stereo on the nightstand.

He unsnaps the clasp on her bra as he pulls her V-neck shirt over her head, exposing firm C-cup breasts. They tumble to the bed, knocking the animals on the floor. She pulls at his belt buckle as his tongue finds her cherry sized nipples. She stares into his eyes, feeling her insides dance at the prospect of further intimacy. She can feel the overwhelming desire to make love to Deangelo.

He slides her gucci jeans off, revealing her sexy pink underwear. He grabs her hands as she reaches for his manhood, and places them above her head. He whispers in her ear, "This is about you." His breath is hot and warm on her earlobe. He plants kisses right below her ear, as his hands, run through her hair. "Point to where you want me to kiss you."

She puts a finger on her lips, then her neck. "Mmmm", she purrs, as her hand travels to her breasts.

As he kisses her, his hand slowly delves into the elastic of her panties, tickling her nest of dark curls. Her hand goes lower, to her belly button, as he rushes with his mouth to satisfy her request. She arches her neck back, as her hand goes lower.

With her legs spread wide, she feels the breath of warm air, enter into her body.

"Deeeeee!" she screams, as he brushes his mouth across her other set of lips. His tongue flicks expertly in snakelike motions, as she shakes uncontrollably.

She reaches out for him again. This time he doesn't stop her. He enters her penetrating her fully, cupping her round ass. Their legs intertwine in slow rythmatic movements. The moist feeling Deangelo feels, cause him to explode. He wouldn't have pulled out, even if she would have asked, like she usually made sure she did. But this time, she didn't ask. They fall asleep in each others arms.

Ring ...Ring . .. Ring ...

The sound of Dutchess phone wakes them up hours later. She struggles to see the caller ID as she wipes the sleep away from her eyes. Deangelo watches on with jealousy and anger building.

"Hello," Dutchess answers in a droggy voice. "Oh, what up cuz...Now?" She looks at the clock on the dresser. It reads 9:26 A.M. "I'm on my way," she says disconnecting the call.

"You jus' gon' disrespect me like that?" Deangelo asks, staring at her wild eyed.

"Boy, that was my cousin Pirelli," she explained, while heading to the shower.

"You sure it wasn't that nigga Ice?"

Dutchess heart crumbles into a million little pieces. She wants to tell Deangelo the truth about where she is going, and what she is doing, but he would never understand.

"I can't believe you asked me that, but I know you didn't mean it." Dutchess tries to kiss him and he turns his head. "Straight up, it's like that," Dutchess pouts.

"Listen baby, I got to get ready to go, heres my phone, call the number back if you don't believe me. I'm not cheating on you." Deangelo refuses to take the phone and heads off to the shower.

After coming out she says, "I love you baby and I'll make it up to you. I'll even go to church with you like you want me."

"You promise?" He asks, knowing she never agreed before.

"Uh-Huh," she responds, finally getting the kiss she was after. Dutchess exits the door, heading to her Uncle Amos' house.

The cladenstine group of Supremacists meet once again. Today's agenda is a discussion of their plans for for further world dominance. Once again the smells of cigars and cigarettes waft through the air, commingling with that of freshly brewed Folger's coffee. They are all seated around an oakwood round table.

"Any news on our plans?" asked Sheriff Jonothan Adams, looking directly at their intelligence source.

"As far as we know things are still moving forward," responded C.I.A agent Nathan Regan, shuffling through a stack of papers. He finds the memo and reads it over. "Basically our superiors want us to continue what we're currently doing and keep the N.A.A.C.P out of the loop until the legislation is passed." They all nod their heads in agreement.

"So there we have it gentlemen, here's what we must do," expressed Judge Milton with excitement. He takes a hard puff on his cigar causing the tip to glow redish-orange, as a cloud billows from his mouth. "We must keep dem darkies in the dark, because we all know Niggers. Almost. Always. Cause. Problems," he elates with a large grin, showing off his wittiness of word play of the acronym N.A.A.C.P. Hearty laughter fills the room as Alderman Donald Hennings wipes the tears from his eyes.

"Okay gentlemen, quiet down," he says inbetween wiping his eyes. "As we know, thanks to our good brother Judge Milton here who continues to display his genius, that nigger Kennytha Baptiste is free. And I pray to God he goes out there and pump his people full of that poison, so them ignorant niggers can keep doing our jobs for us, getting killed or locked up. As long as we take out the head the body will fall. No longer do we need ropes, all we have to do is keep their neighborhoods filled with dope."

Judge Milton takes a sip from his now luke warm coffee, sitting the mug back down on the table. "I don't believe that I could have said that any finer myself. One more issue before I close. I want to know if you cut the grant money in the urban districts Mr. Hennings?"

"Yes, I've taken care of that. I've already transferred the funds into another account to fund the suburban areas."

"Good, so with that being said, this meeting is adjourned."

Pirelli steers the grey Sunfire through the cluttered parking lot of Walmart on Cicero Avenue, pulling up to the front entrance, dropping Erica off at work. Erica is Pirelli's fiancée, who he has been with for the last seven years. Erica and Pirelli have two boys. Erica has a short hairstyle that emphasizes her high cheekbones, sculptured face, and full lips. She's short and petite with crystal brown eyes.

Pirelli proposed to her and gave her an engagement ring the same day he was released from prison. He made a promise to her that he would marry her within a year. She stood by his side faithfully during his period of incarceration, never missing a visit, accepted all his extragant collect calls, wrote him at least once a week, and made sure he kept money on his account. She even took one of the pictures he sent her from prison and had it enlarged up to six feet. She placed the human sized picture on the wall in their bedroom and she'd fall asleep every night staring at his picture.

Struggling on her own raising their two boys, she managed to provide for him to the best of her ability. Pirelli grew to love her more and more for standing in his corner when his back was against the wall. He got caught cheating on her several times, but she always managed to forgive him. She even forgave him for a woman he got pregnant, who had a miscarriage. One thing he learned over the years of incarceration is who really loved him. All the women he cheated on Erica with wasn't no where to be found, when the hammer hit the table leaving him with a 5 year sentence. It wasn't a day that passed by that he didn't regret his infidelity. He realized how much he was hurting the woman he truly loves, with every beat of his heart.

Pirelli has been using her car to get around in since the day of the high speed chase. He called and reported the car stolen the same night. The car is wrecked, but it doesn't matter to him, because he will never claim it.

After two sleepless nights of none stop hustling, he made up for his loss.

"Well, I guess I'll see you later." Pirelli said, leaning over in Erica's direction. He lifts her chin with his thumb and indexfinger, guiding her to his lips, studying her beautiful eyes. His lips softens against hers, tasting her peppermint breath.

"Mmmm," a short muffled moan escapes from her throat. "Let me hurry up and get out of here, before I be late. And don't forget to pick up the boys up from mama's house at-"

"I already know, at six o'clock," he cut her off.

"Good, I'm just remindin' you 'cause I don't wanna hear her mouth. And make sure you be careful. Love you." Erica climbs out of the car, being slapped by the oppressive summer heat.

Before pulling off, Pirelli waits patiently for an elderly woman, pushing a shopping cart full of bags to pass by. The lady flashes a friendly smile, reminding him of his grandmother.

He eases down on the gas turning onto Cicero avenue. He glances at the digital clock on the dashboard.

"I still got a little time left," he thought. For the last two days, he has been looking for another car. Lately he has been frustrated. Dropping Erica off at work and picking up the kids is intervening with his hustle. He decides to stop at the Cadillac dealership on Cicero.

He pulls up on the lot and parks the car. Stepping out of the car, he browses around at the large selection of luxurious automobiles; the blazing sun causes him to sweat profusively. With the back of his hand, he wipes beads of perspiration from his forehead.

"Damn it's hot as a muthafucka out here. Let me go see what they got on the showroom floor," he siad aloud. He enters the building; the soft breeze flowing from the central air system rushes him, slowly drying his moist skin, relieving him. He looks around with a searching gaze, locking his focus on the pearl white Cadillac Escalade in the middle of the showroom floor. The sales representatives, busy assisting customers, doesn't pay any attention to him, as he browses the showroom floor. With his fingertips, he grazes the hood of the Cadillac truck in admiration.

He opens the door climbing inside, melting into the plush interior. He grips the steering wheel, being greeted by the fresh smell of leather. A young female sales representative, notices him sitting in the SUV.

As she prances in his direction her long, curly, blonde hair bounces in the rythmn of her stride. The muscles in her calfs tighten with each step. She is wearing a sleeveless black button-up dress, with one button unfastened, revealing a hint of her cleavage, and a belted waist, that emphasizes her Coca Coca bottle figure.

The clicking sound of her high heel pumps, alerts Pirelli. He shifts his gaze to her, scanning every curve in her body. The woman is the thickset white girl he has ever seen in his entire life.

"Excuse me sir, is their anything I can assist you with

today?" She asked, with a friendly smile, plastered on her face.

"Matter of fact, yes it is," Pirelli replied.

"Well, first let me introduce myself. My name is Jenny." She informed, in her strong sophisticated voice. Pirelli shakes her outstretched, soft; french manicured hand, staring into her baby blue eyes. An electrifying sensation courses through his body.

"Please to meet you Jenny, and my name is Pirelli," he replied in his plesant baritone voice. The powerful and seductive scent of his Polo Double Black colonge embraces the atmosphere.

"Pleasure to meet you Pirelli. So, let me start off by telling you a little about this machine. This beauty right here is one of a kind. It features a six point two liter Vortec v-eight v.v.t engine that delivers four hundred and three horse power, and four hundred and seventeen pound feet of torque. This luxurious truck unlocks a stout zero to sixty time of six point five seconds. Its computer controlled road sensing suspension provides instant response to just about any driving condition. This monster has best in class, highway gas mileage, and is nicely equipped." Pirelli studies the woman's body up and down, listening to her.

"Can I test drive it and see what it has to offer."

"S-Sure," the woman stuttered, noticing his lustful stare.

"May I have your driver license?"

"No problem." Pirelli fishes inside his pocket and introduces his driver's license. He places it into her extended hand and she struts away to retrieve the keys. He locks his attention on her tear drop, shaped ass, as her hips rock side to side.

She returns with the keys and escorts him to another truck of the same model, that's parked on the lot. They climb inside the truck and he zips out of the lot, leaning back in the plush leather seat styling, playing with some of the features bobbing his head to the music. The truck rides smoothly as if it is riding in mid-air.

"So, how you like it so far?"

"I haven't had the chance to get the feel of it yet."

"Oh, you haven't?"

She reaches out a hand and traces the corded muscles from his shoulders, down across his bicep, all the way down his forearm. "Nice shirt you got there." Pirelli glances at her, uncertain what to say, feeling her seductive touch.

"Thanks." She looks up at him, with an impish smile on her face.

As he focuses on the road he hears, "Mmmmm." He looks into the passenger seat and his eyes enlarge at the sight of the woman with her legs spread wide open, stirring her finger in her wetness. She places her moist indexfinger in her mouth teasingly, slowly removing it. "Is this what you want to test drive?" She asked, pulling him by the collar of his short sleeve button up shirt. Her eyes glitens with lust, as she stares into his brown eyes. Her tender lips presses against his, she murmurs against his lips, Her tongue glides along the seam of his lips, seeking entrance.

He gasps at the erotic feeling, her tongue finds its way inside to taste him and to offer pleasure. She hears his gutteral groan as he deepens the kiss, and her moan in response, as he fondles her firm breast. Suddenedly, she grabs his hands pushing him away.

"Wait! What are you doing?" Pirelli looks at her with a look of perplexion. "This is my show. You just sit back and enjoy," he is shocked by her brutally frank speech, and the aggressive sound of her seductive voice. She yanks at the buttons on his shirt, revealing his chisled chest. He feels her warm breath against his chest. Like an animal, she reaches down and unbuckles his belt. He hears the rasp, as the zipper opens. He groans aloud, as her soft hand slides down the front of his boxers. She cups his balls, feeling the soft weight of them in her palm. She stares at his hard mandingo, her eyes wide with astonishment and anxiety. Her tongue teasingly grazes the head of his throbbing erection causing him to swerve into another lane. She slightly tilts her head back, looking into his hungry eyes. He maintains control of the Escalade swaying his head. The music from the factory system fills the air. "You like it?"

"Hell yeah I like it." Pirelli presses speed dial on his Motorola Razor cell phone and places it to his ear. "Ay cuz, I need you to drop off that money. I found a car I want."

"Excuse me sir. Excuse me!" The young female sales representative calls out.

Pirelli sits in the Cadillac Escalade, bobbing his head to imaginary music, with his cell phone to his ear. He snaps out of fantasy land, still bobbing his head.

"Sir."

"Huh." Pirelli looks at the blonde haired woman stupified, still dazed from his daydream.

"This is a floor model; no one is allowed to sit in this vehicle."

"Oh, my fault, I didn't know." Pirelli climbs out of the truck and glances at his watch. ***"I can't believe I wasted all this time. Let me hurry up and get the fuck out of here***."

Dutchess pays the Arabian cab driver and jumps into the car with Pirelli. "What up cuz?" Pirelli greeted Dutchess as they dip out of the gas station.

"Trying to handle this business so I can hurry up and meet this rich white boy at unc's house."

"You make sure you be careful baby girl."

"I'm straight. I know this is a dirty game, but I'mmma big girl. I'm willing to accept whatever consequences comes my way. My daddy taught me a lot when he was living. And whoevers resposible for my father's death... I'mma deal with them, but right now a bitch gotta get paid." Dutchess stressed with a serious facial expression on her face.

"I feel you," Pirelli replied, pulling into the parking lot of McDonald's. He scans the parking lot and spots Chill's candy apple green 66 drop top Chevy Chevelle parked, resting on 26 inch chrome feet.

Chill sits at the table by himself, adjacent to the window with a view of the lot. He peers through the smoke lenses of his Cartier designer frames watching Pirelli, as he struts across the lot. The fresh crispy smell of french fries wafts the atmosphere as Pirelli enters the restaurant. He glimpses around at the large crowd of customers in search of Chill.

A loud ear peircing scream steals Pirelli's attention. He turns around swiftly locking his focus on a three year old little girl having a temper tantum, because her mother refuses to buy her an apple pie.

Spotting Chill, he breaks through the threshold of customers standing in the long line.

"Sup baby?" Pirelli greeted, as they slap palms, shaking hands.

"You know how I do it," Chill replied, taking a sip of his orange soft drink, shifting his gaze out the large glass picture window.

A procession of automobiles floods the drive thru. Chill glimpses around and slides Pirelli a McDonald's bag. Pirelli reaches into his pocket and passes him a thick wad of money, with a rubberband around it, under the table.

"That's the whole fifty five."

"A'ight cool. Just holla at me when you almost out. I see y'all been runnin' through this shit lately."

"Yeah, just a little somethin'."

"Well just hit me."

"A'ight." They slap palms and shake hands and Pirelli exits the building. He jumps into the car and tosses the McDonald's bag into Dutchess lap. She opens the bag and inspects the nine ounces of crystal white powder. A large smile beams across her face.

"It's time for me to shine."

"Make that two of us cuz." Pirelli blurted, staring at an excited Dutchess.

"Naw, I'mma do better than that. I'mma make it hurricane." She retorted, as they blend in with the afternoon traffic, headed to Amos' apartment.

CHAPTER FOUR

Black Jesus' Mercedes-Benz navigates through the heavy rush hour traffic, hugging the road like an inmate on visit.

As the glaring red sun shines down on his 22 inch Dub Esinem Floater's, throwing a reflection off the smooth pavement. The glow from the cars navigation system, illuminates the inside, giving the cream interior a blue tint. The subtle glance, out of the rear-view mirror reveals a black SUV, trailing two car lengths back. The same vehicle has been trailing him for over miles, through various loops and turns. The sounds of blaring horns commingle with that, of loud and soft purring engines, creating a hectic atmosphere.

Making a sharp right unto the Dan Ryan Expressway, the traffic, finally eases up, allowing the Benz, to open up its AMG engine, leaving the black Cadillac Escalade in its dust.

Suddenedly, two Ducati Desmosedici RR's merging from the Bishop Ford Expressway, surrounds the luxury vehicle on each side. The bikes are painted in Rosso GP red, with white number plates on the tail. The matching helmets hide the rider's dreadlocks. They ride with precision with one hand, using the other to point the Heckler & Koch HK53 5.56mm machine guns at Black Jesus' vehicle. This momentary distraction has given the Escalade enough time to catch up, and veer in front of the Benz, causing it to slam on its brakes, to avoid an accident. The screeching tires come to a halt, being replaced by the smell of burning rubber.

Five men hop from out of the truck wearing long leather trench coats, with Rasta Safari hats, exposing every different length of dreads. Pedestrians look on from the passing cars, as they watch a scene in which they think is part of a movie. The leader of the gang signals to one of the other men to open the door. Snatching the door open, he finds a shaking mocha complexioned Trinidadian woman talking on a silver Motorola Razor.

The leader walks towards the woman and grabs the cell phone from her hands. He speaks into the set. "Black Jesus, me need to to talk with you, 79th and Stoney Island, me give you thirty minutes." Click!

Black Jesus arrives at the destination five minutes before the scheduled time. He parks the low key grey pickup truck at the far end of the block in front of a fire hydrant. He exits the S-1O and struts quickly down the street towards Rick's Records and Tapes shop.

He is dressed in tattered clothing, giving himself the appearance of a bum. Two 9 millimeter pistols fit snugly in their holsters, underneath a well worn brown leather bomber jacket. Four clips are tucked securely in the back pockets of his faded stone washed jeans.

As he approaches the corner he watches as a newer model Escalade truck pulls up. Five men jump out and assume various positions. Shortly after his Benz turns the corner and parallel parks behind the truck. A man jumps out turning his back to Black Jesus, as he barks orders through a Motorola walkie talkie. Two motorcycles bend the corner, one of them carrying the girl as a passenger. She appears to be unharmed, which is a good sign, thought

Black Jesus. The woman is escorted into the record store, by one of the riders as the other assumes position outside the shop. Black Jesus recalculates his original plan, now knowing that there are seven accomplices. He now plans to get as close to who he assumes to be the leader, using the element of surprise as his defense. No one seems to notice the bum walking down the street, kicking the crumpled Pepsi can with its faded label. The presence of a bum is a normal occurrence in this area.

"Grrrrr." A stray dog growls from a back alley as Black Jesus walks by, revealing glowing eyes and large white teeth. The clanking sound of the can disturbs his meal. Black Jesus abandons the can in favor of not provoking the dog to give up his rat, and chasing him. Although outnumbered, he walks up on the man who is in charge, maintaining his element of surprise. Black Jesus is the one who is surprised, as he slowly recognizes the man's face.

"Ganja?" the words slip from Black Jesus' mouth in complete shock.

The crack hisses and sizzles, as Tasha sucks on the hollow glass tube from Amos' apartment. Her daughter Kisha plays in the corner of the room with two empty lighters, pretending it is Ken and Barbie dolls. The floor she plays on is littered with burnt matches, ashes, and choreboy. Her mother nods from a tattered armchair. Other pipers occupy two milk crates, while one is asleep on the dingy couch. Amos sits in a chair with a ripped cushion that blocks the entry into the kitchen. The hole in the chair is where he keeps the excess dope.

He reaches into the secret location and pulls out a little for himself. "***I got to make sure the product is still good***," he tells himself, "***Don't wanna be sellin' nobody nothin' I***

wouldn't smoke myself. He runs the long flame from his lighter underneath the spoon, adding a tiny drop of water to the powder. "That's a good girl," he tells the product.

Kisha watches on, as the white piper on the milk crate takes a long drag from the pipe. The smoke swirls from the tip, and floats to the ceiling. The woman next to him nods in and out, scratching her arm in the process.

Amos' fills the needle with water then squirts it out. The needle sucks in the poison. With the rubberband tied tight around his arm, he feels for a sweet spot. A slight dizziness overcomes his body, as the toxins enter into his bloodstream. He nods slightly.

"Amos." He opens his eyes to see Tasha, standing in front of him.

"Let me get a ten pack."

"Where the money?" She reaches into her dingy bra, handing him the musty crumpled bills. He shuffles through the bills. "Man, Tasha, this only seven, I told you no shorts." She licks her chapped lips, that looks as if she was eating white powder donuts.

"I can pay in other ways."

"Nobody want yo' nasty ass." Now she is desperate.

"Come on Amos, please, you know I'm good for it."

"No money, no dope." He hated to be this way, but it was a rule Dutchess had given him.

"What about my daughter then? Get over here Kisha." Kisha shyly walks over and hides behind her mother's leg.

"She's clean, she's a virgin," she added. Amos' face turns red, as the anger boils in his chest, causing him to lose his high.

"You triflin' as hell Tasha, here, take this dope and get out. I don't want yo' daughter, but the state needs to take her from you." He snapped. Tasha doesn't hear a word he said. She grabs the dope in her skinny fingers and rushes to her apartment, down the hall.

"Hurry yo' ass up bitch," she yells to Kisha. Her little legs speed up as she hurries to catch the woman she loves, with all her little heart. "Now sit yo' ass down, and don't you move."

Tasha grabs her utensils from the cabinet. Her plan is to mix the cocaine that she had got from Amos, with the little herion she had left over. This concoction is known as a speedball and she had heard about it from another junkie. The veins on her arm are overly used, so she pulls up her dress she is wearing, exposing her ashy skinny brown thigh. After going through the dopefiend routine, she injects the potion into her bloodstream. She smiles, as she slowly closes her eyes. The drug gives her an euphoria like she has never had before. It was called death. Kisha sits Indian style on the floor, waiting for her mother to tell her she can go to her room.

As the hours pass she falls asleep. The hunger pains in her small stomach wakes her up four hours later. She wipes the sleep out of her eyes with the back of her hands and looks at her mother. "***Mommy sleep***." Kisha thought.

She had once tried to wake her mother after she had taken her drugs, and recieved a vicious back hand. Fear causes her not to make that same mistake again. Although, her stomach feels like someone is stabbing her with a sharp knife.

"***Me hungry***." Kisha comes up with an idea and goes into the kitchen. She pushes a chair up against the stove and climbs on top of the chair. Her tiny hand reaches for one of the knobs. "***Me cook food***."

Black Jesus stares in shock, as he is surrounded by a group of armed men. His shiny 9 millimeter is pointed at the man.

"Put ya weapons down," the man barks the command in his heavy Jamacian drawl and the soldiers immediately follows the order. Black Jesus understands what the man has said and slowly lowers his gun and places it into his holster. "Me name is Zago, Ganja's twin brother." He informed.

Zago is the spitting image of his brother Ganja. He has flown in from Trenchtown, Jamaica to O'Hare International airport. Immediately after learning of his brother's death, he was on the next thing smoking. He left home with a promise of blood-shed to anyone responsible. Zago reaches out his hand in a friendly gesture, which Black Jesus readily accepts. "Me sorry for havin' ta ride down on ya so hard mon, but me didn't know no other way to reach ya," Zago states apologetically. "Me brotha use ta tell me how slick you is," he admitted, trying to ease the tension in the air.

"It's all love brother, yo' brother was always good to me so I hold nothin' against you, except for you holdin' my woman hostage." Black Jesus stated.

Zago speaks into his walkie talkie and moments later January is leaving on her own free will. Her Prada dress clings to her, as she sways to the Mercedes, gaining the attention of every one on the streets. One of the soldiers whips the Escalade around and Zago motions for Black Jesus to get into the vehicle.

The truck circles the block going down 79th street. "Me lookin' for the mon that killed me brotha," he says, blowing a billow of smoke from the ghans he has lit. The windows of the truck makes it appear to be later outside than it really is.

"You and me both." Black Jesus replies, accepting the blunt from Zago.

"Me won't to know if maybe the streets been talkin'." Zago's studies Black Jesus' face carefully, looking for any signs of dishonesty. He's almost sure that Black Jesus did not have anything to do with the death of his brother. The kill was much too sloppy to have come from somebody getting as much money as Black Jesus. The mere fact that his chain was missing from his body told volumes to anybody who was paying attention.

"Naw man, I ain't heard shit, but I got a few of my guys on it. If something shakes, I'll let you know right away. Ganja was good people, and I hate that some lame took him out. So, if there is anything I can help you with, just let me know." Black Jesus stated.

"Me appreciate that mon, and me tellin' ya, when me find the mon who killed me brotha, me gon' make the bomba klaat wish him never been born."

The Escalade circles the block once more. "Where ya won't me to drop ya off at?"

"Right here is good." Black Jesus points to an old truck with a smashed in fender. Zago now knows why people never see Black Jesus creep up on them.

"Me brotha told me you was one smooth rudeboy." Zago states as Black Jesus exits the truck. "Now me have seen with me own eyes." Black Jesus smiles, as he walks to his truck. The escalade pulls off, with Zago in the back. He is lost in deep thought, with only one thing on his mind, revenge.

Dutchess sits on the edge of Amos' bed counting a large pile of money that she made in the last two hours. Traffic has been moving rapidly from the moment she arrived. She gives Amos an ounce at a time, and he conducts all transactions. The majority of Dutchess clientele is middle aged, upper class Europeans.

Amos steps into the bedroom and hands Dutchess a thick wad of money. "I need more." Dutchess takes the money and hand him another ounce, along with her new digital scale that weighs a capacity of one hundred grams. Amos rushes out the room to serve the customers; he has waiting in the livingroom. Dutchess quickly counts the money that Amos handed to her. Before she could finish counting Amos comes back into the room gripping another wad of money.

"I need another one. They lovin' it." Dutchess reaches in her bra and drops another ounce into his extended hand.

He exits the room leaving the strong smell of cocaine base lingering in the air. Looking at the large pile of money accumulating on the bed causes her to smile. She counted a total of $7,700.00 dollars and stared at it in disbelief. This is the best day she had. She's down to her last four ounces within three hours. She averages a little over $1500.00 an ounce. She flips her cell phone open and calls Pirelli. The way things are moving, she know she'll be out soon. Pirelli answers his phone on the first ring.

"What's poppin'?"

"I need to see you again, the same way."

"What!"

"Just like I said I need to see you again."

"You bullshittin' me." he said in disbelief. "I just dropped you off to yo' car a few hours ago." He pauses for a few seconds. "Damn cuz, you caught me in the middle of somethin'. Fuck it, let me get this shit together and I'll hit you right back."

"Now that's what I'm talkin' about. I knew you'll come through for me." 'Dutchess said excitedly.

"You just remember, you owe me one for this one," he responded.

"A'ight cousin, I won't forget about you when I come up. I'm going to make sure your right there with me," Dutchess promised.

"A'ight, I'mma hold you to that. I'll holla at you in a minute."

"A'ight."

"Peace out." Click!

Dutchess stuffs all her money into her purse. "I need to go stash this," she thinks to herself. She steps into the living room and the strong malorderous smell slaps her in the face. "Whew, that shit stank." She blows out a short breath, squeezing her nose with her thumb and indexfinger. "Ay unc."

"Yeah."

"Let me talk to you for a minute." Dutchess said, with a wave of the hand. They step off to the side, out of eye sight. "Here, take this. I'll be back in a minute; I gotta go take care of some business." Amos tucks the packages in his crotch area.

"A'ight, hurry back cause this won't last that long."

"It won't be long, I'll be right back." Dutchess exits the apartment, walking through the dim narrow hallway. She stops in her tracks, sensing something wrong with her surroundings. She smells the atmosphere and inspects the hallway, walking slowly. "***It smells like somethin' burnin' around here***." She follows the smell and spots a cloud of continous smoke, ascending from the bottom of Tasha's apartment door. "Oh my God." She said aloud, thinking about the the little girl that may be in danger. She hurriedly moves to the door and turns the door knob, opening the door. A large cloud of thick, gray smoke pours out of the door into the hallway. Dutchess coughs, being chocked by the smoke. The smoke clouds her vision, making it hard for her to see.

Tasha lies back on the chair dead, faintly visible. "Come baby, where you at?" Dutchess becomes startled as she searches the apartment for the little girl. She drops to her knees crawling on the floor. She can hear a multitude of voices coming from the hallway, as the neighbors panic, vacating the building.

Dutchess spots the little girl lying soundless, on the kitchen floor. Dutchess embraces the little girl, coughing uncontrollably as the smoke clogs her lungs.

The sounds of sirens wail from a distance. Dutchess exits the burning apartment and collapses to the hallway floor, with the little girl in her arms. She regains her breath and gives the little girl mouth to mouth.

"Please baby, don't die like this." Dutchess continues on, trying to revive Kisha and save her precious life.

Neighbors surround her as she carefully pumps her stomach. Dutchess never thought in a lifetime that she'd be using the CPR lessons she learned in high school. "Please God, don't let her die." Dutchess lies against her tiny chest and hears the best rythmn she ever heard in her life, and the soft beat of her heart. "She's alive." Dutchess blows the breath of life into her lungs. Dutchess can hear the distance sound of footsteps and electronic devices. Kisha starts coughing, and breathing on her own. Her eyes flick open, and the first thing she sees, is the woman who saved her life. She cries inbetween her coughs, hugging Dutchess as if she's holding on to dear life. Dutchess embraces her, thanking God for giving the little girl a second chance at life. "It's gon' be okay baby." Dutchess assured, combing her fingers through Kisha's hair. Dutchess kisses Kisha on her smooth forehead, holding her as if she gave birth to her.

"She saved her." A woman happily shouted, with teary eyes. Fire fighters storm through the hallway.

"Everybody out the building."

"Somebody else is in the house," Dutchess yelled, knowing that there is no hope for Tasha. They carefully enter the apartment. Dutchess kisses the little girl one last time, and stares in her baby brown eyes, before vanishing down the hall.

Cheryl Blackwell, lost in deep thought, stares out her office window at the traffic coming up and down Dearborn Street. Today is her first day of work at the federal building, since she took a leave of absence following her husband's death. The office has been painted an off white during her break, with the addition of wood panel strips along the base of the wall. Her Sony Vaio laptop sits on her desk, while its screen saver of dolphins jumping through loops, dances across the unattended monitor. A picture of Lawrence, herself and Dutchess is located at the edge of the desk, next to a flower pot with dead leaves that were once geraniums. Since returning to work, she has been concentrating all of her energy on trying to build a new case against Kennytha Baptiste. She vows to herself to one day be responsible for his demise.

Mr. Sorensten, her boss, barges into her office without knocking, stealing her attention. He is carrying a brown box that sits on her desk, causing her screen saver to return to its normal screen. The image of dolphins is replaced by a picture of Kennytha Baptiste. He takes a seat in the chair, reclining it back with his weight. He pushes his wire-rimmed glasses up to his nose, and takes the folder from the top of the box, handing it to her.

"This here is the new case file your assigned. Scan through it and see if you can make something stick. We really need this one. The government has been breathing down my back, asking where all the money is going. We need results." She stares at him in disbelief.

"***What does he mean we need results, I've been performing excellent since I got here***," she thought to herself. She knows that the money reference was strictly for her sake. It was directed towards the amount she spent for the Baptiste case, only for it to wind up being botched. A million dollars could be spent on one case, as long as a conviction was made, and no one would say a thing. But let a penny be spent in a loss, and everyone wants to know was the penny spent justifiable, she silently complained, looking over the folder. Mr.Sorensten could hear the soft purr of her laptop, when the air conditioning system that keeps the building cool went off.

"What are you working on?" he asked, while trying to peek at the monitor. She quickly minimizes the website, leaving the blue default start up screen for windows XP.

"Oh nothing," she lied. She points at the folder, "This now, I guess." A thin smile creases his face.

"Good, that's what I like to hear. This guy is real polished. The state can't seem to make the charges stick. His name is Kashuan Lewis, but he goes by Ice." Mrs Blackwell laughs.

"What a fitting name for such a buoyant person."

"My sentiments exactly," chimed in Mr.Sorensten. "Let's melt this guy before he gets to be a problem, and everyone who's dealing with him." He rises to leave, and turns to her before leaving out the door. "Oh and Cheryl."

"Yes, mister Sorensten."

"Glad to have you back."

He exits the door and she puts the folder into her desk. For now, Ice is a secondary concern. She kisses her golden wedding ring. "I miss you so much baby." She refocuses her attention back to the computer screen, double clicking on the blue 'E' opening up Internet Explorer.

Her home page is set on Google, the internets largest search engine. Anything and everyone can be found using this service.

She types the words into the white search box as they appear on the screen. "Hiring A Hitman." She presses the the search button, and waits patiently for results.

Moments later an Email with Baptiste's picture is sent to cyberspace.

CHAPTER FIVE

Carmen stands in her bathroom trying to apply a thick layer of make up on her face, to cover the fresh black eye that Tyrone has given her. Having no luck, she decides to fix her hair up in a style that conceals her right eye perfect. The style of her hair mixed with her light brown skin gives her a look similar to Aaliyah's. She takes one more look into the mirror and exits the bathroom. She steps into the small bedroom with scattered toys and Kool Aid stains on the floor. A Power Ranger action figure crunches under neath the heel of her shoe, as she makes her way to the twin size bed. She kisses her daughter on the forehead.

"I love you," she tells her. Carmen loves her daughter very much, and part of the reason she hasn't left Tyrone yet, is because she wants her daughter to grow up with her father. The other reason is because he had told her that if she ever leaves him, he would kill her. As crazy as he is, she believes him.

Closing her daughter's bedroom door softly, she passes by Tyrone lying on the couch sleep, with one hand resting in his pants. The stench smell of old pepperoni floats to her nose. The box is some where lost underneath the sofa. She has been meaning to clean up, but with work and all, it's been keeping her a little more tired than usual. Besides, even if she did Tyrone would just have it messed back up, within a few hours.

"Tyrone," she calls out softly, not really trying to disturb the sleeping lion. Tyrone stirs in his sleep, and then balls up on the couch in a fetal position. "Tyrone," she says again, gaining his attention.

"What?" he answers rudely, wiping the slob away from the corner of his mouth.

"Where the keys at?"

Tyrone has been out all night drinking and partying with the hundred and fifty dollars he stole out of her purse last night, when she was asleep. His head aches from the hangover he received from last nights partying.

He points to the floor, mad because she didn't know that they were in the pizza box. "Right there, damn!"

"I guess I was supposed to know they were in there and not on the key rack," she mumbles under her breath, rolling her eyes at his motionless body.

"What!" Tyrone snaps, hearing her say something.

"Nothin' Tyrone." "***Lord I wish that he would give me a little help***." She silently prays, walking out the house. She looks into the mailbox, finding a piece of mail. A bill from Common Wealth Edison notifying her of the immediate threat of turning off her power. The total amount owed is $832.62, which is in red bold print. She can save them the trip of coming out, by making the payment of $142.32. She tucked the bill into her purse. She will pay them with the money she has hid in her Gucci bag, after going to work. She gets into her brown 1996 Ford station wagon. The barometer reading for the gas is almost touching 'E'. When she went to sleep last night, she had a quarter of a tank. She smacks her hand across the steering wheel. "Damn it Tyrone!" She starts the car and heads to work.

Upon reaching Mahati's African Braiding shop, the building is on fire. Ambulance, fire trucks, and police sirens ring out in the air as the vehicles rush down North Avenue. Many spectators and customers watch as the building goes up in smoke. Parking her car, Carmen gets out and talks to her co-worker Laquita, who is in the front row watching the blazing fire and thick black smoke floating in the air.

"Damn Quita girl, what happened?"

"I don't know fo' sure, but they say Mahati did it." Quita's thick ghetto accent embraces her.

"Why would he do that?" Carmen questioned. Laquita smacking gum in her mouth, she responds, "Girl you know that cheap ass African muthafucka will do anything for money. He tried to do an insurance job, but got caught. Look over there." She points a long skinny finger, with long fake nails towards a cruiser by the curb. Mahati sits in the back seat looking dumb as ever, hanging his bald head down. A piece of cloth from his black, green, and gold Dasheeki is caught in the door.

"Jus' look at his dumb ass," Laquita hisses. Carmen feels dizzy from the realization that she is out of work. Being that she is the sole bread winner for the house, her not working equals no food.

"What we gon' do now, I got bills and a kid to feed at home?" Carmen whined.

"What you mean what is you gon' do?" Laquita corrects her, swinging her wild blonde hair. "Girl you know this hair shit for me is just something I do to keep my parole officer off my ass, about me havin' a job. As soon as I leave here, I'm out there on the stroll, and if you need to make some money, I suggest you get out there and do the same."

"***Sellin' some ass***." That is a new thought for her. Carmen walks away from her girl, thinking she had a lot of nerves to suggest that she become a prostitute. That is the last thing she is willing to do. "***Fake ass Beyonce lookin' bitch***!" she thought, getting into her car. So far today had been a bad day for her. "***It can't possibly get any worst***," she told herself, as she drives to go pay her bill.

The small waiting line inside of Common Wealth Edison is not as bad as most days, but still she grows impatient.

"But I paid my bill last month," the man who is in front of her argues to the woman behind the window. Carmen steps to the next avaialable window, and slides her bill through the slot.

"What can I help you with today?" the elderly brunette behind the counter asks. "Umm, I would like to make a payment."

"Will that be cash, check, or credit card?"

"Cash," Carmen replies, fishing through her purse. The woman types Carmen's information into the computer and reads the tag, someone has typed into her account. It reads, ***Deliquent Account, customer makes excuses, payment due or terminate***. Carmen begins to dump the contents of her purse onto the counter. Loose change, lip stick, tampons, and other various items. She checks once again where she knew she had put the money. "It was here last night," she mumbles loud enough for the woman to hear.

"Sure it was honey," the woman replies unbelievingly. "Just come back when you have it. You have until Friday, then we'll have to shut off umm-k." A thin smile creases the woman's pink lips. "Bye now, have a nice day."

"***Damn you Tyrone***." It was the second time that she had said that today. "***What am I going to do now***," she thought. The thought of stripping or getting out there on the track selling her body entertains her mind. She would do it if necessary to feed her daughter. She doesn't want to, but she doesn't have many options.

"***Oh wait a minute, let me call Sade's crazy ass. I'd rather get on a bus then become a hoe***." Carmen thought as she headed home to confront Tyrone.

Dutchess and her mother are sitting in the kitchen, waiting for Deagelo to arrive. Cheryl gets up, and stirs the ham, and cheese omelet in the black cast iron skillet. The tasty aroma plays with Dutchess' stomach. "You sure you don't want any," Cheryl asks one last final time. Dutchess has been feeling a little under the weather lately, and hasn't had much of an appetite.

"I guess I'll try a little." Cheryl fixes both of them a plate, and sits down across from Dutchess.

"I've noticed that you've been staying out a little later than usual."

"Oh, I got a second job." Cheryl takes a few bites from the well seasoned omelet.

"Mmm, doing what?"

"Working at the gas station."

"The gas station," Cheryl repeated. "That doesn't seem like a good job for a young woman as smart as you are. Why you don't want to go to college?" Dutchess plays with the omelet with her fork.

"You startin' to sound like Deangelo. That's not what I wanna do. I have other plans." Dutchess proclaimed.

"Now, since you don't want to talk about that, let me ask you something."

"What's that?"

"Sex, are you and Deangelo sexual active?"

"Naw ma," Dutchess responds blushing, embarassed that her mother is so blunt. They have a very close relationship, and talk about many things.

"I was just asking, because I'm not ready to be a grandmother."

"Don't worry, you have a long time before you have to worry about that." She finishes her omelet, and feels like she has to burp. She attempts to and starts throwing up. Cheryl looks on with concern. “Wheew, I guess I'm still sick,” she says, cleaning up the mess. She goes to brush her teeth and when she comes back down Cheryl is chatting with Deangelo.

“Well, you ready?” he asks her.

“Yep.”

“Where are you two going?” Cheryl inquired.

“Dang, nosey,” Dutchess replies with a smile.

“I'm takin' her to church Mrs.Blackwell, she needs it.”

“I agree. I knew there was a reason why I always liked you.”

“Whatever,” Dutchess repiles. “Well ma, we'll see you 1ater.”

Cheryl walks them to the door, keeping it open until they make it in Deangelo's car. They pull off, heading to church.

The assassin from a safe distance away, watches through the scope, as Dutchess and Deangelo pass through, the dots. He readjusts his aim at Cheryl, who is standing in the doorway. He expels a deep breath, steadying his hold on his rifle.

“Steady...Steady...Almost...Damn.” Cheryl closes the door. He breaks down his equipment. “***There's no rush. There will be another time***.” He tells himself.

Victory Faith Baptist church is filled to near capacity, as Deangelo and Dutchess walk in, taking a seat in the back row.

They squeeze inbetween two large women. Deangelo

stands up to sing along with the choir.

"This little light of mine, I'm gon' let it shine, let it shine, let it shine, let it shine."

The pastor struts from the back area, in a brown three piece suit taking the podium. The music slowly fades away. She grabs Deangelo, pulling him back to his seat, as they share whispers.

"That pastor is a hypocrite."

"Girl what you talkin' about? I've been comin' here wit' my mother for years."

"Sssh," the big woman says, rolling her eyes at the two. Pastor Mario stands tall, scanning the congregation. It is a packed house, with only standing room remaining. He calculates the potential profit in his head, as the ushers, pass out creme-colored programs. The additional bodies add more heat to the already under-ventilated building.

Pastor Mario takes a deep breath, and closes his eyes, recalling the money sermon, from his memory.

"The bible says, 'For God, so loved the world, that he gave his only begotten son, John 3:16." The swooshing sound of the pages being turned, fill the atmosphere, as the congregation finds the verse. "The Lord, loves you," his melodic voice pours into the pews, enchanting the members of the church.

"Praise the Lord," said the woman next to Dutchess.

"The Lord made a sacrifice, so we could live," Pastor Mario added.

"Amen," came the refrain, "Hallalujah."

Pastor Mario nods his head in delight, seeing that his words are having an effect on the people. "I said, so we can live."

"Yes Lord, thank you Jesus," an elder in the front row shouted.

"So today, we will be reading out of the book of Hebrews." Pastor Mario slips his hand into the breast pocket of his suit, removing his handkerchief, wiping his face. The members of the church fan themselves with the newly received programs.

"You know what, let's forget about Hebrews. I can feel the spirit, roaming around the room today. I'm just going to close my eyes, and let the spirit guide us."

He picks the bible up, and slashes his hand through it. To the members watching, it looks like he is selecting a random page, but Pastor Mario is smarter than that. Earlier, he had creased his bible so heavily, that when he performed his trick, it couldn't help but open to that page. He holds the bible out, showing that he was lead to the book of Hebrews. "This is a sign brothers," he exclaimed.

"***He's goin' to hell***," thought Dutchess.

The woman next to Deangelo rises, being filled with the spirit. The lady next to Dutchess, not to be out done, rises as well, faking a shake, shouting unintangible words. Shortly, the women return to their seats, and the pastor continues.

"We're in Hebrews chapter 13, beginning with verse 15. And as I read it silently in my head, I know that it's truly a message from God himself."

"Praise the Lord!" the congregation shouts.

"It is a message tellin' us what we as followers of Jesus must do. The Lord sacrificed his son, so that we could live through him, so let us continually offer up a sacrifice to praise God ... " He pauses to let the words sink in. "But it doesn't stop there."

"Preach brother preach," someone shouts from the audience.

"Cause in verse 16, it tells us, and do not neglect doing good, and sharing, for with such sacrifices God is pleased." He signals to the ushers. "So what this is saying is, we must make a sacrifice to the Lord today." The ushers are passing around collection plates. "Do what you can to please the Lord." He pulls out the offering dish that he keeps by the podium, holding it high in the air. "Reach deep, fill it up, pile it high, to the sky," he chants.

The dish makes its rounds, he frowns as it is passed to Sister Mary Martha, he knows that she will leave one crumpled bill, a one dollar food stamp. "***Where does she keep gettin them from, they using Bridge cards now***," he thought. Others fill the plate up. Dutchess passes it directly to Deangelo. He puts in a hundred dollar bill.

"What you doing?" Dutchess reaches to get the money from the plate. Deangelo passes it to the woman next to him.

"Not bad, not bad at all." He closes the service in prayer.

Dutchess and Deangelo leave, stopping to have lunch. His flight leaves today, and he promises to return as soon as he saves up enough money. He drops her off back at home. They share a passionate kiss, as he walks her to the door. "I wish you could stay," Dutchess whines.

"I do to."

"Well, alright, call me baby when your flight lands. I love you."

"I love you too the baby."

Dutchess enters the house, heading to her room. She has two book cases. One filled with law books, covered in dust, and the other with urban novels. The acceptance letters from Harvard, Stanford Law, and Yale, sit unopened on her comptuer desk. She kicks her shoes off, and lays in the bed. She reaches her hand out to her night stand and grabs 'The Coldest Winter Ever,' by Sistah Souljah. She reads a couple of chapters becoming thrilled. "That's what I'm talking 'bout get money." The book gives her a motivation, like never before.

◈◈◈

Chaos pulls into Mimi's driveway dropping her off at home after a long night at his apartment. Chaos met Mimi a week ago at Water Tower Place Mall. She lives with her mother and her 12 year old brother. She looks like she belongs on the cover of a Smooth Girl magazine. She has long silky jet black hair, vanilla complexion, a petite frame, and a 36c chest that fits her body perfectly.

"Give me a call later on sweetheart," Chaos said, watching her climb out of the car.

"I'll do that baby. And by the way, thank you for last night," she stated, waving him good bye, as he pulls out of the driveway. Chaos locks eyes with a young boy who is walking through their front yard carrying a basketball.

A fresh breeze of air blows through the windows fluttering Chaos' Enyce shirt, as he rounds the corner. He glances to his right and spots a man with a large frame. His eyes enlarge at the sight of the man, strutting out of a single family residence talking on his cell phone. The diamond Benny & Co watch on his wrist twinkles, as the sun beams on each diamond. The dime sized diamond earrings resting in his earlobes sparkle, accentuating his dark complexion.

Chaos watches him through the rearview mirror, as he jumps into a pearl white Mercedes Benz CLS500, with 21 inch chrome faced Giovanna rims. "Today must be my lucky day," he said quietly. "All this time I been tryna find out where Bricks lay his head, and I bump into this nigga like this. I'mma lay low and watch that house fo' a minute," he thinks to himself. He grabs his cell phone with a devilish smile plastered on his face. "Wait til I tell Slow about this."

Errrk! Errk! Errrk! A procession of unmarked vehicles pull up recklessly from all directions, after receiving a tip from a reliable source. Drug Enforcement Agents, along with A. T. F., pours into the Northside residential building wearing navy blue wind-breakers clutching semi-automatic weapons. The meticulously move through the hallway in a military style formation, with their artillery drawn, heading to the target apartment. Agent Rains leads a groups of agents, approaching the door to Ice's bachelor pad. Hearing a series of moans, Agent Rains places his indexfinger against his lips. "Sssh, I think we literally caught him with his pants down," he whispered to the other agents, wearing a smile on his face. The agents gather around on each side of the door, listening intently to the couple getting their freak on.

"Ooooh, s-sh-it, dad-dy. Ughhh! It's in m-my stomach." Smack! Smack!

"Stop runnin' from this dick!" Smack!

"Ooh, eeew, s-shit. Beat this pussy up. O-oh, I~I'm cummin' again d-daddy. Ooooh! Ooooh! P-Pleaseee don't s-stop!" the woman begs. The clapping sound of flesh reverberates in the rythmn of their movement behind the closed door.

Agent Melinda Dorch's eyes skitters to Agent Rains, as he clutches his his police issued 9 millimeter, with a firm grip, preparing himself for the raid. Hulking shadows dance on the walls as they ease closer to the door. Agent Rains bangs on the door.

"D.E.A, search warrant, open up!" Agent Rains barks with authority, waiting for a response.

"Aaaah, yeah, you makin' me cum again." Smack! Smack!

"Put some pussy juice on this dick."

The couple doesn't respond to the boisterous knock at the door. The sound of their sexual encounter communicates with Agent Melinda Dorch's hormones, making her hungry for physical contact, leaving her legs weak.

"The myth about the blackman must be true. My husband can't even make me scream like that. I can't even remember the last time I've had an orgasm. I've' been faking orgasm for a long time. Maybe Bill should get lessons from him." Agent Melinda Dorch drifts off and regains her focus.

Agent Rains nods his head giving the other agents permission to force their way into the apartment. Two agents position themselves in front of the door, gripping a double handled battering ram. They rear the battering ram and swing with full force. The ram slams into the door making a loud crashing sound, knocking the door off its hinges.

Chaos and Slow leans back in an old model surburban analyzing their surroundings, waiting in the darkness, hoping that tonight be their lucky night. With the windows cracked, all they can hear is the rustling sound of the tall trees. The trees dance from side to side from the force of the midnight breeze. The dimly lit street lights shine, making the tranquil neighborhood faintly visible to the naked eye.

"Man this nigga ain't about to show up. We been sittin' here all day," Slow complained, running out of patience. "I'm surprise the neighbors didn't ... "

"Sssh, hold up," Chaos interrupted him in mid-sentence, as he locks his focus on a car turning the corner. The headlights blare on the various parked cars. A glow of intermittent light shines in the suburban, outlining their frames as it passes by.

"I told you this nigga ain't comin'. I can be at home layin' in some pussy right about now," Slow proclaimed.

"Be patient joe, you know how this shit go. Trust me, this shit gon' payoff real soon," Chaos stated surely, studying the on coming traffic that ocassionally passes by.

"I think that's the nigga Bricks right there," Chaos blurted.

"Where?" Slow asks, looking over his shoulder at a blue Honda Accord, pulling into a driveway.

"Naw, not over there, over there." Chaos points at the Mercedes Benz riding up the "block with its lights off. The mirrored rims chop, reflecting off the concrete pavement. Chaos and Slow leans down in the seats as the car passes by them.

The car dips into the driveway parking on the side of the house. "Yeah, that's him. I told you all you gotta do is be patient. Let's do this."

They quietly climb out of the truck, pushing the doors up without closing them. They make a soundless approach hiding on the side of the single family residence. Chaos clutches his nickel plated Glock .40, with one in the hole. Slow leans back with his back against the wall, holding his 357, with its cooliant system. The red beam shines on the grass as they wait for Bricks to make his way to the front door. They listen to the rattling sound of his keys as he inserts his key into the lock. With perfect timing they step from behind the house. Bricks notice a glint of light and reaches for his gun in fright. Before he is able to draw his gun, Chaos jabs him in the ribcage with the barrel of his gun. "Don't think about it nigga," Chaos said in a raspy voice, biting down on his lower lip. A red doss shines on Bricks' temple as Slow aims the high powered handgun. He removes Bricks' gun from his waistband. "Open the door. You try any slick shit, I'mma blow yo' top off mafucka," Chaos snarls, trailing him into the house, gripping the back of his collar with the barrel of the gun pressed against his temple.

They escort him inside the house, stepping into the pitch black livingroom. "Turn the lights on in this mafucka," Chaos instructs watching his every move. He flicks on the light and the luxurious livingroom becomes visible. Perspiration glistens on Bricks' forehead. Slow searches the entire first floor making sure no one else is in the house. "If somebody upstairs I advise you to tell me now," Chaos suggested, glaring into Bricks' eyes.

"The only person here is my girl. Just tell me what y'all want from me," Bricks responded, hoping that he make it out of this situation alive.

A combination of rising voices pierces the air, as the group of Drug Enforcement Agents scramble throughout the apartment. Agent Rains aims his gun in front of him, scanning the apartment with a searching gaze. Hearing the copule still engaging in their sexual encounter has him confused. He is wondering how they could not hear the blatant entry.

As he eases along the wall nearing the bedroom with his gun in hand, the groaning and moaning becomes louder. He turns the corner taking precaution. "Freeezee!" He shouted, aiming his gun, staring into the bedroom in disbelief. HIs eyes browses the room only to find a neatly made queen size bed and a 42 inch screen television with a porno flick crooning from it.

"Ooh shit baby. Aaaah that pussy was good." He walks over to the DVD player and turns it off. He looks over at the other agents who are staring in disbelief. No Ice, no female companion, and no sex scene.

"Don't just stand there! Search this place inside out," he bellows, his voice expressing his impious mood.

Searching the apartment thoroughly, they find a bulletproof vest, two .45 automatic handguns, and $15,000.00 dollars in cash.

"I want them guns dusted for fingerprints. I'm going to nail that dope dealing scum for whatever I can." Agent Rains stated, as they file out of the sabotaged apartment.

Rachel's eyes flings open at the sound of the whining bedroom door swinging open. Her eyes spread with panic, as she focuses on the two armed intruders guiding Bricks into the bedroom at gun point. She bolts upright in the bed holding the blanket, covering her breast in terror. Her heart hammers at the base of her throat, and a disturbing sensation courses through her body. "W-What's going on Bricks?" She asks, in a trembling voice, staring into the icy eyes of the two masked men.

"Fuck you think goin' on bitch!" Chaos answers before Bricks could reply. "Get the fuck out the bed," Chaos barks, aiming his gun at the startled woman. She hops from the bed with her firm titties dangling, wearing a pair of thongs. Slow gives the woman a lustful stare. She hugs herself trying to cover her chest. Watching her luscious hips rock side to side, Slow finds himself having an erection. A sound unable to be identified brings him back to his senses. He glimpses around, intently listening for the sound.

"Dawg, did you hear that?" Slow inquired.

"Hear what?"

"It sound like somebody else is in here. I know I ain't losin' my mind."

Rachel already knows what the sound is he heard. "***Please God help me***." She silently prays to herself. Slow hears the distant sound again.

"I knew I whatn't just hearin' shit," Slow said in a low tone, creeping into the hallway with his thumper in hand.

"Y'all bett' not make one sound," Chaos snarls.

Slow walks into the room cradling a new born baby in his arms, dressed in a pair of sleepers. "Please don't hurt my baby," Rachel cries, becoming hysterical.

"Bitch shut the fuck up! As long as we get what we came for, won't nobody get hurt," Chaos snaps.

"I got what y'all came for man. Please just, don't hurt the baby," Bricks pleads, "It's down stair in the kitchen."

"Now that sounds better. Let's go take care of this business." They take them down stairs. The infant looks around as if he doesn't have a worry in the world. He has been birth into a cold blooded world known as the devil's playground.

"It's in the cabinet over the sink," Bricks informed.

Slow opens the cabinet and pulls out a small grocery bag filled with money. Slow looks inside the bag inspecting the various denominations. His face crinkles in anger. "Mafucka this ain't all you got!" Slow rants.

"That's everything man, I'm tellin ' you," Bricks lied.

"You wanna play wit' my fuckin' intelligence," Slow opens the microwave with a diabolical look flashing in his eyes, and places the infant inside of it. He slams the door shut and punches the buttons setting the timer on fifty minutes.

"Pleeasse, I'm beggin you, don't hurt my baby!" Rachel cries, with tears spilling from her glassy eyes. She can hear the muffled sound of her baby crying on the other side of the glass sqirming. Slow positions his finger on the start button.

"A'ight! A'ight! ," Bricks shouted, "The rest is in the safe!" Chaos strikes him across the forehead with the Glock .40, making him see a silver blur. He gashes him open with the blow to the head and warm blood runs down his face.

"Hurry up and open it bitch ass nigga, I ain't got all day," Bricks grimaces in excruciating pain, cupping his forehead, staggering towards the safe that's mounted behind the couch. Rachel weeps in the background, fearing for the life of her precious little baby. He pulls the couch away from the wall with trembling fingers. He twirls the combination lock. After turning the knob several directions, it opens. He prepared himself for a time such as this. He reaches into the safe and clutches a .45 automatic handgun, which sits atop bundles of neatly stacked hundred dollar bills. His heart pumps with fear as he takes a gamble with his life. He swiftly shifts his burly structure.

"Fuck you doin' nig-" Boc! Boc! Boc! Bricks fires the gun, waving it haphazardly, stubling to the floor.

Chaos returns fire, letting the Glock .40 clap. A bullet ricochets off the chandelier and rips through Slows neck. The defeatening sound of gunfire and Rachel's earpiercing scream awakes the tranquil neighborhood.

Slow grips his neck, blood leaks through the crack of his fingers as he tumbles to the floor. Chaos peppers Bricks' chest with hot bullets. The upper half of his large frame dances against the wall. Chaos storms out of the side door exiting the house.

Rachel dashes across the livingroom trembling in fright. She trips on a cord, and a ceramic lamp crashes against the floor, bursting in a shard of pieces. She grabs her crying baby out of the microwave nauseated in fear, cradling him.

The strong smell of gun powder lingers in the air. Sirens wail from a distance getting louder and louder. Rachel's knees grow weak. She drops to her knees beside Bricks holding her seed in her arms, thanking God for sparing their lives. She feels the livingroom tilting. She begins to concetrate on her breathing. Tears trickle down her cheeks, coursing down the length of her unblemished carmel complexioned face. She gazes into Bricks' partially closed suffering eyes, as he fights for his life.

"Please don't die on me like this," she whispers. Her

mouth is dry and the words vanish into her throat. Bricks' chest heaves heavily, sucking in and out, as he looks into Rachel's eyes, paralyzed with his back against the wall. His vision begins to blur, and Rachel's beautiful facial features becomes a silhouette, slowly fading away. He sees his whole life flash in his head from childhood to adulthood. A voice echoes through his head. "Son your time has come." His eyes close completely. The only thing he can see now is pure darkness, as imminent death embraces his soul.

The semi-crowded Churches Chicken on 66th and Halstead serve its waiting patrons, as Ice and Chill meet in a secluded booth in the back. Ice sits with his back facing the wall, overlooking the entire establishment. Chill has just returned from the counter with a six piece wing dinner, a side of mash potatoes, macaroni and cheese, two biscuits, and a large Sprite.

"You sure you don't want nothin'," Chill asks, reaching into the grease stained bag removing a wing.

"Naw, I'm good." Ice stares at the bad ass little nappy head boy having a temper tantrum in the seat next to his.

"I said, I don't want this shit!" he yells, throwing the crispy thigh onto the ground. "McDonalds, Happymeal, apple pies," he chants, jumping up and down.

"Boy, do you want me to whip yo' lil eight year old ass!" the dark complexioned woman with rollers in her hair yells at the boy. She takes off her houseshoe, holding it like a whip. He quiets down instantly. Smack! Smack! "That's for actin' like a damn fool!" she hits him twice and stops after noticing Ice staring at her.

"So, what's up with you playboy? What is it you wanted to talk to me about?" Chill asks, while cleaning the chicken to the bone. His voice draws Ice's attention away from the woman.

"Oh it ain't shit, I just wanted to know what's up. I see you been steppin' yo' game up with the wizerk."

Ice is concerned that maybe Chill has been selling weight to an undercover by accident. That may explain why his apartment was raided. In this game, a person can never be too careful. His clientele has never been so large, so why the sudden change?

"***I hope I don't have to kill this nigga***," Ice silently thinks. Chill can read his man vibes, from the look in Ice's face.

"I pick up this new custo," he explains.

"Is it a cop?" Ice bluntly asks.

"Come on dawg, now you know, you and me better than that."

"I'm just sayin', how long you knew him?" Ice sarcastically asks Chill.

"About two months, three at the most." He waves both hands in the air, palms facing up waiting for a reply. "Naw man, we go way back," he lies, "And he, ain't no he, it's a she." Action's brown eyes enlarge as he stare at him in disbelief.

"What? A bitch? What's her name?"

"I don't think you know her man. She one of them fine little pretty hoes, with a fat ass. From the suburbs and shit. Don't even look like she would get into somethin' like this. I don't know her name, but I can get in contact with her."

"You sure she sellin' it?" Ice asks, still in disbelief.

"Well, I don't think she smokin' it all up," Chill replies comically. Ice rises from the table pulling his creme and brown velour jacket to his nose. "Damn this shit smell like dirty grease and chicken. I need to get some air." They walk out of the restaurant and the evening air ruffles the windbreaker outfit that Chill is wearing.

"Yo, I want to meet shorty," Ice tells Chill, as they walk to their whips.

"A'ight hold on, let me call this nigga." Grabbing his Nextel he dials Pirelli's number. "Aye Pirelli this Chill... Can you hear me, this Chill...My man wants to meet yo' cousin...Later tonight...Just call me when you get in the area."

The Greyhound bus station on Canal and Harrison is packed with customers toting their luggage, arriving and leaving. Moe hangs up the payphone. The coins he placed into the phone bounces around rattling, dropping into the return slot. He places the coins back into the phone dialing Bricks' cellular phone number for the umpteenth time. The voicemail picks up on the third ring.

"***Why the hell he ain't answering the phone? He knows he suppose to pick me up today***," Moe thought to himself. Having no success at reaching him, he calls another number.

"Hello," A voice answered through the staticky line. The phone is having bad reception. Moe slaps the reciever against the palm of his hand. "Hello, hello. Can you hear me?" he shouted into the phone becoming agitated.

"Heyyy baby," the female voice greets excitedly. Her voice comes in crystal clear.

"How you doin' sweetheart?" Moe asks.

"I'm okay, what about yourself?"

"I couldn't be no better now that I'm a free man."

"I heard that baby. Why you didn't tell me you were getting out today? You know I miss you."

"I wanted to pop up on you and surprise you."

"So, where you at?"

"I'm at the bus station on Canal and Harrison, I need you to come and pick me up. My man was suppose to scoop me up, but he ain't answering his phone fo' some reason."

"Just stay right there baby, I'm on my way out the door right now."

"A'ight, I'll be in the front waitin' on you."

"Okay baby, bye, bye." Moe hangs up the phone shifting his gaze on the two beautiful women entering the lobby. One of the women is prancing in a pair of knee length black leather Aldo boots with two inch heels. The woman has on a BabyPhat velour jogging suit on and a pair of white BabyPhat gym shoes. Both the women are well proport ioned in all the right places.

"Damn it feels good to be a free man." Dutchess and Carmen stands at the rear of the long winding line of customers waiting to purchase Carmen's bus ticket. Moe steps into the restroom invaded by the malodorous smell of stale urine. Gang lierature written with black magic markers stains the walls, and the tattered stalls.

He steps over a roll of wet toliet tissue, strutting towards the urinal. The sound of running water roars from the faucet, left turned on by previous pedestrians. He stands at the urinal urinating, being tormented by the stench smell of human waste. He hears movement coming from one of the stalls and glances over his left shoulder. "Uuuuuh!" Someone is in the stall strainning, sounding like a retarded Master P.

"Damn put some water on that shit." Moe blurts, pinching his nose with his thumb and indexfinger. He rushes to the sink and washes his hands. He presses the chrome plated button, activating the hand dryer. It makes a loud roaring sound similar to a vacuum cleaner.

Carmen stands in line glimpsing around nervously. "Relax girl, for you give yourself away. I know this is your first time doing this. Just be cool, trust me, after awhile you'll get used to it." Dutchess stated in a conspiratorial tone.

"I can't believe I'm doing this," Carmen said silently. "***This is my first and last time doing this. I just need some quick money to pay my bills, until I find another job***." Carmen mused.

Moe cuts through the crowded lobby. The engine to the Greyhound hums in the terminal, preparing for it's journey. Moe exits the glass aluminum doors standing in front of the bus station. He looks around appreciating the simple sound of car horns blaring, making him aware of this existing world he once took for granted. Automobiles whistle as they travel up and down the busy streets, passing by. He looks at every car that pulls up, anticipating the arrival of his female friend Latina, who he has known for many of years. He once thought she would be the woman he'd marry. Latina stuck by Moe's side religiously from the beginning of his prison term, until the end. Moe has a lot of respect for Latina. When all his so called friends disappeared like the season, Latina maintained her love and loyalty for him. There is nothing in the world that Moe wouldn't do for Latina.

Moe recognizes a familiar face as he peers into a parked car, at a man conversing on his cell phone. He moves his hand to the rhythmn of his speech, like a pimp running his best game. Moe walks up to the car and taps on the window collecting his attention. The man acknowledges Moe and jumps out of the car with a smile growing on his face, pulling at the corners of his mouth.

"What up Moe?" They shake hands giving each other a half hug. "Man they finally released you from that hell hole huh?"

"Yeah, you know they can't keep a real nigga down."

"I hear that baby."

"So, what you been up too?" Moe asks.

"Nothin' man, just tryna get things back in order. You know I ain't been out here that long."

"I see you got on the gray sweat suit and the fresh airforce ones," Pirelli said jokingly. They burst out in laughter.

"Man this ain't shit. You know I'm about to hit the stash and get fresh in a minute," Moe proclaimed.

Dutchess exits the bus station walking in their direction. She sent Carmen to drop off 4 and a half ounces in Springfield, Illinois. They concealed the dope in the lining of her knee length highheel boots. It will be sold for $6,500.00 to one of Dutchess' european customers she met through Amos. "You ready to go cuz?" Dutchess said interrupting Pirelli and Moe in the middle of their conversation, never acknowledging Moe.

"Hey, have some manners and say what's up to my man Moe."

"Hi, now come on lets go. I got money to make." Dutchess stated with a cocky attitude.

"Hold up, give a second," Pirelli said. Dutchess climbs into the car.

"Damn, yo' ol' girl real cocky ain't she."

"Yeah she a cold piece of work," Pirelli admitted.

"Yeah, I like that. She seems like a true go getter."

"That she is, it's in the bloodline. Check this out, I gotta bounce. You got a number I can reach you at. I ain't forgot about what we talked about."

"You got somethin' to write with?"

"I got somethin' better than that." Pirelli flips his cell phone open. He scrolls through the phone and downloads the number to Moe's cell phone shop.

"A'ight, you stay up. I see yo' cuz is ready to go," Moe said with a smile.

"Yeah, I betta get goin'.

"A'ight just hit me at that number."

"A'ight one."

Bianca lies back on the sofa in Carmen's apartment chanting on the phone, twirling a strand of her hair. B.E.T 106th and Park croons in the background, escaping the television. Carmen's daughter Renee lies on her belly with her box of crayons, coloring on her pad of paper. Renee has always been very artistic. Carmen believes that she's going to be an artist one day.

Bianca has been baby sitting for Carmen every since Renee was two weeks old. Bianca is like an aunt to Renee. Bianca loves her as if she is of her own blood. She always buys her gifts for her birthday, and Christmas.

"Gurrrl, guess who I ran into at the club last night?.. Nope, Chill. Umph, he knows he's a fine muthafucka. He was outside in front of the club throwing money out of his car. Mami, that fine muthafucka is paid. I wouldn't mine lettin' papi hit some of this kitty cat." Bianca giggles at the woman's remark on the other end of the line. "Unt uhn mami, you dirty hoe you."

"Tee-Tee," Renee calls, tapping Bianca on her arm, interrupting her conversation.

"What a minute Nee-Nee, I'm on the phone."

"Me wanna show you picture I draw."

"Let me go mami. My bad niece keep buggin me so she can show me her picture."

"Tee-Tee."

"A'ight Nee-Nee. I'mma call you later on mami...A' ight bye mami." Bianca hangs up the cordless phone, placing her focus on Renee. "What is it you wanna show me mami?"

"Me picture," Renee answered, in her young immature voice.

"Let me see it," Bianca said, watching her as she hides the picture behind her back.

"Say please."

"Stop playin' mami, let Tee-Tee see the picture."

"Say please," Renee repeats, teasing her with the picture.

"So that's how you wanna play it. Okay, come here," Bianca said, charging in Renee's direction with an impish smile on her face. Renee takes off running, giggling as Bianca chases her through the livingroom. Bianca grabs her, tickling her on the side, as she clutches the picture in her tiny hands, giggling uncontrollably.

"Heh! Heh! Heh! You c-c-cheat-in' Tee-Tee. Heh! Heh!"

"Let it go." Bianca said, tickling her allover, as she shifts her tiny frame trying to block Bianca's hands.

"O-Ok-ay, okay, Tee-Tee. Heh! Heh! Heh!" Bianca takes the picture from her and analyzes the art work. She looks at the two stick figures on the paper and a car with a red dot on it's hood.

"This is nice," Bianca compliments, and points to one of the stick figures. "Who is this Nee-Nee?"

"That's mommy."

"And who is this." Bianca points to the second stick figure.

"That a police man and police car." Bianca stares at the picture as if she had just seen aghost. "What's wrong Tee-Tee?"

"Nothin' mami," Bianca lied. "I hope Carmen is alright. I knew mami should've told Sade no about takin' the trip," Bianca mulled.

"Ticket please," the pleasant faced bus driver holds out his pale hand, as Carmen attempts to board the bus.

She fishes through her purse, finding the round trip ticket. “Thank you and we hope you enjoy your travel with Greyhound.” She steps onto the bus, feeling the climate controlled AC, glad to be out of the scorching weather. She peers down the aisle, looking for an empty seat. A sea of white faces stare in her direction, hoping she doesn’t choose the seat next to theirs. She curses under

her breath, “Damn, what have I let Sade talk me into, all these bastards look like agents, even the little babies.” Besides herself, there is only one other person of ethnic origin, a Korean woman who sits towards the back. Carmen decides its best not to put up the Rosa Parks demonstration, and heads for the back. The Korean woman is sitting in the seat by the aisle, listening to her Ipod Nano.

“Excuse me, is this seat taken?” Carmen politely asks. The Korean stares at her smiling, showing what Carmen believes to be sixty four teeth. “***Damn, she got a whole nother set***,” Carmen thought to herself. The woman keeps singing her favorite tune, in an off beat foreign tongue. “I guess that means I can sit down.” She climbs into the stiff chair, and glances out the window. A K-9 unit, with the assistance of officers from the Sherriff’s department are running dogs along the bottom of the bus next to hers. “***Shit***.” She looks around nervously, catching the atten tion of a white man, sitting across from her. He is dressed in a black suit, and wears brown hair, in a military style crew cut. They lock eyes momentarily, and then Carmen looks away. Everything was wrong about this picture. She is planning her options for escape, which are very limited, when the voice crackles over the mic.

“I’m sorry for the slight delay, but we have to wait until the Sheriff’s department gives us the okay to depart.”

Carmen watches as the dogs near the bus. There is only one place for her to hide, the small bathroom. She looks back over her seat, the small white sign with red letters, reads occupied. The white man is still staring at her, as he sees the worried look written all across her face. His profession has trained him to be on the look out for such things.

The bathroom door opens, and a large woman wearing a bright orange sundress waddles out. Carmen rushes into the bathroom, locking the door behind her. The smell invades her nostrils, with such a strong force that causes her to become lightheaded. She frowns her face at the foul odor, using one hand to cover her nose, and the other to flush what the big woman should have. She makes up her mind not to come out, until the bus is moving.

Five minutes later, the electronic display, embedded on the front of the bus, switches from Chicago, to Springfield. As the bus edges forward, she opens the door, bumping directly into the well dressed white male. Her eyes enlarge, upon seeing him, and she wants to close the door back, and flush everything down the toliet.

He gives her a warm smile, or was it a knowing smile, she isn't sure. She stands blocking the entrance to the bathroom.

"Pardon me, are you done in there?"

"Huh, oh, yea," she returns to her seat wondering if he knows what she is carrying. Dutchess has assured her that the product was well hidden, and that no one would find it, unless she told them. "He's probably going in there to search," thought Carmen. "It is too late to worry now, whatever happens will just happen." She reclines her seat and slowly dozes off.

"We will be arriving in the Springfield terminal, in three minutes." The mellow sound of the driver's voice awakens her. The Korean woman is gone, getting off at the last stop. Still there is that white man, who was watching her even as she slept.

As the bus pulls into the terminal, he thinks of his approach. This is part of his job, he enjoys the most. He has a strict motto, it is 'Never let them get away'.

Carmen grabs her purse, and falls in line with the rest of the people, waiting to exit the bus. As she takes her first step off the bus, she feels a hand touch her shoulder, and then hears the familiar voice.

"Excuse me, miss."

The sounds of Beyonce, featuring Jay-Z 'Upgrade' plays as Pirelli navigates through the mundane traffic with Dutchess in the passenger seat.

"How you gon' upgrade me, I'm already number one." Jay-Z boasts through the sound system. The sound system makes it sound as if he's in the back seat. Dutchess and Pirelli converses over the smooth melody about upgrading their operation.

"Girl, you somethin' else." The red light they stop at gives them ample time for conversation. Pirelli stares at

Dutchess in total astonishment. "Fa' real though cuz, you know daddy always taught me, if I'm going to do somethin' do it big." Dutchess stares out the window as the light turns green, the mere mentioning of her father causes anguish in her heart. She begins to think about her father. Pirelli's voice brings her back from the tranquility of her daydream.

"You sure you ready for that? You talkin' about a big move."

"What?" Dutchess states, confused for a second, not knowing what Pirelli was talking about. "Ah, naw cuz, a couple of keys ain't no big move, you just thinkin' to small." The words offended Pirelli, but he lets it slide.

"Whatever, but anyway, I was just lettin' yo' ass know

'cause this is what I do. This ain't just some shit I picked up as a hobby," Pirelli barks. Dutchess' eyebrows rises with a questioning look, giving her the appearance of a chinese woman.

"Ah, that's what you think this shit is for me, a fuckin' hobby!"

"Look Sade-" The vibration of Pirelli's Nextel stops him from finishing the sentence. He answers the phone. "What up? ...Who this?" He motions for Dutchess to turn the music down. "Oh, what up Chill? .. She with me right now, why what's up? ..Damn, I ain't never met the boss man." Pirelli jokingly states, but meaning every word. "A'ight, when? .. I'll holla." He hangs up the phone.

"Who was that?" Dutchess questions.

"That was Chill, he said his man wants to meet with you. So here's your chance to get yo' foot in the door and do it big." Dutchess smiles.

"That's the shit I'm talkin' about cuz, big things." she states, with all the confidence in the world.

"I feel you, but look Sade," Pirelli begins finishing where he left off. "This is a rough game, where niggas is playin' for keeps. People gettin' stuck up, locked up, and kidnapped everyday." Dutchess nods her head listening to him attentively. "This game will do three things for you. Make you rich, put you in a ditch, or make you a snitch. Some people die fulfilling all three. So when you say you wanna do it big, just remember the consequences is even bigger. A lot of niggas accept the side that glitter, but when the lights go out and the bottles stop cracking, don't nobody wanna take resposibility for their actions. They don't wanna accept the bitter side of the game and do they time like a man." Pirelli looks at her steadily before turning his head back to the road.

"I feel that cuz, and I know you trying to look out for me, and I appreciate that," Dutchess states truthfully.

"You know I got to look out for my favorite big head cou sin." Pirelli laughs, barely getting his words out. She playfully hits him on his arm. "But serious Sade, you know if Chill fronts you them two thangs, even if the package get knocked you still have to pay for it. Once it's in yo' hands you responsible for paying that money."

"That's why we pay him in full," Dutchess boldly states.

"So you saying you got fourty grand?"

"Yea," Dutchess said. "I know I should have just about that. If not I know I'm close. If I don't, I'll figure out a way to get the difference." Dutchess silently thinks to herself, as they head to meet Chill and his man.

Fear. Every limb in Carmen's body is filled with the stuff, as she awaits her fate. Her knees wobble, and shake, like a two dollar crap game. She turns around locking eyes with the man she spoke with on the bus.

"Hello again, sorry to bother you, my name is Matthew Chapten." Carmen stares at him waiting for a further explanation. "I'm a member of the CLC, the Christian Leadership Conference, and I couldn't help but see the worry and concern in your eyes. I wanted to make sure you was alright. God set it on my mind to stop you."

Carmen's tense body relaxes after hearing the news. "Oh, thanks. It's really nothin', I've just been havin' a bad day," she lies. It was more like a week.

"No problem, and sorry for intruding, I just can't sleep comfortably at night if the Lord puts on my chest to say something to someone, and I don't."

"Don't worry, I understand completely." Actually she didn't, but she said she did, to pacify him. The last time, she had been in church, was for Lawrence's funeral, before that, when she was six and was forced to go by her grand mother. She had acted up so badly that Grandma Reese never took her back.

Through the years of physical abuse, and financial trouble, she has often prayed, but none have been answered. She wants to believe in God, but without any concrete proof of his existence, it's hard for her to do.

Matthew reaches into his briefcase, and removes a flyer, handing it to her. It is a flyer about tonights meeting at the Holiday Inn.

"It starts at six, if you would like to attend, the lord would love to have you there Carmen," he says, his voice filled with compassion. Carmen reads the scripture at the bottom of the page. It reads: ***There is nothing concealed, that will not be disclosed, or hidden, that will not be made known (Matthew 10:26)***.

The words resonates in her mind, as she stares down, at the page. Suddenly, it dawns on her. With her eyes still glued to the flyer, she asks, "How do you know my name?" She looks up, and the man is no where in sight.

She shrudders, as a chill runs through her body. She balls the flyer up, and throws it in the Greyhound terminal trashcan. Many people traverse the lobby area, as she exits the building, to meet up with the paying customer.

Chapter Six

Chinky navigates the uhaul cube truck down Interstate 94. The engine purrs as he exits onto Cicero Avenue. He never notices the white conversion van trailing behind him, from a mile away. The distant sound of a helicopter hums in the air.

Chinky is one of Kennytha's drivers from Haiti. He is an illegal immigrant that Kennytha had smuggled into the country. Chinky is one of his tamed assassins, which will kill with the snap of a finger.

The white conversion van picks up it's pace. Within the matter of seconds, the van is near the rearend of the uhaul truck. Chinky glimpses in the rearview mirror, noticing the van speeding up making it's approach. "Shit!" he mutters in frustration. The van races pass him, with a trail of dust lingering from its tires. "Crazy mafucka drivin' like him lost his mind!" he complained. A great deal of relief travels through his body. Glad that it was just a reckless driver, he continues with his journey, listening to the staticky radio station. Hearing one of his favorite songs, he smacks the dashboard trying to get the station to come in clear. "Come on piece of shit!" Recieving no results, he turns the radio off.

Hearing a semi-truck roaring on the side of him, he

focuses back on the road. The European truck driver flashes a friendly smile, and hits his horn. The semi speeds up, turning into Chinky's lane diagonally, cutting him off. Chinky smashes down on the brakes swerving uncontrollably. A massive group of government vehicles swarms him from every direction, with red strobe lights oscillating on their hoods.

Surrounded by the large group of barking drug enforcement agents, Chinky clenches his 5.8 millimeter. With 50 kilograms of pure heroin concealed in the floor of the uhaul, he knows it's over. If he goes to prison, he knows that Kennytha will hire someone to kill him.

Weighing out his options, he squeezes the trigger of the semi-automatic weapon. A group of DEA agents spill out of the bed of the semi-truck, carrying high powered rifles.

Braaah! Braaah! A shower of bullets peppers the uhaul, shattering the windows. Boc! Boc! Boc! A bullet pierces the tire of the uhaul truck causing it to rock. The thunderous sound of gunfire reverberates as bullets penetrate the uhaul. It rocks side to side, as if it has hydraulics.

Chinky grips his wounded chest, groaning in excruciating pain. Knowing that he is no match against the large number of agents, he puts the barrel of the gun into his mouth, and squeezes the trigger with trembling fingers. His head jerks back from the impact of the gun. Inevitable death grips his soul. He lies in the seat lifeless, with the gun still clutched in his hand. The agent moves towards the uhaul carefully with their guns in front of them. They open the door and his body topples to the ground.

"Fuck, there goes one of the only witnesses that could've brought Kennytha down, fuck!" Agent Rains snapped, raking his fingers threw his hair, dropping his hands to his side in disappointment. He takes a deep breath and signs. "Somebody make a call so we can get this mess cleaned up," Agent Rains ordered, walking off to his vehicle.

Dutchess and Pirelli arrive at the Tavern on Rush. He calls Chill's phone to let him know that they are outside. Inside the bar, Ice has positioned himself at a corner booth, where he can see the front door. Chill rises from his seat and stuts to the front door.

Dutchess enters first, observing her surroundings. Pirelli is still circling the block, looking for a parking spot. She walks directly to the bar, catching looks from men and women as her hips swing seductively. Chill stands at the door as Dutchess passes by. He gives her a lustful stare, but he doesn't recognize her, as he waits for Pirelli, and his female associate.

Ice sees Dutchess through the tint of his glasses as she makes her way towards the bar. ***"Damn, what this stuckup bitch doin' here***," he wonders. He doesn't know, but he figures it to be the perfect time to push up on her. He slides up on her smoothly, placing his hand on her shoulder.

"Keep yo' muthafuckin' hands to yo' self" she spits in a rage of fury, spinning around to confront the unknown. Ice raises his hands like it's a stickup.

"My bad baby, I was just tryna' buy you a drink."

"Well I don't need your hands touching me, or your money to buy me shit!" She snaps with an attitude, cocking her head to the side.

"You know you too cute to be acting so tough all the time." Ice words catch her off guard, causing her to smile.

"Look Ice, I appreciate the compliment, but like I told you before, you talking to my girl, and I don't get down like that. So, what you got to offer me, I'll never need."

"Never say never" Ice warned her.

"You never know who you might need one day."

"Yea, whatever" she said to his back, as he walks off to his table. "***Damn whats taking Pirelli so long***" she thought as she orders a Hennessy Sour. "Can I get a straw please" she asks, as the bartender turns to oblige her request.

Pirelli walks in and gives Chill a simple Gangster Disciple handshake. The GD's as they are called for short, are just one of the many gangs that run shit in the streets of Chicago.

Pirelli waves Dutchess over to where they are standing. Chill takes a long admiring look at Dutchess. "This baby girl, that been moving that white like it's Christmas." Chill exclaims, shocked by her beauty.

"What's ya name Ma?"

"Dutchess."

"Dutchess huh, I like that. Let me introduce you to my man." Chill leads them through the crowd of patrons as a slow Melody plays; compliments of the Dj. Cigar smoke lingers in the air, as people dance rhythmatically.

Ice sits at the table nursing his drink. The ice tinkers against the glass, as they approach. "Ay, this my man Ice, Ice this is Dutc-."

"I know who that is," Ice replied cutting him off. Pirelli and Chill exchange looks of confusion.

"What I don't understand is what she's doin' here."

"I told you earlier what she need." Chill stated.

"Who her," Ice points at Dutchess, "Naw, not her, Beyonce got hoes out here fucked up, they don't need shit from no nigga ever, ain't that right Sade." Ice chuckles as he finishes his statement. Dutchess bites her tongue.

"***Out of all the niggas in the world sellin' dope, why it gotta be this nigga he working for***," thought Dutchess.

"Look Ice, I'm 'bout my business, so if you trying to make money holla at me, if not, that's good too. The shit didn't stop getting produced when you got yours,"

Dutchess boldly stated.

"As long as I get paid, a purple monkey can buy it," Ice replies, standing to leave. "Just let Chill know what you need, and I got you."

Ice and Chill leave Dutchess and Pirelli in the club, as Dutchess explains to her cousin about what has just happened.

"Sade, or should I say, 'Dutchess', what was that all about?" Pirelli asked discombobulated.

"Cuz, the nigga been tryin' his hardest to get wit a sister but he's just not my type. He's a clown ass nigga."

"Yea, a clown ass nigga with a plug. And when and where the hell did this name, Dutchess come from?"

"Remember when you was locked up and you asked me to send you this book name Dutch?"

"Yea, and."

"Well, I brought two of those. One for you, and one for me. And Dutch ran New York and he was a nigga. I'm a female and I'm about to run the Chi, so I decided to be the Dutchess of Chicago." Dutchess stated, rising from her seat.

Looking at Dutchess and thinking about how Dutch ran the streets of New York, he couldn't do nothing but respect her. "Well, if that's how you feel Dutchess, lets do this." Pirelli said with a big smile.

Upon entering the car Ice speaks to Chill. "The next time that bitch calls for something, tell her we out."

Zago steps on the escalator accompanied by his cousin Jabo. They ascend to the second floor of Water Tower Place mall on a minor shopping spree. Zago's long kinky dreadlocks bounces on his shoulders, as they strut inside Footlocker shoe store.

A young male employee dressed in a black and white

uniform looking like a referee greets them. "Welcome to Footlocker is there anything in particular your looking for today?" He politely asked, with a warm friendly smile on his face, chasing a bigger commission.

"No. Me like to browse around fa somethin' me like mon" Zago replied, in his heavy jamaican accent browsing the store.

"If there's anything I can help you with, please feel free to ask." He walks off giving them their distance, standing in hearing range.

After scanning the large selection of tennis shoes, Zago signals for the young eager employee. "Yes sir. What can I help you with?"

"Let me get dese in a size ten rude boy" Zago requested, holding the green and white Adidas running shoe in his hand.

"Give me one second I'll be right back." He returns with the shoes. "Would you like to try them on first?" He asked, clutching the blue and white shoe box, with the Adidas flower printed on it.

"Me straight mon. What ya got ta match dese mon?"

"We got a green and white Adidas jogging suit that match these perfect. What size would you like?"

"Double X rude boy" Zago replied. Zago watches as the beautiful woman behind the cash register serves the awaiting customers.

The employee comes back carrying the jogging suit and pair of shoes. He places the merchandise on the counter to be rung up. The young man stares at the platinum necklace, with its diamond medallion sparkling around Zago's neck.

"How are you doing today?" The beautiful young lady asked while scanning the merchandise.

"Me doin' fine sweetheart. What about ya self?"

"Working hard" She proclaimed, "Your total comes out

to one hundred and eighty-five dollars."

Zago reaches into his pocket and pulls out a thick wad of money. As he shuffles through the bills, she makes small talk. "Nice necklace you got there. My man got the same one." She compliments, recognizing the same necklace in her boyfriends drawer, she seen when rambling for traces of infidelity.

Zago's face contorts realizing what the young woman has just said. He hands her two hundred dollar bills. Analyzing the man's facial expression, she notices an unpleasant look. She stares at him dumbfounded, wondering if she offended him.

"Ya must have man wit' good taste." Zago reads her name tag. "Mimi" he said to himself. She hands him his change and he grabs the merchandise concealed in the plastic Footlocker bag. "Thanks" He replied.

"Thank you too. Please come again."

"***Me be back***." He thinks to himself as he joins the awaiting Jabo.

He notices the icy look in Zago's eyes. "What's wrong wit' ya rude boy?" Jabo asked, knowing his cousin very well. He gazes at Zago with genuine concern.

"Ya never gon' believe dis mon."

The dark blue four door sedan maneuvers through the distill night, virtually unnoticed except for one set of eyes. The owl, that is perched on an olive tree branch, on the left side of the road, can see the car as it moves silently with its headlights off. The moon shines through the branches, casting ghostly shadows on the road. The car's tires hum on the dirt road, as a cool breeze blows from the nearby lake.

The man driving the vehicle scans through the radio stations past the rap, and soft rock, to the classical.

The melody that plays helps him to ease his mind.

Slowly edging the car forward, he pulls over to the side of the bridge. Leaving the car running, he exits the vehicle and walks around to the trunk. He inserts the key, and removes a large bag, the same color as the black gloves he is wearing.

The bricks that he has affixed to the bag gives it it's extra weight as he grunts carrying it. Finally reaching the middle of the bridge, he heaves the bag over its stone railing, watching its fifty foot fall. The splash in the water below temporarily disturbs the ecosystem as fish scatter in different directions. The water turns white from the impact, then returns to black. Lake Michigan is once again calm for the moment. The man removes a flashlight from his back pocket and shines it on the water below. His clothing is black like the water. Seeing nothing, he kills the light and returns to the vehicle.

With the use of a small phillips screwdriver, he removes the license plate, and places a new one on. No one notices his departure, just as he does not notice the bag rising up to the top of the lake, as he pulls off.

Pirelli is seated at the glass kitchen table frustrated. He scrolls through the sixty numbers he has downloaded in his cell phone for the umpteenth time. It has been a long stressful week for him. The entire city of Chicago has been dry of drugs for the last two weeks, since the big drug bust in Naperville, Illinois. The only thing he managed to get his hands on since the bust is nine ounces, which him and Dutchess went half on. The nine ounces turned out to be rerock, and they ended up losing two ounces on the cook. It has been a lot of bad dope in circulation, since the drout begun.

With his elbows planted on the table, he runs his hands over his deep waves, and the length of his face. He can hear the sound of his two sons playing the Playstation3 game system in the livingroom. His cellular phone chimes continuously, vibrating and twirling on the kitchen table. He glances at the caller's Identification, ignoring the call. Seeing the number of one of his favorite customers upsets him. "***Shit I'm missin' all kinds of money. Somethin' gotta break. What the fuck I'm gon' do, these bills kickin' my ass. I can't keep dippin' in my stash. Erica little work check ain't gon' do it. I gotta hurry up and find some work before I start cuttin' into my re-up money.***" The sharp sound of Pirelli's youngest son snaps him out his pensive state of mind.

"Stop cheatin' Rell, it's my turn," Fatman shouts.

"Shut up punk," Rell snaps back.

"I'm tellin' daddy."

"So, gon' and tell then, you little snitch."

Fatman storms into the kitchen screaming at the top of his lungs. "Daddddyy! Rell cheatin'. He won't let me play the game." Fatman complained, in between heavy breathing, with his lips compressed in anger.

"Rell, get in here!" Pirelli barks. Rell walks into the kitchen with his chin buried in his chest, in fear.

"Why y'all in there fightin' over that game?" Pirelli stares at Rell, who is the split image of himself waiting for a response. "You hear me talkin' to you. Look at me when I'm talkin' to you." Plrelli ordered, locking eyes with his oldest son, who is 6 years old. "Why y'all fightin' over that game?" he repeated.

"I 'ont know," Rell whined in his young undeveloped voice.

"What you mean you don't know? Let me tell both of y'all somethin'. As long as I'm alive, y'all gon' share. I bet' not ever catch y'all fightin'. The only fightin' y'all betta be doing, is together, not against each other, y'all got that? Do I make myself clear?"

"Yes." They answer in unison, listening intently to their father.

"And as for you Fatman, don't come in here snitchin' on yo' brother. You know I don't play that snitchin' shit. Now is that understood?"

"Yes daddy." Fatman responded, his baby brown eyes flicking with innocence. "Now y'all give each other a hug and make up." They wrap their arms around each other, displaying true brotherly love.

"I'm sorry Fatman," Rell apologized.

"Me too."

"Now y'all get back to playing the game like big boys."

"Okay dad." They return to the livingroom.

Pirelli's cellular phone chimes again, stealing his attention. Recognizing the number flashing on the screen, he answers the phone. "What up cuzo?"

"What's up with you?" Dutchess asks.

"Same ol' shit, stressin' like a muthafucka. I called everybody I know, ain't nothin' movin'." He informs, with disappointment lingering in his voice.

"We have to do some thin ‘, quick."

"I can try my man Moe again, that's our only hope."

"Moe?"

"Yeah, ol' boy I ran into at the Greyhound station, when we dropped Carmen off." Pirelli refreshens her memory.

"How the hell Moe gon' help us, when he look like he needs help his damn self. I seen that cheap ass grey jogging suit he had on."

"Trust me Dutchess, that nigga is holdin'."

"How you know what he got? And where you know him from?" she inquired.

"I meet him in the joint. We was locked up together," he informed.

"Shit, a person can be all they wanna be in jail."

"Dutchess, chill out, I'ma call him anyway. We ain't got nothin' to lose. I've been callin' the number he gave me, but I didn't get no answer. I heard his man Bricks got killed."

"He probably gave you a bogus number," she assumed.

"Naw, he ain't cut like that. I'ma hit that number one more time."

"A'ight, call me if you hear somethin' 'cause my phone been ringing off the hook. If I don't answer, I'll just call you when get off work."

"A'ight, peace out cuz." Pirelli hangs up the phone and scrolls through his numbers in search of Moe's number. Finding his number he presses automatic dial. The phone rings two times and the soft sophisticated voice of a woman appears on the line.

"Can I speak to Moe ...You got a number that I can reach him at?..Let me grab a pen real quick...A'ight, what is it?.. Got it...A'ight, thanks." Pirelli hangs up the phone and dials the number he just recieved. The phone rings and he waits patiently for someone to answer. Pirelli feels like a dopefiend trying to get his next hit. Just like the dopefiends is addicted to the drugs, Pirelli is addicted to the fast money.

Moe's eyes drifts out towards Lake Michigan as he stands on the terrace to his full floor penthouse sipping on a bottle of Louis XIII Black Pearl. A warm soft breeze passes by like a compassionate spirit, softly whispering in his ears, fluttering the collar of his short sleeve black Prada shirt. His long titanium chain hangs down to his navel with it's iced out medallion attached to it. The muscles in his face trembles, his eyes become glassy as he thinks about Bricks. It has been a week since Bricks was buried. He tilts his head back and takes another swallow of the alcoholic beverage. The warm liquid travels down his throat, his face creases from the powerful kick. He studies the magnificent

Chicago skyline through the lenses of his Prada glasses. The sky is a wrinkled teal green sheet, contrasting with the sunrise. A triangel of birds reconnoiters overhead.

He tosses the bottle over the railing on to the energetic city of Chicago. He musters up his strength and regains his composure. He struts through the glass doors, stepping outside his exclusive penthouse. The skylights above the hallway provides surprising views of the roof-top swimming pool. The aluminum louvers next to the staircase casts patterns of light and shadows on the french limestone floors. The maple kitchen cabinets are placed under long quartz countertops to preserving views of Lake Michigan.

Moe sinks in the pure white butter soft leather sofa with chrome panels lining the base of it. He stares at his huge wall to wall saltwater aquarium, watching all the exotic creatures float around. The glow from the aquarium reflects off the stainless steel pool table with it's white suede top and clear poolballs scattered allover it. Four transparent pool sticks with white tips sits in a stainless steel rack that is affixed to the wall.

He tilts his head skyward laying back with his fingers interlaced across his stomach in a reverie. The sun beams on the rooftop swimming pool. A kaleidoscope of colors from the pool dances on his pecan complexion. Ripples of light reflects in his ebony brown eyes. His cellular phone chimes, snapping him out of his reverie. He leans forward sliding the phone out of it's clip attached to his waistband. "Hello," he answered.

"Can I speak to Moe?"

"Who is this?"

"Pirelli."

"This me. What up wit' it?"

"Nothin' much, just tryna put some thangs together."

"Yeah."

"Yeah, you know itls tight out here right now. I know

you been takin' things a little hard lately, since yo' boy Bricks been gone. I heard what happened, that was some cold-blooded shit they did. I didn't really know him personally, but I heard a lot of good things about him."

"Yeah, that was my man. I remember me and my dawg use to share the same clothes when we was in grade school. I'll never forget how he was there for me when I was down and out. He took care of all my business affairs and dropped clothes off to my kids, making sure they was straight. I'ma really miss him." Moe expressed. He pauses for a second and blows out a short breath of air. "But what it is though?" Moe inquired.

"I need to talk to you face to face whenever you get a little time on yo' hands," he replied.

"Check this out. Meet me at my cell phone shop on seventy first and Pulaski in about forty-five minutes."

"Cool, I'll be there."

"Alight cool."

"Holla." Click! Moe places the phone back into it's clip. "***It's time to get this shit back on track. Maybe I can put Pirelli on. He did always keep it one hundred wit' me. I'ma see how things play out***." He mulled.

Pirelli maneuvers the Sunfire parking in front of Cellular World Wireless. Dutchess leans back in the passenger seat. They wait patiently for Moe to arrive. On coming traffic moves up and down the two way street, whirring by them. The sun beams brightly bathing the streets. Occupied with their own thoughts, Dutchess breaks the silence. "You sure yo' man not on some bullshit?" Pirelli shifts his eyes away from the sideview mirror, plastering his eyes on a paranoid Dutchess.

"Of course, keep yo' cool," Pirelli replied.

"I hope so. But, if not." She cocks her automatic handgun with a devilish look burning in her eyes. "I got somethin' to put him in his place," she declared.

"First all, what you doing with that? And second of all, what you know about that?"

"To answer yo' question I keep my guards up at all times. You can't get relaxed in this game. And to answer yo' second question, I know a lot about this thing I'm holding. It's a Beretta PX Four Storm. It weighs twenty seven point seven ounces and measures, seven by nine sixtenths long, by five and a half high by one and three eighths thick." Dutchess skillfully breaks the pistol down. Her fingers moves quickly as she removes the magazine and clears the pistol of it's ammunition. She pulls down on the two disassembly levers just above the trigger guard. She then releases the slides and permits it to slide forward off the reciever. Turning the slide over, she lifts out the recoil spring and guide as well as the central block. The rotating barrel simply lifts out of the slide. Pirelli stares at her in amazement, as she puts the gun back together, and reloads it.

"Dammn, cuz, you ain't no joke," Pirelli stated.

"You must of forgot who my daddy was. Let me tell you somethin' Relli. I know I'm a female and you might think I'm trippin', but you can't trust nobody in these streets. My daddy taught me to be more than just a school girl. He taught me how to handle myself and defend myself in this dog eat dog world. I know I don't have to sell dope, but I have a reason why I chose to get down and dirty. A lot of men think the game is only made for them and they under estimate my potiential, but I'ma tell you like this." Dutchess pauses for a momentarily and gazes into his eyes with a solemn facial expression. "A lot of people think just because I came from a wealthy household that I'm some type of weak bitch. I'ma be the baddest bitch that ever did it. A few gon' love this bitch, many gon' hate this bitch, but one thing they all gon' do is respect this bitch."

"My bad Dutchess. I guess I still look at you as the little innocent girl that you once was. I didn't know that unc groomed you so well."

In the middle of their conversation a black Dodge Magnum with tinted windows circles the block with the driver and the passenger faintly visible. The car moves slowly moves along the curb, parking opposite of them. Dutchess grips the trigger of the Beretta watching them closely.

"That might be him right there," Pirelli assumed, unable to see the occupants of the unknown vehicle. The engine hums softly sitting motionless. Pirelli waits for someone to climb out of the car.

"Somethin' don't seem right about this," Dutchess proclaimed, scanning her surroundings.

"I think we should bounce," Pirelli said, becoming paranoid and insecure as he appraises the scenery. A sparkle of chills travels through his body. He begins to feel the same as he did when he caught his last dope case.

Dutchess regrets bringing the $40,000.00 in cash. They notice an unknown car turning the corner prowling. "Shit, this looks like a set up," Pirelli thinks to himself reaching quickly.

Sheriff Alderman parks the police cruiser in between Judge Milton's Malibu, and Senator Hennings Chrysler Concord. He is a few minutes late for the monthly meeting as he rushes into the building. Already the atmosphere is tense as he walks into the room in the middle of Judge Milton's speech. "If we can't make them slaves, let's put them in graves." The Sheriff nods his head in agreement as he takes a seat. "We need to keep them prisons filled to capacity."

"How do you propose we do this?" Senator Hennings questioned.

"Easy," roared the Judge. "If a black drug addict gets caught smoking crack in the park, we give him a fed case. If one of them ugly dark pigmented creatures so much as picks up a gun, we give them a fed case," he concluded. "Trust me, I want to be the first to sign my name to such legislation that will authorize such a thing, but isn't small cases like that the states concern?" The Senator wanted to know. "We'll both try them. That way we get a double dip. When they finish with their time with the federal Government, we transport them to state custody. That way we get double the time, for the same crime. Everybody is happy," the Judge elated with a devilish grin.

"Brillant idea, Regan get on the phone immediately and alert the circuit courts in the area," commanded the Senator.

"Actually, theres no need, the practice has been covertly in effect for years," stated Regan. "It has come into scrutiny lately because of the Paris Hilton's and Lindsey Lohan's of the world being charged with simple possessions. The public wants to know why it's possesssion for them, and distribution for others. As long as they continue to think that it's a money issue, we're safe."

"Very well, moving forward on the agenda, any other concerns?" questioned Judge Milton. "Ah, before I forget. I recieved a real sympathetic letter from a family saying in short, that because I was their Senator I should pressure the local police departments to start a regional manhunt for this serial killer, who has been killing and raping little kids. What should do?"

"I remember seeing something about that in the news, tell me what race was the kid?" Judge Milton questioned with concern in his voice.

"Well, my department is leading the investigation, and so far it's been five little black boys ranging from the ages between four and nine," stated the Sheriff.

"Oh, they were black, then I suggest you do absolutely nothing," the Judge stated with no compassion, upon learning the boys race.

"You know Chicago was once a good place to live, to raise a family. Now you can't come outside, because of all the fucking gangs," ranted agent Regan.

"He's right," chimed in Judge Milton. "Their calling themselves organized chapters now. Black this, Latin that. Next thing you know, they'll be applying for tax breaks and going into politics."

"It's funny that you mentioned it, because one of them leaders from one of them nigger cults, had nerve to come and tell me, he could offer ten thousand guaranteed votes in my next Senate election, for a cost."

"Ha! Ha! Ha!" The smoker's chuckle, travels around the room. "You know, theres only one way to do damage to those gangs." Sheriff Alderman stated, his tone becoming serious.

"Oh yeah, and what's that?" They asked in unison. He lowers his voice in a conspiratorial whisper.

"What we must do is... "

Varooom! Pirelli starts up the car, staring at the car as it makes its approach, now visible. The huge chrome grille on the car gleams being touched by the sun, obscuring Pirelli's vision. The sky blue metallic Rolls-Royce Phantom pulls up beside them sitting on 27 inch chrome feet looking monsterous. Moe leans back in the oatmeal leather interior, his deep spiral waves spinning 360. He gazes through the lenses of his Prada glasses that rests on the bridge of his nose. He parks in front of them and climbs out of the car wearing a white and creme Mauri jogging suit, and a pair of matching gym shoes. He stands at the front entrance of the cellular phone shop and sweeps the air with his hand, gesturing for them to step inside the shop.

Dutchess looks at the Rolls Royce as if it has her hypnotized.

“Come on Dutchess,” Pirelli said, feeling secure. They step into the shop scanning the large selection of cell phones in the display cabinets. Moe’s beautiful employee greets them cordially. Pirelli looks at the woman as she prances over to the computer adjacent to the cash register. Her ass bounces vibrantly as she prances in her Christian Louboutin stilettos. Her knee length skirt hugs her hips, tracing her tiny waistline and bubble butt. She has a high yellow skin tone, light brown and gray eyes, and long silky natural brown sandy hair. Pirelli is mesmerized by her sex appeal. Moe and Pirelli slap palms greeting each other.

“Sup baby?”

“Same ol’ shit, tryna make it out here in this jungle.” Moe and Pirelli met when Moe was serving a one year sentence for the state, before starting his federal sentence.

“I hear that,” Moe places his attention on Dutchess. “Oh, excuse me fa’ being so rude. How you doin’?”

“I’m straight,” Dutchess replies. Moe remembers how aggressive she was at the bus station and that’s what he likes about her.

“Straight huh?”

“Yep, that’s what I said.” Moe smiles at her swaying his head slightly. He buries his hands in his pants pockets and looks at Pirelli.

“So, what y’all tryna do?”

“We tryna get two thangs. We been out fa’ a minute. Niggas been sellin’ that bullshit out here since this drought hit. I’m hopin’ you can make it happen for us.” Moe rubs his chin with his thumb and indexfinger pondering. He knows that he can easily get $24,000.00 a kilo because of the drought. If it wasn’t for the 100 kilos Bricks had stashed before he was murdered, Moe would not be able to supply them, without going to his old connect Franko.

"I can make it happen, but we got one slight problem."

"What's that?" Pirelli asked with a puzzled look.

"I don't sell nothin' less than five birds. So, this what I'm gon' do fo' y'all. Just give me what y'all got and pay me the difference later. I'ma charge y'all eighteen thousand a cake."

"That's cool." The sound of his words fills them with concealed excitement. Pirelli feels like he has the shits. Right now Dutchess feels like she can kiss him. His words is like music to their ears. He walks over to the cash register and opens the drawer. He grabs a set of car keys out of it and tosses them to Pirelli. Dutchess goes out to the car and returns with the $40,000.00 in cash, she had under the seat. Moe takes the bag and hands it to the woman on the computer.

"Here, put that in the safe," Moe instructed. The woman walks off to a room in the rear of the shop. "Take those car keys with you and follow the grey Dodge Magnum. They gon' take you to a red Buick. Its five books stashed inside the back seat. When you finish, don't call me. Wait fo' me to call you."

"What you want me to do with the car when I'm finished?" Pirelli asked.

"Do what you wanna do with it." Moe registered the car in a John Doe name. He has over a dozen trap cars to smuggle his dope in. "One more thing before you go. I gotta nice stash left. After that supply is gone, I'm retired from this shit. So take advantage of it. Remember, the game is infested with haters, so make sure you keep yo' grass cut at all times so you can see the snakes comin'."

"I got you joe," Pirelli replied as they walk out the door.

Mimi empties her cash register, and places the money in a small green pouch. Her co-worker looks over her shoulder as she handles the money. Turning off the lights, and pulling the metal gate down, they exit the store. They walk down the hall to the mall's safety deposit box.

"See you tomorrow Mimi."

"Yep, later rich." She responds, heading in the opposite direction. The chill of the night air embraces her, as she exits the building. "Whew, I shoulda wore a jacket." She exclaims, wrapping her arms around her large breast. She spots her tan jeep Cherokee in between two vehicles. After entering the truck, she fastens her safety belt, and turns the ignition. Thump! Thump! Thump! The three knocks on her driver's side window causes her to jump. "Damn it Rich," she gasps, holding her hand against her heart. "You scared the shit out of me." The truck window slowly descends. Rich stares sheepishly at the pavement. His scaggily brown hair, covering his pimpled white face. He is out of breath as he speaks.

"Sorry Mimi, but I rushed over here to catch you before you left. I need the keys to open in the morning."

"Oh," replies Mimi, her snarl disappearing from her face. She reaches into her knock off Louis Vuitton purse that Chaos had given her from a robbery. She passes him the keys, with a smile as fake as her purse. "I forgot, here you go."

"Thanks Mimi," he said, but she never hears him, as the window rolls up, and she pulls off.

As she heads home, she scans the stations until finally resting the dial on 107.5 WGCI. She turns the volume up as Donnell Jones croons, "Where I want to be."

"This is my shit," she squaks, singing along with the melody in a high off pitched voice. "But when you love someone, you just don't treat them bad." She is engrossed with the music that and never notices the dark colored SUV following closely behind.

Chaos takes the last sip of the Old English 40 oz. bottle, and hurls it into the grass. It mingles with the other debris. The state of being pissy drunk has become a habit for him, every since his partner was killed. Dressed in dark Ecko jeans, black Timberland boots, and a Black t-shirt with Slow's picture on the front with the words, "Rest In Peace." He waits impatiently for Mimi's arrival.

"Damn, what's takin' this bitch so long," he wonders aloud. He takes out his cell phone dialing her number. It rings three times then goes to her answering machine. "I bet this dumb hoe got that music blastin' and probably can't hear the phone." He says, frustrated, redialing the number again, and getting no response. "Shit, I gotta piss like a muthafucka," he exclaims, going back into the house.

After using the bathroom, he decides to wear the chain he robbed Ganja for. "Fuck sellin' this shit, I'm rockin' this," he declares boldly, liking how the chain glimmers in the mirror. His phone rings, stealing his attention from the necklace. "Where you at ...How come you didn't answer the phone when I called?..What I tell yo' ass about that damn music, never mind, I'm on my way out." He said, discon necting the call.

Chaos steps outside and struts to Mimi's Cherokee with Ganja's chain dangling from his neck. As he reaches for the door handle on the passenger's side, a Cadillac Escalade dips into the driveway blocking Mimi in. The blaring headlights on the SUV blinds Chaos' sight. A group of men pours out of the truck aiming high powered handguns and assualt rifles. Chaos backpedals with his hands in the air. His eyes stretches wide open as he looks at the image of Ganja in disbelief.

Chapter Seven

Ding! Dong! The sound of the chiming doorbell garners Pirelli's attention. He rises from the leather sofa to answer the door. "Who is it?" he asked, looking out the peep-hole.

"It's Tiera," a soft feminine voice travels from behind the door. Pirelli unfastens the chain on the door, ushering the woman into the apartment.

"What up baby girl?" Pirelli said, closing the door. Tiera is Erica's older sister. Tiera is 5'0 tall, 125 pounds, brown skinned, and well proportioned in all the right places.

"Nothin', just comin' to get them bad ass kids."

"You can say that again," Pirelli added. "Aye Man-Man, y'all come on, yo' mama here," Pirelli shouts down the hallway to the back room, where they are playing Playstation3.

"A'ight, here we come," Man-Man answered, still playing the game.

"Y'all hurry y'all ass up, I ain't got all day," Tiera barked. Pirelli has been waiting all day for her to come and pick them up so he can help Dutchess cook up their dope and serve his awaiting customers. His phone has been ringing off the hook with desperate customers.

Pirelli's two sons follow behind Man-Man, Tiera's 13 year old son. Man-Man is very observative, and watches everything around him. His father is a local heroin dealer named Cakes, from the Westside of the city. He is a member of the Travelers. The Travelers is an organization that rides under the 5 point star.

Man-Man has his baseball cap cocked deep to the left, imitating his father. “A’ight Joe,” Man-Man said, walking out the door.

Pirelli sways his head. “***That boy gon’ be just like his father***.”

“A’ight.” Just before Tiera exits the door, Dutchess steps into the apartment, carrying a grocery bag. “Aye girl.” Tiera said, walking out of the apartment, along with the kids.

“Aye,” Dutchess replied. Pirelli closes the door behind them.

“We gotta hurry up, everybody been blowin’ up my phone.”

“Shit, yours. Mine too.” Dutchess added, placing the bag atop the kitchen table. Pirelli retrieves all of his cooking utensils out of the cabinet. A cake mix blender, a digital scale, a box of Arm & Hammer, a Pyrex pan, and a large silver spoon. “What you need all that shit for? Amos don’t do it like that,” Dutchess stated with a questioning look on her face.

“Let me handle this. I’ma ‘bout to introduce you to the stretch game. Whenever it’s a drought, you have to take advantage of it. This is a time when you make a quick come up and get rich. We probably one of the only ones in the city gettin’ bricks for eighteen thousand a piece. We can break two bricks down and sell the rest in weight. We can easily sell a brick for twenty six thousand,” Pirelli explained. He removes the kilo out of the grocery bag. He puts on a pair of latex gloves to prevent the dope from getting into his pores. He can’t afford a dirty urine, his parole officer would revoke his parole in a heart beat.

He cuts the kilo open, removing it from its wrapper. Dutchess finally conquered the dream of every street hustler, getting her first chicken (Kilo). Pirelli places the powdered brick into a large ziploc bag, grinding it up, by pressing the large spoon against the ziploc bag, breaking it down into fine pieces. He pours it into the Pyrex pan. Dutchess has never seen that amount of cocaine get cooked at one time. He weighs up 252 grams of baking soda and pours it into the Pyrex pan along with the cocaine. He pours a cup of warm water into the pan and stirs it with the spoon. He plugs up the cake mix blender, activating it. The roaring sound of the cake mix blender drowns out the television crooning in the background. He puts it into the pan mixing up the substance. After giving it a good mix, he turns the knob on the stove. The fire shoots up dancing under the Pyrex pan. Pirelli adjusts the fire, giving it just enough fire so it doesn't crack the pan. The dope foams up and breaks down slowly, transforming into oil base. He shuts the fire off and blends it on level two. It begins to thicken, looking like yellow cake mix. He turns off the blender and presses a button releasing the wired wicker stems letting them rest in the semi-hard dope. He pours a glass of ice water into the pan and the dope locks up, hardening around the wired wicker stems. He grabs the tips of the wicker stems pulling the thick layer, pie like chunk out of the pan. Dutchess stares at the large chunk of dope in amazement.

"Now, this is what you call Betty Crocker," Pirelli bragged, sitting the dope on top of several paper towels to dry. He breaks it by hand, listening to the loud snap, as he drops various chunks on the digital scale individually, weighing up the dope.

After weighing up all the pieces, it comes out to be a little over 45 ounces. He brought back an extra 9 ounces. Dutchess does the math in her head on what she would profit off each bird and it causes butterflies to form in her stomach.

"You ready to get this money cuz?" Pirelli said excitedly.

"You damn right I'm ready to get this money."

"Well, lets do this."

ONE WEEK LATER

Donnavan hangs up his phone in frustration. He hasn't had any dope in the last three weeks. Everytime he call his connect all he recieves is the voicemail. He even tried other people he knows, but he still came up empty handed. He became so desperate that he even tried getting his hard, and that's something that he never does. He likes to get his dope in powder form so he can get all the extras.

Donnavan steps out of the apartment noticing all the traffic coming in and out of Amos' apartment. "***Maybe I can holla at Dutchess, she might know somebody. She's been crackin all week***." Donnavan struts to the door and rings Amos' doorbell. He can see the peep-hole darken as someone peeps through it. The chain rattles on the door and Amos opens it. A strong malorderous smell coming from the apartment leaps through the ajar door, slapping Donnavan in the face. He fans the smell away from his nose.

"What's up Donnavan?" Amos greets, "come on in."

"Is Dutchess around?" Donnavan inquired. "Yeah, what's up?"

"I need to talk to her about some business."

"Hold up a sec, let me go get her." He walks away, stepping into the back room. All the dopefiends in Amos' livingroom pays no attention to Donnavan. He recognizes one of his customers fixing her pipe, preparing herself for a hit. Dutchess steps out of the bedroom wearing a two piece BabyPhat skirt set that clings to her hips, accentuating every curve in her body. Donnavan scans her 34-26-40 frame from head to toe in admiration.

"Damn sweetheart, you wearing the shit out of that skirt set," Donnavan complimented, eyeing her candidly. He licks his pink lips, doing an impression of LL Cool J.

"Thank you for the compliment, but what brought you my way? My unc don't owe you no more money do he?"

"Naw, it ain't nothin' like that. The reason why I came is because I needed to see you. I'm tryna get me some work. I thought maybe you might know somebody that can plug me."

"I might be able to help you . What you tryna get?" Dutchess asked.

"I'm tryna get a nine piece of soft. I usually get a half of thang, but my money lookin' a little funny right now."

"I tell you what. How long would it take you to get seven thousand?" Dutchess asked. Without giving it no thought, Donnavan replies.

"Just give me five minutes, all I got to do is run to my apartment."

"A'ight, well meet me back here in five minutes," Dutchess instructed.

"You sure you can get it?" Donnavan questioned.

"You ain't said nothin' but a word Don. Hurry up and get yo' money together."

Donnavan walks out of the door and returns with the seven thousand dollars. Each thousand has a rubberband around it. Dutchess picks up one of the stacks and counts up a thousand dollars.

"You good." Dutchess drops the bag with a chunky brick inside of it on top of the kitchen table. "Huh, take this." Donnavan picks the bag up and examines it.

"Is it all here?" he asked.

"Of course," Dutchess replied. He reaches into the crotch area of his jogging pants and pulls out a pocket sized digital scale. He breaks the chunky brick down into individual pieces weighing it up. It comes out to 252 grams.

"Damn baby, you right on the money." He puts the dope back into the bag, ready to jump in the air and click his heels. "You just made it snow baby girl. For now on, I'ma call you Snow." Donnavan stated, walking towards the door placing the dope in his crotch area.

"Naw'll Don, I'm cool. Just continue to call me Dutchess," Dutchess stated with a serious look on her face.

"Okay, okay, okay. One more question though. Is it all gon' come back?"

"Go find out," Dutchess replied.

"A'ight, I'll holla." Donnavan exits the door excited, and heads to his apartment.

Erica is lying under the sheets tossing and turning. She is having a hard time getting to sleep, worrying about Pirelli. For the last couple of weeks, he has been staying out all night hustling. He would be so exhausted when he comes home, so tired that he would fall straight to sleep without making love to Erica. She would smell his clothes and go through his cell phone thinking that he was out cheating on her. Erica's biggest fear is Pirelli not returning home one day. She knows that the lifestyle he is living comes with pain and pleasure. Pirelli has made many promises to her that he is going to quit selling drugs after he makes one more move. One more move turned into many more.

The television croons and a soft blue glow shifts around on the ceiling. Hearing the springs in the bed squeak from Pirelli's body weight, grips her attention, awakening her from her sleep. She turns over and her mouth drops open, as if she has just seen a ghost. Pirelli is sitting on the edge of the bed counting a large pile of money that covers almost half of the bed. She rises forward with a questioning look on her face. She has never seen that amount of money in her entire life.

"Pirelli what is you doing?" Erica asked, staring at him like he just robbed a bank.

"What you mean what I'm doing? I'm countin' money," he replies, "You act like this is the first time you seen me countin' money."

"I hope you didn't do nothin' crazy," Erica stated.

"Baby stop gettin' all paranoid, you know I ain't did nothin' crazy. The game is good to me right now, that's all. I'm done after I bust this last move."

"I'm done after I bust this last move," she mocks him, "You keep on tellin' me that Pirelli. Don't you think you made enough money already? You told me when you was locked up that you was done with this mess," Erica exclaimed.

"You know I gotta take care of my family and give y'all the best," Pirelli said, placing bundles of money inside a Timberland shoe box.

"Baby... I don't care about money. I just want you here with me and the boys ...We can't afford for you to leave us again. All the money and material things in the world means nothin' to me. I just want you to promise me that you're done after this," Erica expresses how she truly feels, with a serious look plastered on her face. He studies her ebony brown eyes, seeing all the pain and anguish buried deep in her soul. Her eyes flick with genuine sadness, as she stares at him in silence, waiting for him to respond.

He leans over and pulls her to his chest, holding her head against his heart. She can hear the pumping sound of his heart, playing it's soft music. He combs his fingers through her hair, tucking her silky hair behind her ears.

"Baby I promise I'm done, just give me two more months. I just wanna get us a nice home and start a business so we can be straight. I want my boys to have what I never had. It is never my intentions to cause you any pain. I would never hurt you in no type of way. The only thing I have to live for is you and my boys. Besides that I have nothin' else to live for." Pirelli expressed. He brushes her hair back and plants a kiss on her forehead. "Just be patient baby, I promise you its gon' be over in a minute. Now help me count this money so I can get some rest."

They counted a total of $243,554.00. Pirelli can't believe that he have close to a quarter million dollars in cash. The drought season has been good to him. Moe has been fronting Dutchess and Pirelli 10 kilos at a time for eighteen thousand dollars each. Pirelli and Dutchess came across a line of clientele in Milwaukee, which helped them increase their profits. They get more per kilogram when their clientele comes from Milwaukee.

Pirelli stashes all the money in empty shoe boxes, except for $3,554.00, which he gave to Erica to deposit into her bank account. Erica returns to the bedroom after using the rest room, looking sexy as hell in her silk chemise and matching thong, by Mary Green. Her luscious hips sways as she makes her way back to the bed. Her plump booty hides her thong, slightly jiggling, as she plants her knee into the bed crawling to her favorite side of it. Pirelli catches an eye full of ass, as he watches her climb into the bed. She grabs the remote to the television off the nightstand and browses through the channels. Pirelli peels off his attire and crawls into the bed beside her. He rubs her thighs feeling the softness of her skin. They gaze into each other's eyes, silently like they are the only two people in the world. Their lips inches towards each other slowly. Pirelli's lips take hers with fervid urgency. They kiss each other like wild animals, clinging to each other's trembling limbs. Everything inside of her cries for him. He slides her thong to the side, feeling her moist, silky pubic hairs. He massages her clit with his middle finger.

"Ummm, baby, yeah," Erica moaned, rubbing her hands across his deep spiral waves. He peppers her smooth silky flesh with warm moist kisses, inching his way to her wetness, burying his face between her warm thighs. He captures her swollen clit with his soft full lips, twirling his tongue. "Ummm, I want you bay," she said in her sultry voice. She humps his face squirming wildly, arching her back. He cups her ass so she can't resist. "Oooh, bay," she cups the back of his head. He licks and sucks her pussy like it's the most important thing in the world. "Ooooh bay, you a-about to m-make me come," she cries. A warm sensation sizzles down her spine to her toes. The world explodes inside of her. Pirelli swallows all of her warm juices. He blows cool air on her clit, driving her crazy. The sensation is magical. Her chest sucks in and out, as she heavily pants. He triggers all of her hormones. He puts two fingers in her hot pussy finger fucking her, gently sucking her clit. He tries to talk to her in between licking her clit, but his words are smothered by her pussy bumping against his face.

They bodies shift in a 69 position with her on top. She tucks her lips around her teeth and engulfs half his mandingo inch by inch. She follows his dick with great enthusiasm. She holds his throbbing love muscle in her tiny hands, licking his balls teasingly. They moan simultaneously tingling allover.

Pirelli grazes her puffy pussy lips with his tongue, smacking her ass. "Ooh shit! Pirelli. Y-You s-sucking the hell out of m-my pussy." He spreads her ass cheeks open, grazing her asshole with the tip of his tongue, rubbing her clit in unison. "Oooooh Pi-relllli." Hungry for his loving, she moves forward kneeling over him, grabbing his fully erect dick, guiding it inside of her. She slowly lowers her body, looking over her shoulders into his eyes. She springs up and down like a frog, making all sorts of sex faces. She reaches behind her with both hands, balancing her weight, spreading her ass cheeks apart. Pirelli tilts his head forward, watching her sexual juices glisten on his dick, as she rides him. She stops on her way up with the head of his dick inside her wet pussy. Her pussy tightens, gripping his dick as she manipilates her vaginal muscles.

"Uuuh shit baby. I love when you do that," Pirelli blurts, watching her as she makes her ass cheeks bounce, as she kneels over him with half of his dick in her.

Erica is a woman in the streets, but in the bed she is a freak. Even though Pirelli sleep with other women on the side, he never met a woman with a pussy meaner than Erica's.

Pirelli turns her around onto her back taking control. He rests her legs on his shoulders sinking deep inside of her fist tight pussy, grinding against her pubic bone, feeling all pussy.

"Ooooh, it's in my stomach b-baby." Erica makes all kinds of faces, handling the dick like a soldier. He delivers her powerful strokes, beating up her pelvis muscles. He turns her around on all fours. A sheen of sweat covers their bodies. Hitting it from the back, he spreads her ass cheeks, seeing a creamy streak of cum on his dick. He bites down on his bottom lip beast fucking her. Her firm round bubble ass jiggles with the rhythmn of his strokes. All the muscles in his back flexes. His arms snake around her tiny waist, his grip tightens, he drills her harder and harder. His mouth drops open as he releases his sexual juices inside of her. "Ooooh shit baby." They moan uncontrollably, as she throws her pussy against his pelvis. They cum together and escapes to a world of ecstasy.

A dark green convertible Jaguar XKR with tinted windows, races down the pitch dark road, on Interstate 30. The car slows down and the window lowers on the driver's side. The driver tosses a black trash bag out the window, into the middle of the road. It speeds off playing loud music.

An older white man with gray receding hair drives down the road in an old model station wagon, with his German Shepard in the back seat. The dog has dingy fur looking like it's older than his master.

As he cruises down the road, he doesn't notice the trash bag lying in the middle of the road. He runs over the bag and hears a loud thump underneath his car and smashes down on the brakes, sliding on the gravel. He hears something dragging under his back tire. He pulls to the side of the road and steps out of the car chewing tabacco.

"What on earth was that?" he said aloud walking to the rear of the car, seeing the bag half way under the back tire.

The crickets hum in the darkness in unison. Traffic whirs by him occasssionally with blaring headlights. The dog jumps around in the back seat of the car hyper, barking at all of the cars passing by. The man kneels down and tugs the plastic bag, pulling it from underneath the car.

"Damn litter bugs, always throwin' their trash in the middle of the road," he said aloud. The bag rips as he pulls it. He examines something that looks like a hairy pizza. "Looks like a dead animal." He picks it up with his thumb and indexfinger taking a closer look. A strong malodorous smell slaps him in the face. "Uugh shit!" He drops it back on the ground and springs back in fear, back pedaling, staring at Chaos' smashed head, with its eyeballs missing. He moves hurriedly jumping into his car. He puts the car into to gear and speeds off.

Dutchess peers through the tinted lenses of her Dolce & Gabbana glasses, moving through traffic in her brand new pearl white Bentley coupe GT. She leans forward in the plush leather interior placing Kanye West's CD into the disc player. She hears the muffled sound of her cell phone chiming in her Hermes Birkins purse. She reaches into the passenger's seat grabbing her purse. She unzips it and answers the phone.

"Hello ...Nothin', on my way to drop off some new clothes to Ms. Walker for Keisha...A'ight, just call me later on...Okay." Dutchess flips the phone closed and tosses it back into her purse.

Dutchess has been looking out for Keisha every since she saved her life from the fire. Dutchess turns up the music hearing one of her favorite rap songs. Kanye West's "You Can't Tell Me Nothing," pumps out of the factory sound system. She hits the turn signal switching lanes, bobbing her head to the rhythmn of the music. The bright rays from the sun kisses her Tiffany & Co. diamond watch, as she grips the steering wheel.

Ice sits at the red light in his convertible Cadillac XLR chanting on his cell phone. He notices a beautiful woman in a Bentley two cars behind him. Dutchess weaves through the traffic pulling beside him. Ice recognizes Dutchess immediately and his mouth drops open, with his attention drawn to her. She lifts up her sun glasses and nods her head assuringly, with a slight smile pulling at the corners of her mouth. The pink diamonds in her ring glistens, as she holds her glasses revealing her greenish and gray hypnotic eyes. Her nickel sized nipples bulges through her House Of Dereon halter top.

Dutchess and Ice lock eyes on each other. Ice says something she can't understand because of the volume of the music. She turns down the music.

"What was that you just said?" she asked.

"I said, I see you moved up in the world," Ice repeated. He eyes her car candidly in admiration. "You gettin' 'em like that."

"If that's what you wanna call it. I just had to step my game up, if you know what I mean. I'm a big girl now. I'm done playin' childish games," Dutchess proclaimed.

"It look like I should be messin' with you. Want you gone and plug a nigga with some of that work. You know it's tighter than a virgin's pussy out here."

"Just talk to Chill, he still have the number." The light turns green and Dutchess sheilds her eyes with her glasses and smashes off. Errrk!

"Aye, Dutchess, hold up I'm serious!" Her long silky hair flutters in the wind as the warm summer breeze slaps her in the face. She caresses the .40 Glock she has in between her legs, with it's laser grips. She knows in this game you gots to stay on point.

"***That nigga must be crazy if he think I'm fuckin' with him.***" The chrome 22 inch shoes on the Bently coupe chops as she bends the corner.

Detective Herra sits at his desk reviewing the case file from the Lake Michigan homicide. No matter how many times he goes over it, he keeps coming up with the same worthless results. He slams his fist down on the desk, knocking over his cup of coffee.

"Damnit, what am I missing," he screamed, as he watches the Taster's Choice brand sink into the tan carpet. For some reason, it reminds him of blood, which gets his mind going. He traces the image in his mind. The bag the body was found in had a small hole in it, which means that blood had to seep into whatever vehicle the killer transported the body in. It could have been a motorcycle, or a truck, but most likely it was a car. In fact, he is sure it is a car, because he had found faint tire tracks, he believes belong to a car. The only thing he isn't sure about is the model, but even now he has narrowed it down to two. He is making more progress now, than he has in days. His brain is in hyper mode, like a computer. The thought strikes him instantly, "the computer." The boy's parents had said that their son spent a lot of time on the computer. He had sent it with the rookie down to forensics. "What's taking him so long?" he thought.

An officer at another desk distracts his attention, a burly man with a resemblance to Burt Reynolds. "Hey Herra, you ever narrow those makes of cars down, so we can run a search through the terminal?"

"Yea, it's between a Malibu and a C-" He's cut off by the rookie entering into the office, out of breath.

"Detective Herra, come quick, you going to want to see this." Without giving it a second thought, Detective Herra rushes out the door. He is led to the computer department. "We ran a trace on the computer and found out that the little boy had been chatting with someone named SD Freak. We have all the logged conversations. It's pretty sickening," the rookie stated.

"How do we get in contact with this sicko," questioned Herra.

"We don't have to."

"Huh? -What you mean?" The rookie points to the computer with a blonde female officer typing on a keyboard.

"The sicko got in touch with us." Herra walks over to

the screen.

"What's the sicko saying?" The blonde looks over her shoulder.

"Nothing illegal yet, just friendly conversation."

"Sheriff Alderman," Herra calls out to the superior, seated at his desk, "Find out if you can run a trace on the sicko's computer to find his location.

"Will do," replied the sheriff, typing commands into the computer in front of him. Herra returns his attention to the blonde.

"Keep him talking, give the sicko your age, and see if the monster bites." The blonde follows the instructions and types the words as they appear on the screen.

Jim07: Hi my name is Joey and I'm nine, what's yours?

SDFreak: Hi Joey, my name is Elmo and I'm nine also want to be friends.

Jim07: Cool I like riding bikes and running, but I don't have a bike.

SDFreak: My mom just bought me a brand new bike, you can use it if you want.

Jim07: How can I get it.

SDFreak: Well you can't come to my house, but I can ride my bike to your house. Where do you live?

Jim07: I don't know if I should tell you.

SDFreak: Come on, I probably live right by you.

Jim07: 47th and MLK.

SDFreak: I'll meet you on the corner tomorrow.

Herra pats the female officer on the shoulder. "We got the sick bastard now, good work." Herra stated. He looks over in Sheriff Alderman's direction. "Did you get the trace on the location?"

Don't worry, we'll get him tomorrow, I'll have a team watching the whole area.

The cranberry red Range Rover maneuvers through Galewood, with its huge mirrored rims chopping smoothly, flickering and reflecting off the concret pavement. Dutchess leans back in the leather ivory interior conversing on her Nextel. The diamond braclet on her wrist glistens as she activates the sound system with the remote. The LCD screen spits out the dashboard with a soft glow. The 15 inch Memphis Elvis subwoofers delivers a soft deep bass. Pirelli veers the truck down a oneway street, with three trained young goons trailing behind them in a Monte Carlo. Dutchess and Pirelli scrutinizes the area in search of new territory to expand their lucrative drug empire.The area is empty of rival gang members, due to a 30 count federal indictment. The area has been dry for the last three weeks.

Scanning the neighborhood, Pirelli sees an old school 69 Electra sitting motionless, with its 26 inch chrome rims windmilling. The driver of the car chants on his cell phone and rounds the corner.

Dutchess notices a dark complexioned man with a bald fade, leaning inside a Ford Contour conducting a drug transaction. He steps away wearing a white t-shirt, fresh white Airforce ones, and a pair of baggy jeans. Pirelli looks at him and recognizes the man.

"I was locked up in Joliet with the nigga. I don't really know him, but we might be able to work somethin' out. Let me step to him and see what's up," Pirelli said, hopping out of the truck with his heater tucked in his waistband, under his Enyce shirt. Hearing the sound of Pirelli's Jordans striking against the graveled ground garners his attention. He turns around and recognizes Pirelli.

"Don't I know you from some where?" the man asked, towering over Pirelli with his frail 6'0 frame.

"Yeah, from Joliet," Pirelli answered.

"So what brings you around this way?"

"I'm tryna spread the hustle. I heard this was open turf."

"Hold up dawg, I'm holdin' this down over here now Joe. I hope you ain't tryna step on my toes."

"Naw, it ain't like that playboy. I don't knock nobody hustle. I'm not here to take nothin' off yo' plate. I'm here to offer you a proposition that can help you make mo' paper." Pirelli explained.

"A proposition, mo' paper." The man frowns up right.

"That's right, a proposition and mo' paper."

"How the hell you gon' offer me a proposition. I run this shit around here now. I was here before you thought about comin' over here."

"Well, I didn't come over here to debate with you. I came to discuss business."

"My man just left, that's the only connect I need."

"Before you make that decision I think you might wanna talk to my partner," Pirelli said, gesture with his hand. Dutchess steps out of the truck in a velour body suit. The man looks at the beautiful Goddess as she makes her approach with one hand behind her back.

"I know you don't expect fo' me to talk to a bitch about my money," he ranted, loud enough for her to hear.

Pirelli stands face to face with the man chewing on a toothpick, with his fitted New York Yankee's cap tilted to the right, shading his eyes. The DMX look alike glances at the M&P .40 Smith & Wesson she clutched in her hand. "I guess you gon' shoot me huh?" he snapped, his face crumples, flushing with anger. Under estimating the beautiful young woman, he continues to bark. "Go ahead, shoot me mafucka! It want be the first time I been shot!" He lifts up his shirt exposing the old bullet wounds on his chest. "You see this," he bangs his fist against his chest emphasizing, "I been shot four times already! I'm not scared of no mafuckin' pistol!"

Dutchess levels her gun to his chest. She glares at him with an icy stare and bites down on her lower lip, squeezing the trigger. The .40 Glock flashes in her hand singing a song promising death. He staggers backwards doing a death dance, as the bullets slices through his chest area. His lifeless body topples to the ground after being shot five times.

"Dammnn, that make nine times you been shot now," Pirelli declared standing over the lifeless body.

"Yeah, but you know what?" Dutchess asked.

"Whats that?"

"This time he won't be gettin' back up."

She walks off, showing no remorse for the man. She stops on the side of the Monte Carlo, gaining the attention of the three goons.

"What up Dutchess?"

"After today, this is y'all area." With that being said, they jump in the truck heading to their next location.

The small investigation room that Ice is sitting in is sweltering with heat. It was actually designed to be a hot box. There are no windows, only cinderblock walls, leading up to a shabby ceiling. The only air that comes into the room is from the crack underneath the door.

Agents that work in the building, has a inside joke about the room. They call it "Hell on earth." At the moment however Ice doesn't find anything funny about the suffocating conditions. Michael Jordan probably had less sweat on him after playing in two overtimes, than Ice has now. His t-shirt is completely soaked. He sits in the chair, with his head down, on the metal table, extending from the floor. The steel door opens, blowing in a gust of cool air, as it mixes with the warm and muggy.

Agent Rains, walks in wearing plain blue jean pants, in a crispy white Oxford shirt. He slams the folder, he is holding on the desk by Ice's head, startling him.

"So, what can you tell me?" Agent Rains asked.

"I ain't got shit to say to you, I want my lawyer. You muthafuckas ain't got shit on me," retorts Ice, his face snarled.

"Ha! Ha! You dealers always humor me. I guess Hollywood is partly to blame, the rest is ignorance. Your looking at a lot of time. The more you tell, the less time in the cell, so come on spit it out."

"I ain't some country nigga, I know my rights, I want to holla at my lawyer. You ain't got no sells on me," Ice screamed.

"Clearly you don't understand or know shit about conspiracy, but with it, all we need is one person to say you sold them dope. Be it a dopefiend, a worker, or an enemy. So what you have to say now tough guy?"

"Same shit, just slower so you can understand, I... want...my...lawyer."

"Who Markkus Steingold, we have him on wire taps, accepting money for illegal acts. That's money laundering. Now him, he's cooperating, because five years is to long for him, and he also don't want to lose his license. Just like I know one decade is too long for you." At the mention of his lawyer's name his head lowers in defeat.

"A'ight, what do I got to do?" His face becomes solemn.

"What can yo give me on Kennytha Baptiste, we've already heard about the funeral home and cemetery."

Ice shakes his head, "Nope, I can't do that, hell naw. I ain't tellin' on him or nobody from my hood, I got a reputation. And you know that Kennytha will kill me."

Agent Rains flips through a photograph book on the desk. "You know him, or him," the agent asked, pointing at the mug shots of several alledged drug dealers. Ice studies the pictures and names. One nigga named Cakes, the other Magyk. He doesn't really know much about Cakes, so he isn't about to give him up either. He stares at the brown skinned man with braids.

"What this say Mag- what?" The agent snatches the photos, "It's pronounced Magic and if you don't know what it says, you don't know him, and your wasting my time. Now either you give me somebody I can work with or your going down for felon in possession of a firearm, and money laundering. The guns we found in the apartment, which was registered in your name and the fingerprints we got off the gun belongs to you. Now do you think you can convince the jury that you are innocent? If you take a plea bargain, the federal Government will enhance you for your background so that never see day light again. Now, either you stop playing games, wasting my time and give me somebody I can work with or," he runs his finger across his neck. Ice is racking his brain trying to come up with somebody. Suddenly a picture of Dutchess pops into his mind.

"I told her this game wasn't made for a woman." He thinks to himself. "Now tell me the name I need to know."

Detective Herra peers through the binoculars, as the elderly man dressed in a blue sports coat and slacks guides a chrome bike with training wheels across the graveled parking lot. He is stationed across the street at the Marathon gas station. An old Ford pulls up beside him, and two detectives get out slamming their doors.

Reese Washington and Tom Clay are partners. They both are in their early forties. Despite the difference in skin color, Reese being black and Tom white, they are like twin brothers. Both weighing 250 pounds and standing 6'4.

Reese was once a professional football player in the Canadian league prior to joining the force.

"What's goin' on chief?" Reese asked in his southeren

drawl. Herra passes him the binoculars.

"Fuckin' sick bastard," he mouthed, passing them to his partner. Tom takes a peak, shaking his head.

"Whaddaya need us to do?" he asked.

"Tom, I need you to watch the perimeter, just in case he tries to make a run for it," he said.

"Ha! Ha! With that limp he has, I don't think we have to worry about that," stated Reese.

"You might be right, but I don't want to take any chances. I want you to confront him Reese. I'll back you up, the man is extremely dangerous," Herra stated.

Tom goes to his position, which is only a few feet to his right. Reese is busy crossing the street. Herra is suppose to be watching Reese, but his attention is on an old bum coming from the left side of the parking lot. He appears to be saying something to the man with the bike.

Herra abandons his post to stop the bum from interfering with the sting. Reese has picked up his walk, turning it into a fast trot towards the man. His long arms swing wildly as he waves his gold detective shield, while shouting. Rocks forcefully discharge from the ground with each stride. Herra is still busy with the bum. The man does not hear Reese's shouts, but sees him when he is only 10 yards away. The sight of seeing a black man charging at him and screaming scares the shit out of him. He reaches for his hip, just as Reese dives in the air. "Reese, look out," Tom shouted. Boooom!!

Black Jesus steers the white four passenger golf cart over the grassy manicured surface of the 18 hole golf course, moving along a huge man made pond. The smell of freshly cut grass greets his nostrils. Ice sits in the front passenger seat nervous, wondering why Kennytha called a special meeting.

"***Maybe he found out about the debriefing I had with the feds. Nah, whatn't nobody around when they picked me up. Maybe this is about the losses we been takin'***." All sorts of things is racing through Ice's head.

Mr. Taylor the funeral director sits in the back of the cart trying to figure out what's on Kennytha's mind. His head swivels as he scrutinizes the scenery. Black Jesus knows there is something wrong because the only time Kennytha calls for an emergency meeting, it's for one reason only, betrayal. He knows that whenever someones crosses Kennytha, he can be coldblooded like a woman with a broken heart.

Black Jesus spots Kennytha and his caddy struuting to the tee. He notices somebody else seated in Kennytha's golf cart. He can't identify the other individual because of the way the person is facing. Pulling up closer, Black Jesus recognizes the heavyset man with his receding hairline, and his salt and pepper neatly trimmed beard. He's only saw the man a couple of times since Kennytha's, uncle Sa-far, who blessed him into the game at an early age and let him over see his empire, after severing years of dedication. Safar is the man behind the scene. He never speaks one word in the presence of anyone in the organization, but Kennytha.

He stares at the three men with a watchful eye, smoking on a thick blunt. Slowly, he blows out a billow of smoke that makes is facial features faintly visible.

The shining sun causes Ice to squint. He adjusts his Gucci visior, shielding his eyes. His diamond and platinum teeth blings between his parted lips.

"Me be wit' ya in minute. Me me take me last shot." Kennytha stands beside his caddy, who is perspiring heavily, carrying the 40 pound bag full of golf clubs on his back. Kennytha is dressed in a white Ralph Lauren hat, a pair of white golf shoes, and thin white cloth gloves.

The caddy hands him an iron golf club. Kennytha lays the club diagonally across his left palm. He relaxes his thumb and forefinger with his other fingers gripping the shaft. With both feet, he forms a line parallel to the intended flight, positioning himself in a stance known as the square.

They watch him closely as he displays his skillful ability. Kennytha always plays golf when he has spare time on his hands. Kennytha's shoulders does a 90 degree turn and his hips does a 45 degree turn. His right leg and his flexed knee supports his body weight. His left heel rises slightly off the ground. Playing a par 4 hole, he hits the ball 225 to 250 yards down the fair.

Mr. Taylor whistles, watching the golfball high in the air, no longer visible. "You hit that ball better than Tiger Wood," he complimented, trying to ease the tension floating in the atmosphere. Aftering watching the ball disappear, Kennytha turns around facing the three men. He stares at them with a dreadful look burning in his bloodshot red eyes.

"Me gonna get straight to da point. Me shipments been gettin' caught up. Me just lost fifty kilos of heroin. Dis organization is infested wit' a rat, now it's time me do a little exterminatin'," he declared, slowly scanning the faces of the three men standing shoulder to shoulder. Kennytha received a trip from one of his inside resources, who is employed by the federal government. He locks his focus on Ice, intently staring into his fear stricken face. Intoxicated with fear, he does the best at concealing his guilt. His heart races and his palms are immersed with sweat. Kennytha shifts his attention to Mr. Taylor, glaring at him, stepping closer. He bites down on his lower lip in anger. The veins in his forearm flexes, as he swings the iron golf club. Whack! The golf club strikes Mr. Taylor across the forehead. He back pedals, cupping his forehead, howling in pain. Blood seeps through his fingers.

"Please Kennytha, I'm tellin' you I didn't have nothin' to do with it," he pleaded. Whack! "Aaaww, plea-" Whack! Whack! Whack! Kennytha's lenthy dreadlocks dangle to the rhythm of him striking Mr. Taylor brutally, with the iron golf club repeatedly. Mr. Taylor sprawls in the grass groaning in pain, with his shirt drenched in blood.

"Me…kill…you…ma…fucka!" Kennytha barks inbetween striking him. "Me…told…you…don't…fuck… me!" The golf club becomes a silver blur, as he swings it haphazardly. Kennytha fractures every bone in his face. Mr. Taylor tries to look through his blood soaked eyes.

He balls up in a knot, and receives a vicious blow to the temple, that steals his life. Kennytha looks down at the brutally beaten man in disgust, watching his lifeless body on the ground, with his nerves still twitching. Kennytha towers over him with bloody hands, and his white Polo shirt stained in blood, still gripping the bloody golf club. He hog spits on a dead Mr. Taylor. "Piece of shit!"

Kennytha's slender built caddy walks up to him. "Here you go boss." He hands him a dry towel. Mr. Taylor's assistance with the federal government cost him his life. Kennytha was able to seize all of the survelliance tapes stashed at the cemetery, before they were able to reach the hands of the federal government.

The clicking sound of Kennytha's butterfly knife snaps Black Jesus and Ice out their trance, taking their focus off the dead body. Kennytha looks at Ice revealing a devilish grin.

"Cut him tongue out of his mouth." He drops the butterfly knife into Ice's trembling hand. Ice knows that if he refuses Kennytha's demand, he can end up just like Mr. Taylor, a dead soul.

The impact of their bodies colliding and smacking against the gravel, created a thunderous booming sound. Tom makes it across the street with his pistol drawn. Reese, after hitting the man with a professional flying tackle, aims his gun at the man's head, while rummaging his free hand through his pocket. The man shakes with fear, as he stutters to save his life.

"I-I-I wwwas ju-just tryin' to turn my radio down." Reese removes the Ipod Nano from the man's hip, just as Herra, the other bum, and Tom walk up.

"God he smells like shit," Reeses complained, holding his breath. The only thing new about this guy is his clothing. Everything else is old and dirty. His fingernails, hair, and skin.

"You find any weapons?" asked Herra.

"No, just an Ipod, and a crumpled fifty dollar bill."

"Just as I figured, this fella here just let know that his pal here is a bum, and that they were paid fifty dollas each to come here."

"Oh yeah," Tom replied skeptically, "Where's your friend now?"

--- 182

"All I know is he said to give you guys the MP-what's-a-mah-jig?" the scraggily haired bum, said pointing to the device in Reese's hand. Reese puts on the headphones listening intently. The robotic voice startles him.

"Oh there you are. I was wondering when you were going to make it." Reese looks around the parking lot, searching for the culprit.

"***He has to be around here some where***," Reese thought. The voice continues.

"The shame is, while you three are harassing bums, I'm getting ready to enjoy my latest victim. Say hi Joey."

"Helloooo," the voice is childish and immature.

"You fucks thought I was fucking stupid. Come here

Joey. Come sit on Santa's lap, and tell him what you want for Christmas."

Reese throws the MP3 player down, unable to stomach any more. He lifts the bum up from the ground by his collar. "Listen here you dirty son of a bitch! What does this guy look like?"

"I don't know, it was dark, I couldn't really see."

"Tell me!" Reese shouts, raising his left fist.

"He was black," the bum lied in attempt to save himself. Reese throws him onto the ground.

"Fuck," Herra shouted, angry they didn't get their man.

When the bums get three blocks away scraggily hair says to dirty skin, "Hey, how come you didn't tell him the truth?" Dirty skin reaches into his pocket as they enter the liquor store removing the crumpled bill.

"I can give you fifty different reasons," he said with a yellow grin. "Besides, it's what he told me to say."

Chapter Eight

Dutchess and Pirelli are in a single family residence packaging large quantities of cocaine, preparing it to be distributed throughout the city. Dutchess rented the house under a fictitious name to protect herself from any possible criminal charges. 23 kilo wrappers sits on the carpeted livingroom floor in a pile. Dutchess cuts open another kilogram of cocaine, being attacked by it's a strong odor.

"Ugh, this shit stank. It smells just like piss." Dutchess wrinkles her nose, fanning the smell away. Wearing a pair of latex gloves, she breaks the corner off the brick she has in her hands and tosses the solid chunk into a Ziploc bag. Pirelli stares at her with a puzzled look on his face.

"Ain't you gon' put it on the scale and weigh it up first, before you put it in the bag?"

"Naw, for what, it's all there," Dutchess replied.

"Give me that." Pirelli grabs the bag from her and removes the chunk of dope from the bag, preparing to weigh it up.

"I'm tellin' you it's nine ounces. I been doin' this shit long enough now," Dutchess said with confidence.

"Yeah, me too, but this gotta be done right." Pirelli stated, dropping it on the digital scale. The numbers on the screen scrambles and stops at 252.8 grams. Dutchess leans over his shoulder and reads the measurements.

"I told you." She said, her lips curved in a deep smile.

"You still a little over," Pirelli said.

"Don't trip, the extra eight tenths is in courtesy of me. You know we gotta take care of our customers."

"Yeah, I hear you." Pirelli added, grabbing another kilo.

Two hours of silence passes by and they are down to the last 5 kilos. Dutchess breaks the silence, becoming frustrated with the digital scale. "This scale is too fuckin' little, we need a bigger one," she complained. The numbers on the digital scale scrambles off balance. Every time she resets the scale, it bounces down to -2.3 grams. "What the fuck is wrong with this scale!"

"The batteries might be low," Pirelli assumed. Dutchess continues fixing on it, trying to get it to work. Getting it on all zeros, she drops a nickel on top of it to check its accurancy. The scale shuts off completely, and she becomes agitated. She smacks the back of it against his palm.

"Fuck this shit!" Dutchess snapped, flinging the scale across the livingroom. It crashes against the wall breaking into pieces. "From now on we done breakin' down birds," she proclaimed.

"What?" Pirelli blurted with an unpleasant expression plastered on his face.

"You heard me. It's time for us to move up in the game. I'm turning all the smaller clientele over to Donnavan. Either way it goes, the money still comes back to us."

"Hmph," Pirelli eyebrows points upward, "If you say so." He flashes his pearl white teeth, liking the sound of it.

"I don't care if its four thirty in the morning and somebody calls for a bird, I want them served. Our services will be available twenty four hours a day. It's supply on demand," Dutchess stressed.

"I guess in other words, you sayin' work, work, work, until yo' fingers hurt." Pirelli humorously said. They fall into uproarious laughter. “Hell yeah.”

“Well lets take this shit to the stratosphere then cuzo. You know I’m with you one hundred percent.” Pirelli added, placing 2 kilos in a Footlocker bag.

“Let’s get this shit started. I’ma go drop these off to T-Mac. I’ll holla at you later.”

“A’ight.” Pirelli exits the house with his thumper planted in his waistband.

Knock! Knock! Knock! “Hold on mami, somebody at my door,” Bianca said to Dutchess over the phone. “Who is it?” Bianca shouted, walking to the door in her nightgown.

“Pizza delivery.”

“What? I didn’t order any pizza,” she said peeking through the doorview at the man holding the pizza box.

“Is this apartment 103F,” he asked, looking at the yellow receipt.

“Yea, that’s my apartment.”

“Well this is your pizza.” She unlocks the door and two masked men charges into the apartment aiming pistols at her head shouting. “Bitch, where it’s at!”

Dutchess hear Bianca’s ear-piercing scream over the phone and the crashing sound of glass. Dutchess knows why they are there. Dutchess has been paying Bianca to stash dope in her apartment for her. She hangs up the phone and smashes down on the gas pedal to her Bently GTC making her way to Bianca’s apartment.

At the next meeting, the Klan members each hold a copy of the Sunday Chicago Sun Times. Their total concentration is on the front page article, entitled, “Area’s

Gang Violence Sky Rocket's."

The amount of bloodshed in the streets of Chicago, is at an all time high, based on reports received from the local precints, and joint Gang book magazine, endorsed by Mayor Daley. This unexpected hike in numbers is due primarily to four local gangs warring against each other in retaliation. Latin Kings vs. Black P Stones vs. Mickey Cobras vs. Gangster Disciples.

At this time we are not sure of the source of this commotion, but we do know that it has no signs of ending soon. 1000's of innocent bystanders have been injured, or killed in the process, mostly in the low income African-American neighborhoods.

"This is beautiful, Alderman you are a genius," Judge Milton elated. "Look what we have accomplished by only taking four worthless lives and blaming it on another group."

"Fucking World War three," Agent Regan excitedly added.

"Four people and over one thousand injuries and deaths. That's a twenty five thousand percent return on our intial investment," stated Senator Hennings.

"With numbers like that who needs a stock market, let's get people to invest money for guns and drugs in the block market," added the sheriff, with joyful laughter.

Dutchess breathes heavily with her. 45 automatic cluthched in her hand. She inches her way towards Bianca's ajar door with caution. Listening closely, she hears no movement inside the apartment. She steps into the apartment scanning the living room for any traces of Bianca. She spots shards on the floor from the broken lamp. Getting closer to Bianca's bedroom, she hears a muffled moan. She enters the room seeing a struggling Bianca with duct tape on her mouth, handcuffed to the radiator. Dutchess examines her ripped gown, blackeye, and the cigarette burns on her arms. Tears flow from her eyes as she lies on the floor looking like a helpless puppy.

"Oh shit, who done this to you Bianca?" Dutchess said kneeling down over her. She strips the the duct tape away from her mouth.

"T-They robbed m-me. They t-took everything mami. II tried to lie to them, b-but they w-was hurtin' me," Bi-anca cried with her chin buried in her chest in defeat.

"Don't worry about that. It's nothing but material shit, I can make up for it. I'm just glad that you're alright." Dutchess sincerely expressed, embracing a crying Bianca with a hug.

"Let me get you out of these handcuffs." Dutchess goes into the kitchen in search of utensil to pry the handcuffs. off of her.

Pirelli is on the phone in the bedroom talking to a female as Erica walks into the house from a long days' work. She heads towards the kitchen, then remembers she has to call her sister Tiera. She picks up the cordless phone and hears the giggling voice of a white girl.

"It's only cheating if we get caught, and I'm very good at what I do," the woman said. Erica has a good mind to say 'Bitch!' and get it popping from there, but she bites her tongue, listening to the exchange. Every word spoke breaking her heart farther.

"You sure we can get away with it," Pirelli asked.

"Yea, unless you plan on tellin'."

"Look, I'm going to be honest, this is my first time doin'

somethin' like this, I got money, I just don't want my girl to find out." Erica feels as if she is about to pass out.

"As long as I get paid, I don't care how we do it. Whatever is best for you. How about you meet me in a half hour at the House of Blues."

"Alright, I'm on my way."

Erica hangs up the phone. She bumps into a rushing Pirelli trying to head out the door. He tries to give her a kiss and she turns her head. "Straight up," Pirelli said, wondering why she has an attitude.

"Where you off to in such a hurry?" Erica questioned

"I gotta go meet Dutchess," he lied. She thinks about the times he said he had to meet Dutchess, or was going out on business.

"***Was he with this bitch all along***?" She thinks to herself.

"Yeah, yeah, yeah, whatever!" Erica said.

"What that's suppose to mean?" he asked, throwing on his jacket.

"Just what I said." She crosses her arms across her chest, rolling her eyes skyward in frustration.

"Look baby, I gotta go, don't wait for me, I'll be in a little late." Erica looks at him like he's crazy. He leaves out the door and she falls to the floor crying. Pirelli has no idea of the pain his conversation has just caused Erica, as he goes to meet the woman.

Deangelo leans back in his leather high chair behind his desk staring at a picture of him and Dutchess on the day of their prom. He has been thinking about her every since he returned to California. His new position as a real estate broker has been keeping him busy.

He picks up the phone and calls Dutchess. The phone rings several times and the voicemail comes on. "The

Nextel customer you are trying to locate is not available, please leave a message." Beep!

"Hey baby, this is Deangelo. I was just callin' you to let you know that I really miss you andi can't wait to see you again. When you get this message please return my call. Bye baby, hope to hear your voice today." He hangs up the phone and removes a stack of papers from his desk drawer preparing to close a multi-million dollar deal in the next hour that will make him fifty thousand dollars richer.

THE NEXT MORNING

Pirelli zips out of the parking lot in his old school 73' Chevelle Laguna, with its custom built 496 Chevy big block Stroker engine. The floormasters growls as he accelerates. Rell and Fatman sits in the back seat playing their Nintendo Ds. Erica fishes through her Charles David purse pulling out her lip gloss. She pluckers her full lips, applying the lip gloss to them.

Pirelli jumps on the expressway headed to Riveroaks. He bounces his head to the music, drifting off into his own little world. Today is a special day to him. He managed to take the dope game to another level. He's having the best time of his life. He is no longer on parole, due to him keeping his nose clean, he received an early discharge.

Erica's eyes focuses on something lying in the middle of the road. "Pirelli watch out!" Erica shouts sharply, startling him and the boys. He cuts the steering wheel quickly causing everyone's body to shift. He misses the dead deer lying in the middle of the road.

"Whew, that was close,"Pirelli said.

"You betta watch where your going before you kill us in here," Erica stated. Erica wrinkles her nose. "What the hell is that smell?" she asked. Pirelli shrugs his shoulders focusing on the road.

"I don't know."

"Uuuugh, that's Rell mama, he pooted," Fatman blurts, moving away from Rell fanning his nose. Rell leans over and playfully strikes Fatman on the shoulder.

"You got the fart touch."

"Nuh, uun." Fatman taps Pirelli on the shoulder passing it on. "Daddy got it now." Pirelli looks over in Erica's direction and she reads his mind.

"Don't even think about it baby." She smiles, crossing her fingers exposing her French manicured custom multicolored fingernails.

"Nan, nan, daddy got the fart touch," Fatman sings in his adolescent voice.

"Boy, it smells like somethin' died in yo' stomach," Pirelli said comically. They all erupt in laughter. Fatman holds his stomach laughing uncontrollably.

"Boy y'all somethin' else," Ercia added.

They arrive in front of a European style home parking in the horse-shoe driveway behind the Lexus LS460. Erica looks at the home admiring its flawless manicured lawn. "This house is beautiful baby. I never knew you had family that stay out here. They must have paid a fortune for this place. I can't wait until we move out of that small house of ours. Our house don't even have to be this big."

"Y'all ready to party boys?" Pirelli inquired, looking in the back seat.

"Yessss," they chorused.

"Come on then, what y'all waitin' for?" They climb out of the car. A cool breeze of wind sweeps the atmosphere, the leaves on the manicured trees rustles.

"The last one to the door smells like a rotten egg," Fatman blurts.

"Wait, hold up," Pirelli said, holding his hand up

stopping them in their tracks. "Ain't you gon' have some manners and give the birthday boy a gift?" Rell pats the pockets of his Rocawear jogging suit.

"How we gon' get hima gift daddy? We don't have no money in our pockets."

"You don't need none. You know I got y'all back. Daddy gon' always look out for his boys," Pirelli said. He pops the trunk and hands them gifted wrapped packages.

"What about mama?" Erica asked jokingly.

"You know I got you too ma." He hands her a small square package. She puts it up to her ear and shakes it.

"Dang nosey, you act like it's for you."

"Aw, my fault baby, you know me," Erica said with a flawless smile. She struts to the front of the house in her Bottega Veneta pumps looking sexy. Pirelli loves the way her Roberto Cavalli jeans fit and her classy beige blouse. Her silky black hair flutters in the wind and her diamond earrings dangles in her ears. Pirelli walks behind her in his Gino Green Global blue jean suit. He steps in front of them and rings the doorbell. The sun strikes the Russian cut diamonds in his Presidential Ambassador Icelink watch.

A white woman answers the door dressed in a gray two piece business suit, with long athletic legs. She has her long blonde hair in a ponytail. She reveals a friendly smile and ushers them into the house. "How are you today Ms. Fowler?" the woman greets Erica in a friendly mannerism.

"I'm doing fine," Erica replied. Erica's face contorts as she wonders how the woman knows her name. She shakes Pirelli's hand.

"Dad I thought you said we was comin' to a party?" Rell interrupted. Erica scans the living room admiring the crème colored carpeted floors, the 88 inch projection screen that over looks the living room, the heated marble floors, and the exclusive chocolate leather and aluminum couch set made by Ralph Lauren.

"Let me escort you all to the party." The woman prances in front of them, leading them to the dining room area. Upon entering the huge dining room, Erica freezes in her tracks drawing a deep breath of air, covering her mouth.

"Oh…my…God." Her eyes stretches open as she plasters her eyes on the 10 foot human sized family portrait of her, Pirelli, and the kids. The picture overlooks the glassy cherry oakwood table that is situated with a brass plates and silverware. A large crystal chandelier hangs from the cathedral ceiling above the table. The table is set for four individuals.

"Welcome to our new home baby." Pirelli said, wearing a smile on his face. Erica stands there speechless. Tears of happiness glistens in her glassy eyes, spilling over her eyelashes, flowing down her face freely. Pirelli captures her chin forcing her to look into his eyes. "Baby I promised you that I was gon' get us a new place. All I wanna do is give you the best that life has to offer." She stares at him through her blurry visual and smiles.

"Thank you baby."

"You don't have to thank me. I'm giving you what you deserve." She lifts her lashes meeting his steady gaze. Their lips merge together and they linger in each other's arms.

"Yuck, mama and daddy kissin'," Fatman blurts, covering his eyes. They laugh at him in between their kisses.

"Oh,there's one more surprise." Pirelli remembers, "Open y'all gifts."

"Huh, our gifts," Rell said in confusion. "I thought the gifts was for the birthday boy."

"It ain't no birthday boy, I tricked y'all." They move hurriedly unwrapping their gifts.

"Wow! Xbox." Rell shouts excitedly. "What daddy get you Fatman?" Rell asked.

"He got me some new controllers for the Playstation 3."

"Yeah, Thanks dad. What daddy get you mama?" Rell asked. Erica opens the small package and cracks open the small velvet jewelry box. A large diamond engagement ring sparkles, causing her to squint.

"Oow, mama that ring is pretty." Fatman complimented.

"Let me see mama," Rell said, looking in her extended hand. Pirelli kneels down on one knee.

"Baby, we been together for many years and I want to know...will you marry me?"

"Oh yes Pirelli." The two of them kiss and hug forgetting about the woman standing in their presence. She looks at them glad to see a happy family.

"I guess I better get going," she interrupted, gaining their attention.

"Oh, I forgot that you where still here," Pirelli said. "I forgot to introduce you two. Jessica, this is my fiancé Erica, and Erica this is Jessica. This is the woman that I was on the phone with when you was ease dropping on me. I knew you was on the phone. Jessica is a real estate broker. She made it possible for me to buy this house. She also helped me decorate the house," Pirelli explained.

"Nice to meet you Jessica," Erica said.

"Nice to meet you too Erica. Pirelli told me a lot of good things about you. The two of you have been through a lot. I sincerely wish you both the best. Maybe one day when I meet Mr. Right, I will get married. I know it will be no time soon."

"You never know Jessica, love comes in mysterious ways," Erica stated.

"I guess your right about that. Well, let me get going, I have a closing to attend to. I have to meet with my client."

"A'ight. You take it easy Jessica, and thanks for your help. I really appreciate it."

"No problem. And once again, it was nice meeting you Erica, take care." Jessica's heels clicks against the marble floors. The sound of the closing door replaces her footsteps.

Moe leans back in the leather seats of his Roll Royce waiting for Dutchess to arrive. Dutchess turns the corner in her Bentley GTC with the top dropped. She pulls into the lot parking beside him. Moe greets her with a friendly smile as she approaches his car. She opens the door and jumps inside with her Dolce & Gabbana sunglasses reasting on her forehead, revealing her colorful eyes that hypnotize every man that crosses her path.

"What up Moe, why you need to see me?" Dutchess asked.

"I need to make you aware of a few things," Moe replied, staring through the windshield at the children on the basketball court playing basketball.

"Like what?" Dutchess questioned, looking at him trying to read his mind.

"Remember I told you and Pirelli to take advantage of what I had to offer you?"

"Yeah, I remember."

"Well, that time has finally come and from this day I'm now retired from the dope game. One thing I learned about this game is that you have to get in and get out while your ahead. The game don't promise you nothin'. The federal government is playin' for keeps. We make it, they take it. Playin' the game and being successful is like playin' the lottery. A lot of people always sat that the game has changed, the laws changed, and the niggas that's playin' this game. I don't know what yo' plans is, but I just wanted to let you know that I'm officially out the game for good."

Dutchess glimpses out the window. "So I guess you tellin' me I need to find a new plug," Dutchess asked.

"That's right," Moe said. "I got bigger plans than this, it's time that I take this to Hollywood." Moe reaches under his seat and pulls out a laptop. He flips it open and the screen lights up. He punches a couple of keys on the keypad and hands it to Dutchess.

"What is this?" Dutchess asked.

"That's a movie that I'm workin' on called 'Devils Playground'. Me and my man Jeremy started puttin' that together in the federal joint. We found a couple of investors to help us put this demonstration together. We even got 50 Cent on line. We about to bring this thing into fruition and blow up," Moe proclaimed.

"I like that. I'll give y'all my support when it hit the movie theaters, but ya'll need to write a story about my life." Dutchess said jokingly.

"That's what it's all about, givin' support, and I tell you what, if you ever get the chance to sit down and chop it up with us, anything is possible baby girl"

"Since you mentioned support, why don't you introduce me to yo' connect so I can continue my hustle," Dutchess suggested.

"My connect? You askin' me for a big favor ain't you?" Moe massages his chin in deep thoughts. "Hmmm, I think I might be able to help you. But you have to promise me that you won't mess up my reputation."

"I promise you I won't destroy yo' reputation."

"Well, that means that we have a deal," Moe stated.

Chapter Nine

A soft compassionate breeze whispers in the darkness. Leaves flutters on the trees, making a soft crackling sound. Cheryl Blackwell turns her Lexus into the driveway. Pulling up along the side of her residence, she shuts off her headlights. She grabs her briefcase off the passenger's seat. Making her way out of the car, she thinks about how lonely she has been ever since Sade moved into her own apartment. Her Jimmy Choo high heel pumps click, as she struts to the fron door. She never notices the Nissan Pathfinder passing by at a slow pace.

Flashes of light reflects off the octagon shaped window, gaining her attention. Glimpsing over her shoulder, she spots the red Nisssan Pathfinder turning thr corner. It's taillights disappears into the darkness. She could swear that somebody was taking pictures of her. She quickly shakes the thought from her head.

"***Maybe I'm just tired from working on my upcoming case.***" She steps inside the house and ends her night with a long hot shower.

A mix throng of customers mingles at separate tables conversing inside of Home Run Inn on Kostner Avenue.

The delicious smell of pizza colognes the air. Dutchess is seated at a booth by herself. She sits back patiently waiting for Franko to arrive.

Today will be Dutchess' first time meeting with Franko. Franko is Moe's old connect, who helped him make it to where he is. Moe informed Dutchess about Franko, letting her know that he is a man with zero tolerance and very powerful. He has what they call dope boy magic in the hood.

Dutchess' eyes browses around the restaurant as she stares at the sea of faces surrounding her. She takes a swallow of ice water, tapping the table top with her French manicured fingernails. She tilts her head peering through the large glass windows observing a red pick up truck parking beside a white Chrysler Sebring. A Mexican man in his late forties steps out of the pick-up with his shiny jet black hair combed to the back, with a gray streak. He has a thick waxed mustache, various gold chains, gold rings on all fingers, a snake skin cowboy belt with a belt buckle the size of a saucer, and a pair of snake skin cowboy boots. He fits the same description that Moe gave her of Franko.

He walks into the restaurant strutting in Dutchess' direction. Dutchess stares at the Hispanic man who seems to be moving in slow motion as he makes his approach. He smiles cordially with one of the whitest smiles Dutchess has ever seen. He stops at her booth towering over her with his muscular frame.

"How you doin' Dutchess? Mine if I join you?" he inquired, staring at a beautiful Dutchess.

"I don't care, have a seat. You the one who wanted me to meet you here didn't you?" Dutchess replied, looking up at him. He pays no attention to her bold remark. In a way he likes her style. He never had antone talk to him like that before. Right away he notices that she has a lot of courage. He seats himself across from her. He glimpses at the cleavage that's peeking out her blouse. He studies the Chopard watch on her wrist with floating diamonds in it.

"Me like your watch. You seem like a woman with good taste," he complimented in his Spanish accent.

"I didn't come here to talk about my watch. I came here to talk about business. I don't have all day Franko."

"Slow down me lady. Me gon' get down to all that. First me want to break down my rules."

"Okay, break it down than." A waiter walks up to their table interrupting their conversation.

"Excuse me, is there anything I can do for you?" the waiter asked politely.

"Yes. Me will take an order of bread sticks, and a Pepsi," Franko informed.

"What about you ma'am?"

"I'm straight."

"Okie dokie, I'll be right back with your order." The waiter walks off.

"Now back to what me was sayin'. These are my rules. Me front you two hundred and fifty kilos. You got up to ninety days to make it disappear. If you're not finish by ninety days me call you. If you're finished before ninety days you call me. Never call me under any circumstances, other than being out of supplies. If you break me rule," Franko snaps his fingers, "me be finish doin' business with you just like that."

The waiter returns to the booth. "Here you go sir." He places the basket of hot bread sticks on the table. "Enjoy," he said and walked away. Franko reaches into the basket and grabs one of the bread sticks. He takes a bite off of it scanning a few faces in the restaurant.

"You see that man over there?" Franko nods in the direction of an Hispanic man sitting at a booth by himself, pretending to be reading a newspaper. He lowers the newspaper and locks his eyes on Dutchess.

"Yeah, I see him." Dutchess answers.

"That's a very dangerous man."

"Oh yeah." Dutchess points out the window. "You see that car right there?" A Dodge Stratus passes by the window slowly. The limo tinted window on the driver's side rolls down and one of Dutchess' goons nods his head slightly with a serious look on his face. The window rolls back up making his image invisible. She points her finger in another direction. "You see that man in the work uniform cleaning the windows?" The bald headed man looking like Mr. Clean nods his head. "He's train to go at anytime."

Franko cracks a smile, impressed with Dutchess'set up. "Me very impressed. For you to be a woman you got more balls than a lot of men me ran across in this business. Moe told me a lot of good things about you, but I'm goin' to make somethin' clear to you." Franko's face crinkles, "Don't you ever cross me."

"Is that suppose to be a threat?" Dutchess asked, watching him as he rises out of his seat.

"No that's not a threat. Me don't make threats. Me make promises." He hands her a small 4x6 envelope and slides it in front of her. "Me send your shipment real soon. Have a nice day my friend." Franko said, strutting towards the exit. Dutchess opens the envelope staring at multiple pictures of her mother Cheryl Blackwell. Her blood boils and an angry look flashes across her face. She glares out the window. Franko or his pick up truck is no where in sight. She slams her fist against the booth knocking over her glass of ice water.

"Muthafucka!" she snapped. Several customers turn in her directions at the disturbance. She rises from the booth and exits the reataurant.

ONE WEEK LATER

The sound of machinery reverberates in the garage. Dutchess and Pirelli stands around a late model Mercedes Benz truck. They watch closely as a burly built white male operates an air driven panel cutter. He carefully saws the car in half. The truck was imported from Mexico, by Franko's sophisticated drug smuggling operation.

They expertly removed parts from the truck and replaced the weight with numerous packages of pure cocaine. That's their way of getting the drugs pass the U.S. customs. This is the first shipment Dutchess received from Franko. They take the whole truck apart, removing the packages. Dutchess picks up one of the square shaped packages and examines it. Franko sent a total of 250 kilos. Pirelli stares at the large quantity of cocaine and his kness begins to buckle.

"How we suppose to move all of this shit in ninety days?" Pirelli inquired.

"Easy, put the word out there and give out the best numbers in Chicago. At twelve thousand and five hundred dollas a piece we can't lose," Dutchess responded.

"Well, let's make it happen than." Pirelli stated with a smile on his face.

Every since Carmen had met the preacher on the bus, she has taken up reading her bible as a pastime. She even convinced Tyrone to go to church with her one day. That day, the preacher spoke on cherishing the black women, God's greatest creation. The sermon had already broken him down. Through misty eyes, he apologized for ever putting hands on her. It was something he had said many times before, but something inside of her told her that he was sincere this time.

"***Maybe there is a God***," Carmen thought. For her, life couldn't be better right now. Tyrone has transformed back into the man she fell in love with back in highschool. She has begun to lose a few excess pounds she has been carrying around. She has been slowly stacking her money to open up a hair salon. She told Dutchess about her new happiness, and her girl was happy for her. She made it a habit to share verses with Dutchess as she runs across them. Dutchess believes that it's a higher power up there, she just doen't believe in the bible.

"Too many inconsistencies," Dutchess had said to her, when she tried to explain Immaculate Conception, the way Jesus was born. "Believe what you want, but Mary was fuckin' plain and simple." Dutchess stated to her one evening. That's what she liked about her girl, she never bites her tongue. Always keeps it real. That was the difference between her and Bianca. And speaking of Bianca, "***Where is she at anyways***?" Carmen thought, finishing up a verse in the bible. She is sure that the break in at Bianca's house was staged. She just doesn't have enough proof to confront her. Dutchess was pissed, but the black eyes and cigarette burns Bianca had on her legs was enough to convince her. Carmen isn't so sure, and she made another mental note to check into it.

Lately Carmen has even begun to dress sexy, but today she dresses down, giving herself the appearance of an elderly black woman. She looks at her watch.

"Damn I'm runnin' late," The disguise helps her to be more inconspicuous, as she makes her drug runs. She fixes her wig and slides into her blue granny dress, complete with white ruffles at the bottom. She exits the room and gives Tyrone a kiss. "I'll be back later baby, I got a run to make."

"A'ight, be careful."

"Come give momma some suga," Carmen said to her

daughter, who was lying on the carpet with her feet in the air coloring. Renee gets up and gives her mother a hug and a kiss.

"Mommy, I want you to see my picture," Renee said in her immature voice.

"Not right now baby, mommy late, I'll see it when I get back." Renee pouts her lips.

"But you always say that and never look."

"I will this time baby, show daddy. Mmm-k?"

As Renee runs to get her picture Carmen exits the door. "Look daddy," she says handing the picture to Tyrone, who is occupied with the video game. He grabs it in his hand, never glancing at the picture. He hands it back to her as he continues dominating the computer in the latest NBA Live.

"Yep baby, uh-huh, that's pretty." Renee takes the picture from his outstretched hand and continues finishing the master piece.

Bianca throws the cell phone at the wall, smashing it in multiple fragments. After becoming a regular user of cocaine, she was introduced to heroin, something that gave her a stronger high. The only problem was when she couldn't find any stuff. The pain she feels is somewhere between cramping and menopause. Tears streams down her face as she fights off the sickness. She lies on the floor in yeaterday's dirty designer clothing, balled in a knot. Her stained white blouse hangs loosely on her soulders. She draws six old cotton pieces and takes a hit of the poison. It's not enough to cure her sickness, but it's enough to get her moving again. The sickness she feels from being separted from the H, makes her want to commit suicide. She picks up a pencil and paper and begins to write.

Dear Dutchess,

First let me start by sayin' I'm sorry mami. You never been anything but a good friend to me. I was always a little jealous of you. Here you was, accepted to college and you didn't even go. Do you realize how bad I wanted to go to school, but couldn't afford it? And while I was sleeping around with this guy and that guy, you had a solid relationship with Deangelo. I know this sounds selfish of me, but at least you got the chance to have a papa. When you started making all of your money, did you ever say here Bianca girl, take this money and go to school? No! But you did treat me like your punta. A female dog, a mule! Keep this over your house. What if the cops would've came? I would be the one going to jail. All for what, the little money you gave me? The clothes? The jewelry? The car? The new apartment? I'm not making no excuses for what I done, but when the opportunity came along for me to make some real money, I took it. SURPRISE! The home evasion was staged. I know your mad, but

I was the one who lost out on the deal. Two black eyes and being burned with a cigarette. All that shit for $5,000.00. Well, that money was gone a long time ago. And Pickle, well he promised he would make sure I never run out of product. I guess that was a lie. Look at me now. I don't want you to feel sorry for me just understand and forgive me one day.

Love Bianca XOXOXOXO

A tear falls from her face, landing on the letter, leaving a small damp circle. "***If only Pickle would've answered***

his phone." She stares at the prescription bottle filled with little white pills. She glances at the letter. She crumples the letter up, and throws it on the floor. Some things are better left unknown, she contemplated while plotting her next move. She walks to the couch picking up the black cordless phone. She calls the person who has never been anything to her except a friend. She knows that she can count on her to come through. She almost made a terrible mistake killing herself, she reasoned. "***Besides, there is no herion in hell***," she thought, waiting for Dutchess to pick up and come to her rescue.

Carmen exits out the door. She knows that she should stop neglecting her daughter. She makes another mental note to start spending more time with her. A cold breeze scuffles down the street. She gets into her car and drives to the Greyhound station, parking a half block away. She passes by the elderly black man with a cane, sitting on the bench. He smiles and waves, and she waves back as she crosses the busy street. She opens the door and is greeted by the warm air. She glances behind her and notices a strange thing. The old man with the cane is running full speed towards her. Before she can react she is surrounded by a team of DEA agents.

"Your not the only one who can dress up like they're old," the young agent says, removing his fake gray wig, mustache, and beard. A female agent searches her and finds two kilos of cocaine strapped to her body.

"Take her down to the station. By the way, you are under arrest. You have the right to remain silent. Anything you say can and will be used against you." He smiles as he reads her Miranda rights to her. Too many cases had been over turned on appeal from agents failure to do so. "Good job." He pats one of the agents on the back as Carmen is driven downtown.

Carmen has been under investigation for the last two months. As the crusier moves through traffic she thinks about the last verse in the bible that she read. "***The Lord giveth and he taketh away.***"

Music erupts from the JL Audio sound system of Pirelli's brand new Escalade ponding hard. He can feel it's pulsating rhythm in his chest. The loud deep bass rumbles, vibrating the surface of the earth, punching the concret. Pirelli bobs his head to the rhythm of Young Jeezy's CD 'Inspiration'. The 7 inch LCD monitors glows along with the 27 inch Sharp drop down flat screen. The custom chrome Cadillac grill and it's chrome accents glimmers as he bends the corner on a one-way street, garnering the attention of everyone on the block.

Pirelli has become known as a brick layer on the Southside of Chicago. Almost every hustler on the Southside is familiar with Pirelli and Dutchess' name. Cheryl Blackwell knows Sade as Sade, but the streets know her as Dutchess, the notorious queenpin.

Pirelli parks in the middle of the block on Claremont behind a 72 Chevy Caprice with a watermelon coloered paint job, sitting on 26 inch mirrored rims. Bump! Bump! Bump! Bump! Pirelli's high powered sound system sets off the car alarm on the old school Chevy. A french vanilla complexioned female stands in front of a single family residence waering a pair of tight fitting Apple Bottom capris, accentuating every curve in her body. Pirelli plasters his eyes on the girl, undressing her with his eye balls. Her round breast stands up perfectly and her dime sized nipples bulges underneath her Apple Bottom halter top. She chants on a pre paid cell phone, staring at him with a lustful gaze wavingat him. Pirelli blushes and returns the wave with a smile. She places one hand on her luscious hips poking it out like she's posing for the camera.

You can tell from her shapely front that she has a stupid booty. It looks like if her tiny waistline gets any smaller it's going to disappear.

Pirelli sees a shadow in his peripheral visionand shifts his gaze to the passenger's door. "***Damn I'm Slippin'***." A dark complexioned man with a bald fade reaches for the door handle. Pirelli hand glides to the door panel, grazing the custom suede and leather upholstery, as he hits the powered locks, unlocking the passenger's door. He hops into the truck sinking into the leather interior. The rich bass knocks loudly, shaking the seats and the rearview mirror. T-Mac feels like someone is giving him a back massage. Pirelli grazes the indigo blue screen on the dashboard, turning the volume down to level one, so their conversation can be audible.

"What up T-Mac?"

"Nothin', just tryna break bread," he replies with a leery look in his eyes. He reaches inside his denim LRG pants pulling out a bulgy plastic bag, tossing it into Pirelli's lap. "That's the whole forty-six stacks I owe you."

"Cool." Pirelli said, placing the bag under the seat next to his clapper, (Gun).

He met T-Mac through Sheena. Sheena is T-Mac's sister who he met two months ago at the check cashing place. She was sending her brother Corvette some money through Western Union. Corvette is T-Mac's older brother, who is serving a 30 year prison term for 50 grams of cocaine base. Pirelli asked to borrow her ink pen and began flirting with her. He filled out the same blue form as well, sending his man Silk a thousand dollars like he promised. Silk is serving 22 years in the feds at Milan F.C.I. awaiting his appeal. Sheena and Pirelli exchanged numbers. On their first date Pirelli let her know that he has a family at home. Sheena respected his honesty and they continued their relationship with an understanding.

"Man, who is shortie over there in those capris?" Pirelli questioned, licking his lips like L.L. Cool J.

"Man, that's Micole hot ass. She only fifteen years old," T-Mac informed.

"Damn, these young girls getting' thick ass hell. I wouldn't have never guessed that she is only fifteen. If she was three years older I would've snatched her up. Shit, I see why these niggas be out here messin' with these young hoes." Pirelli stated, looking through the windshield. T-Mac glimpses around like he is up to something. "You a'ight?" Pirelli asked with a puzzled look on his face.

"Yeah, I'm straight." His words are not convincing. Pirelli starts feeling uncomfortable.

"Let me get up out of here. Just hit me tomorrow," he said.

"A'ight, I'll do that." T-Mac climbs out of the truck looking around, stalling like he is looking for somebody.

"***Man, what this nigga on. He act like he tryna set a nigga up or sumpthin'***." Pirelli activates his rear camera system, Bluetooth ready. He pulls off paying no attention to a waving Micole. He turns the corner exiting the neighbor-hood with caution. He looks at the screen of the in dash monitor noticing a black Crown Victoria trailing behind him at a distance. He begins to tremble trying to keep his composure. "***I knew it was somethin' about that grimy lookin' ass nigga. I let Sheena talk me into messin' with her shiesty ass brother***." He picks up his pace trying to lose the car. He glances at the screen again in search of the car. Everytime he switch lanes, the Crown Victoria switch lanes.

He cuts through an alley jumping onto a side street.

The V8 engine roars as he accelerates. His huge 28 inch mirrored rims flick as he turns multiple corners losing the car. He makes it to his bachelor pad pulling into the driveway. He reaches under the seat grabbing the plastic bag and his gun. He drops the gun inside the bag with the money. He jumps out of the truck walking briskly with the bag in hand. The two heavy platinum chains hanging from his neck clings together as he struts into the house. He stashes the bag under the couch and blazes up the half of blunt he left sitting in the ashtray to relax his nerves. He sits back on the black leather sofa in a zone.

After ten minutes passes by, he hears someone knocking at his door. His heart drums against his chest. Quietly, he pads over to the window. He hears the crackling sound of a walkie talkie. He peeks through the curtains and his heart beat quickens at the sight of the black Crown Victoria parked in the driveway, behind his truck.

"Oh shit!"

The officers waste no time processing Carmen into the county jail. Within minutes she is out of the granny dress and into an orange jumpsuit. A white plastic band with her picture, date of birth, and prison number dangles loosely on her wrist. She is led into the interrogation room by two tough looking cops.

"My, my, my, it sure would be a shame to go down for someone else's drugs, wouldn't it Mick?" Steve asked his partner upon entering the freezing cold room.

"Sure would be," Mick coyly responded. "Especially as young as she is right now," he added.

"Hell Mick, by the time she gets out that dress she had on will be what others her age are wearing." Steve said with a crooked grin plastered on his face. Carmen glances down at her arm noticing the goose bumps for the first time. Were they from the cold air or is she just nervous, she wondered silently. She makes upin her mind not to give up Dutchess, the officer's voice snaps her back to reality.

"We know that you're a small fish in a large pond. Give us the person we need, that we're looking for and you walk out of here right this minute," stated Mick.

"That means we forget all about those forty years," added Steve.

"***Damn, why did this have to happen when things were going so good in my life***?" Carmen thought to herself. Having a young daughter made things even more complicated for her. Then there is the issue of loyalty to Dutchess. A kind of a friendship, which deserves the most loyalty? Carmen takes a deep breath coming to a difficult decision. "The person that y'all need..."

Pirelli debates with himself trying to decide if he should open the door or not. "***It's only one car, it can't be nothin' serious. They need a search warrant to come in here. Fuck it, let's see whats up***." He unlocks the door staring at a beautiful female officer who has a flawless copper skin tone, almond shaped eyes, perfectly arched eyebrows, and full lips like Fantasia, and long microbraids.

"Is there aproblem officer?" Pirelli inquired, putting on his best performance. Seeing the officer, he is able to relax. The smell of marijuana emits throught the ajar door, mingling with her nostrils.

"Yes, there is a problem." He watches her as she sniffs the air. She drawsher police issued 9 millimeter. "Turn around and put your hands behind your back you criminal," she barked. He turns around following the officer's instructions. She slapps a pair of cold handcuffs around his wrist restraining him.

"What did I do officer?" he asked,as she walks into the house placing the gun back into her holster. He turns around facing the officer.

"Did I tell you to turn around!" she snaps, shoving him in the chest area. His chain makes a metallic cling, as he falls to the sofa back first. She unfastens his belt hurriedly as if she is in a race. She tugs at the waistband of his Azzure jeans, pulling them down. His rock hard dick rests on his navel. She grips his dick mesmerized by the size of his long, thick, brown crooked dick, with it's thick veins.

She nibbles on the mushroom-like head of his dick, teasing him. He feels the warm soft texture of her tongue. She simultaneously licks his heavy balls, jerking him off. She gives him a seductive stare and twirls her tongue, lubricating her full succulent lips. She shakes her head and tucks one of her microbraids behind her ear. She envelopes the full length of his dick, licking his balls. Warm saliva trickles down his balls. She manipulates the muscles in her throat like a true skull master. Her head swerves wildly as she makes slurping sounds. She alternates in between gentle and aggressive sucks, taking him inch by inch, stretching her jaw muscles as wide as she can, and almost getting lockjaw. Humming, she rotates her head side to side. The warm juices in her mouth sings a song,

Pirelli tilts his head back, resting the back of his head on the couch, with his eyeballs rolling in the back of his head, like a man on his way to heaven. Groans of ecstasy escape his parted lips. Pirelli loves her vicious head game. He arches his back humping her face.

"S-shit, you suckin' the h-hell out of this d-dick Sheena." Sheena is a freaky bitch who likes to take control in the bedroom. Pirelli loves her aggressive ways. She reels her head, disheveling her hair.

"You like the way I suck this big dick don't you?" Sheena snarled. She pulls off her belt and her pants fall to her ankles, putting her Coca Cola bottle shape on display. She sits her walkie talkie atop the glass end table. She loops the elastic of her thong with her thumbs, pulling them off. She trips on her foot clumsily, her round ass jiggles, as she catches her balance. Turning around with her back facing him, she toots her tear dropped shaped ass in his face and her furry pussy. It looks like she has a small monkey in the thigh-lock. She reaches between her legs playing with her pussy, looking over her shoulder. Her pink morsel of flesh glistens as she spreads her puffy pussy lips. It looks like the inside of a strawberry.

Sheena holds one of Pirelli's knees guiding his dick into her wetness. Her face contorts as she lowers her pussy taking all the dick like a champ. She clenches her teeth as she rides him holding both knees. She baths his dick with her sexual juices. "Mmm, baby. You got me wet as hell." Her juices slide down the side of her legs. Pirelli never seen a woman cum like Sheena. He looks at the tattoo on her ass cheeks, sinking deeper inside of her. When she comes down, he comes up. Their bodies make a clapping sound as their flesh connects. "Ooh, give me this dick!"

"Squad 52 come in," her walkie talkie crackles.

"Shit!" Sheena reaches for the walkie talkie panting heavily.

"S-Squad fifty t-two to dispatch," Sheena speaks into her walkie talkie with Pirelli's dick buried deep inside of her.

"We have a robbery in progress on seventy first and Stoney. Suspect is five foot ten, approximately 210 pounds, blackmale, wearing blue and black."

Pirelli continues to grind under her."Ten f-four." Sheena replied. "I got to go baby, sorry we can't finish. And by the way I told T-Mac to hold you as long as he could, just in case you thought he was up to somethin'."

"I knew he was up to somethin'. Don't be gettin' a nigga all noid like that." Pirelli proclaimed Sheena removes the handcuffs. She kisses him on the lips and storms out the door.

Pickle leans back in his brand new foreign whip chanting on his Motorola cell phone. The air conditioner hums in the background, fluttering his shirt collar. Pickle is a local dope boy from the Westside of Chicago. He used to be a small time street peddler until he was connected with a major supplier he met through his Puerto Rican freak. Seeing his potential to move large amounts of dope, the plug decided to front him multiple kilograms of cocaine.

"Man, fuck that bitch, I ain't givin'her shit! I don't respect no broad tryna play a man's game anyway. She don't got no business on these streets. She bet not come to me talkin' no crazy shit. If she do I got somethin' that will solve the problem." Pickle glimpses out the window, wondering what's taking Myhria so long to come out the house.

"Man this bitch need to hurry her ass u-" Seeing her stepping out the door, he stops before he could finish his sentence. He brings his call to an end.

"Yo' here come ol' girl." Pickle listens to the caller, nodding his head in agreement.

"A'ight fo' sho', fo' sho'...yep." He hangs up the phone and stares at her doll like face, down to her pretty French manicured toes, that are exposed at the tips of her Louis Vuttion sandals.

Carmen leans back in the chair waiting for the officers to return to the interrogation room. She never thought that she would be in this type of situation. The only thing she keep seeing is her daughter's innocent face. "***I can't leave my baby out there to live without me. Who's going to take care of here while I'm gone away? In fourty years my daughter will have to take care of me***." Many thoughts race through Carmen's head.

The officers return with a cell phone and a recording device to record Carmen's phone call. "Are you ready to set the deal up?" Mick asked, wearing a large smile on his face, exposing his rotten tooth. Carmen thinks about Dutchess and her heart drops in her stomach.

"Yeah, I'm ready,"

The officer hands her the phone. She dials the number that Dutchess gave her in case of an emergency. The phone rings several times. Mick holds a listening device to his ear anxious for a drug bust.

A woman answers the phone with a strong professional voice. "Butler's Law Firm, this Sandy speaking, how may I assist you?" the woman asked. Mick's face wrinkles up in confusion.

"This is Carmen Ellis, tell Mr. Butler I'm in custody. I'm at t-" Click!

"Fuck is you doing? Get her the hell out of here and put her back in her cell!" Officer Mick barked. The other agent snatches her out the chair and places the cold handcuffs around her wrist.

"Fuckin' crackers, I'll never sell my people out. Y'all can't keep me forever." Carmen's voice fades away as she is escorted down the hall and back to her cell.

The loud rich bass escaping the 12 inch Memphis Elvis subwoofers blitzes Dutchess' ears, as she leans back in the passenger's seat of Pirelli's Cadillac truck. He reaches to the sky and presses a button on the roof of the truck. The sunroof rolls back allowing the rays from the sun to seep into the inside of the truck. Their heads swivel, as they search for Wilcox and Fransico Street, in search of their prey, after receiving a tip from a reliable source.

"Fransico gotta be somewhere around here," Pirelli proclaimed, driving in circles. "Fuck it." Pirelli becomes frustrated; he presses one of the buttons on the rearview mirror. The sound system automatically shuts off and a ring tone hums through the speakers. A sophisticated feminine voice disperses from the speakers.

"Welcome to ON Star, how may I help you?"

"I'm tryna find Wilcox and Fransico," Pirelli informed.

"Right now your located on Wilcox and California, is that correct?"

"Yes,"Pirelli replied.

"Continue traveling West and you should run right into Fransico. Is there anything else I can help you with sir?" the woman cordially asked.

"No, that'll be it."

"Thank you for using ON Star." The voice fades away being replaced by deep bass. Pirelli rounds the corner on Fransico, driving slowly. Pirelli spots a dark green Quarter to Eight with its butterfly door propped up in the air on the passenger's side.

"Aaaw, there go that nigga right there," Pirelli blurted, pointing his finger in the direction of the foreign whip.

"I'm about to delete that bitch ass nigga! I'm tried of him playin' with my money. How the fuck he gon' buy a new car and he ain't paid me my money. Pull up on that mutha fucka!" Dutchess snaps, her eyebrows pointing to her cute little nose. Pirelli can see the icy look in her colorful eyes.

"Hurry up, pull up on him," Dutchess said, reaching under the seat grabbing the black stainless steel .45 automatic ACP. Errrk! Pickle jerks to attention to the sound of the pearl white Cadillac truck pulling beside him recklessly. Dutchess aims her gun at his head.

"Oh shit!" Pickle shouted, smashing his foot down on the gas pedal hauling ass. Errrk! The tires on the BMW squeals and the rearend swerves uncontrollably. The pink diamond ring on Dutchess' trigger finger glistens as she squeezes the trigger.

Boc! Boc! Boc! Boc! The deafening sound of the firearm leaves Pirelli's ears ringing. Bullets buzzes pass Pickle's ears like angry hornets. The back windshield shatters, peppering the back seat with broken glass.

Myhria cowers in the passenger's seat screaming in rage.

Boc! Boc! Boc! Dutchess continues cracking at her target, through the passenger's window of the Cadillac truck. She holds on to the door with one hand to keep her balance, as Pirelli speeds behind the BMW. Boc! Boc! Boc! Boc! The high powered handgun jerks in her hand. Boc! Boc! Boc! Boc! Boc! The BMW slams into a telephone pole on the side of the street. Thick clouds of smoke billows from the crumpled up front end of the car. Anti-freeze leaks out of the radiator underneath the car.

Pickle squinches in severe pain laying on the air bag. Four spider-like holes are in the front windsheild of the bullet riddled BMW. Dutchess ejects the empty clip and slaps in a full clip.

"Hurry up Dutchess, you know them people probably already close by," Pirelli stated. Dutchess climbs out of the

Escalade planting her Christain Louboutin stilettos on the surface. She can hear the sound of the startled woman in the car, weeping in pain. The sound of her heels clacks against the pavement. She looks at a groaning Pickle, with a frigid stare.

"Please ... I promise you ... I'll pay you...yo' m-mon-" Boc! Boc! Boc! Dutchess disregards his plea and shoots him three times in back of the head, execution style.

Myhria tilts her head back and looks at Dutchess with glassy eyes breathing heavily, grimacing in pain from the repercussion of the car crash. Dutchess looks into her eyes feeling sorry for the girl. She would like to let her live, but she knows that it can cost her freedom. Being very familiar with the law, she knows not to leave a witness behind.

She aims her gun to the girls head. "This ain't nothin' personal ma. Sorry to say, you just was with the wrong nigga at the wrong time." Boc! Boc! Boc! She prances away in her BabyPhat cuff mini skirt, with her curveous hips swaying back and forth. She jumps into the truck. "Let's get out of here."

Chapter Ten

The rustling sound of money fills the air as Pirelli feeds the IBM electronic money counting machine with twenty dollar bills. He takes every five thousand dollar stack and wraps a rubberband around it. He counts out fifty thousand dollars and shrink wraps the money air tight, with the Food Saver, placing each vacuumed sealed plastic bag into cardboard boxes.

The long hours of organizing the money has him exhausted. He yawns, stretching his arms above his head. He leans back on the leather sofa, and looks at all the bulgy duffel bags filled with money that haven't been counted. Pirelli never thought that there would be a time in life that he would get tired of counting money.

"***I been countin' this money so long it looks like my fingers turning green." Pirelli blows out a short breath. "I need to take me a break***," he said quietly to himself. Stepping over boxes and bags, he makes his way to the kitchen and grabs a bottled water. He tilts his head back, his throat bounces, as he takes a long swig. He struts over to the window with his lengthy titanium necklace swaying on his chest. The rays from the sun leaps through the blinds, kissing his custom diamond medillan, as he peeks through the blinds watching the oncoming traffic. He never noticed the unmarked car with government plates on it. It was sitting across the street for two hours. After looking out the window he yawns. “Uugghh, let me finish gettin’ this paper together.”

Dutchess veers into the parking lot in a blue trailblazer, parking at the front entrance of ‘So Fresh So Clean’ laundrymat. She climbs out of the truck and opens the back door on the driver’s side, removing two bulgy book bags, a box of Tide washing powder, Downy, and bleach. A woman holds the door open for her, as she totes everything inside, placing it next to the washing machine. She unzips one of the bulgy book bags and empties the clothes into the coin operated washer, placing coins into it. She flips open her Nextel and hits speed dial, calling Pirelli’s number. The phone rings and goes striaght to the voicemail.

“***Why the hell he’s not answering the phone? He usually answers my call. I hope there’s nothin’ wrong.***” She calls the number again receiving no answer. “***Maybe he’s tryna get the money together***.” Flipping the phone closed, she takes a seat at a table next to the window. She grabs an Ebony magazine off the table on the side of her and flicks through the pages, occassionally glimpsing out of the window. A Nissan turns into the parking lot pulling beside the Trailblazer.

Donnavan climbs out of the Nissan wearing a dingy blue khaki suit, carrying a bulgy book bag similar to the two that Dutchess has. Seeing him make his approach, Dutchess drops the magazine on the table and struts to the washer pretending like she is checking her laundry. Donnavan stops the washer beside hers, feigning like he doesn't know her, placing his book bag on the floor besides hers. "How you doin' miss?" Donnavan greeted.

"I'm doing okay," Dutchess replied. "Is anyone using this washer?"

"Naw, go ahead, help yo' self."

Donnavan opens the book bag and removes a small amount of clothing, dropping them into the washer. They discreetly exchange their book bags. Dutchess removes the clothing from the washer and throws them into the dryer. None of the customers noticed the drug transaction that just took place. Dutchess gains the attention of the woman who held the door open for her.

"Excuse me miss, can you keep an eye on my clothes until I get back? I have to rush to the school and pick up my kids," Dutchess lied.

"That's no problem, I understand, trust me I got three kids of my own. Besides, I'll be here for a minute anyway," the woman informed, with a friendly smile on her face.

"Thanks, I really appreciate it," Dutchess thanked, picking up the book bag that Donnavan sat beside her.

"A'ight sir, see you later."

"A'ight ma'am," Donnavan smiled, sliding the book bag that contains 15 kilograms of cocaine. The woman stares out of the window as Dutchess places the book bag into the back seat of the truck. "***For her to have kids she still got a nice shape. It doesn't look like she ever had kids***," the woman pondered, wishing that she could say the same about herself. Dutchess pulls out of the parking lot with approximately a half million dollars in cash. Donnavan paid her for the 15 kilograms in full and paid his debt.

Considering the fact that Pirelli did not answer the phone, Dutchess circles the block several times, analyzing her surroundings. She pulls into the driveway parking behind Pirelli's Ford Focus that he uses for his trapper. Dutchess and Pirelli never drive anything flashy to the safe house.

Dutchess grabs the book bag out of the back seat. She steps into the house and drops the bag on the floor in anger, staring at a sleeping Pirelli. He has a duffel bag full of money under his head, using it for a pillow, with money scattered all over the floor beside the couch.

"Pirelli!" Dutchess shouts his name, standing in the doorway. He awakes from his sleep, startled by the sound of Dutchess' harsh voice.

"Huh, what?"

"What you doing? You know we gotta have this money counted and ready for Franko," Dutchess scolded. She glances around the room at all the duffel bags and unorganized bundles of money. She looks at her watch. "Shit! It's one thirty, that mean we only got two hours to count the rest of this money, damn Pirelli. How far did you get?" she asked. His forehead crinkles as he ponders, trying to remember where he left off.

"Damn, I loss count."

"Shit! How the fuck we suppose to count three point five million dollars in the next two hours, shit! Start countin' I'ma get the other money machine." Dutchess retrieves the other electronic money counting machine. Moving quickly they feed the machines. The rustling and ticking sound of the money machines is the only sound that can be heard.

A hour passes by and their still two million dollars away from their targeted number. Suddenly Pirelli's money machine jams. "Damn!" frustrated, he removes the money trying to get it back on track. Unfortunately he is unable to get it to work properly. "Shit! We really in trouble now. This one broke down on me." Dutchess glances at her watch.

"Damn, we only got one hour to have this shit ready. Start countin' it by hand," Dutchess suggested.

"What! Count it by hand, is you crazy?"

"You heard me, I didn't stutter."

"How I'm suppose to count all this money by hand by myself, it's impossible for us to finish countin' this money in the next hour," Pirelli proclaimed.

"You not doing it by yo' self." Dutchess grabs her cell phone. "I'm callin' the whole team. Nothin' else moves until this is done."

"Well, lets do this," Pirelli added, flicking through a bundle of money, moving faster than a bank teller.

ONE WEEK LATER

T-Mac climbs into the pearl white Cadillac truck meeting Pirelli in their usual spot, down the block from his mother's house. Dope heads traverses the block trying to come up with a hustle to support their addiction. A slender built man in his mid-thirties walks up to the passenger's side of the truck knocking on the window, collecting T-Mac's attention. He presses the power button on the door panel lowering the window slightly.

"What?" T-Mac said, looking at the man as he flexes his jaw muscles from side to side with snot leaking from his nose.

"Yo' T-Mac, I thought you w-was gon' give me a wake up." The man said while scratching his thick nappy beard. Pirelli begins to feel uncomfortable knowing that he is riding dirty and that the jump out boys can pull up on him at anytime. Dutchess warned Pirelli over and over about riding dirty in his truck. A young blackmale driving a sixty thousand dollar truck with large rims and a banging system is quick to be stereotyped and pulled over.

"Man don't you see me tryna take care of some business," T-Mac stated, glaring at a fiending dopefiend

Rick. "Man get yo' dopefiend ass away fro-."

Errrk! A black van pulls up recklessly with its side door sliding open. Dopefiend Rick sprints through someone's yard hauling ass. Pirelli moves quickly, but not quick enough. He stares at the group of tamed sharks aiming a chopper (M & P 15T) and high powered handguns, wearing blue bandannas, concealing their facial features. They surround the truck gripping their guns with their hands laced in black leather hitters.

"Get the fuck out the truck bitch ass niggas! Before I blow y'all muthafuckin' wigs back!" One of the armed men barked, aiming inside the truck. Pirelli holds the long 357 Magnum in his hand between the console and the driver's seat.

"***I should take one of these niggas with me***," Pirelli thinks to himself, ready to die for his shit. A vision of Erica and his boys flashes in his head. He lets go of the pistol seeing that he is out numbered. "***I ain't about to die for this materialistic shit***." Pirelli lets go of the gun and unlocks the door. One of the gunmen snatches Pirelli out of the truck at gun point. He smacks the shit out of him with the pistol. "Aaw shit, muthafucka!" Pirelli cursed, grimacing in pain.

"Give me this hoe ass nigga!" The gunmen yanks the two platinum pieces off his neck. "Take that watch off too," he said in a raspy voice. Pirelli can hear T-Mac on the other side of the truck groaning in pain. Pirelli removes his watch and hands it to the gunman. "Now lay on yo' stomach and count to a hundred," he snarled. Pirelli follows the man's instructions feeling humiliated in front of the whole neighborhood. All sorts of thoughts races through his mind, as he lay on the ground with a throbbing headache.

"***These niggas fucked up if they let me live to see anotha day***." While lying on the ground Pirelli notices someone peeking out their window watching all the commotion.

Errrk! Errrk! The gunmen pull off in Pirelli's Cadillac truck with two kilos, two platinum chains, an Icklink watch, $60,000.00 in cash, and his favorite pistol that he nicknamed 'Solve 'em'. They set him back close to $200,000.00 without the truck. T-Mac lays on the ground rocking back and forth holding his swollen lip, looking like Eddie Murphy in the movie "The Nutty Professor."

"Hoe ass niggas hit me in my mouth," T-Mac complained. Pirelli recognizes something different about T-Mac, all of his rose gold jewelry is gone.

"***Damn, they fucked yo' lip up***." Pirelli wants to say, but he keeps the comment to himself.

Pirelli is heated, but at the same time he feels good. Not because they let him live. He is happy it was them instead of the police. He would rather die on the streets than to go back to the pentientiary, sitting around a bunch of men telling their war stories and bragging about what they claim they had or got on the streets.

"Dawg you a'ight?" T-Mac inquired, rising from the ground holding his lip.

"Yeah, I'm good. Who got a phone around here? I need to call a cab."

"Come on, we can go to mom's house and use the phone," T-Mac suggested. For some reason the whole block is quiet.

"That's cool, let's bounce."

THREE HOURS LATER

A loud thunderous sound reverberates on Claremont where Pirelli and T-Mac was robbed. The block is full of activity and back to normal. Everyone glimpses over their shoulders searching trying to see where the sound is coming from. It's a sound that everybody in the hood is familiar with, but they never heard anything like this before.

A black BMW 760 rounds the corner driving reckless on 24 inch chrome Varance wheels beating hard with dark tinted windows. Tupac's "Picture Me Rollin'" rips through the subwoofers bouncing against the pavement. The chrome rims sparkles in the semi-darkened streets. Micole stands outside on the porch in a pair of low rise, hip hugging, bootylicious jeans with the red elastic of her thong exposed. She stares at the BMW closely, along with everyone else on the block. The BMW stops in front of T-Mac's mother's house. A man sitting in a lawn chair on T-Mac's mother's front porch, rises from his seat in curiousity.

The door to the BMW pops open and Pirelli climbs out of the car wearing a long thick platinum chain, with an iced out medillan the size of a hockey puck. His diamond sprayed Dibur watch glistens as he tucks his brand new nickel plated 357 Magnum in his waistband.

"W-What up man? W-Who you lookin' for?" the man inquired. Pirelli looks at him remembering him from earlier, when they were being robbed. The man stares at him paranoid like he want to run.

"I'm lookin' for T-Mac." Pirelli replies, picking up a bad vibe. Dopefiend Rick glances at the brand new BMW that Pirelli purchased through his personal car dealer. He never has to worry about the paper work or the IRS getting involved. He dropped over a hundred grand on the BMW like it wasn't shit to it.

"H-Hold up, I'll get him." Dopefiend Rick said. He walks into the house through the side door. Pirelli leans back in the leather interior glancing at his diamond bezeled watch. Pirelli starts feeling that vibe again and wonders what the hell is taking T-Mac so long to come out of the house. T-Mac struts out of the door and jumps into the car with Pirelli.

"Damn joe, you clownin' ain't you?"

"You know how it go baby. Big thangs poppin' and little thangs stoppin'," Pirelli retorted.

"You came back at these hatin' ass niggas." T-Mac stated through his swollen lips, grimacing in pain.

"I ain't came back yet. I gotta set an example or niggas gon' think I'm soft."

"I feel you."

"I just came to let you know that I got you tomorrow. I'ma hit you with two bricks so you can make up for that loss you took."

"Aaw, good lookin' out Joe." T-Mac thanked him. "Those stupid ass niggas didn't even pat me down. I had twenty five stacks tucked in my pants."

"Damn Joe."

"Yo', I'ma pull out of here. I'll holla at you tomorrow."

"A'ight cool. I'll be at moms house all day." They slap hands doing a GD handshake showing each other love. T-Mac exits the car going inside of his mother's house. The car system rumbles as Pirelli pulls off turning the corner. He never notices the car moving behind him at a fast pace, until it veers into the right lane trying to pull beside him. Heavy traffic crosses at the intersection giving him no where to go.

"***Fuck, I got somethin' for them mafuckas***." He elevates the 357 Magnum with his finger on the trigger, aiming at the blue PT Cruiser. Before he could pull the trigger, he recognizes three beautiful females waving, trying to flag him down. Being familiar with the passenger, Pirelli lowers his gun sitting it in his lap. Micole shouts from the passenger's side.

"Pull in the gas station." Pirelli zips into the gas station with the three females lingering behind him.

"***I know this young girl don't call herself tryna get at me.***" He thinks to himself as he watches her make her way to his car. She jumps into the car looking like Ciara with a body like Serena Williams. Her Babyphat perfume fills the air.

"I know you probably wondering what a young lady like me want with you." Micole said in her soft voice, sounding like Michel'le.

"Yeah, you right, I am a little curious," Pirelli replied.

"I'm gon' put it to you like this." Micole peers through the windsheild at her friends sitting in the car. Pirelli tries to read her mind. "I seen what happened earlier when you got robbed."

"That was you lookin' out the window?" he asked.

"Yep, that was me. I even know who set you up."

"What!" Pirelli blurted.

"I know who set you up. But you have to promise me that you didn't hear it from me."

"I promise I want mention yo' name. Tell me who did it."

"T-Mac set you up," she informed.

"How you know that?" Pirelli asked.

"Because he the same one that set my brother up to get robbed two years ago. But you got lucky."

"Why you say that?"

"Because they killed my brother. But nobody can prove that T-Mac had somethin' to do with it."

"So still tell me how you know that he was the one that had me set up?" Pirelli repeated.

"Because thirty minutes after you left the same black van pulled behind his mother's house. Four dudes got out of the van."

Everything is starting to make sense to Pirelli. "Dopefiend Rick was in on it too. That was T-Mac's way of keepin' me distracted until the van pulled up. That's why that dopefiend muthafucka was actin' all nervous when I pulled up to T-Mac's mother's crib." Pirelli puts it all together.

"Check this out baby. You don't have to tell me no mo'. Huh, take this." Pirelli hands her a thousand dollars for her information. "Look, you take that and buy you somethin' nice. Play like we never had this conversation. Is that understood?" Pirelli asked, looking at the young lady, staring in her eyes.

"It's our secret. I'll never talk about this day ever again. Just make sure he pays for what he did to my brother."

"Don't worry about it, I got you. Gon' and join your friends."

Micole leans over and kisses Pirelli on the cheek. She wishes that she was a little bit older. "Thank you." She hops out of the car and joins her friends. Pirelli smashes out of the parking lot contemplating, pulling his plan together.

THE NEXT DAY

Pirelli struts to T-Mac's old school Chevy Caprice dressed in a black tailor made Giorgio Armani suit, with his hands buried in his pants pockets. His Armani dress shoes drums against the pavement. He jumps into the car joining T-Mac.

"What up P?" T-Mac greeted, bobing his head to 50 cent's 'Many Man'.

"What up?" They shake hands curving their fingers at the tips.

"What you all dressed up for? You on yo' way to a funeral or somethin'?"

"Somethin' like that," Pirelli replied, removing a paper bag from under his blazer. He tosses the bag into T-Mac's lap. The bag rustles as he looks inside of it, seeing a large amount of money. A look of confusion forms on his face. "That's for yo' mans you had rob me. That's the twenty five thousand that they forgot. Next time you have somebody do a job, have them do it right."

"Hold up. What you talkin' about P?" T-Mac inquired, playing dumbfounded. Pirelli reaches into his inside pocket of his blazer, pulling out a Zino Platinum cigar and a lighter. He strikes the lighter lighting his cigar. He exits the car blowing out a cloud of smoke. T-Mac hears the sound of a pump clacking. He shifts his gaze to the driver's window wide eyed staring into the barrel of a chrome six shoot Iceberg pump. T-Mac springs back with a frightened look etched on his face. Every bone in his body claps.

"Which one you want, a open casket or a closed casket?" Ducthess asked, in a gruff tone, squeezing the trigger of the canon. Boooom! The loud unrestrained sound of the pump startles the bystanders, catching them offguard. A series of screams slices through the air as innocent bystanders zigzag running for safety. The scuffling sound of feet slides across the ground. A haze of gunsmoke is the only thing that is in between T-Mac and Dutchess. Brain matter and shards of glass is scattered on the floor and the passenger's seat.

Dutchess prances in her high heel pumps with her eyes faintly visible behind the lenses of her Dolce & Gabbana sunglasses. A crisp breeze sweeps the air, lifting Dutchess' skirt revealing her shapely legs and thighs as she prances in a casual manner. The smell of her Euphoria Calvin Klein perfume trails behind her, lingering in the air. A person would never think that a woman as beautiful as Dutchess could be so dangerous and deadly. She cuts inbetween two houses disappearing into the alley.

Chapter Eleven

A white semi-truck bearing the name Smith Beverage & Co, moves down 69th and Western, pulling in front of Treatz corner store. A small car lot is located on the other side of the block. A group of teenagers hangs around in front of a barbershop slanging rocks. One of the teenager struts briskly to the curb and picks up a crumpled up Dorito bag. He removes a small sack of rocks out of it, and meets up with an approaching car, stopping in the middle of the street conducting a small drug transaction.

Big Homie stands on the side of the barbershop with his hands tucked in the pockets of his navy blue Pelle Pelle coat, fingering the trigger of his P229 semi-automatic handgun. His long french braids hangs out of his skull cap. He scans his surroundings with vapors billowing from his face.

Big Homie is a member of the Gangster Disciples who has been living in the neighborhood as far as he can remember. He watches the driver of the semi-truck unload a variety of sodas, placing them on a dolly pushing them into Treatz corner store.

Treatz used to be owned by the Arabs until a robbery took place, leaving the owner and his wife in a blood bath. The store has been closed for years. Everybody that had it ended up dead.

Dutchess purchased the corner store through a corrupt real estate broker. The broker set up the paper work so nothing would lead back to her. He also set up the paper work to keep the IRS from investigating the purchase exceeding more than $10,000.00.

Lately Big Homie has been noticing a lot of flashy cars pulling up to the corner store staying for long periods of time. All of the unusual activity causes him to become suspicious.

"I know they sellin' weight out that mafucka. How they gon' just come and set up shop in our hood like that? It ain't going down like that, hell naw. " Big Homie thought to himself watching the uniformed driver climb back into the truck pulling off. Big Homie walks off with ice crunching underneath his Timbs.

Dutchess steps from behind the bulletproof booth and locks the doors joining old man Bennie and Pirelli. Bennie is an old head who served 15 years in Stateville state prison for first degree murder. Bennie is 6'2 with a muscular built. Bennie is Pirelli's mother's ex-boyfriend who helped raise him for the first 10 years of his life. Bennie would remind you of Ving Rhames from the movie 'Baby Boy'.

Dutchess has been dealing with Franko for nine months and this is the third shipment he has sent her. She stands beside Pirelli as he grabs a six pack of Coca Cola. He cuts the can open inspecting the 12 ounces of cocaine that is compressed in the Coca Cola can. Each six pack contains 2 kilograms of uncut cocaine. Franko sends her 250 kilo-grams of cocaine every ninety days. After ninety days, he contacts her to check her status. If she's done before the ninety days, she calls him.

Dutchess notices a piece of plastic hanging out of a Diet Coca Cola 12 pack box. Curious, she rips the box open, removing a zip-loc bag.

"What the hell is this?" She asked, holding the package towards Pirelli. He shrugs his shoulders.

"I don't know." He opens the package. He stares at multiple finger sized packages wrapped in ballon wrappings.

"I know exactly what it is," Bennie stated, looking at the package. "It's a kilo of heroin." Dutchess reaches inside the other 12 pack boxes pulling out 20 kilograms of heroin.

"What the fuck Franko expect for me to do with this? We don't have not one heroin customer on our line. I don't know nothin' about heroin, I never sold this shit a day in my life. I don't even know what a kilo of this shit go for on the streets. I don't know where to begin," she stressed.

"They go for eighty thousand a piece," Bennie blurted.

"What! Eighty thousand. How I'm suppose to move all this shit in the next ninety days?"

"Maybe you should call Franko and see if he sent you the wrong thing," Pirelli suggested.

"I can't call Franko. He made it clear to me not to call him under any circumstances, except if I'm done. He said that's the only exception. If I don't follow his instructions he'll stop my supply," Dutchess explained.

"That's some serious shit right there. That heroin will make a nigga rich over night. Once you cut it up it's worth even more." Bennie informed, telling her the little that he does know. Dutchess knows it has to be cut if it's coming from Franko. Everything he sends her is always pure. If she doesn't cut her cocaine, its purity would kill anybody who comes across it. She has to have her own kilos wrapped and re-stamped after receiving her shipment.

Pirelli massages his goatee in deep thoughts looking skyward. "Mmmm, I think I might have the answer to our problem." Pirelli flips open his cell phone and scrolls through the numbers he saved in his phone.

Erica sings along with J-Holiday's 'Put You To Bed' as she cruises down the expressway on her way home from work. Erica goes home everyday after work and takes a nap before picking up the kids from her mother's house. She maneuvers her Audi A8L exiting the expressway. She thinks about the trip that her and Pirelli took to the Bahamas and the gifts he showered her with. She became accustom to their extravagant lifestyle and stopped pressuring him about when he's going to stop selling drugs.

The custom ring tone escaping Erica's cellular phone embraces her attention. She looks at the number flashing on the screen. "I wonder what Tiera want. She knows that I'm usually sleep at this time." She answers the phone. "Hello." Erica holds the phone to her ear, listening to the sniffling sound of Tiera. "Girl what's wrong with you? Why you cryin'?" Erica questioned with genuine concern.

"M-Me and Rob got into it again. H-He hit me in front of Man-Man. I can't stand his punk ass. I'm done fuckin' with him," Tiera exclaimed.

"Girl you always say that when y'all get into it."

"I mean it this time. Don't nobody hit me in front of my damn son."

"I'ma come and pick you and Man-Man up, I'm on my way to mama's house to pick up the kids. Y'all need to get away from there for awhile. You need to get some time to yourself and figure out what it really is that you want in life."

"I'm straight Erica. I don't wanna invade you and Pirelli's privacy," Tiera protested.

"Girl I don't wanna hear that mess. You ain't invading our privacy, we got a lot of room over here. You and Man-Man can stay in the guest room, so pack y'all stuff."

"Maybe I do need to get away from here for awhile. I'm so tired of running into all the wrong men. Sometimes I wish I had a man like Pirelli. You lucky to have a man like him, who knows how to treat a woman."

"Don't get it twisted. We have our share of problems too. We just work our problems out and got an understanding," Erica replied.

"I wish me and Cakes could get back together, but he to damn hoeish," Tiera stated.

"You know a man gon' be a man. It's in their nature to cheat." Erica replied, staring in the rearview mirror at an unmarked car that has been trailing behind her every since she exited the expressway. It's the second time in the last week she noticed that car. The first time she thought maybe they thought she was somebody else. "Let me get off this phone girl. I'll talk to you later on when I come get y'all, so make sure you be ready." Erica said, keeping a close eye on the car.

"Okay."

"A'ight, bye, bye." Erica presses end and tosses the phone into the passenger's seat. She makes a couple turns and the car turns off.

The custom paint on the Range Rover gleams as it trails behind Cakes' box Chevy Caprice, chopping on its chrome 26 inch rims. He leads the Range Rover to the Rockweil Garden's Projects. The projects was torn down and reconstructed, it use to be highrise buildings. The neighborhood is prodominantly Vicelords and Travelers.

Pirelli and Cakes arranged a meeting for him to meet with Cakes' crony Magyk. (Magic) Magyk is a five star universal elite of the Travelers and a major heroin dealer. He served an 81 month federal sentence in the past and is now back on top of his game.

The mundane sound of traffic floods the streets. The entire neighborhood is full of activity. A group of thugs stands on the block on point, wearing leather coats and hoodies, shielding themselves from the cold wind. Thin layers of snow covers the grass.

Pirelli and Dutchess are seated in the Range Rover scanning the group of serious faces that seems to be mean mugging them, with their hands buried in their pockets.

Cakes steps out of his car and greets all the young soldiers with their fitted caps tilted slightly to the left. He struts to a banana yellow Hummer H2 with its windows foggy. He knocks on the driver's side window gainning the attention of the driver. The door swings open slowly and a large cloud of marijuana smoke floats in the air. Magyk steps out of the Hummer standing 6'1, sporting a yellow Laker's fitted cap broke deep to the left, with his long french briads snaking out of it, resting on his shoulders. He embraces Cakes with a half hug. His diamond Techno-marine Hummer watch twinkles on his wrist, being kissed by the sun. He looks over at Dutchess and Pirelli with pinkisk red eyes, gone off that hydro. They saunter to the Range Rover and Dutchess steps out of the truck in her tight fitting Escada jeans and a pair of Cesare Paciotti suede studded boots turning heads. She climbs into the back seat letting Magyk and Pirelli sit in the front seat. Dutchess doesn't like anyone to sit behind her. Cakes join her in the back seat.

"Magyk, this is Pirelli my man I've been tellin' you about. And Pirelli this is my man Magyk who can help you with yo' problem," Cakes introduces them. They shake hands nodding their heads.

"What up Joe?" they greet each other.

"Oh yeah, my bad. Magyk this beautiful woman right her, name is Dutchess," Cakes informed. "Dutchess huh. How you doing baby girl?" Magyk greeted, staring into Dutchess' green and grayish hypnotic eyes. Dutchess nods her head without saying one word. "So, what's the proposition you got for me?" Magyk asked.

"I got a deal you can't refuse," Pirelli stated.

"And what's that?"

"I'm willing to give you bricks of heroin for seventy stacks a piece and double whatever you buy. You can owe me the other half, but I need to know if you can handle the load?" Magyk looks at Pirelli as if he had just insulted him.

"You must don't know why they call me Magyk," he replied.

"Naw, I'm not aware of that. You tell me why they call you Magyk?"

"They call me Magyk because everything I touch, I make it disappear," he snaps his fingers, "Just like that."

"So what about if somethin' happen to my merch?" Pirelli inquired.

"See that house across the street?" Magyk pauses for a moment as Pirelli locks his focuses on the house.

"Yeah I see it."

"Up there in that attic I got a sniper on point twenty four seven. Five-o don't even come through here, we got this shit on lock."

Pirelli nods his head liking Magyk's style and confidence. Magyk reaches into his inside coat pocket, pulling out a business card. His diamond five point star medillan sparkles, slightly exposed underneath his leather coat.

"Here take this. That is my number. Whenever you ready just hit me and give me the instructions and I'm there." Magyk stated. Dutchess' eyes glides over to a young frail boy no older than eleven years old, riding on a four wheeler with 22 inch triple gold wired Dayton rims, heading in their direction. He hops off the four wheeler holding a cellular phone in his hand with a baby nine millimeter tucked in his waistband. He taps on the passenger's window gainning Maygk's attention. Magyk rolls down the window.

"What up Mo?" Magyk said calling him what all

Travelers and Vicelords call each other.

"You got a phone call Mo." Magyk grabs the cell phone and rolls up the window.

"Holla at me," he answered the phone. "A'ight Mo. One." He hangs up the phone. "Yo' I'ma holla at y'all. Bring me five of those thangs. I got three fifty waitin' on y'all, so that mean I'm expectin' ten of those thangs."

"A'ight, I'ma hit you in a minute," said Pirelli.

"A'ight Joe." They bump fist and Magyk climbs out of the truck continuing with his business.

Ice sits in his house chatting it up with Chill. "Dig this Joe, shit is fucked up in the streets," Ice stressed.

"What Baptiste talkin' about?"

"He on some other shit right now. Call that bitch Dutchess and see what she on."

"And what I'm supposed to say?" Chill questioned.

"Ask her what up on that work, she expecting my call. I ran into the bitch a while ago in traffic," Ice proclaimed.

"A'ight," Chill stated unbelievingly. Chill takes out his new Nextel. Chirp! Chirp!

"What up Chill?" Chirp!

"Yo' my man Ice tryna holla at you." Chirp!

"Just come down to Treatz, I got y'all. Chirp!

"A'ight shorty, one."

"You heard her Joe, lets roll," Chill said grabbing his Avirex jacket from the couch.

"Hold up real quick, I gotta grab somethin'." Ice runs to his bedroom grabbing the wire transmitter from off the dresser. He places the new state of the art audio and video device around his neck. No one would suspect that the platinum chain with its large diamond shaped medillan is really a wire.

Ice exits the house wearing baggy black Roca wear jeans, a red, black, green, and yellow Bob marley T-shirt, and crispy black Italian Air Force Ones. He throws on his matching black Pelle Pelle jacket as he exits the door. Chill is leaning against the Cadillac XLR, in denim Enyce pants. His blue and black Polo shirt flutters lightly in the wind, where it is exposed from his unzipped jacket. Eeerp! Eeerp! Ice hits the locks letting him in.

They arrive at Treatz. There is a lot of traffic going in and out of the building. Customers walk out with soda cans and bags of chips, with smiles plastered on their faces.

Ice and Chill struts inside the building. An off duty police officer on Dutchess' payroll pats them down,

searching for wires and weapons. Ice's heart skips a beat as the guard runs his hand across his chest. He relaxes moments later when the guard signals to a worker behind the glass that their clean. They are led into a secret back room. Butt-naked women wearing white masks remove cocaine from packages, placing it in various labeled chip bags.

The air in the room is cold, which causes the women with mocha skin tones cherry tomato sized nipples to stay hard. "You see that Chill, that bitch winked at me."

"Which one?"

"The one with the tiger prints on her inner thigh, with the trimmed heart shaped pussy hairs," Ice stated excitedly.

"Damn Joe, you stalking hard to notice all that," Chill clowned, as they are escorted into the next room. Dutchess is seated behind the table. She stands to greet them in tight Babyphat spandex pants that hugs against the contours of her pussy lips.

"***Damn that shit look like it's throwing up the Black Power sign***," Ice lustfully thought to himself. Ice and Chill takes a seat right across from her. Ice sits upright in his chair, remembering not to slouch. The agent had warned him, not to slouch, because dooing so could potentially distort the video feed. His job is simple. All he has to do is get her to agree on a price for the drugs, then say the code words, and the troops would rush in. It would buy him six months of freedom.

"I appreciate this Dutchess, I didn't think you was gon' see me," Ice truthfully stated.

"I wasn't, I was thinking about spinning you at first. You know how you did me." Her voice dripping with sarcasm.

"It wasn't even like that," he lied.

"Un-huh, whatever, but like I said, I ain't into childish games, so what can do for you?" she asked impatiently.

"I need four of them thangs." She rolls her eyes. Her bodyguard with the Mr. Clean bald head behind her laughs.

"Nigga stop playin'. I don't do nothin' less than five. I'm using them scales they weigh the obese with," she boasted.

"What's the ticket?" Ice asked.

"Well since it's a drought season, I'ma need twenty three a piece." Dutchess watches his facial expression change.

"What! Twenty three, I can't get it cheaper?" He seems to be talking to his chain. Before she can make a counter offer, he spaeks to his chest again, raising his voice. "I said, I can't get it cheaper?"

"What the fuck!" Dutchess screams as the door blasts from its hinges. Agents flood the room with their weapons drawn.

"Get on the fucking floor now!" Dutchess and her bodyguard, and Chill are thrown forcefully to the floor.

"What the fuck is going on Ice!" Chill screamed, with his head mashed against the floor.

"Rat muthafucka!" Dutchess screams over and over. "You dead you funky rat muthafucka!"

Ice awakes from his dream smiling. He reaches out to his nightstand, and grabs the chain that the feds have given him. He has already used it to successfully set up one local drug dealer for practice. If things go smoothly for him, as they did in his dream, and his first trial run, he will have no problem staying on the streets. He was bugging out when he was told by the agent that he would receive a percentage from each bust. He looks over the Confidential Informant Brochure packet.

Dear Mr. Lewis,

Welcome to the Sell and Tell program (SAT for short) Earn a lucrative lifestyle by doing what you love to do best, selling drugs. Enjoy all the luxuries of the game, without the pain. In addition to your monthly payment, you will receive special access to thousands of recently seized cars, planes, houses, and boats. Our two tier program makes it easy to go from a regular CI, to a super CI, in as few as two years. Once you reach this status, and 95% of our participants do, you will begin to receive even greater rewards, including free medical and dental.

Send this form back today and receive two limited Edition DVD's, "Secrets from the greats," and how one man took down the mob and made super CI overnight. Hurry and don't delay, start your career today.

Ice sits the letter down. "Fuck they givin' me a license for this shit," he said to himself. He picks up the phone and calls Chill. "Aye Joe I need you to call Dutchess...Yeah it's urgent."

Dutchess grips the steering wheel to her 1984 Buick Limited moving through the heavy traffic on Interstate 94. The cold wind whistles through the slightly cracked window that is off track. The heater is on full blast comingling with the cold breeze, pouring into the car. Every since it started getting cold outside Dutchess hasn't had time to get it fixed.

For the last two weeks Dutchess has been short on her drug supply. She is wondering why Franko haven't gotten in contact with her. Franko usually call her in ninety days like clock work, if she is not finished. This is the first time he has ever been late with his phone call. It has been exactly 103 days and she hasn't heard anything. She has 4.3 million dollars of Franko's stashed at one of her safe houses.

Dutchess takes a detour through Lincolnwood making sure that no one is trailing her. She does this every time she goes home. She even removes the chip from her cellular phone so she can't be tracked by the government's satellite system. Deangelo is the only one that she communicates with on her home phone.

She pulls up on Crawford and parks her trap car. She jumps out of it and struts down the block, jumping into her Bentley coupe. She makes another detour jumping on Interstate 41, making her way to her 1.8 million dollar mediterranean style home in Skokie. Pulling up to her heated three car garage, she presses a button on a small device. The garage door ascends exposing her Range Rover, and her Volkswagon Phaeton. She pulls inside the garage parking beside her Range Rover. Automatically the door decends and it becomes dim. She steps out of the car being greeted by the smell of brand new rubber tires and fresh oil. She enters the luxurious residence through a door that leads to the kitchen. She steps across the heated marble floors making her way to the stainless steel refrigerator.

She tosses her leather Versace purse on the marble counter top island. The interior lights in the refrigerator shines on the floor as she grabs a cold bottled water. She tilts her head back taking a long swig of the water. After satisfying her thirst, she heads to her mastersuite.

Tiera turns off the shower with beads of water drizzling down her flawless carmel complexion. She steps onto the heated marble floor in the guest bathroom. It has been a week in a half since Tiera has been at Erica and Pirelli's house. Tiera is envious of Erica because she has something that she never had, a good man like Pirelli to take care of her and treat her like queen. Tiera woke up in the middle of the night on many different occassions walking pass Erica and Pirelli's mastersuite, hearing the gratifying sound of their sexual encounter, on her way to the bathroom. The sound of their love making would remind her of how lonely she is.

She dries herself off and wraps the towel around her naked shapely frame. The dry towel accentuates her curvaceous body, barely covering her round plump booty. She steps out of the bathroom barefooted, prancing like a black stallion. She turns the corner bumping into Pirelli. He struts behind her on his way to the mastersuite. Tiera intentionally drops her towel exposing her naked frame. Pirelli stops in his tracks staring in disbelief.

"Ooppss," she whispers, bending down doing an "All pussy in your face" pose. A paw print tattoo crawls up her thighs. She peeks through the eye opening senuous gap between her thighs, seeing the expression on Pirelli's face. She picks the towel up wrapping it back around her.

She walks off vanishing into the guestroom. Pirelli came close to dropping the jar of Dill pickles in his hand that he went to get out of the refrigerator for a pregnant Erica. He finds himself becoming aroused from the visual of Tiera standing in front of him butt naked. He shakes her image from his head and walks off. He never looked at Tiera in a sexual way before. He knows that was just the nature of man taking its course.

***"I think I betta keep it real with Erica and let her know about this. I noticed her lookin' at me a couple of times. Yeah think I betta gon' and tell her before it get out of hand.*"** Pirelli comes to a decision. He steps into the mastersuite holding the jar of pickles that Erica has been craving every since she came home from work. She lays on the bed rubbing her stomach, watching 'Love & Basketball' on DVD. "Baby I need to talk to you about somethin'. I don't know how t-"

"Oh baby come touch my stomach, hurry up, the baby is kicking." Erica shouts excitedly cutting Pirelli off. Pirelli sits on the edge of the bed rubbing her stomach gently. He feels the baby moving around.

"Damn baby. The baby act like she ready to come out of there now." He chuckles and the baby stops moving. He opens the jar of pickles and feeds it to Erica.

"Mmm," she takes a bite of it. "Baby what you need to talk to me about?" Erica asked, chewing on the pickle. Seeing the glow in Erica's eyes and considering her pregnancy, Pirelli decides it will not be a good time to tell her. The stress can cause her to have a miscarriage.

"I just been wantin' to tell you that I love you baby. I can't wait until we get married, like I promised you," he lied.

"I can't wait either baby. I've been thinking about that lately myself. After I drop this load our dream will come true. Me and Tiera was talking about how she is going to help me arrange the wedding." The sound of Tiera's name startles Pirelli.

"Oh yeah. I'm glad she is willing to be very supportive. Let me change into somethin' more comfortable baby, so I can sit back and enjoy this movie with you." Pirelli said, changing the subject. He changes his clothes and jumps into the bed cuddling up with the love of his life.

Duthcess is cuddled up underneath the Versace blanket in her king sized canopy bed, sleeping peacefully. The fire place crackles, illuminating the mastersuite, reflecting off the glass walls that gives her a beautiful view of Lake Michigan. Her house phone chimes awakening her from her sleep. She reaches for the phone knowing that it has to be Deangelo because he is the only person that has her number.

"Hello," she answers the phone in a weak voice, half sleep.

"Puedo hablar con nieve," a man speaks in spanish.

"What!" Dutchess shouts, unable to comprehend what the man is saying.

"Puedo hablar con nieve," the man replies in spanish.

"Whoever the fuck you is, I'll appreciate it if you stop playin' on my fuckin' PHONE!" Dutchess hangs up on the caller and balls back up under the blanket. The cordless phone rings over and over. Dutchess tries to ignore it, but the sound of it starts to irrate her. She snatches the phone in anger. "Didn't I say stop playin' on my fuckin' phone?" Dutchess snapped.

"Calm down my friend. That's not nice way to answer your phone." A man says in a rich spanish accent.

"Who the hell is this callin' my house at five o'clock in the fuckin' morning?"

"It's me, your good friend Franko." The fire crackles in the fireplace dancing in Dutchess' angry eyes.

"How the hell you get my numb-"

"Don't waste time askin' me that question. You know me have connections all over the country. Just come and open door my friend." Franko said cutting her off.

"What! Open my door." Dutchess rises from her bed slamming the phone down in anger. She throws on her silk nightgown and her leather Versace slippers. She reaches under the pillow grabbing her Glock .40. She struts briskly to the glass elevator, wearing an angry facial expression, looking like a baby devil. She peers through the glass elevator doors as it descends to the lower level of her residence. She exits the elevator sinking into the thick plush skyblue carpet, prancing across the livingroom. Glimpsing out the large picture window, she sees a maroon four door Lincoln Continental with three hispanic males sitting inside of it.

She opens the door gripping the handgun staring at Franko, who is standing in the doorway dressed in a pair of jeans that fits him just right and a pair of leather cowboy boots, with gold tips. Ducthess' arched eyebrows points to her cute little nose as she snaps on Franko. "What the fuck is wrong with you showing up at my damn house where I lay my head! I don't conduct no fuckin' business at my house!" Dutchess lets him inside the house before her nosey neighbors start peeking out of their windows.

The community she stays in is predominantly white and she is one of the very few blacks that lives in the area.

"Me ran into a slight problem, so me needed to talk to you face to face," Franko explained, picking up one of her expensive sculptures. "Nice place you have here Dutchess," Franko places the sculpture back on the ledge of her marble fireplace. His eyeballs browse around the house.

"I don't wanna hear that shit Franko, tell me why you're here?"

"Me came to thank you for your business and your loyalty to me and my people. Me sending you your regular and somethin' extra to show you my appreciation. Me people will be to pick up cash."

"I have your money for the heroin you sent too. You know I don't sell heroin. I never sold that shit before."

"You mean to tell me you sold all that heroin already?"

"Of course, what I suppose to do, hold on to it?" Dutchess replied looking into Franko's eyes.

"I'm very impressed, you passed my test. You never seem to amaze me."

"You know I'm a woman that's all about that paper," Dutchess said.

"Well my friend, the same rules apply, nothin' changes. Me guess I'll get going. Sorry for disturbing you and awakenin' you out of your sleep my friend. Me was in the neighborhood so I thought it would be disrespectful if I didn't drop by to say hello to my good friend." He opens the door and exits the house.

"Franko!" Dutchess called out.

"Yes my friend," Franko answered, turning around looking at Dutchess.

"Thank you." This is the first time he has ever seen Dutchess smile.

"Your welcome."

"One more thing Franko."

"What's that my friend?"

"Can you please not come to my home, I'll appreciate that," Dutchess asked respectfully.

"Me apologize Dutchess. It'll never happen again," Franko promised.

"Thank you."

"No problem." Franko winks his eye at her and flashes a friendly smile. He closes the door behind him. From that day Duchess finally realized that Franko has a lot of power. Franko is an experienced veteran who has been in the game for many of years. Dutchess returns to her mastersuite falling back into a peaceful sleep.

Chapter Twelve

THE WHITE CORRECTIONAL INSTITUTION

Carmen leans back on the bunk in the two woman cell, reading an Ebony magazine. Her cell mate Jalisa sits on the bottom bunk braiding her hair. Carmen was represented by attorney James Butler, one of the most powerful African-American attornies in the Midwest. Considering the fact that Carmen was in possession of 2 kilograms of cocaine, James Butler put a motion in to suppress the evidence for illegal search and procedure. The judge denied the motion along with Carmen's bail. The prosecutor argued to the judge that Carmen was a flight risk. So therefore Carmen remained in custody.

James Butler knew that he couldn't take Carmen case to trial. With an all white jury there was no way that he could prove beyond a reasonable doubt that the two kilograms found on Carmen's person didn't belong to her. He arranged to have lunch with the prosecutor and talked him into giving Carmen a 2 year plea bargain, which meant that she had to serve 1 year and do the other half on parole. Carmen took the plea so that she could hurry back home to her daughter.

Carmen hears the sound of footsteps and keys jingling

in the hallway, alerting her that a correctional officer is on the deck. The footsteps stop and the guard stands at the door to her cell. The correctional officer shuffles through a small stack of mail. The officer kneels down and slides two letters under the door and walks off delivering the mail to the other inmates.

Jalisa rises to her feet hoping that some of the mail belongs to her. She picks up the two letters and scans the front of them. A look of disappointmeht registers on her face as she hands the letters to Carmen.

"Here you go Carmen. I guess somebody has some love out there. I ain't got no mail in almost two weeks," Jalisa complained. Carmen reads the front of the letters and opens the one with Tyrone's name on it.

Dear Carmen,

How are you holding up in that hell hole? I know it ain't easy baby, but you got to stay strong. I want you to know that I miss the hell out of you and I can't wait for you to come home. Renee is doing real good. Your friend Dutchess gave your mother some money so that she can place Renee in an art class. Renee always asks about you. I pick her up from school everyday and drop her off to your mother's house. I found a job the other day making ten dollars a hour. I spend time with our daughter every weekend. Renee wanted me to send you the picture that you promised her you was going to look at before you left out the door and never made it back. I couldn't believe the picture when I first looked at it. God always try to give us signs. Well, I'm going to close this letter.

Love Always,
Tyrone

Carmen unfolds the drawing that her daughter drew and her eyes stretches open in disbelief, as she stares at the artwork. Renee drew a picture of a man holding a kane wearing a badge around his neck and a stick figure of her mother in handcuffs. Carmen was so shocked that she placed the letter from Dutchess on the bed and fell into deep thoughts.

Big Homie has been watching Treatz corner store religiously for the past few months. At first he wasn't sure about the business conducted behind them walls, but when he seen several local drug dealers coming in and out, he knew what time it was.

"***Fuck this, they gettin' too much paper***," he mulled, rubbing his hands together to beat the cold weather. They was making so much money that he brought his childhood friend Pain along. Pain is another big black ugly dude from the area. "This is our hood, they got us fucked up settin' up shop on our block, and we ain't gettin' paid." Pain who is usually drunk as he is now nods his rock shaped head in agreement.

Dressed in all black, the duo watches from across the street as Bennie walks to his dark green Cadillac DTS. The snow crunches softly underneath his Stacy Adams. Just as he inserts his key, he feels something a little colder than the weather press up against his bald head. Bennie holds his hands in the air dangling his keys. "Here man you can have the ride."

"I don't want the ride, we want what's inside," Big Homie barked in a raspy Ja Rule like manner. The mention of the word "we" let Bennie know that this situation is a little more serious than he thought. He glances at the accomplice sizing him up. He is large, but Bennie feels he can take him if need be. They walk Bennie back to the door.

"I ain't got the code," Bennie lied. Whack! Big Homie strikes him in back of the head with the Glock . 40.

"Maybe that will help you remember." It did too, cause soon as Bennie gets off the ground he wastes no time entering the four digit code disalarming the system. A car goes down the street startling the robbery in progress. The car slows down in front of them. "Walk this nigga in P, I'll handle this," Big Home instructed.

"Excuse me," the white man said rolling down the window of his Audi. "Sorry to bother you, we'er lost. Can you give me directions to Michigan Avenue?"

"Yeah, just make a left up there on Western, go down to the light, and make a right," Big Homie replied quickly to get the man and his wife moving.

"Thanks buddy." Big Homie glances at the out of town Alabama plates as the car pulls off. "Wow, he was friendly," the man said to his wife pulling off. He had no idea

that Big Homie had sent him to a dead end street with nothing but hungry vultures. Blocka! Blocka! The gunshots seizes Big Homie's attention as he runs towards the door of Treatz.

A cloud of light slices through the darkness, outlining various tombstones that are scattered all over the cementary, glazed with snow. A gray automobile moves slowly along the pathway. The car halts near a gravesite. A woman steps out of the car dressed in a black lengthy leather coat, holding a red rose. She leaves the engine running with the headlights shining.

She kneels down in front of the tombstone, sticking the stem of the rose in the ground with tears flowing freely down her beautiful unblemished face. Even though reality has sunk into her head, she's still having a hard time believing that the man she loves dearly is gone. Ever since he was murdered her life haven't been the same. Her heart suffers in pain daily. She's taking everything out on the criminal's everyday that she is at work. She can't count all of the sleepless nights that she has had every since he has been absent from the world. With her french manicured hands, she dashes the tears away from her eyes.

"I miss you so much, this is all my fault. If it wasn't for me you would still be here. I know who did this to you and he's going to pay for it. I know God say thou shall not kill, but I have to do what I have to do. It's an eye for an eye," she spoke to the dead man as if he can hear her. She rises to her knees being attack by the cold late night breeze. She climbs into the car with one thing on her mind, vengence.

Pain's gun slides across the floor to Big Homie's feet, as he enters the shop. Moments before, Bennie has just gorilla smacked the shit out of Pain knocking the pistol from his hand.

Blocka! Blocka! Bennie hits Pain directly in his forehead. Big Homie returns two wild shots, one of them catching Bennie in the shoulder. The powerful impact knocks him through the glass counter, as shards of glass fly every where shattering on the concrete floor. Big Homie rushes over to Bennie. He shoots him two more times in the chest. Bennie's body bounces on the floor like a basketball. Big Homie turns to check the register. He wasn't leaving out empty handed. Blocka! Blocka! With his last ounce of strength before dying, Bennie shoots Big Homie in the back of the head introducing him to death.

Dutchess steps out of the bathroom with a dry towel wrapped around her body. She prances to the walk in closet searching through her large selection of attire. Olivia invited her to Kennytha's boat party. Olivia was complaining about how Dutchess has been treating her like a stranger every since she quit working at the check cashing place. Dutchess accepted her invitation knowing that this is her chance to get close to the man who is allegedly responsible for the assassination of her beloved father.

Finally dressed to impress, she grabs her cellular phone noticing a missed call. She looks at the number. ***"I must've missed Deangelo's call when I was in the shower. I'll just call him tomorrow,"*** She thought to herself before exiting her luxurious residence.

The party on the boat has no signs of ending soon, as Dutchess, Bianca, and Olivia steps out of the Range Rover. The massive yacht is perched just off the lake, and requires a speed-boat to reach it. Even the speed-boat is luxurious looking in all green with a golden stripe.

Bianca squints her eyes looking at the triple deck white monster in the water. "Damn papi doin' it way big," she commented, stepping onto the boat. The water isn't the only thing that's wet, as her gold digging glands goes into overtime. Dutchess stays silent as they coast towards the yacht. Her mind is on other things beside partying. The sailor reaches the yacht and helps them onto a lower level.

Every baller, shot caller, and professional hoe is in attendance. Bianca quickly disappears into the energetic crowd.

"Be right back mami, there go papi from the Bulls," Bianca shouted in Dutchess' ear. The pulsating rhythmn from the custom sound system shakes the floor. Dutchess and Olivia laughs at their girl.

"That girl is a hot mess," stated Dutchess.

"Who you telling girl." Olivia replied, grabbing two champagne flutes from a half naked woman carrying a silver tray. She passes one to Dutchess and sips it slowly, taking in her surroundings. "What you thinking about girl?" Olivia asked.

"Huh, oh nothin'," Dutchess lied staring into the large glass mirror in front of her.

On the other side of the mirror is the V.I.P lounge, where Black Jesus is seated, with his face buried in between large titties. On the other table is a fresh line of cocaine and drinks. He snorts a line of powder off the woman's silicone titties. The cocaine temporarily paralyzes his senses. He watches the exotic beauty sway her hips seductively through the two way mirror. He rises from the chair dismissing the blonde bombshell with a wave of the hand. Pleasure can be received at any time, but opportunity comes once in a life time. He signals for one of Kennytha's men to summon the beautiful Goddess.

Dutchess feels a light tap on her shoulder as R-Kelly's 'Grind for me' pours out of the yacht's acoustic speakers. She spins around and the man places his hands in the air.

"I don't want no problems baby, but the Birthday boy sent me to get you," he explained, trying to pacify her. One thing the streets do is talk, he is aware of her reputation as well as her temper. Ordinarily Dutchess would have spazzed out on the man but things are swinging her way better than she could have ever planned. Olivia turns to follow them, but when they get to the door she is stopped. "He only mentioned Dutchess." The man stated.

"Go ahead girl, if you need me I'll be by the bar," said Olivia. Olivia was always the nosey type. Walking off, Olivia pulls out her cellular phone and goes into the restroom.

Dutchess enters the room and the man follows behind her closing the door. She sees the crystal flakes on the table. Black Jesus watches her eyes. "You want some?" he asked.

"Naw, I'm straight," Dutchess replied, crossing her arms in front of her chest. Black Jesus glances at the diamond bracelet wrapped around her wrist that reads 'Head Bitch In Charge'.

"I'm not goin' to waste your time. I like yo' style." Black Jesus thought out his words carefully in his cocaine clouded brain. "Right now your doin' yo' thang, but together we can put the whole Midwest on lock. Everybody in the ghetto is searching for a Black Jesus." He lets the words linger in the air. Just in case this is a trap, Dutchess decides to play it safe.

"Don't you work for ol' boy?" Dutchess inquired.

"As I was sayin', we can put the whole midwest on lock." If she wasn't sure before, she is sure now. Black Jesus is planning to make a run for power. He did his homework on Dutchess and he's positive she will be on his side if, and when the revolution starts. Many questions races through Dutchess' mind.

"***Why would he be tellin' me this? Does he know somethin' about my father***?"

"I'll have to think about that and get back with you," Dutchess said reaching for the door handle.

"Don't think about it for too long, the time is now," he proclaimed, as she steps out of the room going one way and the security another. Mintues later Black Jesus has his face once again submerged between titties.

Dutchess meets back up with Olivia at the bar. "What that nigga wanted with you?" Olivia questioned.

"Nothin', he's just coked up, crazy as ever, and tryna get down with a boss bitch."

"Did you run into Ice back there by any chance? I been looking all over for him. He told me he was gon' be here," Olivia stated.

"Naw I ain't seen him," Dutchess replied. She feels another tap on the shoulder. "What!" She spins around with an attitude back to her usual self. In her midst is a young goon wearing the same black outfit as the last one.

"The boss wanna see you," he informed.

"Here we go again," Dutchess mumbles under her breath. He leads her to the third deck. Kennytha leans back on the leather sofa surrounded by his entrougage of women and goons dressed in a red two piece Versace suit with matching crocidile shoes. His long kinky dreadlocks rests on his shoulders.

"Finally me eyes meet the legendary Dutchess. Me know you is real hustler." He stands up knocking one of his goons out of the seat across from him. "Here take a seat," Kennytha instructed. Dutchess feigns a smile at the display.

"***I can't believe I'm standing in front of the man that's responsible for my father's death. I have my chance to murder this muthafucka right now***." Dutchess mulled, staring at him.

"Me know you real hustler cause you out sell me workers and have some of my people afraid to do business in certain areas. So me say to me self how come me don't kill her?" Dutchess arched eyebrows crinkles as she stares into Kennytha's cold black eyes. Her blood boils as his words soak in her brain. No fear is sensed on either side. "So me have long talk with me uncle." Safar leans back studying Dutchess from head to toe. Kennytha scribbles on a sheet of paper and slides it across the table. Dutchess scoops it up staring at the numbers written on it.

"What's this?" she asked with a puzzled facial expression.

"Me know you dealin' wit' Franko, and him taxin' ya, so me offer you deal you can't refuse." Dutchess doesn't know if this is a threat or what, but she knows that you should never bite the hand that feeds you. "Me uncle want you to switch to the winnin' team." Dutchess looks over to the old man with a yellow grin.

"No disrespect to you or your organization, but I have to think about that. I can't just go against the grain," Dutchess stated.

"What ya mean go against the grain; Me got da whole world in me hands. Me had D.E.A in me hands 'til they turned rats. Dis is me world. Let me show you what me do ta people da crosses me." Kennytha signals to one of his workers. They bring in someone with a pillow case over their head. The pillow case is removed exposing Black Jesus' bloody face. His eyes are swollen shut. A fuming Dutchess stares at Kennytha who has confirmed his guilt. "So tell me Dutchess how do me know you not the police?" Dutchess focus glides over to the two men holding Black Jesus up. He mumbles underneath the duct tape. Dutchess begins to have a flashback.

Lawrence kisses Dutchess on her forehead. "I'll see you later Pooh-bear."

"A'ight dad. Don't forget my graduation is later on tonight."

"Forget, I wouldn't miss it for the world."

"You promise?"

"Yea, I promise." Dutchess stood in the doorway watching the only man she has ever loved. The one who raised her, taught her how to ride a bike, and drive a car. Dutchess peered through the screened front door. She watched her mother pullout of the driveway waving goodbye to her father. An older white woman jogged pass their residence with her puppy running along the side of her. The rearend of her mother's pearl white Lexus GS430 was no longer in her view.

Lawrence climbed into his navy blue Denali and placed the key into the ignition. He blew a kiss to his pride and joy, as he turned the key slowly. Kabooooom! The truck exploded shaking the earth with a loud thunderous rumble, as blazing fragments of Lawrence's shredded truck showered the well manicured lawn and driveway.

"Noooo! Dadddy! Noooo! Dutchess cried uncontrollably.

The sound of Kennytha's voice brings Dutchess back to reality. "You not answer me question. How do me know you not police?"

"I'm gon' show you that I'm not the police." Dutchess moves with swiftness pulling the silvery .45 automatic from the waistline of one of the men holding Black Jesus by the arms. Guns click from every direction as Kennytha's security detail draw their weapons. Dutchess' face crinkles in anger as she clutches the gun aiming at a fearless Kennytha. "I'm far from a police," Dutchess proclaimed. She aims the gun at Black Jesus and squeezes the trigger. His head jerks backwards as a bullet rips through his forehead cracking his skull. The deafening sound leaves their ears ringing. One Kennytha's men mouth drops open in disbelief. Black Jesus is sprawled on the ground like he is nailed to the cross. Dutchess maintained her composure with an idea rooted in her mind. She contemplated on killing Kennytha right there on sight, but she knows that now isn't the time. She tucks the gun back into the man's waistline. "Now do that answer yo question?"

Kennytha lips curve into an evil smile.

"Now that's what me like." Kennytha's men lower their guns as they read their superior's mood. "Me give you couple days to make decision." Dutchess exits the area walking in a surreal motion. Her Manolo Blahnik boots clacks becoming a distant sound. She spots Ice and Olivia sitting at the bar hugged up. She approaches the couple.

"Heyyy girl, where you run off too?" Olivia asked, being nosey as usual.

"I had to set the record straight with somebody I always wanted to meet."

"Oh yeah." Ice and Dutchess give each other an evil look.

"You seen Bianca?" Dutchess asked.

"She somewhere around here whoring around," Olivia replied.

"Well, I'm going to head out. Are you gon' be okay?"

"Yeah girl. I'ma leave with Ice."

"Well, I'm gettin' ready to leave. Do me a favor and make sure Bianca makes it home safe."

"Don't worry I'll make sure." They embrace each other in a friendly hug saying their goodbyes. As Dutchess makes her way out of the door she crosses the path of a white man carrying a puppy in his arms.

"***Damn it look like I seen him some where before***." She thought to herself. She begins seeing a visual of the white lady jogging pass their house with a puppy the day her father was killed. Dutchess couldn't believe it, everything is all starting to come together.

Two men walk into Sorensten's large office. He is sitting behind an antique cherrywood desk reviewing files. The carved wooden legs of the desk are sunk into the plush beige carpet. The two men glance around the room admiring the portraits of Sorensten shaking hands with Presidents of the past and present. So engrossed with the case in front of him, he does not notice their presence.

"Utt umm," the taller one of the two men clears his throat gainning the attention of Sorensten. He looks up and begins to twirl the silver fountain pen he was writing with between two fingers. "Can I help you fellas with something?" His voice perturbed that the secretary would send them in unannounced.

The shorter one said, "This is a delicate matter. Is it safe to talk here?"

"Of course, pull that door behind you closed, and have a seat." The men supply their credentials, and then explain why they are there. "Oh, I see. Very well then," replied Sorensten.

"Now you understand why we must do it this way?" commented the shoter one.

"Indeed." Sorensten replied pressing the intercom button on his desk. His secretary quickly responds over the loud speaker.

"Mr. Sorensten I'm sorry about sending-"

"Never mind that gross negligence on your behalf, alert security and send them to my office immediately," Sorensten interrupted. Three minutes and thirty three seconds later two security guards knock on his door. "That's them gentlemen. Shall we?" The rise from their seats and follow Sorensten out the door.

Cheryl stares at the notes strewn across her desk. From informant testimony and police intelligence everything is pointing towards one person. Why would anyone even get involved in drugs was beyond her. She thinks about Sade's friend Carmen being picked up by the state for drug charges. It seems unreal to her, but she isn't surprised. The incident confirmed her beliefs. "***It's not Carmen's fault, it's just that when a person doesn't grow up with both of their parents in a stable environment, they usually look to crime***." She silently thought to herself. The statistics are clear to her. "***Just look at Bianca, grew up with one parent, and it's obvious that she is strung off drugs***." She decides that she will have a talk with Sade concerning her friends. The statistics speaks for them selves. "***Now compare those two with Sade***," she thought. Yes growing up with both parents definitely reduced bad habits and crime.

The knock at her door startles her. Mr. Sorensten walks in with two men and the security guards behind him. She looks up from the case file. “Is there a problem?”

“We have a slight situation Cheryl,” said Mr. Sorensten.

“I’m really working hard at bringing this Dutchess character down,” she stated.

“She really doesn’t know,” said one of the agents.

“Know what?” Cheryl hears the news and closes her eyes. It’s all she can do to keep from crying.

Pirelli parks his BMW in the heated horseshoe driveway. He hops out of the car wearing a brown leather Al Wissam coat, denim Al Wissam jeans, and a pair of Kenneth Cole Reaction shoes. He totes a bulgy nylon gym bag. He spots the mailman leaving his residence, after placing mail inside the mailbox.

“Good morning Mr. Blackwell,” the mailman greets him with a friendly smile.

“Good mornin’,” Pirelli replied. The sun shines hard melting the thin layers of snow that coats the grass. Pirelli leans forward picking up the Chicago Tribune off the porch. He steps in the house hearing the faint sound of two females giggling. He cuts through the foyer stepping into the livingroom in shock. He stares at Man-Man leaning back on the leather sofa in between two teenage white girls eating popcorn with his feet crossed on the cocktail table. Their eyes are locked on the 88 inch projection screen. Popcorn is scattered allover the carpet. He recognizes the long platinum chain on Man-Man’s neck with it’s iced out charm. “Man-Man what the hell you call yo’ self doin’?” Pirelli inquired.

“Aaw, what up playa?” Man-Man greeted Pirelli.

“Playa ... Nigga if you don’t get yo’ feet off my furniture. I don’t know where the hell you think you at,” Pirelli snapped. The two blond haired girls rise from the sofa storming out of the front door. Pirelli trudges over to Man-Man and removes the chain from his neck. "Don't let me catch you goin' through my shit again. If I catch you again I'm gon' knock yo' little ass out," Pirelli warned. He looks around scanning the livingroom. "Clean this mess up right now before I knock yo' little grown wanna be ass out," Pirelli threatened.

"Mannn unc you be trippin'," Man-Man said, bending down cleaning up his mess.

Pirelli hears loud music coming from the back area. He gazes through a set of glass doors. He spots Fatman and Rell playing in the indoor pool with the baby white tiger that he bought Erica for her Birthday. He opens the door stepping on the deck. He shuts off the CD player. "Get out this damn swimming pool and get y'all ass in the house. I bet y'all ain't even did y'all homework yet? Y'all know I don't play that shit. Don't let Man-Man get y'all asses whipped around here," Pirelli ranted, walking back inside the house. He makes his way to the mastersuite stepping inside the closet. He slides the clothes to the side exposing the eEmpire safe that only opens from his fingerprint. He touches the screen and the safe opens. He unzips the gym bag placing bundles of money inside the safe along with his exclusive jewels. "***A couple more moves and I'm done with this shit.***" He says to himself. He sits on the edge of the bed and unfolds the newspapers. His eyes enlarge as he reads the front page. His heart drops in his stomach. The triple homicide and large amount of drugs and money found at Treatz corner store made the front page. His cellular phone vibrates on his waistline. "***Shit, what Sheena want? Maybe she got some information for me about this situation.***" He answers the phone. "Hello."

"Baby what's going on?" Sheena asked.

"I don't know what's going on."

"I need to talk to you baby, it's very important. Meet me

in back of my mother's house tonight and be careful."

"I'll be there," Pirelli promised.

"I'll see you than baby."

"A'ight." Pirelli hangs up the phone. "Shit! Everytime things start goin' good somethin' unexpected happens," Pirelli talks to himself. He rushes out of the house to use a payphone just in case his phone is tapped. He called Dutchess and informed her of the bad news.

LATER THAT NIGHT

Pirelli maneuvers his big body BMW into the dimly lit narrow passageway. He pulls beside a green dumpster awaiting Sheena's arrival. Every since he read the newspaper article he has been paranoid. He took a long detour before he arrived to Sheena's mother's house. He had to reassure himself that he wasn't being followed. He reaches inside his coat pocket producing a pack of Newports. He doesn't smoke cigarettes, but he needed something to relax his nerves. He ran through a half pack of cigarettes within the last four hours.

The ascending fire from the lighter dances making his face visible in the darkness of the car, as he lights the cigarette. A bright orange dot shines in the darkness as she takes a long draw of the cigarette. He glimpses around nervously surveying his surroundings. He notices a set of eyes glowing behind the bushes. "Fuck is that?" he whispered to himself. A cloud of light illuminates the narrow passageway startling the cat behind the bushes. The cat scurries away vanishing into the darkness.

"Shit, I'm trippin'." A paranoid Pirelli shifts his gaze to the rearview mirror with a watchful eye, as a car makes its approach. The bright headlights shine inside his car outlining the interior. He squints his eyes trying to adjust to the blaring lights. He hears the sound of the cars engine humming softly as it nears the rearend of his BMW. The headlights die out and the engine falls into silence. Seeing that it's Sheena, Pirelli hops out of the car.

The cool breeze presses his shirt against his chest, as he strides towards her vehicle. She steps out of the car with silent tears rolling down her cheeks. The midnight breeze carries the scent of her perfume.

Pirelli wraps his arms around her giving her a warm embrace. Slowly and gently he rakes his fingers through her hair. She shoves him in the chest with all of her strength pushing him away from her. "Why Pirelli?" she ranted, her voice close to trembling.

"What you talkin' about?" he responded, staring into her red-rimmed eyes. "***I hope she didn't find out I had her brother murked***."

"You know what I'm talking about you bastard!" She snapped rummaging through her purse. She stares at him sharply gripping a glistening .44 mag. "Rick told me that you and that bitch Dutchess killed my brother!" She shouts angrily in tears. Pirelli extends his hands in the air backpedaling.

"Hold up baby, let me explain," he pleaded choosing hiswords carefully.

"Explain what! How you killed my little brother! How could you do this to me!" Her hands tremble uncontrollably as she continues to aim the gun at him. Pirelli bumps up against the dumpster knocking over an empty beer bottle. Knowing that he has no way out, his heart drums against his chest and his mind races 30 million miles per second.

"***I guess this is the end for me. I knew I should've brought my strap***." He watches as she slowly pulls back on the trigger.

"See you in hell motherfucka," she snarled. Pirelli

sees a flash of light. The ear-splitting sound of gunfire reverberates. His eyes close and his body springs back. For some reason he doesn't feel any pain. He opens his eyes staring at Sheena lying on the pavement in a river of blood. Her . 44 mag is still clutched in her hand, as she lies on the pavement beside her car lifeless.

Pirelli's eyes settle on a female figure that is silhoutted against the moon gripping a nickel plated handgun. Her facial features are unrecognizable. The woman prances closer to him looking like an angel making its approach. He recognizes the woman immediately.

"Micole," he blurts out. He can't believe his eyes, the young woman from the neighborhood that has a crush on him saved his life. The sound of sirens wails loudly and a young Micole disappears into the darkness.

A caravan of patrol cars races through the area responding to the gunfire. A patrol car pulls into the narrow passageway shining its search lights. The globe of lights bounces around scanning the premises. The beaming lights shine on Pirelli obscuring his vision. He sheilds his face with his hands blocking the light. An authorative voice travels through a loud speaker. An officer jumps out of the squad car with caution, with his gun aimed directly at Pirelli. The officer spots a lifeless Sheena who he recognizes as his co-worker. He shouts into his radio, "Officer down!"

A large group of patrol cars pour into the narrow passageway. "Put your hands on top of your head and slowly turn around," the officer barked, aiming his police issued 9 millimeter Sig & Sauer in front of him with both hands inching towards Pirelli. The officer grabs Pirelli with a solid grip, handling him rough.

"Hold up! You hurtin' my fuckin' arm!" Pirelli snapped grimacing in pain.

"Stop resisting mother fucker!" Pirelli rebels as the officer slaps the handcuffs around his wrist cutting into his flesh. A group of officers join in slamming him against the hood of his BMW.

"Get the fuck off me!" he shouts angrily. They taped off the crime scene with yellow tape. They search the premises thoroughly. Pirelli closes his eyes trying to escape the unpleasant realities. Three officers escorts him to a patrol car. As they attempt to place him in back of the squad car a voice attracts their attention.

"Turn him loose." Officer Friendly turns around staring at a clean cut man dressed in a double breasted designer suit flashing a gold badge. He strides in their direction. Pirelli stands in his tracks confused. Pirellil's chest raises rhythmnically, with each inhale inflating the front of his shirt.

"Excuse me sir, who are you?" Officer Friendly questioned.

"I'm special agent Rains from the Drug Enforcement Agency. Your prisoner has a federal warrant." He locks eyes with Pirelli.

"Well, well, well, look who we have here. Mr...Pirelli... Blackwell," he said slowly. Mr. Rains makes a gesture with his hand and two men dressed in two piece suits takes Pirelli into their custudy. "I'm going to put it to you like this Mr. Blackwell. You can help yourself right now by telling us what we need to know about Dutchess or you can do this the hard way. Just in case you don't know. With a record like yours, you automatically qualify for career criminal, which starts you at thirty years to life."

"Man fuck you and do what you gotta do. I promise you by time this is over with my attorney will have you checking parking meters for the rest of your career," Pirelli proclaimed, unknowledgable of the federal system.

"We'll see when this is all over," Agent Rains said as they haul him away.

Many customers traverse Fogo De Chao Brazilian Steakhouse. The fresh smell of seafood colognes the air. Silverware and glasses clinks together, intermingling with the clattering sound of contending conversations.

Kennytha is seated at a neatly arranged table accompanied by two of his armed men. Dutchess made all of the reservations earlier that afternoon after calling Kennytha. Dressed in a two piece Prada suit, with his lengthy dreadlocks in a ponytail, he scans the semi-crowed restuarant. Dutchess enters the restuarant wearing a red silky wig that accentuates her unblemished skin, a one piece designer skirt, and a pair of Chanel high heel pumps.

Kennytha tilts his head watching the beautiful goddess make her approach. The waiter escorts her to the table she had reserved for this meeting. Before seating herself Kennytha's men pat her down for weapons or any electronic devices. Dutchess hasn't been carrying any firearms since Pirelli showed her, the newspaper article about the three dead bodies, money, and drugs being discovered at Treatz.

She sits face to face with Kennytha concealing all her anger she has buried deep down inside her heart. Finally the day has come for her to revenge her father's death. She thought everything out carefully. Kennytha sits in between his security. The men have their artillery concealed underneath their blazers. Kennytha lights his Zino Platinum cigar. In silence, he studies Dutchess through the ribbon of cigar smoke. "So, me assume dat you ready ta join me team." Kennytha stated in his heavy Caribbean accent.

"Maybe," Dutchess replied feigning a smile.

"What ya mean maybe? Me know ya wanna join winnin' team. Me not no fool."

"Like I said, maybe," Dutchess said wearing a solemn expression. The waiter appears to the table with a bottle of fine french wine. He fills both their glasses. He displays a friendly smile and discreetly winks his eye at Dutchess before heading to the kitchen area.

Dutchess takes a sip of the wine. She glances at the glowing clock that reads 7:05. Coming close to the time for her to retaliate, she meticulously calculates her every move.

"How many birds can you gurantee me at one time?"

"Me can gurantee you as many thangs as you can handle. Me got da whole world in me hands. Whatever you want me can get," Kennytha proclaimed with a diabolic smile. Dutchess looks at the clock again. She counts silently in her head preparing herself for her next move. She slowly places her hands under the table. The high pitched sound of the fire alarm garners everyone's attention in the restuarant. A small group of employees storms out of the kitchen area shouting. Thick smoke fogs the restuarant.

"Fire!" Everybody out!" Yelled the waiter that winked at Dutchess. Dutchess snatches the two twin Heckler & Koch .380 autos that is duct taped under the table. Everyone in the restuarant rushes towards the exit in a disorderly fashion forming a stampede. This gives Dutchess enough time to handle her business. Kennytha and his men focus on the chaotic scenery that is unfolding right before their eyes, no longer focusing on Dutchess. She holds a gun in each hand aiming directly at Kennytha.

"That DEA agent you had killed ... that was my father muthafucka!" Kennytha's men reache under their blazer after realizing what is transpiring. She squeezes the trigger of the handguns hitting her targets. The sound of gunfire coughs. People scream and shriek, dropping to the ground racing in all directions away from the terror of instant death. Boc! Boc! Boc! Boc! Fire discharges from the muzzle of Dutchess' guns as bullets spit. Her hands jerk repeatedly as she continues to fire.

Two bullets rip through Kennytha's chest area. The impact hurls Kennytha's body against the wall. He holds his chest grimacing in pain cursing. One of Kennytha's men tries to aim his gun at Dutchess, but he isn't quick enough. She put two holes in his forehead sending him staggering backwards crashing into a table. Bottles of wine crashes against the floor foaming. Kennytha lies against the bullet riddled wall stainned with blood.

"B-Bitch... Y-You...gon'...die fa d-dis," Kennytha managed to say through all of the excruiating pain. Dutchess stands over him clutching the two handguns.

"Oh yeah. Well you about to die first. See you in hell muthafucka!"

"M-Me tell you father you say h-hello," he said with a devilish grin. Boc! Boc! Boc! Boc! Boc! Dutchess fires into his chest giving him the remainder of the clip. Kennytha and his men lay on the floor in a puddle of brownish red blood. Dutchess casually prances away. Broken glass crunches under her high heel pumps. She exits the restaurant through the fire escape.

A woman waits near by the restuarant waiting on Dutchess as she instructed. The woman is slender due to her drug addiction and her health. Her body has been suffering in unbearable pain. She was once very attractive until her heroin addiction and Aids got the best of her.

The doctor told her that she would be lucky if she lives for another two weeks. The doctor's estimate has to be right. Her bones are aching so bad she feels like she will not make it for another twenty four hours.

Dutchess meets up with the woman and hands her the orange chin chilla, the red haired wig, and the two hand guns. The woman puts on the wig and the chin chilla. Through all the pain the woman smiles at Dutchess revealing her rotten teeth, adjusting the wig. She feels beautiful for the first time in years.

"How do I look?" she asked Dutchess. She gazes into the woman's pain filled eyes for a moment before answering.

"You look beautiful," Dutchess answered, feeling sorry for her. Dutchess wraps her arms around the woman embracing her with a warm hug.

"Thank you for the money. My kids can finally go to college and be comfortable. This is the least I can do for them. All I did was cause them so much pain over the years. It really hurt me to know how I neglected them," she sincerely expressed. The faint sound of sirens brings them back to the situation at hand.

"I guess it's time for me to go. I'm glad we was able to help each other. I'm sorry that it have to end like this." Dutcess said with heartfelt words.

"Don't be sorry baby, this is life. We all have to die some day. Now you get goin' sweety," the woman replied. Dutchess struts off, her high heel pumps clicking against the pavement becoming a faint sound as she distant herself. A police car zooms pass her with the waiter in the passenger seat pointing to the woman in the orange chin chilla wearing the red wig. Dutchess paid him good money for his assistance. He will never have to worry about money for a long time.

Dutchess jumps on the El-train mixing in with the throng of patrons. She scans the cluttered train searching for an empty seat. She finds a seat beside a well dressed white man with gray hair. The man has his eyes glued to a Chicago Tribune. He glimpses at Dutchess and flashes her a pleasant smile. She cracks a short smile in return. She peers through the window of the train plastering her eyes on the cluster of patrol cars blocking the streets off. Red and blue lights pulsates, glistening in her eyes. The train moves forward with a loud rumbling sound. She closes her eyes and lets out a short breath of relief.

After five minutes of pondering she arrives to her destination. She climbs out of her seat. The man lowers the newspapers admiring an attractive Dutchess. Her designer dress clings to her body tracing the sensual curves of her hips. The man's eyeballs dances as he studies her exiting the train. He turns the page of his newspaper seeing a picturing of a beautiful woman wanted for a large drug conspiracy. His eyes widen and his mouth drops open. He shifts his gaze to the window staring at Dutchess as the train pulls off.

She prances away turning several corners. Making it to her trap car, she hops inside of it. Her cellular phone chimes under the seat. She fishes under the seat grabbing the phone.

"Hello," she answered.

"Girl I been looking for you all day. The feds picked up Ice two hours ago," Olivia sniffles over the line.

"Why you cryin' Livia?"

"Because I don't know what to do without him."

"Don't worry it's gon' be okay."

"I need you to come meet me somewhere. I have something I need to tell you. I don't know if they have my phone bugged." Olivia stated.

"Okay be cool. I'm gon' call you from a payphone and tell you where to meet me at," Dutchess said.

"A'ight. Make sure you be careful girl."

"I will. You just relax, I got yo' back," Dutchess sincerely stated.

"Okay." Dutchess hears an echoing sound before the line goes dead. She rolls down her window tossing the cell phone into the street. She rides off on her way to assist her friend.

The mellow sounds of Sade's song 'Cherish the Day' pours out of the car speakers. Dutchess leans back in the driver's seat singing along with the lyrics waiting patiently on King Drive. Olivia pulls up slowly parallel parking in between a Dodge Neon and a Ford Focus. She walks briskly, covering her hair with the newspapers. She didn't want to mess up her perm. The smell of wet concrete floats in the atmosphere. She climbs into the passengers seat joining Dutchess.

Olivia leans into Dutchess' seat giving her a long sisterly hug. It seems as if she doesn't want to let her go. The last time Olivia gave her a long hug like that was when Dutchess loss her father. Dutchess starts to feel strange. Rain drums on the windsheild commingling with the crooning CD player. "What's wrong Livia?" Dutchess inquired with genuine concern.

"They took Ice and Chill is on the run. After they took Ice I stopped at the gas station to get some gas and something caught my attention," Olivia informed.

"And what was that?" Dutchess asked with a look of curiousity. Olivia hands her the Chicago Tribune. Dutchess flicks on the interior light reading the newspaper. She stares at the picture of herself on the front page. She closes her eyes sways her head in disbelief. "***This can't be happenin' to me.***"

In the middle of reading the article a gold Lincoln Navigator slices through the night at full speed with it's headlights beaming. Dutchess tilts her head in the direction of the truck being blinded by its headlights.

Dutchess hears a click she recognizes. Without looking she snarls, "Bitch you set me up!" She stares at the approaching vehicle. It comes to a screeching halt. Dutchess hears a combination of voices.

Four men jump out of the truck wearing plain clothes, forming a semi-circle in front of Dutchess' car. Olivia aims her black police issued 9 millimeter at Dutchess. She shifts her gaze locking eyes on Olivia. "Bitch you ain't no police. You nothin' but a gold digging hoe!" Olivia studies her colorful eyes seeing all the anger building up inside of her. The superior DEA agent raises his voice sharply.

"Step out of the vehicle with your hands up!"

"Make this easy on yourself Dutchess. I'm sorry it had to go down like this. I was investigating Ice and you came into the picture. You was never the target in this ongoing investigation. I'm really sorry, but I have to do my job," Olivia proclaimed. "Please step out of the car. Make it easy on yourself. I promise I will help you get the best deal." Olivia feels the sting of tears pricking at the back of her eyes, and closes them tightly fighting back the deluge of emotions that threatens to engulf her. She grew close to Dutchess during the long months of working by her side.

"Fuck you and your deal, I ain't did nothin' to break the law!" Dutchess snapped.

"Get out the fuckin' car now! This is Your last warning!" the agent barked in a gruff tone.

"This shit ain't over with bitch!" Dutchess solemnly declared. Reluctantly, she climbs out of the car with her heads in the air. They apprehend her, placing her in handcuffs. Several different thoughts fill her head. She knows that it's going to be one long ride.

Pirelli and Earl are sitting at a make shift table playing a hand of casino. Casino is a card game that is played by prisoners throughout state and federal institution; it is a two player game. There are five ways a player can accumulate points. That is by collecting the ten of diamonds(3 points) the duece of Spade (2 points), any of

the four aces (1 point each), and collecting the most spades (1 point), and collecting the most cards (1point). Therefore the maxium number of points available is 11 points. The game starts out with the dealer dealing six cards to himself and his opponent. The cards are played out, then four cards are dealt out thereafter, until the deck of cards run out. The player being dealt to throws a card from his hand face up onto the table. If the player has a card with the same value, he can pick it up, or use another card from his hand to build on the card on the table. If he can't do neither, he must place a card onto the table, and then the opponent can utilize the same options.

They took a plastic trash can and turned it upside down, placing a piece of cardboard on top. Earl places a seven of hearts onto the table. Pirelli looks to the ceiling, trying to remember what has been played. After thinking, he throws out a jack of diamond, and Earl picks it up with the jack of club. Pirelli plays a five of heart.

"Can I get next?" A dark skinned brother with braids asked, interrupting their game.

"Now Dre you know you can't beat me in this." Earl boasted, with strong confidence.

"Bet a book then?"

"A what?"

"A book of stamps nigga." Dre stated, pulling out a thick roll of stamps. In the streets they have big faces, but in prison the currency is first class flags with .41 cent denominations.

"I don't gamble." Earl cops out, while deciding his next play.

"That's what I thought nigga, you all talk."

"You got next Joe," Pirelli blurted, intervening on the situation that have the potential to get way out of control. For some reason Pirelli took a liking for Earl. They met the same day Pirelli made it to the 21st floor of MCC Chicago. Earl reminds Pirelli of himself, when he was in the state joint. A young wild gun-slanger with a pistol case.

Earl slaps a three of spade onto the seven of heart already on the board.

"Ten," he says, utilizing the option to build.

"What color is yours?" Pirelli talks shit as he removes the ten of diamonds from his hand and pick up both cards. Pirelli knows he has a ten in his hand because you can't build with a number you don't have.

"Damn!" Earl shouted, playing his ten of heart to the board next. "I knew you had it."

"Nigga you didn't know shit or you wouldn't have build it, you card dummy," Dre clowned. "Only nigga in the B.O.P (Bureau Of Prisons), that can let cards out think him," Dre added.

"You won this one P, I got next. I need to go use the phone any ways. When I get back I'ma beat you like you was in 'Roots'." Earl procliamed, as he struts to the phone in his orange jump suit. Earl had a bail hearing last week and the magistrate judge granted him a $5,000.00 bail with the conditions of the electronic monitoring. Earl's cousin promised to post his bail, due to the fact that the gun belonged to him. Being that his cousin had a long criminal history and would've been in the guideline range of 15 years to life, Earl sacrificed his freedom knowing that he would get a much lighter sentence.

Earl dials his cousin's number. The phone rings four times and his cousin's voicemail comes on. "This call is from a federal facility. This is a prepaid call, you will not be charged for this call. To accept please press five. If you do not want to accept this call please hang up n-" The line falls into silence.

"Hello ...Hello."

"***I know this nigga didn't just hang up on me***," Earl said to himself calling the number back. The phone rings two times and his cousin answers the phone.

"This call is from a federal facility. This is a prepaid c-." The line falls into silence and Earl's blood begins to boil. Icewater starts flowing through his veins as he entertains the thought of revenge. "***I know this bitch ass nigga ain't dodging my calls.***" Earl calls the number repeatedly getting nothing but the voicemail. "I can't believe this hoe ass nigga playin' games wit' me," Earl muttered. He bangs the phone against the ledge of the booth in anger collecting the attention of all the inmates standing around. "I'ma kill that bitch ass muthafucka Joe, on everything I love!" he says to no one in particular as he walks away from the phone, leaving it dangling from it's chrome spiral cord. He takes a seat in front of Pirelli with his chin in his chest, swaying his head.

"Sup my nigga?" Pirelli asked, staring at an angry Earl who has his fist balled up, biting down on his lower lip. He blows out a deep breath of air.

"Man, my cousin on some hoe ass shit dawg. I took this case fo' on that nigga me and shit." Now he wanna keep avoiding a nigga, hangin' up on me and shit."

"Man, that's some slimy ass shit he doin'," Pirelli added. "Man I'm tellin' you, when I get out this muthafucka it's on. All I asked that nigga to do was post my bail."

"You know how it is when you down and out. It's out of sight out of mind. Niggas feel like they can't be touched because you on lock. It's very few that keeps it one hundred." Pirelli stated.

"Man I'll do almost anything to get up out of this hell hole and back at that nigga." Earl stressed.

"Just give it a little time, he might come through for you."

"Yeah right. That rotten ass nigga left me for dead. I promise you I'ma get at that nigga. He gon' pay fo' this shit." Earl's words sinks into Pirelli's head as he thinks about his own issues he have to deal with.

Dutchess sits behind the defendant table with Krauger Strauss the high priced cocky lawyer that her mother has retained for her. To the public he is a hero, but to many prisoners he is known for selling out his clients.

Cheryl sits in the front row of the crowded courtroom with a constant stream of tears rolling down her face. Dutchess is dressed in a black skirt set business suit. "Hear ye, hear ye, all rise for the honorable James E. Milton, you are now hearing case number 50030-7, the United States Of America vs. Sade Lynell Blackwell." The clerk informed. Judge Milton exits his chambers and struts to his seat.

"You may be seated," he informs the court. He picks up a large stack of papers, and begins to read the front page, adjusting his glasses on his nose as he does so. "Okay, can I have the appearances of both counsels listed on the records starting with prosecution?"

"Glenn Stevens, AUSA, for the Northern district of Illinois to my immediate left is DEA agent Rains." The deathly pale, beady-eyed Italian prosecutor responded.

"Very well, and the defense." Dutchess' lawyer rises to his feet.

"Attorney Krauger Strauss, from Strauss and associates. To my left is the defendant Sade Blackwell, sitting next to her is my private investigator Tim Greene." Cheryl glances over at her boss sitting behind the prosecution table. She couldn't fault him, he was only doing his job. Still it made her angry.

"Thank you Mr. Strauss, now that we got that out of the way. Let's get down to business, shall we?"

"Excuse me your honor, before we get under way I'd like to file a motion withdrawing from counsel in this case," Attorney Strauss interrupted. The court erupts in an uproar.

"Order! Order in the court!" Judge Milton bangs his gavel restoring calmness. "Approach the bench Mr. Strauss." The judge turns on the fan, preventing their conversation from being heard as they whisper in hushed tones. Strauss returns to his seat as they turn off the fan. "Given the nature of the information I have just received, and to prevent this case from being overturned on appeal for ineffective assistance of counsel, I have no choice in the matter than grant your motion for withdrawl."

"Thank you your honor."

"As for you Ms. Sade Blackwell, have you secured alternate consel?" Deangelo walks into the courtroom late taking a seat beside Cheryl. Dutchess rises from her seat.

"I have your honor."

"Okay, and who might that be?"

"I will."

"Excuse me!"

"I will be representing myself." The courtroom breaks out in pandemonium at the news.

"Objection your honor, she can't represent herself," prosecutor Stevens hollered over the spectators multiple conversations.

"Order!" The crowd quieted. "On the contrary, pursant to the sixth amendment of the United States I can and will," stated Dutchess defiantly.

"Assuming I permit this fiasco in my courtroom the law still requires you to have competent counsel, who will serve as your co-counsel?" Dutchess doesn't have a plan for this question, but she doesn't have to. Suddenly, without realizing it, Cheryl is off her feet saying,

"I will." Now Mr. Sorensten is up and out of his chair.

"Objection your honor, she is an employee of the United States government."

"Ex-employee," Cheryl corrects him, "My resignation papers will be on your desk within an hour, but for now I quit," she yelled.

"Order!" Judge Milton yells calming the war. Mr. Sorensten's face flushes red.

"Your going to regret this," he warns.

"Obviously you people think this courtroom is some kind of circus. This type of behavior will not be permitted in the future. Now I understand that emotions are running high, but we have rules and procedures that must be followed. Is that understood?"

"Yes your honor," Dutchess and the prosecutor said simultaneously.

"As for you Ms. Blackwell, I'm going to permit you to represent yourself, but as I've warned, my courtroom is not a circus, so just as I have removed your counsel today, I'm at the liberty to remove you. Is that understoood?"

"Yes you honor."

"Very well, the defendant is now remanded back to the custody of the United states Marshall services, where she will remain until November 10th, the commencement date of the trial." Judge Milton bangs his gavel, and the Marshalls escort Dutchess out of the courtroom back to her cell in MCC Chicago.

Dutchess lays on her stomach stretched out on the lower bunk srutinizing her court documentations. She shuffles through her discovery packet searching for any errors in her case, trying to develop the perfect strategy to defend herself. She blocks out the combination of noises that pierces the atmosphere, throughout the crowded dorm. Her bunk mate Denise is taking a shower. Denise is awaiting sentencing for a fraud case. Dutchess and Denise get along real good until she tries to convince her not to go to trial.

Dutchess takes her yellow high-lighter and traces over various contradicting statements. In the middle of writing notes, Jessie interrupts her.

"Dutchess! They callin' you for a visit," Jessie informed.

"A visit. I wasn't expectin' no visit until tomorrow."

"Well, the C.O just called yo' name for a visit," Jessie said standing in her bunk area leaning against the bunk, eying her backside. Jessie is one of the many dikes in the dorm. She came on to Dutchess when she first arrived to the dorm. The other female inmates were already familiar with Dutchess before she stepped a foot in the dorm, from seeing her face numerous times flashing across the television screen. The correctional officers and the inmates treat her like a celebrity. She has been indicted as Chicago's first queenpin. The Chicago Tribune in front of her reads, alledged queenpin and self-made millionaire indicted on drug conspiracy charges.

Dutchess stands in front of the mirror fixing up her disheveled hair, combing it to the back placing it into a long ponytail. She approaches the officer's station.

"You ready Ms. Blackwell?" the female officer asked.

"Yeah, I'm ready." She opens the main door that leads to the elevator. She steps into the elevator dressed in her orange jumpsuit. A tall dark skinned correctional officer sitting in a chair inside the elevator looks at her.

"Visit right?" he asked.

"Yeah." He presses a button and the elevator descends making a squealing sound, as if it's about to break down. The doors open as the elevators stops at its destination. Dutchess steps out of the elevator and checks in at the guard's station. A clatter of contending conversations fills the visiting area.

Dutchess scans the large pool of visitors in search of her visitor. A man rises from his seat smiling, dressed in a gray double breasted Canali suit, Testoni two tone leather wing-top shoes, with a tappered fade, and goatee meticulously groomed, accentuating his ebony complexion. Dutchess flashes her white kodak smile making her way to him. Her heart hammers at the base of her throat, racing with happy anticipation. She closes the distance between them. His arms snake around her tiny waist. She rises on her tippy-toes kissing him, fitting her body to his, She closes the distance between the two. He gives her a long sensuous hug.

They take their seats across from each other. The prison set it up this way, so they could watch to see if anyone was trying to pass contraband to a prisoner, and to limit the amount of contact between the visitor and the inmate. A row of vending machines sits kitty corner to Dutchess back. Deangelo reaches in his pocket fishing for tokens he exchanged dollars for.

"Do you want anything to eat, or a drink or something?"

"Naw, I'm good", Dutchess replied.

"You sure, I see they got some White Castle Burgers in there with cheese, he added, like it was some type of grand prize bonus.

"I'm positive", Dutchess said starring at him. There are many things racing through her mind at this precise moment. So many things that she wants to tell him, but not sure of how to formulate the words to come out of her mouth.

"What you thinking about?" Deangelo asked her, snapping her back into the realities of prison. For a moment, and just a moment, she had escaped from the confined cinderblock walls, while looking into his eyes.

"Nothing", she lied. "I was just thinking how handsome you look."

"Come on now baby. I mean, I know I clean up nice, but you just look like you got a lot on your mind. I was just asking you a question, and you didn't even respond.

"What was it?"

"It wasn't nothing important, but talk to me, what

you thinking?" "How a person can never realize how important a person is until you are divided by space. One thing I finally learned is who truly loves me and who don't give a shit about me. I really love you and have a lot of respect for you Deangelo, but you don't have to put yo' life on hold for m-"

"Ssh," Deangelo cuts her off by placing his fingers against her lips. "Don't start that baby. Let me set the record straight. I disagree with your decision to represent yo' self in trial, but like I said I'm here for you through thick and thin. If yo' life is on hold, that mean my life is on hold. I love you and nothin' will ever change the way I feel about you. I might mess around every now and then, I'm just keepin' it real, but ain't no piece of pussy gon' ever stop me from comin' to see you, writing you letters, and accepting yo' phone calls. I want you to remember that sex don't have nothin' to do with love. I can sit here and lie to you and tell you what you wanna hear, but that's not my style. I'll never let another woman come in between us. True love will manifest through all adversities. Life is full of trials such as these, that tests our inner strength and the love and devotion for one another, "Deangelo sincerely expresses himself to Dutchess with heartfelt words. He can see a fire sparkling in her eyes. A smile decorates her beautiful face. Her facial expression turns into a solmen look.

"Deangelo I know I never really expressed myself to you." She pauses and gazes into his eyes, her eyes becoming misty. "I want you to know you're the light of my life, the nourishment of my soul, the essence of my being and you give me the strength to carry on. I don't know what I would do without you. Sometimes I wonder how could God be so cruel and let this cold-blooded world come in between us." A tear flows freely down Dutchess' cheek. Deangelo leans over the table that divides them, and wipes the tear with his thumb. He watches her silently for a moment.

"Don't worry baby I'm here for you through all your hard times." She stares at him through the blur of her soaked eyes, his eyes confesses the truth of his heart. "It feels like a part of me is missing without you. My friends don't understand the torment I suffer, being without you physically."

"Ms. Blackwell, bring your visit to a end," the correctional officer stated, interrupting them.

"Well, I guess we gotta end this for now baby." They rise from their seats and embrace each other as if it's the last time they would see each other. She watches Deangelo as he exits the door, feeling like a part of her has left with him.

Pirelli gets off the elevator on the 21st floor returning to his assigned housing unit. He just came from a professional visit with his high powered attorney Johnny Hewitt, who is the most popular attorney in the state of California. Pirelli paid for all his traveling expenses and hotel fees. They scrutinized Pirelli's discovery transcripts and listened to 25 recorded conversations that doesn't incriminate him in no type of fashion. Pirelli never mentioned anything about drugs, not even in cold words. Johnny Hewitt informed Pirelli that there is only one strong piece of evidence that the government has against him, and that one piece of evidence can place him behind bars for the rest of his life.

Pirelli's heart beats painfully, and his head throbs with every beat. "***I can't believe she doing me like this after all the things that we been through. I gave her the world. How could she betray me? We ate at the same table together, we slept in the same bed, we got kids together. Shit! We even spent that money together, we laughed and cried together. I love that woman more***

than life itself. How can her heart be so cold? God why? Erica why you doin' this to me? I thought you loved me?" Several different emotions fills his head as he wrestles with his thoughts. He starts to feel nauseated. Hurt is smoldering in Pirelli's eyes. He walks to the phone in search of an answer. He dials their house number. Erica answers on the second ring.

"This call is from a federal facility. This is a prepaid call you will not be c-"

"Hello," Erica's soft voice takes the place of the recording.

"Why Erica?" Those are the only words that Pirelli is able to muster. Erica takes a deep breath.

"Baby I'm sorry. You know I love you with all my heart. I don't wanna do it, but they threatened to take our boys. I can't l-let them take our boys," Erica cries over the phone, sniffling in deep pain. She loves Pirelli dearly, but a woman's love for her children has no limitations.

Hearing the pain in Erica's shaky voice tugs at his heart. "Baby I know you didn't mean to cause me hurt. You was just doin' what you thought was best for the kids and our unborn child. I just wish...you would've discussed it with me first. You gon' and do what's best for you and the kids. I'm givin' you permission to do it. I want you to know that I still love you, nothin' will ever change that. You're my dream manifested in the flesh. I love you more than my... last breath. I made a lot of bad decisions in my life...but fallin' in love with you ain't one of them. We just have to deal with it and hope for the best." She hears the pensive tremor in his voice as he expresses himself.

"Baby I'm so sorry, I really mean that. It's gon' be so hard being out here without you." Erica truthfully said. The muscles in her face tremble as she struggles with her words. "I-I promise I'll bring t-the boys to s-see you as much as possible."

"Just be strong love. I-I know you gon' be there for..."

She can hear the rustle of air as he expells a deep breath through the phone. “Me.” He realizes that his relationship and his world is about to crumble right before his eyes. Erica. The love of his life has become one of the things he hates from the core of his heart, a rat. Truthfully, to him there is no way she can justify snitching. The feds have no case without her testimony. From this very day their relationship has depreciated.

Pirelli knows he has to make one of the hardest decisions in the world. It’s either lay down and do a life bit without the possibility of parole, or have his baby mama who is carrying his unborn child put out of her misery.

“It’s hard knowing that I won’t be around to see my children graduate from school and go to college. I will never have that chance to teach them how to be a man. But...I know you will be the best mother you can be. I just want you to know that I love you, and if you ever need my advice I’m here.” Pirelli said. His mouth promotes sincerity, but his heart promotes anger. He hears the faint voice of his youngest son in the background.

“Mama is that daddy?” She nods her head yes, staring into the eyes of her innocent little boy, who doesn’t understand that his life is about to make a dramatic change. “Can I speak to him?”

“Yeah, but hurry up, he don’t have that much time left on the phone.”

“Okay.” She hands him the phone. “Heyyyy dadddy!” he shouts excitedly.

“What’s up little man?”

“Nothin’.”

“You being a good boy in school?”

“Yeah. When you comin’ back home daddy? I miss you.” Pirelli falls into silence. His heart jumps into his throat, his soul in turmoil. Tears brim in his eyes spilling down his pecan complexion, rolling down his cheeks. Tears drop on his orange jump suit marinating in it, looking like ink stains. "Daddy when you coming home?"

"Real soon buddy. Put yo' mama back on the phone, love you."

"Love you too daddy, here mama, daddy wanna talk to you," he said, handing her the phone with his tiny hand. The phone clicks, indicating that the call is about to be terminated. Pirelli wipes his faee with the collar of his jump suit.

"Hello," Erica said, holding the phone to her ear.

"Yeah, I'm here. I guess I'll call you tomorrow."

"Baby please forgive me. You know I love you."

"I know baby. I love you too." The phone goes dead. Pirelli hangs the phone up trying to restrain his tears. Earl notices Pirelli strutting away from the phone with misty eyes.

"Yo P, what up?"

"Nothin' dawg, just going through a thang. I need to holla at you later on," Pirelli stated.

"A'ight. Just holla at me when you wanna see me."

"A'ight," Pirelli replied, heading to his bunk. He climbs into the bed trying to sleep off the unpleasant realities.

"Mail call!" the correctional officer shouts, standing in the middle of the day room. Dutchess rises from her bunk and secures her legal material inside her locker. The female inmates form a semi-circle gathering around the female officer. Each of the inmates anticipates on their name being called. Some of the inmate's doesn't bother to go to mail call because they assume that their name will not be called. To most of the inmates, mail call is the only thing they have to look forward to everyday. It's the only thing they have to comfort their lonely hearts.

The officer shuffles through the thin stack of mail placing it in alphabetical order. She calls out names, handing out mail.

"Anderson."

"Pass."

"Donaldson."

"Pass."

"Ellis."

"Pass."

Dutchess' heart drops into her stomach, the feeling of loneliness invades her. "***I wonder why Deangelo haven't written all week. He said he sent me a letter five days ago. Maybe he lied to me. I see what Pirelli was talkin' about now. People act like you don't exist no more when you on lock down***." Dutchess ponders, watching the stack of mail get thinner and thinner. Knowing that the officer put the mail in alphabetical order Dutchess begins to head back to her bunk to sleep off her depression.

"Blackwell!" Dutchess hears her name and turns around feeling excited, knowing that it has to be a letter from Deangelo. She grabs the letter out of the officer's out stretched hand. She scans the front of the envelope. It reads, "Confidential open in the presence of inmate" stamped with red ink. "***This some mutha-fuckin' legal mail***," Dutchess said to herself feeling frustrated. Dutchess opens the envelope and shakes the legal documents.

"Hold on I have something else for you here," the officer said, eying the two letters in her hand. "Here you go." Dutchess takes the letter into her palm smelling the rich scent of Deangelo's colonge. She moves through the threshold of inmates heading to her bunk feeling special. She never notices one of the inmates watching her every move. Dutchess sits at the edge of the bed and puts the letter to her nose inhaling the pleasant fragrance lingering in the letter. She unfolds the letter reading Deangelo's heartfelt words.

Dear Sade,

I pray that this letter land in the palms of your hands with perfect timing. I hope you are in a good state of mind, upon receiving this paper conversation. Myself, I'm dealing with this dilemma the best way I can. Everyday is another day seperated from the woman I truly love. Another unbearable day without your presence. I'm standing on a line between sanity and insanity. I have to keep telling myself she's real, this is real, our love is real, and the end will come. A good day for me can turn bad in the blink of an eye, a tick of the clock, or a beat of my heart. I'm on an emotional rollercoaster that changes it's course without warning or consideration for my mental state. Through this whole ordeal I haven't shedded any tears yet. Attacks of depression, despair, confusion, and frustration hits me and consumes me from the bottom of my feet to the top of my head. At times I just want to curl up in my bed and sleep the pain away. Sometimes I can't even sleep. There is even days that I have to make my heart beat and my lungs take oxygen. Suicide is never a thought in my mind, but dying of loneliness is always possible.

It's funny when I'm with you time goes by quickly and when I'm not with you, it doesn't move fast enough. Love is by far the most powerful emotion. It is the most mysterious and difficult to regulate. I want you to know that I love you and please don't ever doubt the love I have for you buried in the depths of my heart. If it's not real, it ain't me. I'm that nigga that's going to have your back through all of these adversities. I was down with you when you was up, I'm going to be

down with you when your down. I know there's many people who are lonely everyday without love and passion in their lives, so as this whole ordeal is, I know that what you and I share is the most precious of all gifts. I know God molded you just for me. I wear our love like a badge of honor. I want you to understand that I am in prison along with you. I am also doing this time, and the only thing I'm guilty of is loving you. Whenever your feeling down and out just remember I'm here, I love you, and I'm a true soldier to the end.

Love always,
Deangelo

Dutchess slowly folds up the letter. She feels her eyes watering, and closes them tightly, trying to fight back the tears. She smells the letter one more time visualizing herself being held by Deangelo. "I love you Deangelo," she whispers.

"What you say Dutchess?" Denise asked from the upper bunk.

"Nothin', I was just talkin' to myself," she admitted.

"Don't be down there gettin' all emotional."

"Girl shut yo' ass up, ain't nobody gettin' emotional," Dutchess lied. She knows that in her environment she can't show no signs of weakness.

Dutchess is in a deep sleep with Deangelo's letter clutched in her hands. She squirms under the sheet balled in a knot. "Mmmm, Deangelo." She moans thinking that Deangelo is caressing her back. Coming to her senses her eyes flick open. "Bitch what the hell is wrong with you? Get yo' fuckin' hands off me!" Dutchess protested, brushing Jesse's hands off her.

"Bitch you know you want me to suck that pussy!" Jesse barked, waking all the other inmates in the unit.

Jessie struggles with Dutchess as she resists mightily. Dutchess knows that she is no match for the heavyset six foot gaint. Jessie slaps Dutchess with a back hand disheveling her hair. All the inmates in the unit shout, drawing attention to the guards. Denise watches the fight and gives Dutchess no assistance whatsoever.

Jessie smacks Dutchess in the head and she becomes dizzy from the impact of the powerful blow. She sits on top of Dutchess and throws another blow and busts her nose. Dutchess reaches under her pillow. She knew that this day would come. She grabs the pad-lock and swings with all of her strength. She bashes Jessie across the forehead gashing her open. “Aaaw, you bitch!” Jesse shouts rolling over off the bunk, onto the floor. Dutchess can hear the sound of walkie-talkies, rattling keys, and the rustling sound of the officers making their approach.

“You done fucked with the wrong bitch!” Dutchess grabs Jessie by the collar of her orange jump suit striking her repeatedly.

“Break it up now!” the lieutenant bellows. Dutchess’ orange jump suit is full of Jesse’s blood.

They were both placed in handcuffs and escorted to medical for examination. After being treated, they where placed on solitary confinement. Dutchess did two weeks on 23 hour lock down and was placed in another unit for security purposes.

Earl weaves through the evening traffic in his boxed Chevy Caprice fighting against time. He has his electronic monitoring box in a bookbag keeping it in close range so it can appear that he never left his house. The electronic device is operating off its back up battery, giving him 45 minutes to accomplish his misson. If he does not return home within 45 minutes, the electronic device will alert the pretrial service department, which they will call his residence to check on his whereabouts.

Earl made a promise to Pirelli for posting his bond and by all means he will fulfill his end of the deal. He turns the corner parking in the middle of the block, pulling behind a red Durango. He leans back in the driver's seat reaching into the console. He removes a block triangled barrel 9 millimeter. He sits the gun on his lap and scans the area staring intently at his target location. He glances at the time on the dashboard. "***I got thirty five more minutes to pull this off.***"

A dark green late model Monte Carlos SS pulls up seizing Earl's attention. He watches the car closely examing the beautiful woman as she climbs out of the passenger's side. Her silky permed hair bounces as she struts to the door with her purse in hand. She fishes for her keys. "***This is perfect timing.***" Earl slides out of his car with the gun tucked underneath his jersey. His number 4 retro Jordans glides across the pavement as he makes an inaudible approach.

"Blackwell get ready you have a visit," the guard yelled struting down the hallway, giving an answer to his thoughts.

"Damn, I hope that ain't Erica. That would only complicate things" The decision to have her killed wasn't a easy one, but he'd be damned if he was going to spend the rest of his life behind bars. As long as Earl keeps his promise he'll be a free man within a week. She was their main witness, eliminate her and the case would crumble.

"You ready Blackwell?" The guard asked standing in front of his cell in a tight brown uniform.

"Yeah. Who is it?" he asked trying to knock the wrinkles out of his orange jump suit.

"You'll find out when you get there. Control pop cell seven," the burly guard speaks into the walkie-talkie. Clack! The guard opens the cage as the whining sound of the rusted bars fill the air. "Turn around boy," the hillbilly guard commanded. This was just another reason Pirelli have to get out of here.

"***This cracka' then lost his mind***," Pirelli thought, as he bites down on his lower lip, coldly between clinched teeth. The officer slaps the cold handcuffs onto his wrists.

"A'ight you know the routine boy, follow me." Pirelli shakes his head, it was all he could do to keep from hurting him. They take the elevator down and get off on the 10th floor. Another guard takes over, and leads Pirelli to a glass enclosed room taking his handcuffs off at the door.

"Damn he put those on tight," the female guard commented staring at the red marks around his wrist. Pirelli rubs his wrists then opens the door.

"I got good news and I have bad news. Which do you want to hear first?" Attorney Johnny Hewitt asked Pirelli as he entered the small visiting room reserved for attorney/ client privileges.

Johnny Hewitt was known as the criminal's attorney because he was as much a criminal as the ones he represented. He is short and fat with a face like Donald Trump. He is wearing his trade-mark, a cheap polyester suit. Where he spent his money from all the high profiled clients was anybody's guess, but it sure wasn't on his wardrobe.

Pirelli shrugs his shoulders as he leans back in the chair. The jump suit hugs his well toned body. "I don't know, tell me somethin' good." As much as Pirelli is paying him, good news is all he should ever receive. Hewitt reaches into his matching brown leather briefcase. The rustling sound of papers can be heard as he nosily shuffles paperwork around. He hits the latch at the bottom opening a secret compartment. He looks over his shoulder at the guard paying no attention to him.

"Ain't no cameras in here right?" Pirelli quickly glances around the room.

"I don't see shit."

"A'ight here." Hewitt slides him five colored balloons filled with marijuana. "You gotta dry swallow them. You can do it right?"

"This ain't my first bit." Pirelli swallows them one by one like M&M's. This is just another service he offered his clients. This supplemental income allows him to pay for his young girlfriend on the side Porshe 911.

"That ain't the good news I was talkin' about," he said as he removes a letter from the briefcase. "The good news is that the prosecutor faxed me this letter, stating that he's dropping the case against you. They've lost their star witness."

"***Damn that little nigga move fast***," Pirelli thought. His body is filled with mixed emotions. One part sad, the other happy he's about to be free. He tries not to show the happiness. "Yeah, what happened?" Hewitt shifts uncomfortably in his chair avoiding eye contact with Pirelli. This is what he hates most about his occupation. There was hardly ever good news. "And for the bad. I really hate to be the one to tell you this, knowing that you and Erica were-I mean expecting a baby," he clammered.

"What's up, did somethin' happen to Erica?" Pirelli asked revealing a mask of fake emotion. It wasn't good enough for an Oscar, but definitely a nomination.

"Yeah, she withdrew her plea bargain with the feds. Her guidelines are eighteen months to twenty four months for obstruction of justice. She just couldn't bring herself around to testifying against you. Now that's what I call love. Isn't that great?" Pirelli stares at him with his mouth wide open. A blank expression written across his face. “Hey, what’s wrong with you? Cheer up, gimme anotha fifteen thousand and I’ll guarantee she’ll get probation.” Pirelli can’t hear a word he’s saying. His head falls to his knees as he places both hands on the sides of his head.

“Ahhhh,” he screams. His elbows planted on his thighs. “I fucked up,” he mumbles under his breath. “Everything is going to be alright. I’ll have you-”

“What time is it?” Pirelli interrupted. Hewitt glances at his silver Fossil watch. “It’s a quarter to eight. Why?” A glimmer of hope enters his body as his head rises. There was still time.

“C.O.” he yells, gainning the guards attention.

“Yeah, what is it?”

“Take me back please,” he requested. Moments later he is escorted back to his floor. He is striped searched then taken back to his cell. The inmates who are locked in their cells have littered the hallways with leftovers from their meals. Apple cores, empty milk cartons, and potato chip bags line the shiny floors. “Excuse me C.O, I need to use the phone,” Pirelli said once he was back in his cell with the doors locked.

“And people in hell need ice water,” the guard retorted. Pirelli keeps his cool.

“I only need two minutes, it’s an emergency.”

“Nope!”

“Come on man, I’m begging you, the phone is right behind you,” said Pirelli, pointing to the portable phone next to the wall, that is far from his reach. The guard sees something in his eyes, and he walks to the phone.

“If I let you use this phone everybody else on this floor will want to use it. Ain’t that right?”

“Yea ... Hell yeah ...You damn right.” A sea of voices shout back.

The guard places the phone back on the receiver. “I was

gotng to give it to you, until your friends messed it up for you," he says walking away.

"Come on C.O please." The sound of his footsteps walking away tugs at Pirelli's heart. "Come back you bitch muthafucka!" With each fading step there goes his hope. The guard gets to the end of the floor.

"Florez, clean this place up," he yells to his orderly as he passes his cell, going through the door to the officer's station.

Inmate Florez is one of the many orderlies working at the jail. In some institutions they are called trustees. Their jobs include cleaning the floors, and assisting the guards with laundry issuing, and the passing out of food trays. For their help, they are rewarded with small monthly stipend, and have the priviledge of keeping their cell doors unlocked. Florez is the worst kind of orderly. One who some where along the way forgot that he is an inmate. A short Mexican with dark hair, and a mouth full of gold. It is rumored that he was caught with over 800 kilograms of cocaine. He told on his mother, his two brothers, and even his deceased uncle to get his small five year sentence. Still this was too much time for him, and he is working on getting that number reduced.

He grabs the broom and dust pan from the utility closet. It isn't a day that goes by that he isn't tormented by the other inmates. "Watch out y'all Lieutentant Florez is on the floor," shouts an inmate from his cell. A round of laugther is heard as others throw out wet rolls of toilet paper and dead batteries onto the floor.

"I just got one question. How you gon' tell on yo' mama?" A light skinned dude asked.

"Aye y'all leave 'em alone for a minute," Pirelli shouted.

"Nigga who is you super saver snitch!"

"This Pirelli nigga!"

"Oh my bad P." The laughing quieted down.

"Aye Florez, let me holla' at you for a minute."

"I ain't gettin' you the phone P."

"Man, just come here." Florez walks the length of the hall stoppping at Pirelli's cell.

"What's up?"

"I need you to get me that phone." Florez turns around sweeping the floor. "Look man, come here!" Pirelli screamed gainning his attention. "This shit is an emergency and on my dead momma's grave if somethin' happens because you didn't give me the phone, you might as well not even look forward to getting' released."

Florez's knees wobble, and if he hadn't used the bathroom, he would have pissed on himself. "Get me that phone, and I got four ballons filled with weed for you later on." There was no sense in giving him all five Pirelli thought. "I'ma give you five minutes, after that I gotta put it back. I don't want the guard seeing you with it, and lose my job."

"A'ight bet," Pirelli agreed. He passes him the phone.

"Where the weed at?" Florez asked.

"I got you later, I just came back from a visit." Florez nods his head. He knew it would be a while before Pirelli shitted the ballons out.

"I'll bring you some coffee." Florez volunteered knowing it would help him go to the bathroom faster.

"A'ight," Pirelli says as he picks up the phone dialing his house number. As the phone rings, he can only hope that he is not too late.

Johnny Hewitt sits in his car wondering what in the hell was wrong with Pirelli. He reaches into his glove compartment to retrieve the drugs he has put up for his other client. "Oh my God!" he gasps as he realizes his mistake. He gave Pirelli the wrong batch. Pirelli will probably never notice it, he thinks to himself. He decides to act on the lesser of the two evils. Instead of trying to warn Pirelli, he starts up the engine, and heads to try and catch his dealer. "There's still time to make a trade," he thought.

Omar parks his Monte Carlos SS behind his house after dropping his girlfriend off in front so she wouldn't have to struggle through all the tall grass behind the house. Churp! Churp! Omar activates the alarm system on his car. He moves along the side of the single family house with his long french braids snaking down his shoulders, hanging out of his Miami Heat fitted cap.

Making his way to the side door, he hears a click he recognizes and freezes in mid-stride before the cold steel of a gun barrel presses against his temple. "Sup cousin? Long tims no see," Earl said in his deep raspy voice. Omar spins around slowly with his hands in the air.

"Earl," Omar said, his face flashes with fear.

"Yeah, that's right, it's me muthafucka," Earl snarled aiming the gun to his head, flexing his trigger finger. He looks at him sharply in silence, as he back-pedals with his hands in the air.

"Hold up Earl, I know you salty at me. I-I swear was gon' bail you out. I ran into a-a few m-money problems," he stutters.

"You expect for me to believe that bullshit."

"Omar!" his girlfriend shouts his name from inside the house. Earl glimpses over his shoulder in the direction of the distant feminine voice. Seeing that Earl has taking his eyes off of him, he swiftly turns around and sprints like a jack rabbit running from its prey. Hearing the rustling sound of Omar's flight plans, Earl chases behind him. Boc! Boc! The melody of gunfire slices through the atmosphere gripping the attention of the neighbors.

Omar topples to the ground howling in pain, holding his bullet wounded leg. "Aaaw shit!" Omar writhes on the ground groaning and cursing. "Come on cuz, you know I was comin' to get you out of there," Omar lied, pleading for mercy. Earl bashes him across the head with the pistol.

Omar cups his head feeling dizzy. His vision becomes blurry and everything in his sight begins to see-saw. He holds his head grimacing in pain, with a pink welt on his forehead. Earl towers over him looking like a demon. He levels the gun to Omar's head.

"Rest in peace muthafucka!" Boc! Boc! Boc!

20 MINUTES LATER

Earl stands on his toes feeling along the solid oakwood door, searching for the keys to Pirelli's European style home. Pirelli informed him of the spare key that he keeps hidden above the door and gave him the code to shut down the security system.

"***Shit! I'm runnin' out of time***," he thinks to himself. He finds the key and enters the house moving quietly through the marble foyer. He follows all the instructions that Pirelli gave him. He shuts down the system and pads across the plush carpet soundless. A loud musical tone startles him coming from his rear. He spins around locking his focus on the cordless phone chiming a customized ring tone. His beady eyeballs bounce back and forth, as he admires the huge luxurious livingroom that reminds him of the houses he seen on MTV Cribs. This is his first time ever being in a house this size.

He browses around looking at the framed family pictures of Pirelli, Erica, and their two little boys.

Erica squirms in her sleep. Her pregnancy keeps her tired. She comes home every day after work, and takes a nap before picking up the kids. She places the pillow over her head trying to drawn out the sound of the ringing phone.

Earl creeps through the hallway looking like a cat burgular. He hears the phone ringing repeatedly becoming louder and louder as he makes his approach towards Erica's room.

Erica continues to squirm underneath the satin sheets irritated by the sound of the phone. She is hoping that it would stop ringing, but unfortunately it doesn't. She knows that Pirelli doesn't call at this time because he knows her daily routine.

Earl pushes the door open slowly staring at a sleeping Erica tossing and turning in her sleep. "***Maybe that's Pirelli tryna call? It must be something important***?" Erica thinks as she makes her mind up to answer the phone. Half sleep she reaches for the phone noticing the intruder standing in the doorway.

"Come on baby pick up," Pirelli talks to the phone as it rings to the answering machine. Erica's voice vibrates through the phone. "You've reached the Blackwell's resid-" Her voice is cut off by the automated B.O.P. system, "You have a prepaid call-" Pirelli hangs up dialing the number again. Pirelli can hear the sound of somebody picking up the phone just as the guard makes his way down the hall.

Just as she picks up the phone off the receiver, she hears an unfamiliar voice. "Don't answer that phone." She turns her head staring at the dark skinned intruder. Her eyes wide open like headlights.

"Wh-Wh-Who are you?" Erica inquiries in her trembling speech.

"I'm a very close friend of Pirelli. He sent me to introduce you to Nina," Earl replies staring at the beautiful woman shaking in fear. The seed Pirelli planted in her womb twirls around in her stomach reminding her of its life developing inside of her.

"N-Nina who?" She said with a puzzled look.

Earl removes the black 9 millimeter from his waistband pointing it at her head. "Nina Ross, the only friend I got."

"Pleaseee. Nooo, don't kill me, I-I'm pregnant," Erica pleads, holding her hump underneath the flower printed maternity shirt, trying to protect the unborn child. Earl's heart starts to weigh heavy as he looks into her glassy eyes. A part of him wants to let her live, but he made a promise to Pirelli. He knows that if she lives to testify on Pirelli, it will cost him his entire life behind bars, and Earl wouldn't wish that on his worst enemy. Erica sits in the bed helpless, crying.

"Pirelli told me to tell you that he loves you, and he truly hates for it to end like this. He said he will make sure you have the best burial money can buy and that the boys will be safe." Earl unable to look Erica in the eyes grabs a pillow.

"Plleaseeee. W-wait. I-" Earl covers her face with the pillow drowning her out, disregarding her plea. She moves around wildly, resisting. He puts the muzzle of the gun against the pillow and squeezes the trigger. The gun

jerks in his hand, it's gunfire muffled as the bullets rips through the pillow entering her head, cracking her skull. She lays in the bed motionless with her life draining out of her head, marinating in the mattress. Feathers float in the air like leaves falling from a tree in the first week of fall.

Earl looks at his watch. "Damn, I gotta hurry up before this box start beepin'," he mumbles. He moves hurriedly out of the house, knowing that he will one day reap what he sow for the hideous crime he just committed.

"Gentlemen, it is customary that we close out the final meeting of the year with a little history, so we never forget those that came before us," Judge Milton elated, fully dressed in his all white robe. His blue eyes shine brightly behind the hood. He glances around at his klan brothers in full attire. A thin smile creases the cloth. He holds a black book with three golden K's stitched on the cover high above his head.

"This here is the book of life. There are things in this book that the darkie must never become aware of. But the beauty of it is, they have been so well conditioned by our ancestors that they will reject anything that is contrary to what our people embedded in them. So even if it is lost, we will not panic. Each person will get a turn to share a piece of the history starting with the senator." The senator takes the book from the judge and begins to read.

"Brothers, did you know the bible was created by one of the brothers?" The other members gasp.

"No way," stated the sheriff in total bewilderment.

"Indeed, it says here that it was created as a guide for the slave master, and an instrument to keep slaves oppressed. Knowledge is power so we prevented them from reading anything except for the bible, signed T. Rowley. I can't make out the year," Said the senator.

"Unfucking real," stated Regan.

"Wait, there's more. It says refer to the book of John, chapter thirteen, verse 16. A slave is not geater than his master. This message was directed to future brothers and simply meant we are not equal to Negros. The message was received and great brothers of ours created the three-fifth clause, which stated that they are three-fifths of a human being, which in my opinion is too much." The senator passes the book to agent Regan. "Luke chapter seventeen, verse seven through ten, is a message directly to the brotherhood. I will break it down, but you are welcomed to pick up the bible yourselves and read the raw form, as the brother laid it out."

"Give us the good word," Judge Milton begged.

"It says basically, you don't reward a slave for doing what he was created to do. And once they are finished with their daily chores, to keep them broken down, you should make them say, 'we are good for nothing slaves. What we have done is what we ought to have done'."

"That's not really in there is it?" senator Hennings questioned.

"Here's a bible look for youself," Regan said handing him a green standard King James version of the bible. His fingers move hurriedly through the pages creating a whipping sound.

"Well I'll be damned." he said with his mouth gaping wide. Agent Regan passes the black book to sheriff Alderman. "Did you know that the word black represents beauty and power? And it wasn't until one of our brothers gained control of the publishing industry that we were able to associate it with evil?" They all shake their heads in agreement. Sheriff Alderman passes the book to Judge Milton. He closes the book and stares around the room.

"I was going to share a fact from the history book, but that is the past. I'd much rather deal with the future, and incorporate ideology from the past."

"Speak brother." Came the refrain. "I'm angry brothers and I believe I speak for all my people when I say we all have the right to be angry. We missed out on slavery, but that doesn't mean our ancestors after us have to. Now I'm not proposing we write another bible, no that will never work. But what we can do is make tougher laws, give out more time, and bury them Negros under the jail. Now that the crack law is about to change, we have to find another way to substitute the crack law. We prepare our kids to be lawyers to sell them out, judges to sentence them, and guards to give them the ultimate taste of being a slave master."

"It's beautiful," commented the senator.

"Excellent idea," added agent Regan. The only one who was lost to the plan is Sheriff Alderman.

"The plan is brillant; the only thing I don't understand is how we will keep them committing crimes once they learn how much time is being given out?"

"Haven't you been listening to what I've been saying? Our ancestors conditioned them well, certain things have been embedded into the Negro. I have faith that they will continue to commit crimes. As long as we create hunger, there will be crime. Not because they desire to do evil, or even for financial gain. They will do it simply because it is in their nature to be bondage.

The first day of trial is the day in which the jury is selected. Dutchess watches as seventy potential jurors fill the courtroom.

"That's crazy only one of them black," she whispers to her mother seated next to her.

"I told you what we would be up against. If we use our strikes right, we can pick a fair jury."

The next half hour is used learning names and personal references. Many people have already been missed as Dutchess and the prosecutor take turns using their remaining strikes. "We only have one remaining. I think we should get rid of the man in the cowboy hat," said Cheryl.

Dutchess quickly scans over the small pool of people remaining.

"I think number twenty seven." Cheryl flips through the pages in front of her finding juror number twenty seven's information. Name: Jim Crower Age: 76 Birthplace: Mississippi-moved to Chicago.

"Hmmm, he's old enough to have had slaves himself, where he at?" questioned Cheryl.

"Look straight ahead, you see the cowboy hat?"

"Uh-huh."

"Okay, second row, one, two, three, spots to the left in between the muslim lady wearing the scarf and the hispanic man with his head down." Cheryl follows the directions with her eyes coming to the pinkish red face with big beady eyes.

"Oh yes definitely your right."

"Excuse me your honor, we would like to strike number twenty seven," Dutchess said rising from her seat.

"Very well," said Judge Milton.

"Juror number twenty seven, you are excused, we appreciate you for taking the time out of your busy schedule to come down here today. Mr. Crower slowly gets up, and limps to the double doors, exiting the courtroom. "Well that concludes today's festivities, we will start bright and early tomorrow morning," Judge Milton informed.

Over the course of the next two weeks, many witnesses take stand. Tons of exhibits are introduced into evidence. The icing on the cake had come when Ice took the stand. Dutchess had caught him in so many lies that it was ridiculous. Before continuing her cross examination, she glances at a man wearing a free Dutchess t-shirt with a beanie on his head and a long beard. The man recently became a Suni Muslim. The man nods his head at Dutchess. He has been coming to her court appearances faithfully. She knows him very well. He knows that he could've easily been a part of Dutchess' indictment if she were a rat.

"So are you trying to tell me and the ladies and gentlemen of this courtroom that you are not receiving anything in exchange for your cooperation-umm I mean testimony today," Dutchess snapped, "It's it true that three months ago in September your house was raided, and the search produced weapons and drug money in violation of 18 D.S.C 922(G), felon in possession of a firearm."

"Umm, Umm," Ice stuttered, looking towards the prosecutor for answers.

"And Mr. Lewis, while your thinking up an answer can you explain to the jurors why you're not in prison at this current time?" Dutchess employed a loud merciless style of cross examination known as brucifixion.

Needless to say, Ice's credibility as a reliable witness was ruined, giving Dutchess a small victory that day. The other evidence they presented to the courts was circumstantial at best. Still going into the final day of arguments, the government is slightly favored to win. Today is the last day of the trial, the government and defense last chance to make final lasting impressions on the jury.

AUSA Glenn Stevens, tall and lean, wearing a dark blue Armani suit and starched white shirt rises from the prosecution table. He walks in front of the jury box, getting as close to the jurors as possible. They can smell his minty breath as he speaks.

"I'll try not to take up too much of your time. This stage of the proceeding is called the closing argument. You'll hear from me first, and then the defense will get their chance. Then finally I'll get the last say. This case is simple. To give you a brief recap, we have a young woman born to a well off middle class family. Mother was a prosecutor, father was a DEA agent. She knows very well that drugs are illegal. What has me puzzled is why she would even get involved in such scrupulous activities in the first place. But we are not here to determine the when, hows, and whys of her motives. I believe we have produced overwhelming evidence against the defendant in this case. From raids of houses, officer testimony, and rather you believe his story or not, a direct accomplice. All I can ask you to do is weigh the evidence."

Stevens holds his hands in front of him, palms facing up. He raises his left hand to the ceiling and lowers his right to the floor. "The imbalance is obvious and therefore you should return a verdict of guilty. Thank you."

Dutchess rises from the defense table, her hair swept back in a ponytail. She is dressed in a tailored beige pant suit. As she glides over in front of the jurors, she commands the attention of the juror's eyes before beginning.

"Before I start, by a show of hands, how many people have been promised something by someone only to have them renig on their promise?" Each juror raises their hands respectively.

"Okay good, as I speak to you keep in mind the feeling when you were disappointed and let down." She walks to the defense table and picks up a paper Dixie cup filled with water and takes a sip, clearing her throat. "When the government first opened up their case they promised to provide clear and convincing evidence as to my guilt. A promise that they have failed to keep. There was evidence of numerous raids introduced into evidence. However, what was not proven is that those apartments and houses belonged to me. There are no incriminating wiretaps, unless you want to believe the government's version of the conversation." She walks to the defense table and Cheryl hands her the cassette tape labeled exhibit 20. She takes it to the cassette player that has been set up in front of the juror's box. She presses play. Ring! Ring! Ring!

"Hello," the voice answered. Dutchess presses pause.

"For the record this voice has been identified as Anita Walker, the other voice you will hear is mine." She presses play again.

"How are you doin' Mrs. Walker? This is Dutchess."

"Oh, hey Dutchess, I'm doin' fine. Kisha was just asking about you."

"I don't know if I'll be able to make the party, but I'll have the cake dropped off. I'll probably get her next weekend."

"Alright, well I'll explain it to her."

"Thanks Mrs. Walker."

"Uh-huh, bye now."

"Talk to you later." Dutchess turns the machine off.

"This was part of their clear and convincing evidence." A small chuckle escapes her lips, as she shakes her head from side to side in disbelief. "As the evidence and witnesses I introduced proves that Mrs. Walker is the woman who adopted Kisha, the little girl whose life I saved from a burning building. Is it a crime to keep in touch with someone who has lost her mother and needs all the love and emotional support she can get?" Dutchess stares into the juror's eyes searching for an answer. "Kisha was having a birthday party and I sent a cake from a restaurant on the Southside called Original Taurus Flavors. A receipt for the purchase was even produced. A simple act of kindness. But the government presented a different theory. They told you that this was a drug deal and that I was speaking in code. If you remember on the third day of trial Agent Rains testified that this terminology is consistent with that employed by drug dealers trying to disguise their transactions."

She paused letting the words sink in. "Then they brought you testimony from Mr. Lewis. Testimony that was riddled with inconsistencies and false pretenses. You were here, you seen his body movements when he was on the stand. He was fidgeting, and stuttering. These statements are facts they can be proved beyond a reasonable doubt. The government's case against me can not be. Mr. Lewis commits a federal crime, yet he's allowed to walk in and out of the courtroom at free will. When the prosecutor took his position he took an oath to prosecute crime, yet he let's known criminals walk back into society. More broken promises. I know by the showing of hands that this isn't the first time being let down, but today you can fight back. By returning a verdict of not guilty you'll be doing just that. Thank you." Dutchess walks back to her seat and the prosecutor rises to finish his rebuttal.

"There are two types of evidence, direct and circumstantial." He does his hand display again this time keeping them even. "Neither weighs more than the other." He juggles his hands slightly keeping them leveled out for emphasis. "That's the beauty of the law. The defendant is correct, we don't have direct evidence linking her to the houses that were raided, but we provided circumstantial evidence through witness testimony, and accomplices. Just because her name isn't on the lease doesn't mean she didn't control it. All it means is that she is smarter. From her performance in the courtroom it will tell you that we're dealing with a mind that is well diversed in the law. She knows that by putting her name on a legally binding contract in an illegal venture, it can cause problems." Mr. Stevens paces in front of the jury box driving his point home. "As for Mr. Lewis we never said he was squeaky clean. Sometimes because of the complexity of prosecuting those who are higher up in the food chain you have to make a deal with the devil, figuratively speaking I can assure you that he has not escaped punishment and neither should the defendant today. As you are deliberating I just want you to remember as your going over the evidence, direct evidence doesn't weigh one hundred pounds and circumstantial twenty, they weigh the same. Therefore your verdict should be consistent no matter which you decide to base your decision on, neither one or both. Thank you." Stevens takes his seat as Mr. Sorensten pats him on the back.

"Well there we have it, I'll dismiss the jury now, so they can begin their deliberations," Judge Milton stated. Dutchess gives Cheryl a hug, and is then led back to the holding cell by two U.S Marshalls.

Five hours pass by, then she hears someone yell verdict. Dutchess is escorted back into the courtroom. She smiles at Deangelo, who has been there since day one. The jury comes through a side door and fills the jury box.

"Has the jury reached a verdict?" questioned Judge Milton. The jury foreman stands.

"We have your honor." He is the same man that was wearing the cowboy hat that Cheryl wanted to eliminate at jury pick. He has an arrogant demeanor, almost like he's happy. The deputy takes the paper from the foreman and hands it to the judge. He looks it over, and then passes it to the clerk of courts. A dark haired woman with lisp. She has a strong resemblence to Roseanne Arnold. She reads the verdict. "Case number 50030-7, the United States of America vers-s-us S-S-ade Lynell Blackwell, we the jury find the defend-ant..."

"Guilty...Guilty...Guilty." Pirelli stirs in his sleep as the voices resonate in his dream.

"Why you kill mommy daddy?" His youngest son

Fatman asked in a whining voice, his image being replaced by his mother.

"Who's going to watch the kids now?" Her face contorts in a fist of rage giving her a demon like appearance. Pirelli jumps up from his sleep, sweating profusely. He stares wildly around the dark cell, staring at the battered bluish grey cinderblock walls.

Most people wouldn't have noticed the steady rhythmn of the dripping water in the rusted metal sink, but he is painfully aware of it. Especially after smoking the marijuana his attorney brought him mixed with the PCP. Everything has a voice from the jingling keys as the officer makes his rounds to the man's high pitched snore in the next cell. They all seem to be asking the same question. "Why Pirelli?"

"Leave me alone!" he shouted to the darkness.

"Man shut yo' ass up, we tryna sleep crazy ass muthafucka!" A man yelled from three cells down being awakened. The guard struts down the range waving his flashlight into each cell as he count, whistling his country tune.

"Cut that bullshit out C.O!" another inmate yelled.

"It's six o'clock, you people should be up. Make me." the redneck hillbilly arrogantly stated, whistling louder. Pirelli looks out the bars in his cell and scrambles backwards, falling on the floor. To him the C.O looks like Erica. The C.O. flashes the light in Pirelli's cell.

"Blackwell, what's wrong with you boy?"

"Stay away from me Erica!"

"Hey boy what are you doing, put that down." The C.O. screams into the walkie-talkie. "Control this is Palmer, pop cell seven hurry!"

"Erica I'm sorry."

"Wait a minute damnit! Control hit the locks!" Pirelli wraps the white sheet from his bed around his neck. It is tied to a pipe that runs through each cell. He stands on the metal chair that is connected to the desk. Click! Click! The locks on the cell are opened just as Pirelli steps off the chair. His body compluses violently then goes still. The guard reaches him a second too late.

Pirelli's high priced attorney struts into the federal-building holding an envelope. He takes the letter out and waves it in front of the guard's face. "Do you know what this says?" The guard takes the letter reading over it

"It's a court order from the judge," the lawyer adds not able to wait for him to finish. He has worked hard on the motion he filed for his client. "You see that bold print at the bottom, it says granted. I want my client out, and I want him out now."

The veteran guard wants to snap the lawyer's skinny neck. "Well your going to have to serve these papers to the coroner's office. Your client committed suicide last night." The lawyer's face flushes in disbelief.

"***Damn, how am I going to get the other twenty thousand he owes me now***?" he thought.

"You've got mail." Detective Herra's desktop computer chimes as he logs onto the internet. His body flinches, being startled by his computer talking. He has been using America Online (AOL), for a year in a half and still isn't use to it. It took eight years to get him to try it out. It has been the same for him, with the cellular phone. He just doesn't like things to change. He was born on a farm in Mexico and he'd prefer to do without the latest technology. A friend of his had told him once you experience the internet you'll never want to do without it. That same friend had made the same comment to him about marriage. He is divorced now. The only reason he is on the computer is because the rookie had taught him how to run checks on felons through the internet. He could do without e-mail, too much spam. Still it intrigued him to see who the messages are from. He double clicks on the mailbox icon. "You've got mail," the computer repeats showing him the new messages in his inbox. The first message wants him to click here for free xxx pictures. It was enticing, but the second message caught his eye. The subject line read, "Hiring a hitman." The message isn't new, but it is for him, seeing as he hasn't checked his messages in a while. He had forgotten that his Email address is listed on his business card. When he had given Cheryl the card and she didn't call he wrote her off, and figured she didn't need help. Now as he reads the detailed message with Kennytha Baptiste's picture, he isn't sure. In the Email she says she may have proof of him hiring a hitman. She goes on to express concern about the powers that be, who control the politics.

And that in the event of her death, forward this Email to the proper authorities.

"Damnit!" he cursed under his breath. He knew she was safe because he had recently seen her on T.V coming from her daughter's trial. The question is how long will she remain safe.

With the verdict in the trial expected today something tells Herra this will be the day the hitman strikes. He can feel it in the depths of his soul rather it's divine or cop instinct. He doesn't know which. What he does know is that he wants to try and prevent tradgedy from happening. He glances at his watch 3:02pm.

"Mi Dio." My God he says in spanish finishing the rest in English. "I hope I make it on time."

Across town an unknown man is using his computer, destroying all incriminating evidence against him. He drags his dirty picture library to the recycle bin icon with the aide of his mouse.

"Are you sure you want to delete these items?" The computer asked. With no hesitation he clicks yes. He then clicks start then control panel...Internet...Tools...He deletes all cookies, then the temporary Internet files. Then he clears the IP history. Finally he inserts a floppy disk. A message pops up on the screen. "Are you sure you want to reformat your hardrive, all files will be lost." The man clicks yes and leaves the computer to do it's job.

Sheriff Alderman and the rookie detective are riding down the highway responding to a call by a hunter finding a body in the woods. They get out of the car and take the two mile walk plunging into the thick wooded area. Mosquitoes swarm in large packs, as they chop their way to the reported site.

"I ran a back trace on the computer from the first victim," the frail red haired rookie commented.

"And Rex?" The sheriff questioned, placing his hand on his hip, as he stops in the middle of the woods.

"Well, I found the most oddest thing. It traced back to your-aargh!" Before he could finish his statement, sherriff Alderman had pulled his gun and fired directly into his chest. Clutching his chest with his eyes wide in horror Rex begins to cough up blood as he tries to speak. "It was you all along." Blocka! Sheriff Alderman's pistol throws up once more silencing the naive rookie.

The sheriff takes a deep breath then presses talk on his walkie talkie. "Oh my God, help me, he's trying to kill me. It's Rex. Officer down, help me, Rex is the killer," he lied. Sheriff Alderman removes Rex's pistol from his holster, and places it into Rex's lifeless hand and squeezes the trigger. The first three shots go wild. The forth, he shoots himself in the shoulder.

"Aargh, stupid son-of-a-bitch!" He walks ten feet away and collapses to the ground. He smiles to himself, knowing help is on the way. In a few minutes he will be recognized as the hero who stopped the serial rapist.

"I'm Peter Davis channel seven news, and word has just come in that a verdict has been reached in one of the largest indictments ever issued. Our own anchor woman has the scoop. Let's tune in to her now. Karen are you there?"

"Thank you Peter and good afternoon Chicago, I'm Karen Bradley reporting for channel seven news. I'm standing here outside of the federal courthouse where the alledged queenpin Sade Lynell Blackwell also known as Dutchess is scheduled to be walking out at any moment. Once again for the viewers that are just tuning in.

I've received confirmation from my producers and the jury has reached a verdict of not guilty. I repeat not guilty. As you know if you have been following the case in the papers the media was not allowed into the courthouse. But I hear from a close confidential source that it was indeed a sight to see. Statistically wise the federal government has a 99.8 percent conviction rate, yet Ms. Blackwell was able to defy the odds while representing herself."

"This is amazing, does she have any former education in the law?" Peter inquired. He is the background voice.

"Apparently not Peter. Outside of an acceptance letter

from various top universities. There is no record of her attending. She is the daughter of a former prosecutor and high ranking DEA agent if that helps you answer your question," Karen informed.

"I have a feeling that every law firm in the city will come calling. Well keep us updated as things progress," said Peter.

"Your probably right and will do. Hold it on another note here she comes now."

A professional assassin lurks in a vacant apartment building of a tall high rise building on Dearborn Street. Wearing a pair of black leather gloves, he expertly assembles his high powered assualt rifle. He levels the assualt rifle and closes one eye staring through the scope with a watchful eye. He searches through the throng of spectators with the red dot focusing on his target. "***Come on bitch get the fuck out of my way, you blocking my fucking target***," the assasssin muttered in frustration.

Dutchess hears a cacophony of high pitched voices as she exits the front entrance of the federal building accompanied by Mrs. Blackwell and Deangelo. The deafening sound of the roaring crowd greets them as newsreporters and cameramen rushes in their direction. Car horns blare from all directions and taxi cabs crawl through the congested traffic.

"Ms. Sade Blackwell is it true that you never attended college?"

"Is it true that you supplied the entire southside of Chicago with narcotics?"

"What about your relationship with the reputed kingpin Mr. Kennytha Baptiste?" Various newsreporters continues to shoot questions at her, but she refused to answer.

"Move out our way please!" Deangelo bellowed, holding Dutchess' hand escorting her through the massive crowd. Dutchess' feels like a caged animal being studied by another species. The sea of bodies, slowly, reluctantly parts, making an opening. Dutchess and Deangelo plaster their eyes on a blue mercedes with dark tinted windows moving at a slow pace. The window slowly descends revealing a dark complexioned middle aged Haitian man with a clean shaven head. Dutchess instantly recognizes Kennytha's uncle from the boat party. "Safar." He makes an imaginary gun with his thumb and indexfinger pointing in her direction. He frames his lips in an o-shape, "Poww!" Reading his lips, Dutchess knows that he just made a threat. The driver's window slowly ascends concealing his identity.

Deangelo's street instincts kicks in causing him to scan his surroundings for danger. He quickly shifts his head looking in all directions. Everything seems to be moving rapidly. He looks skyward on his left and notices an irregular flash of light coming from a window. "Dutchess get down!" Deangelo's voice thundered.

Gunfire claps over head as he pushes Dutchess to the ground, shielding her with his muscular frame. The crowd of spectators scramble in panic taking cover. A woman screams loudly clutching her daughter. A U.S. Marshall crouches taking cover, skillfully waving his gun around analyzing the chaotic scenery. Mrs. Cheryl Blackwell kneels beside Deangelo's late model Denali truck. Bullets rip into the walkway beside Dutchess and Deangelo. They lay on the pavement entwined. The gunfire falls into silence.

"Baby are you okay?" Deangelo asked, receiving no response. Mrs. Cheryl Blackwell crawls along the sidewalk making her way to the two of them. "Baby say somethin' please," he uttered, lifting his body kneeling over a bleeding Dutchess. He cradles the love of his life in his arms with tears flowing freely down his face. Cheryl flips open her cellular with trembling fingers calling 9-1-1.

Detective Herra arrives on the scene minutes too late, and rushes over to a bullet wounded Dutchess. "Shit." he mumbles under his breath.

"W-We need an ambulance please hurry! My baby just got shot!" Cheryl cried. She drops the phone and goes to comfort her daughter. A large group of people crowd around witnessing the tragic incident.

"Baby please don't die on me like this. I love you. I can't live without you," Deangelo said wholeheartedly, rocking back and forth holding her in his arms. Dutchess lifts her lashes meeting his steady gaze in silence. His heart beats painfully in his chest. He starts to feel light headed. Blood leaks from the corner of Dutchess mouth.

"Be strong for mommy baby. It's going to be okay," Cheryl proclaimed, beside Deangelo on her knees rubbing Dutchess' hand.

"I-I'm t-tryin'," Dutchess manages to say struggling with her speech. Deangelo gently strokes her long silky hair. Dutchess' eyes slowly closes.

"No Dutchess, don't leave me alone. Remember we suppose to get married. Remember all the good times we had. Remember that first kiss. It can't just end like this," Deangelo sniffles in between his tears holding her in his warm embrace. She can no longer feel her body and her world becomes complete darkness.

EPILOGUE

A black Maybach crawls down the semi-darkened oneway street on North Avenue and Laramie. A taxi cab slows down and stops in the middle of the oneway street in front of the Maybach blocking its way. The driver of the Maybach tries to wait, but he becomes frustrated. He blows the horn in anger cursing at the taxi cab driver. The blaring horn splits the air.

Ice leans back in the leather recliner seats of the federally seized Maybach he received from the 'Sell and Tell' program. With a license to sell dope, he feels untouchable. Ice took over the streets of Chicago with the government's assistance. With Dutchess and Kennytha out of the picture, he became a millionaire over night.

He is enjoying the company of his Puerto Rican mami, who he has been blowing dope with all day. Ice unzips the flier of his white Prada trousers. He cups the back of the Puerto Rican woman's head. The vvs's in his Jacob & Co watch dances as he guides her head to his throbbing erection. She swirls her tongue around his mushroom shaped dick head and licks down his shaft. Her warm juices trickles down his balls, as she gives him some of the best head on the planet. She slurps on his dick taking it to the throat. A warm gratifying sensation courses down his spine. She swerves her head wildly chasing him with great enthusiasm.

"Damn Bianca, y-you s-suckin' the shit out this big dick mami," Ice complements her on her skillful ability. A hard bump against the Maybach causes their bodies to jerk uncontrollably. The forceful impact cause Bianca to bite down on his dick. "Aaw shit! Bitch!" Ice cursed, grimacing in pain gripping his crotch area. He turns his attention to a group of Arabian men and a blackman wearing a beanie. They climb out of the LandRover clutching Kalashinikov AK47's with its curved magazines. The armed men fill his vision. Donnavan has anticipated this moment every since he witnessed Ice testify at Dutchess' trial. Intoxicated with fear, Ice recoils feeling like a cornered animal.

Anger gleams in Donnavan's eyes as he stares at the Maybach with its dark tinted windows. Donnavan joined the suni Muslims and retired from the dope game after Dutchess' run in with the feds. One of the Arabs shouts in Arabic. "Allahu Akbar!" They elevate their guns in unison spraying into the extravagant vehicle. The deafening sound of the roaring machine guns chatter. Bullets blows out the tires on the Maybach causing the car to lower. The shower of bullets rocks the car. Bullets rip across the windows spraying glass and bullet fragments everywhere. The shattered windows makes the inside of the car visible. Ice holds the door panel for support, trying to climb out of the car. His white Prada suit is drenched in blood. Bianca's bloody corpse lays in the bullet riddled seats. The shower of bullets from the high powered machine guns chopped the driver's body in half.

Ice bleeds profusively, moaning in protest and in pain. His body is numb from all of the potent cocaine he has been blowing through out the course of the day. Donnavan moves closer to the Maybach firing the chopper. Ice's body bounces against the door as bullets rips through his flesh. Ice's body is nailed into the door under the fusillade of bullets. The gunfire stops, shells clings on the paved street, and gunsmoke lingers in the air. Bloody hand prints and shoe prints stains the leather interior. Ice's lifeless body is slumped against the door. His long platinum chain dangles from his neck with its diamond medallion chipped. The bullet riddled Maybach looks like swiss cheese. The classic mafia style shooting left Ice lifeless. Ice's own mother said he would grow up to be nothing but a hoodlum or either in jail or someone would shoot him. Her assumption proved to be accurate.

GRACELAND

"***Any man can father a child but it takes a real man to be a father***". A tear falls towards the ground inside of the cemetry as Amos remembers the last words Pirelli ever spoke to him. Rell and Fatman stand next to him with tear streaked faces holding a bouquet of red rose. Amos received custody of the two following the death of Pirelli and Erica. At first he was going to allow the state to take custody of them, until his addiction reminded him of the money he could get for housing them. After they arrived at his house, he took a liking to the pair. They reminded him so much of the young Pirelli that he often accidentally called each one his name when talking to them. His urge to use cocaine dwindled daily. Instead of smoking up the money Dutchess had given him, he used it to buy Rell and Fatman new clothes and video games. For the first time in his life he felt needed.

Rell and Fatman solemnly drop the roses on the ground where Pirelli and Erica's tombstones are stationed. "Grand dad can we go back to the car now?" Rell, asked in his youthful voice.

"Go ahead, I'll be there in a minute."

Their footsteps echo in the quiet night. Amos drops to one knee in the prayer position and closes his eyes. A short prayer escapes his lips.

"Dear God, I'm not good with this so bare with me. I don't know if you really exist...But if your up there I'd appreciate it if you gave my son a message. Tell him I said...Aah forget this."

Amos stands up and looks towards the dying moon. "Listen Pirelli, if you can hear me I just want to let you know that I love you and miss you. I know I was never a father to you, but I promise you and Erica, I want let y'all down in being a father figure to Rell and Fatman. Oh, by the way I've been clean for thirty seven days now. I know it's not a long time, but it is a start. I don't want your kids-my grand kids seeing me on that stuff. Just know that I'm trying to do the right thing and I hope you forgive me for not being a real man." Amos brushes the dirt from his pant leg and heads toward the car believing in his heart that Pirelli forgave him.

TRINIDAD

Tall ascending palm trees sway being pushed by the cool soft compassionate breeze. The crystal blue water ripples slapping against the shore forming a mist. The sun melts down on Deangelo's hersey brown skin, as he pushes a beautiful woman in a wheelchair. He leaves a long trail of footprints and wheel tracks in the sand. His straw hat shades his facial features from the rays emitting from the beaming sun.

The newly wedded couple passes by two children building a sand castle. A slender built white woman wearing a pair of sunglasses is stretched out on a chaise longue sun tanning.

"Baby that looks like a nice spot over there," Dutchess said pointing to a secluded area. Dutchess is paralyzed from the waist down. The doctor said she has a 95% chance of never walking again.

"Well, let's do this sweetheart," Deangelo agreed. He gave up his career so that he can take care of the woman he loves dearly. He bathes her, cooks for her, and all of the above.

He removes the picnic basket and blanket out of her lap. He flicks the blanket open laying it on top of the sandy ground. He lifts Dutchess out of the wheel chair. He lowers his body planting his knees on the blanket. The large rock on Dutchess' left hand glistens, representing her marital status. She feels that life can't get any better. On the day of their wedding Dutchess gave Carmen the keys to a beauty salon that she purchased and remodeled for Carmen as a gift for her loyalty. Deangelo and Dutchess lay on the blanket, her back leaning against his chest as they enjoy the panoramic views. The distant sky burns blue and pinkish. Deangelo caresses her stomach feeling the life of their unborn child moving around. He turns to her with an expression so reassuring, so loving, and protective. He knows that there is a God out there somewhere because his prayers were answered.

"You see that baby? It's beautiful ain't it?" he said staring at the beautiful contrast in the sky and the pretty blue water slapping against the shore being kissed by the faintly shining sun.

"Yes baby," Dutchess answered.

"Now this is what you call the finer things in life. The simple things that people take for granted every day. I thank God for allowing us to breathe this fresh air, and for allowing us to be together. All I want to do is grow old and gray with you and be the best husband to you that I can possibly be," he pauses for a second studying her eyes. "When God molded you he had to be thinkin' about me. I know your not perfect, but you're perfect for me. No matter what, I will never hurt you baby. It's me and you until death do us a part," Deangelo sincerely expressed with heartfelt words. They look into each other's eyes in silence. He grips her chining her to his. They kiss passionately wrapped in each other's arms as if they are the only two human beings on this earth.

HIGHLAND PARK HOSPITAL

A miracle is an event that is held to be supernatural because it appears inexplicable. No one understood this more than the man occupying bed number six, located on the sixth floor. His chest heaves as the machines blow air into his lungs keeping him alive. A combination of drugs flow into his veins, as the huge bag of liquid slowly drops into the I.V.

Outside his room nurses move around checking flow lines, and tending to I.V bags of other patients. Nurse Betty Demure made her rounds cheering up patients like any other fifty-eight year old grandmother would do. Considering the overall atmosphere in the hospital, her high spirited mood was a welcoming sight. She whistles a tune to herself as she comes to a stop outside room six reading the patient chart.

Name: Kennytha Baptiste
Status: Coma

She turns the knob entering the dark room. "The first thing we need to do is let some sunshine in here," she said, walking towards the blinds, pulling them back. Large rays of sunshine wash the room. A monitor goes off beeping sharply as a red and green light flickers and glows. She rushes to the machine pressing the rest button, bringing the controls back to normal. "There we are," she continued the conversation as if Baptiste is listening. "Now where were we?" she inquired while changing the bandages on his chest. "That's some nasty wounds you have there sonny boy. Your lucky to be alive. Yes you are." As she applies the last bandage she looks down and smiles, a gentle caring look. "You gotta be careful young man, it's a devil's playground out there. But don't you worry, I'll have you better in no time.

Book Titles	Price/Quantity
Money & The Power (Now Available)	$15.00_____
Dream (Coming Soon)	$15.00_____
Change The Game, Part 1&2 (Coming Soon)	$22.00_____
Powder (Coming Soon)	$15.00_____
Bootleg (Coming Soon)	$15.00_____
Crumbz to Brickz (Coming Soon)	$15.00_____

Acknowledgements

Jeremy Drummond (Flint, Michigan)

Maurice Hawthorne (Milwaukee, Wisconsin)

Jason D. Brantley (Milwaukee, Wisconsin)

Dedication (Jay)

Gabriella A.

Mom + Dad

Theresa Cousins

Dorothy Jones

Terry Flenory

Dedication (Moe)

Sade Hawthorne

Maurice Jr. Hawthorne

Laretta Hawthorne

Brian Hawthorne (R.I.P.)

Maryion Hawthorne

Larry Hopson

Made in the USA
Charleston, SC
17 June 2010